ISLAND FLING WITH THE TYCOON

THERESE BEHARRIE

A MAN YOU CAN TRUST

JO MCNALLY

MILLS & BOON

First Published in Great Britain 2019
by Mills & Boon, an imprint of HarperCollinsPublishers,
1 London Bridge Street, London, SE1 9GF

Island Fling With the Tycoon © 2019 Therese Beharrie
A Man You Can Trust © 2019 Jo McNally

ISBN: 978-0-263-27262-8

0919

MIX
Paper from
responsible sources
FSC™ C007454

This book is produced from independently certified FSC™ paper to ensure responsible forest management.

For more information visit: www.harpercollins.co.uk/green

Printed and bound in Spain
by CPI, Barcelona

...ing an author has always been **Therese Beharrie**'s ...eam. But it was only when the corporate world loomed ...ring her final year at university that she realised how ...on she wanted that dream to become a reality. So she ...t serious about her writing, and now she writes the ...nd of books she wants to see in the world, featuring ...eople who look like her, for a living. When she's not ...riting, she's spending time with her husband and dogs ...n Cape Town, South Africa. She admits that this is a ...erfect life, and is grateful for it.

...o **McNally** lives in coastal North Carolina with one ...undred pounds of dog and two hundred pounds of ...usband—her slice of the bed is very small. When she's ...t writing or reading romance novels (or clinging to the ...lge of the bed), she can often be found on the back ...rch sipping wine with friends while listening to great ...usic. If the weather is absolutely perfect, Jo might join ...r husband on the golf course, where she tends to feel ... more competitive than her actual skill level would ...gest.

...e likes writing stories about strong women and the ...n who love them. She's a true believer that love can ...quer all if given just half a chance.

You can follow Jo pretty much anywhere on social media (and she'd love it if you did!), but you can start at her website, jomcnallyromance.com

Also by Therese Beharrie

Tempted by the Billionaire Next Door
Surprise Baby, Second Chance
Her Festive Flirtation
A Marriage Worth Saving
The Millionaire's Redemption
The Tycoon's Reluctant Cinderella

Conveniently Wed, Royally Bound
United by Their Royal Baby
Falling for His Convenient Queen

Billionaires for Heiresses
Second Chance with Her Billionaire
From Heiress to Mum

Also by Jo McNally

Nora's Guy Next Door
She's Far From Hollywood
The Life She Wants

Discover more at millsandboon.co.uk

ISLAND FLING WITH THE TYCOON

THERESE BEHARRIE

For Grant,
who routinely helps me turn my dreams into reality.

Thank you for Greece.

And for our Greece group and the wonderful tour
guides in Mykonos and Santorini.

Thank you for making a dream—
and this book—possible.

CHAPTER ONE

FIVE MINUTES.

It wasn't long to wait. Things happened, even to drivers from five-star resorts. Or was it five-star accommodation? A five-star villa? Piper Evans wasn't sure. Her brother Liam had used all those terms when he'd told her she'd be staying there. The name of the place was Pleasure Villas, though that wasn't in any of the pictures he'd sent. Either way, Liam had hyped it up so much Piper could have sworn he was trying to get her to move to Greece rather than stay a week for his wedding.

But that was Liam. Or it had been Liam since they'd reconnected after their father's death. Enthusiastic, sincere. Responsible...? She wasn't entirely sure how to answer that. He hadn't been, once upon a time. He was getting married now, though, and marriage didn't exactly scream irresponsibility.

And yet she was still waiting at the airport for a driver he had been meant to arrange for her.

Ten minutes.

Why had she left the task to Liam anyway? She knew how he could be. She had countless examples of him letting her down. Sure, it seemed like he'd changed. The getting married thing, and all that. Or had she only wanted to believe that?

No, she thought. He *had* changed. Mostly since he'd met Emma, his fiancée, but still. Before their father had died, she and Liam had been in touch once, maybe twice a year. Then Liam had started dating Emma, and he'd been in touch more. Piper occasionally met up with them for meals. She wouldn't go so far as to say they were erasing the past, but this was a start. Enough of one that she could see how Emma influenced Liam.

Their relationship had lasted longer than any of Liam's previous ones. The one-year mark had come quickly, and he was still deeply in love. Then the engagement, planning a wedding—all within six months—and her brother wasn't running.

She tried not to feel resentment at that. Rather, she focused on the hope that surged inside her. Liam's relationship with Emma proved people could move forward regardless of their past. Maybe that meant she could, too. One day, she might finally be able to erase the marks her father had left on her life, her relationships, like Liam had.

Except it was now twenty minutes since she'd arrived, and her driver still wasn't there. Which meant her brother hadn't organised her a ride to the accommodation, as he'd assured her several times he had.

She let out a breath. Forcibly relaxed her clenched jaw. She searched the car park of the small Mykonos Airport, looking for anyone who could be looking for her. But, as had been the case for the past twenty minutes, no one seemed to be there without a purpose. She walked back through the sliding doors, circled the small waiting area. She saw only one person.

He'd been there when she'd landed. He held a sign that said Sunset Resort and wore a glowering expression behind dark sunglasses. Something about him made her shudder, and she was immensely glad she wasn't staying at Sunset Resort.

She pulled her eyes away from the stranger, sighed and pulled out her phone. She'd bought an international SIM card for this very reason.

Maybe you don't believe Liam has changed after all.
'Hello?'

'Liam,' she said, relief making her voice breathy. 'I'm so glad you answered.'

'Did something happen? Are you okay?'

'I'm fine.' She began walking to the sliding doors again, dragging her bag behind her. 'I've just been waiting for almost half an hour for the driver you arranged.'

'You have been?' he asked. 'That can't be right. Are you sure?'

'Considering I'm here alone—have been for the last thirty minutes—yes, I'm sure.'

'I'm sorry, Pie,' he said, using the name he'd given her as a child. She still hated it. 'Someone should have been there right when you landed. I gave Caleb your flight details. He's been tracking you, and there's no way he'd make you wait.'

'Caleb?' she said, wondering why the name sounded so familiar.

'Yeah, Caleb. Emma's brother.'

'Oh, *Caleb*,' she said again, as if she knew the man and hadn't only heard his name.

To be honest, Piper thought him a fantasy. Emma talked about her mysterious older brother whenever they got together, yet Piper had only met Emma's younger siblings. For all she knew, Emma had made up this mythical tale of the protective, kind older brother who'd taken care of them after their father died.

Piper had done that with Liam. When her father had refused to let her leave the house or made her jump through hoops when she wanted to study, she'd pretended Liam hadn't left home as soon as he'd got the chance. She'd told herself he was working hard to get her out of the situation he'd escaped.

She hadn't indulged such fantasies for long. Maybe this

wedding was finally the opportunity for reality to eclipse Emma's fantasy, too.

'Let me give him a call and find out what happened.'

'Okay.'

Liam hung up without saying goodbye, which would have bothered her more if he hadn't done so for her sake. A moment later, she heard a ringing from behind her. *Close* behind her. She turned. Found her head shifting up to look at the man with the sunglasses before he answered his phone.

'Caleb,' he said in a voice that made her skin feel prickly. He listened, then nodded. 'I have it handled.' He finished the call, though Piper could still hear speaking coming from the other end.

They looked at each other. Piper's heart began to pound. It jumped into her throat when her phone rang. She brought it to her ear without breaking eye contact.

'Yeah?'

'Pie, Caleb says he has it handled. I have no idea what that means, but—'

'It means he's here,' Piper interrupted. 'My ride's here.'

'Did you say *he's here*?' Liam asked, tone incredulous. 'As in, you think Caleb is there to pick you up?'

'Yes.'

'That can't be right.'

'Hold on.' She lowered her phone, pressing it to her chest. 'Are you Emma's Caleb?'

'Yes.'

'You're here to pick me up?'

'Yes.'

She narrowed her eyes. 'Yeah, it's him,' she said, speaking into the phone again. 'I'll see you soon.'

'Pie? Piper!'

'What?'

'Be careful.'

'Be…'

But her brother had already ended the call. This time, she didn't mind because she barely noticed he had.

He was having a day. Caleb Martin did not have days.

He had successes. Wins. But this morning the catering company his sister Emma had hired to cater the rehearsal party—because a dinner was too small for her grandiose wedding—had cancelled because some pop star had hired their services instead. Emma had come to him in a panic and, though Mykonos wasn't his home, Caleb had had to call in favours with every Greek contact he had to replace the caterer.

Since he didn't have that many Greek contacts, it had taken nearly all morning to find someone else. Then, as if sensing his vulnerability, his driver had handed in his resignation. Apparently, the demands of the wedding were too much for the local to handle. The man clearly wasn't used to responsibility.

Caleb hadn't had the choice. He'd been forced into duty the moment his father had died and he'd been made guardian of his three young siblings. Perhaps that was why he didn't have patience for the driver quitting. Or perhaps it was because the man had done so minutes before Liam's sister was supposed to land. With everyone running around preparing for the party that was two hours away, Caleb had no choice but to do it himself.

But she'd been late. Or not late, he thought, looking at the woman peering up at him. Confused. Though how she could be confused when he was the only man standing in the damn airport, Caleb had no idea.

'So, you're picking me up?' she said, bright brown eyes looking at him curiously. He couldn't figure out if they were light brown or dark brown, or a mysterious mixture of the two. All he knew was they stood out against her skin—another interesting shade of brown—and that they tempted him into forgetting his annoyance.

'Since I'm the only person in this airport with a sign,' he said, voice harder than he'd intended, 'the answer is obviously yes.'

She studied him before she answered. 'Two things. One, you're holding a sign that says Sunset Resort. The place I'm supposed to be staying at is called Pleasure Villas.'

Her cheeks turned a pretty pink colour. It almost distracted him from what she'd said. He looked down, cursed when he saw she was right. He'd grabbed the wrong sign from the seat of the car his driver had used.

Great.

'Two,' she continued as if she hadn't paused to make him feel like a fool, 'I was the only person standing out there for the last half an hour, too. If it was obvious that I should have noticed you, surely the same goes for you?' Her eyebrows rose. 'At least I have a legitimate excuse for not speaking to you. I didn't know you'd be coming. But what's your excuse? Didn't you at least look at a picture of me?'

No, he hadn't. Nor did he have an excuse, which she knew, based on that self-satisfied look on her face. He didn't know how he could find the arrogant expression appealing. How he could be fascinated by the easy curves of her lips. He hadn't even got to those intriguing eyes yet and he could feel his body leaning in, giving in to the desire to be closer to her.

He shut it down like a mousetrap on a mouse.

'If you're done, we can go.'

Amusement flickered in her eyes, but she was wise

enough not to respond. She merely nodded and gestured for him to lead the way. He kept his complaints about the bad luck he was having to himself, though his mind went haywire, thinking about everything he should have been doing instead of fetching a snappy soon-to-be relative.

No, he thought immediately. She wouldn't be his relative. Good thing, too, or the way his body was still demanding to be closer to her would be criminal.

Grunting, he took the handle of her bag. When he was met with resistance, he looked at her.

'Is this going to be a problem?'

'You tell me,' she replied mildly. Which, of course, only annoyed him more.

'I'd like to help you with your bag,' he said through his teeth. 'Would you give me the great pleasure of doing so?'

Her expression changed then. So marginally that if his attention hadn't been focused on every twitch of her features he wouldn't have noticed it. Her lips pursed for a second; the lines around her eyes became more distinct. Tension fluttered across her face, disappearing almost as soon as it appeared.

When she looked at him, her eyes were dull. Inexplicably, his stomach dropped.

'Why?' she asked him, her voice steady despite the tension. 'Why do you want to carry my bag?'

'Not because I don't think you can do it,' he replied, watching her closely. It caused another minute change—a ripple of pleasure. But surely she couldn't take pleasure from him thinking she could do something as simple as carry her own bag? 'I help my sisters with their things all the time.'

'I'm not your sister.'

The words were soft. Softened something inside him, too. The annoyance went up another notch.

'No, you're not.' He waited a beat. 'Perhaps I wanted to be a gentleman.'

'Something tells me being a gentleman isn't a top priority for you.'

He didn't wince, but he wanted to. She was right. He'd been acting like a jerk since they'd met. But the knowledge of it didn't change that he was annoyed. That that annoyance wouldn't allow him to be soft and kind with her. Although it did give him an excuse to give her what she wanted. What, apparently, was important to her.

'Fine,' he said after a beat, releasing his hold on her bag. 'You can do it yourself. The car's this way.'

He walked away, pretending not to notice her shocked expression.

CHAPTER TWO

EMMA'S BROTHER WAS not quite as mythical as she'd made him seem. He was very much human, Piper thought, unashamedly studying him as he drove.

His jaw was locked, the sharp angles of it more pronounced because of the tension. Most of his expression was still obscured by his glasses, though she could tell he was glowering. The glasses seemed necessary for that—or, rather, the expression seemed necessary. She hadn't seen anything other than it since they'd met.

It wasn't her fault he'd had the wrong sign. And maybe she should have asked him, but she never approached strange men. She steered away from men in general, actually. Found it to be a good rule since she didn't trust her own judgement.

The first man she'd trusted had manipulated her whenever she'd allowed it. When she hadn't, too. The second man she'd trusted had abandoned her; she still hadn't forgiven her brother for that, if she was being honest. As for the third man…

She'd chosen Brad, and somehow he'd ended up being exactly like her father. She'd paid for that. Was still paying for it in the form of caution and rules and the constant fear of falling for the wrong person again.

She sucked her lip in, looked out of the window. Her trip down memory lane had extinguished her curiosity about the man beside her. Instead, she focused on the actual lane they were driving along. It was an apt description for the narrow road they were rattling down. Caleb handled it with a confidence she wasn't sure the road warranted.

She wanted to tell him to slow down, to give way to

the large buses driving the curves of the narrow road. To watch out for the scooters zooming past them at what felt like every turn. But her voice wouldn't work. She suspected it had something to do with feeling vulnerable, and the fact that she didn't want him to know she was.

It seemed to be an unofficial mark of their short relationship, this vulnerability. Her inability to speak because of it. Back at the airport, when he'd assumed she'd wanted him to carry her bag without asking, it had kept her from accusing him of taking control like the men in her past. It had also kept her from blurting out a thank you when he'd told her he believed she could do it herself, *unlike* the men in her past.

That difference was why she'd been surprised he'd given in so easily. Nevertheless, her entire body had braced for the argument she'd thought would come. They'd been inevitable before, with Brad. And he'd disguised control with gentlemanliness, which was part of why it had taken her years before she'd seen it. It wasn't the only reason, but still, she was careful because of it. She didn't take anything at face value any more. She couldn't trust herself to.

The car jerked to the side as a bus took a narrow corner wide. A sound escaped from her lips.

'We're fine,' he said curtly.

'I didn't say anything.'

'You made a noise.'

'It was involuntary.'

'We're still fine.'

'So you say,' she muttered, refusing to look out of the window on his side as the bus loomed over them.

'You shouldn't have come to Mykonos if you're afraid of tight roads.'

'I couldn't get out of it.'

'You tried?' he asked, surprise making his voice lighter.

'Everything. But Liam had an answer for every concern.' She looked at him. 'Some of that was because of you,' she said accusingly.

'I didn't do anything.'

'Aren't you paying for the extravagant wedding?'

'Well, yes, but—'

'I couldn't afford to come here by myself.' She sighed at the idea. 'It was a legitimate excuse. Then Emma's magical unicorn of a brother swoops in and suddenly I have no reason to back out.'

Caleb made a strangled sound that would have been amusing had another bus not rounded the corner. She hissed out a breath.

'You didn't learn your lesson from the first bus?' he asked darkly. 'We're fine. This is how people drive here.'

'Doesn't mean I have to like it.'

'That's true.'

He pulled back onto the road. She closed her eyes when it seemed as if he was still too close to the walls keeping them from falling off the edge of the cliff.

She had an intense wave of nostalgia for home. In Cape Town, South Africa, she had a choice about what kind of road she wanted to drive on. It wasn't the standard, these narrow and inclined roads. No, the standard was wide open spaces with plenty of lanes to feel safe in.

'Piper.'

She opened her eyes at the sound of her name. She hadn't expected it. Hadn't expected to like the way he said it either.

Piper.

She heeded the warning of her inner voice and steeled herself.

'What?'

'Worrying about traffic means you're missing the view.'

'I live in one of the most beautiful cities in the world. I've seen views.'

'Just look.'

She did, but reluctantly. Made sure he knew it, too, with a little exhalation and roll of her eyes. The sharp intake of breath she took once she looked out over the stone walls wasn't contrived though. She hadn't been lying when she'd told Caleb about the Cape Town views, but that didn't mean she couldn't appreciate new ones.

This one was particularly stunning, the vast blue ocean stretching out, broken up by rocks and islands in the far distance. On the island itself, white buildings stretched up at different layers, marked by the blue shutters she associated with Greece though she'd never been there before. Interspersed were stretches of brown land, green trees, pink flowers. It was striking and, she had to admit, it distracted her from the drive.

When they went down a curving gravel road she held her breath. Moments later he stopped the car, and she exhaled.

'What if the place had been further down?' he asked dryly.

'I probably would have fainted and you could have done the gentlemanly thing and left me in the car to fend for myself.'

There was a beat before she thought she heard him chuckle, but he climbed out of the car before she could check. Good thing, too. If she saw him smile, or do anything other than glower, she might have to pay attention to the buzzing that had been in her body since they'd met. At the moment, she was blissfully ignoring it.

She'd practised hard on that ability for the last two years. She was pleased it was working.

'Would you like me to get your bag out, or do you want

to do it yourself?' he asked when she joined him at the back of the car.

Oddly, the question touched her. It made her feel... understood, though that made no sense.

'I'll do it,' she answered, to be safe.

She climbed in, pulled at the bag. Pulled again when it didn't budge. It took her a second to realise it was stuck. Panic made her fingers clumsy as she tried to loosen the bag. Pride prevented her from asking for help.

She waited for Caleb's sigh. For the dip of the car that told her he was coming in to help. To take over because, obviously, she couldn't be trusted to do anything herself.

This is why you should leave things to me, Pipe,' Brad had told her whenever something like this had happened. *'You can't do it by yourself.'*

It was funny that she'd heard versions of that from her father all her life. When Brad had outright said it though, she hadn't listened to the alarm going off in her head.

Gritting her teeth, she pulled with all her strength. The bag came loose, but the momentum had her falling back. A hand pressed against her back, but was removed as soon as she was steady. She got out of the car, her face burning despite the triumph of exiting with her bag.

'Nice job.'

She lifted her chin. 'Please don't make fun of me.'

'I wasn't,' he said sincerely.

There was a shriek from somewhere behind them, ending the conversation before she could think about why his answer warmed her.

'Caleb, you *did* it!' Emma exclaimed, launching herself at him as he turned to face her. 'The caterers arrived an hour ago and everything seems to be going smoothly.'

He pushed at a braid that had flown over her face when

she finally let go of him, and smiled. 'Of course, Em. What choice did I have?'

'Ha,' she said, poking him in the stomach. Then her eyes moved to Piper and softened. 'Piper! It's so lovely to see you!'

Emma went to hug her future sister-in-law. Caleb expected Piper to wince. To put distance between her and his affectionate—sometimes overly so—sister. But she opened her arms and squeezed Emma tight. His heart squeezed, too. He ignored the sensation.

'Em, you look beautiful,' Piper said when she leaned back.

Emma beamed at her, smoothing the strapless blue dress she wore before flipping her hair over her shoulder. 'I still have to have these styled,' she said, lifting a free braid.

'And I have to have the whole of this styled,' Piper replied, waving a hand down her body.

Emma laughed.

'Em, it's less than an hour before the party starts,' Caleb said. 'You need to get your hair done and leave. Your guests will start to arrive soon and you and Liam have to be there.'

'Yeah, yeah,' Emma said, rolling her eyes good-naturedly. 'It's not like my hair is going to take long.'

'Is Jada doing it?' Caleb asked, thinking of his baby sister.

'Yes.'

'Then you need as much time as you can get.'

Emma's expression turned thoughtful. 'True.' She kissed Piper on the cheek before doing the same to Caleb. 'Show her to her room, please, Caleb. Liam's already at the beach, welcoming guests.'

She stuck her tongue out before Caleb could say anything, leaving behind a restlessness in the silence.

'You should probably show me to my room,' Piper said eventually.

He acquiesced without reply.

He heard her intake of breath when they walked onto the Pleasure Villas property. It was like when she'd seen the view of the ocean, the island of Mykonos earlier. A gasp at the beauty. So simple, too, as if she hadn't seen something like it before. Or perhaps as if she could still appreciate beauty like it, despite seeing it in her home, as she'd claimed.

But even he, jaded as he was when it came to beautiful places, appreciated Pleasure Villas. Tall white buildings with blue shutters surrounded a bright blue pool. At almost each of the assortment of buildings, green leaves and pink flowers pressed against the white paint. Some crept up, along pillars. Others stretched over from one building to another. The greenery around the pool created an oasis he'd never had the opportunity to enjoy, too concerned with privacy than to strive for relaxation.

He wondered if that would be the case for Piper. She seemed closed off, private, though her tongue was sharp. But then he thought of how eagerly she'd opened her arms to his sister, how she didn't seem to be hesitant or resistant with Emma, and he didn't know. His first impression of her was challenged by almost every other moment he spent with her. As someone who prided himself on reading people quickly and efficiently, he didn't like that she was such an enigma.

Then again, he wasn't buying property from her as he did in his business. That was where he relied on his people-reading skills. Perhaps he needed to calm down. Not that thinking that helped him *to* calm down.

'Here you go,' he said, taking the key from on top of the door frame and opening the door.

'You left the key there?'

'It's safe.'

'Hmm.'

It was the only comment she made as she pulled her bag into the house.

There was another gasp when she was inside, and he felt a strong sense of satisfaction. He'd done some work on the inside of the villas when he'd bought them. Not enough to change the feel of them, but enough that he could be proud when someone liked them.

It had been no small feat to get Adrian Anagnos to sell this place to him. In Mykonos, businesses remained locally owned for the most part. There were none of the fast food places that had taken over most of Europe. Most of the restaurants and properties were family owned. It was how Mykonos had survived the recession, a fact they were quite proud of.

When he'd learnt of this, Caleb had been determined to get a foot in the door. He'd worked with Adrian when the man had come to South Africa, interested in investing in property. Their relationship had been purely professional until, one day, Adrian's daughter had been robbed in Cape Town. Adrian had been in America on business. With no one else to assist her, Adrian had called Caleb, who hadn't given it a second thought.

Things changed then. Adrian invited Caleb on a boat trip one day in Cape Town to thank him. Dinner became more frequent, and Adrian became a mentor. Caleb didn't use that term lightly—it felt like a betrayal to his father, whose business Caleb had taken over when Chad Martin had died thirteen years ago. But Caleb had grown to like and respect Adrian. The older man felt the same about Caleb.

When Adrian had invited Caleb to Greece for his daughter's wedding, Caleb had stayed at this very property. It was one of several Adrian owned on the island. Caleb had liked it so much he'd enquired about purchasing it. It had taken two years before he'd finally worn Adrian down. Eventually, the man had stopped laughing at Caleb; now, Caleb was the owner. It was a deep disappointment that Adrian couldn't make Emma's wedding.

'This is… Wow,' Piper said, drawing him from his thoughts.

'Yeah, I thought the same thing when I first saw it.'

Piper ran a hand over the couch, looking from the cobbled tiling up to the sea-themed décor. She took the two steps up to the open-plan kitchen, walked out to the small courtyard at the back, then into the main bedroom with its en-suite bathroom. With wide eyes she walked out and stared at him.

'Are all the rooms in the villa like this?'

'Pretty much, yeah.'

'Wow,' she said again, setting her hands on the small blue table in the kitchen. 'How could you afford to rent this place?'

His lips twitched. 'I didn't rent it.'

She gave him a look. 'Liam told me you arranged for accommodation.'

'Technically true, although I didn't have to arrange much. I simply didn't hire it out for this week.'

'You didn't…'

He could see her brain working as she trailed off. Enjoyed that brief moment of shock when she realised what he meant.

'You own this place?'

She spoke in a whisper. He smiled.

'I do.'

'Holy cow.' She blinked. Repeated the action in rapid

movements. 'I...guess I understand why Emma went so extravagant with the wedding now.'

'Liam wanted the wedding to be big, too,' Caleb reminded her, as if he had to defend his younger sister.

'Yeah, but Liam wanted it because Emma wanted it.'

'Why do you sound so judgemental?'

'I'm not judging anyone,' she said, straightening her spine. 'I'm only saying that if I had access to literal paradise—' she lifted a hand, gestured around them '—I'd want to have a big destination wedding, too.'

'You're definitely judging her.'

She met his eyes. 'If you tell me you've never once judged Liam because of his choices, personal or professional, I'll tell you the truth about whether I'm judging her.'

Caleb thought back to all the things he'd seen Liam do—things he hadn't agreed with. Two failed business ventures in the year and a half since he and Emma had started dating. A lack of a spine when it came to even the vaguest prospect of conflict.

The only reason Caleb had felt comfortable with the wedding going ahead as planned was because Liam was completely in love with Emma. And he made Emma happy. Otherwise, Caleb might have had to step in, like his father would have, had the man still been alive...

Piper was smiling when he looked at her again.

'I'm going to get ready for the party. Please close the door on your way out.'

Piper dusted a hand over the olive-green dress she wore. It was simple, with thin straps, and revealed more of her breasts than she'd ever shown before. But it had pockets, ended mid-shin, and the colour popped against her skin.

THERESE BEHARRIE   25

She couldn't bring herself to change, despite the situation with her breasts.

She lifted her hand to her hair, which she'd had to tie up into a ponytail since she'd worn it that way on the flight over. There had been no time to wash and blow it again. She'd tied it up, flattened the front of it with gel and straightened her ponytail until it was a sleek curtain to her mid-back. With one last look in the mirror, she grabbed her clutch and opened the door.

Right to Caleb Martin.

They both took a step back. Both sized each other up in the silence that followed. He wore light blue pants and a white shirt. It accentuated the brown of his skin, the broadness of his shoulders, the dark black of his hair. He'd shaved since they last saw one another, so the sharp angles of his face were even more striking than they'd been that afternoon. Or perhaps that was because he no longer wore sunglasses, and for the first time since they'd met she could see his eyes.

When her stomach flipped at them—they crinkled at the sides as he patiently waited for her to finish her perusal, done with his own—she wished he'd brought the glasses again. His eyes were kinder than she'd thought they would be. They were also sharp, light, and the combination of that expression as well as his outfit...

It was a good thing she'd practised her self-control. Fanning herself would have been inappropriate.

'What are you doing here?' she asked when she was finally done staring. No, that wasn't true. She wasn't done. She simply knew what was proper.

'Emma asked me to escort you to the party.'

'Why? Is it complicated to get to the beach?'

'It is not.' Amusement shimmered across his face, a

potent addition to the gorgeousness she was already distracted by.

'Is she trying to set us up?'

His eyes widened comically, the determined shake of his head following in a similar manner. 'No. No, of course not.'

'You're denying this a lot.'

'Doesn't mean it's not true.'

It would probably annoy him if she disagreed—so, of course, that was what she wanted to do. She walked out of the door, closed it behind her. Primly, she folded her hands around her clutch.

'I don't know. You came to fetch me from the airport. You showed me to my room. Now you're escorting me to a party. This must be a date of some sort.'

'It's not a date,' he said. 'It's…being courteous. Which I'm deeply regretting.'

'You're the least courteous person I've met, Caleb. You telling me you regret being courteous proves that.'

'Has anyone ever pointed out how contrary you are?'

Why can't you do as you're told, Piper?

A question she'd heard far too often in her twenty-six years, in various forms.

'All the time,' she said lightly. Fighting for that tone. 'Though you think it an insult. It's not. I try to be contrary whenever I can, so someone pointing it out to me is a compliment. Shall we?'

She started walking, not bothering to check if he was following. She could almost hear his irritation with her. It thrilled her in a way it shouldn't have.

To be fair, some of what she'd said had been for the sake of contrariness—he was so easily riled!—but some of it had been true, too. She'd spent most of her life obeying people. Her mother had died when she was young, leaving her and her brother with a father who didn't want to be one. Keaton Evans had never said so, but she could only assume that was the reason for his awfulness. People who wanted children didn't force them into behaving in certain ways, did they? Surely they allowed their children to become whoever they wanted to be. They let them test the boundaries, drawing them in when the child went too far.

But not Keaton.

Keaton had a strict routine for them to follow. So strict, in fact, that if either of them strayed from it they were punished. No outside time. Food in their rooms. Being kept separate from one another. Since they had no friends, not really, Piper and Liam had become friends. At least they had been in those first few years. Not talking to one another was torture then, which their father knew. It was how he'd kept them in line.

There was no testing the boundaries in the Evans house. There were *only* the boundaries. If they were broken, Piper or Liam would be punished. At least Keaton had been simple in his cruelty.

As they'd got older, Liam began to rebel more, and things got bad. Eventually, Liam had got a bursary to university and moved out. Their father had forbidden him from coming back. Forbidden her from seeing him. They'd lost touch, even when she'd joined Liam at university two years later. By then she'd allowed her father to crush her spirit of rebellion. Of independence. She'd only got it back three years later, when Keaton had died.

Then she'd welcomed another manipulator into her life.

'It's hard to insult someone who doesn't have the decency to be insulted by things that normal people are insulted by,' Caleb commented from beside her. She hadn't even noticed he'd caught up. Now that she had, she could feel his presence like the light breeze caressing her skin.

'That's the point,' she replied. 'I don't get insulted,

and that way I take away the power from the person trying to insult me.'

'Sounds like you've practised it.'

'I have,' she told him simply, before stopping at the top of a steep decline. She let out a breath. 'I knew these heels were a bad idea.'

'I wouldn't say so,' his voice rumbled.

Her flesh shot out in goosebumps. And she remembered, for the first time, that she'd forgotten to put on the nipple covers she'd bought for the dress when she'd realised she couldn't wear a bra with it. She resisted angling her body away so he wouldn't know the effect his flirtatious remark had on her. It would be giving him power. On principle, she couldn't allow that.

'Well, I do,' she said determinedly. 'How am I supposed to make it down this path without breaking an ankle?'

'Take them off.'

She wrinkled her nose. 'Then I'd have dirty feet when I have to wear my shoes again.'

'You could wipe them off.'

'That won't help.'

He stared at her for a moment. 'You're strange.'

'Tell me something I don't know.'

'Well,' he said, 'you do have another option, though I don't think you're going to like it.'

'What is it?'

He turned to face her, his expression so satisfied that she wanted to give him whatever answer he didn't expect from her. Until she heard his suggestion.

'I could carry you.'

CHAPTER THREE

HE'D DONE IT on purpose. He wanted to ruffle her feathers when she seemed so composed. Perhaps not his most honourable decision in life, but he'd been honourable enough. When his father had died thirteen years before, he'd stepped up and taken care of his siblings, who'd been eleven, nine and seven years old. He'd only been eighteen at the time—he'd been the result of a teen pregnancy, the cause of a quickie marriage, and his parents had only had his siblings once they were more settled—and he'd been forced into being a guardian and entrepreneur when he'd taken over his father's business.

So he could afford a little dishonour. Particularly when it came to a woman who intrigued him.

Piper stared at him, those beautiful eyes big and bright and bold against the odd green of her dress. If he'd seen that shade in a store somewhere, he wouldn't have taken a second look. Or he might have, but only to be offended by it. Now, though, on Piper... It made her skin look as if it had been bronzed. And it flattered a body he'd been trying not to pay attention to since they'd met.

Her breasts were full and out on display, though he was trying not to pay attention to them either. He wasn't sure if it was because it would get him into trouble if he did, or if he was trying to be polite. But the straps of her dress rested over smooth, strong shoulders, the waist of it clinging to her ribcage then flaring out. The heels he'd teased her about earlier did excellent things to the legs the dress revealed, though there wasn't much of them to see.

She wore no jewellery, only the lightest of make-up, and the way her hair was tied up accentuated the angles of her face. It made her look innocent, despite her pink lips curving. Despite her high cheekbones, almost demanding her eyes to crinkle even when she wasn't smiling. When she did and those cheeks lifted, her eyes narrowing... He'd learnt his lesson after the first time. Now, he simply braced for the breath he'd lose.

'You're teasing me.'

'Maybe,' he answered.

'Not maybe—yes.' Her eyes flickered to his face before moving back to the steep path. 'This is payback for me not being offended by you.'

'What is?' he asked innocently. 'This decline? I don't control landscape, my dear.'

'Don't call me that,' she said, though her words lacked heat. 'It's condescending.'

'It's not. "My dear" is a phrase of affection.'

She snorted. 'Now I know you're being condescending. You certainly do *not* feel affection towards me.'

He wasn't sure how to respond. The truth was there was a slight niggling in his chest that made him feel something for her. He didn't know if it was affection or if he'd merely suppressed his annoyance.

'Okay.'

He blinked. 'What?'

'Okay, carry me.' She stepped closer to him, giving him a whiff of a scent that reminded him of wild flowers. 'You're still offering, aren't you?'

'I— Yes, of course.' He cleared his throat. Did it again.

She smirked. 'Something wrong, Caleb?'

In one quick movement he scooped her into his arms. Her hands went around his neck with a quick exhalation, and he caught the smell of mint on her breath. It made his body tingle—though that might have been due to the fact that she fitted in his arms perfectly. He tried not to think about the soft flesh of her thighs against his bottom arm, or his hand on her perfect waist.

While he was at it, he resisted the desire to put his nose in her neck, to get more of that intoxicating perfume she was wearing. Or did she simply smell that way? Could someone's natural scent be this heady?

Caleb.

He kept himself from groaning now, too. His entire body had gone tense from the control he was exerting. But he thought of all the times he'd had to exercise control in his life. It was interchangeable with responsibility in his family, it seemed. Like during that phase when Tate, his brother, had refused to eat anything besides pizza. Caleb had refrained from buying anything else—including pizza—if Tate didn't eat at least one nutritional meal a day. There'd been a week where things had been touch and go, but it had worked out.

Then there was that time Jada had consistently got up late for school. No matter what Caleb had done, they'd arrived anywhere from fifteen to thirty minutes late. Jada had got detention and Caleb had received numerous notes about punctuality. Eventually, he'd refused to put the hot water on in the mornings if she didn't get up by six. He'd stood guard over the switch since it meant the entire house didn't get warm water. After three days of the Martin siblings going to school without showers, the collective effort of him, Emma and Tate had forced Jada to get up on time.

He smiled at the memory.

'You're enjoying this?'

It took the question to realise his trip down memory lane had distracted him from the woman in his arms. Now that she'd spoken, he realised it wouldn't work again.

'No.' He took the first tentative step down the hill.

Once he got his grip, he took another. 'I was thinking about how my sister's getting married.'

'No, you weren't.' She continued before he got the chance to ask how she knew. 'What are you feeling about it?'

'Affectionate. Nostalgia.'

'That's it?'

He looked down. 'What are you feeling?'

'I don't know.' There was silence as he took the next few steps. 'I'm happy for Liam and Emma. They obviously care about one another. Liam's changed a lot since they've met.'

Caleb tried not to snort at that. Piper narrowed her eyes.

'See, you're not only feeling affection and nostalgia. You don't like my brother?' she asked after a beat.

'I do.' He took a breath, another step. 'It's not that I don't like him. I certainly wouldn't have allowed him to marry my sister if I didn't like him.'

Her body stiffened. Even when he looked down at her, saw her face taut, saw her actively try to relax it, he still felt her tight muscles in her arms.

'What?' he asked. 'What did I say wrong?'

Her eyes met his. There was an inexplicable disappointment there. His stomach turned.

'Nothing,' she replied. A bald-faced lie. They both knew it. Neither of them addressed it. 'Are we done?' she asked quietly a moment later. Caleb turned, saw they were, and lowered her gently.

'I didn't mean to upset you,' he said when she was on the ground again.

'It's fine.'

'It's not fine, clearly.'

'It's not fine,' she told him, giving him a sad smile. 'But it doesn't matter.'

He wanted to tell her it did, but he had no reason to. He locked his jaw. Didn't bother prying it open when she'd obviously made up her mind. Nothing he could say would make her more receptive to his words. He was sure of it because that stubborn furrow in her brow told him she didn't only feel sad.

He started walking again, along the narrow path that led to the beach. It was covered with sand, more so the closer they got, but he didn't turn around to offer assistance. If she wanted to be stubborn, she'd have to deal with the consequences of it.

Again, not his most honourable decision, but something about Piper rubbed him up the wrong way.

Or the right way.

He grunted at the voice in his head. He didn't need a reminder of the attraction he felt for her. He could still feel her body in his arms. Could still smell her. Still had the desire to bury his nose in her neck. Maybe brush her pink lips when he drew back, taste that mouth, the curve of it—

His thoughts abruptly stopped when he got to the beach. There were people here and if he continued down that path he'd surely embarrass himself in front of all of them. He glanced over his shoulder to check that she was still okay. She seemed to be, though the pull of her lips made him think she wasn't pleased.

Good. Neither was he.

He grabbed a glass of champagne from the nearest waiter and drank.

Piper had to give it to Emma and Liam: extravagance could be quite beautiful.

Once she'd got over being left to fend for herself down that sandy path—which, in hindsight, was probably fair.

What could he have done, carried her the entire way?—
she was able to enjoy it.

The setting was magnificent. An entire stretch of the
beach had been reserved for the party, which allowed for
generous decorations. Emma and Liam had taken advantage. A large portion of the beach had been covered in
wooden planks. A long table sat on the planks, decorated
with greenery and candles, along with a bar and round
cocktail tables.

On the sand beyond it were wooden squares, stacked
and decorated to form smaller tables. The area was full of
them, scattered with round comfortable-looking cushions
as seats. Candles and fairy lights illuminated the area,
which would need the light in a few moments. Currently,
the sun was lowering in the sky, casting an orange glow
over the ocean. It was breathtaking.

'Pretty, isn't it?'

Jada, Emma's younger sister, came to stand beside her.
She was a picture in a light blue dress, her short hair
straight around her face, large navy earrings in her ears.

'It is,' Piper said with a smile. 'So are you.'

Jada blushed. 'You're just saying that.'

'I happen to mean it. But what does it matter if I'm
just saying it?' she asked, bumping her shoulder against
the young woman's. 'I'm surprised you were allowed to
wear blue.'

Jada laughed. 'I had to. Not the same shade as Emma's
dress, of course, but since Emma wanted the wedding's
theme to be "shades of blue" this worked.'

'It certainly does.'

Piper scanned the small crowd. Most of the people
she didn't recognise. Her mother had been an only child
and she and Liam had never got along with their father's
siblings or their children. Unsurprisingly, Liam hadn't

wanted them at his wedding. Surprisingly, he had wanted her there.

She supposed that might be too harsh. They'd seen each other often enough in the last five years that her invitation was warranted. The surprise? That was her resentment talking. Her memories of how he'd abandoned her to fend for herself for two years.

It slipped in, even when she was trying to be positive.

The truth was that if it hadn't been an all-expenses-paid trip to a Greek island during the school holidays when she wasn't teaching, Piper would have stayed at home. In some ways then, she was glad she'd been forced to be there. She needed to move on. Her father was dead. Had been for five years. That time long surpassed the time she'd spent alone with her father after Liam had left. She had to let it go.

She wasn't sure why she couldn't.

'Where are they?' she asked suddenly, not seeing them in the crowd.

'Over there.'

Jada pointed to a section of the beach that wasn't a part of the evening's celebrations. Piper clearly saw the two of them—Emma in her blue dress, Liam in a blue shirt and black pants—but something about it didn't feel right.

'Are they...are they arguing?'

Jada sighed. 'For the last ten minutes.'

'Did something happen?'

'Nothing I can think of. I mean, Em did get really quiet while I was doing her hair, but I thought that was nerves.'

'Cold feet?' Piper wondered out loud.

'I don't think so. I'm sure Emma would have said something. She's not exactly a great keeper of secrets.'

Piper studied the couple. It was clear they were arguing. Her brother's shoulders were squared back, as they always were when he felt attacked. She'd grown used to the stance. Had used it as a warning sign to stay out of his and their father's way.

'You're staring,' a quiet voice said from her side.

Piper turned to see Tate join them. He followed their gaze.

'You are, too, dummy,' Jada said without heat. Her tone was laced with worry.

'It's obvious.'

'Should one of us go check it out?'

'No,' came a new voice. Piper hadn't needed Caleb to answer his sister's question to know he was there. She'd felt him join their group. Her heart had sped up. Her body had become a little more aware. 'Let's give them a moment to sort this out.'

There was a long silence as they heeded the instruction. Piper didn't do so happily. She was worried by the disappointment that had washed over her earlier. When he'd spoken about 'allowing' Emma and Liam to marry. Before that moment, she'd almost forgotten she wasn't supposed to be interested in him. She'd been too distracted by the easy strength of his arms. By how he didn't only seem to be carrying her because he'd provoked her, but because he was a nice person.

But nice people weren't controlling. That trait reminded her too much of her father for her to make that evaluation. It was too much like her ex-boyfriend, too. The blurred lines with Caleb meant she needed to keep her distance. She couldn't repeat the mistakes of her past. She couldn't let her mind linger on *niceness*.

'Should we stop staring?' Jada asked into the quiet.

'Yes,' Piper replied. No one moved.

Then it happened.

Liam's hand paused as it ran through his hair, before

dropping with such a force Piper didn't know how it hadn't taken him to the floor. Emma took a step forward. Liam didn't move. She took another, resting her hands on his chest. Liam stepped back. There was a beat. Then her brother turned and ran.

Through the tables on the sand, past the wooden planks and all the guests who were there to celebrate with him and Emma. Past his future in-laws, who were staring at him in bewilderment. Past Piper, who watched him with a sinking feeling in her stomach.

But not surprise. No, not surprise.

Moments later, they all watched as Liam jumped onto the dock, onto a boat that had just been untied. He exchanged a few words with the man at the helm. Soon he was gone.

An uncomfortable silence settled. Then came Jada's trembling voice.

'Did he…did he just run away from Emma?'

CHAPTER FOUR

SHE WAS GOING to kill her brother. She'd make it swift, painless, because he was family. But he deserved death for this. Running away from his fiancée on the evening of their rehearsal dinner. Four days before their wedding.

Since she was the only one of his family there, it automatically put her in the spotlight. Taking in the three pairs of eyes staring at her, she finalised the plans for his death.

'Did your brother run away from our sister?' Jada demanded now, a clear distinction between *them* and Piper in that question.

'I was watching, same as you were,' Piper said with a calm she didn't feel. Her heart was pounding in her ears. She forced herself to take a breath when she realised she'd stopped inhaling and exhaling.

'Why?' Tate asked.

'Why was I watching with you?'

'Why would your brother leave our sister?'

'Tate.'

Caleb spoke softly, but the twenty-year-old reared back as if his brother had shouted. They exchanged a look, and when Tate looked back at Piper there was shame in his eyes. She wasn't sure if she felt sorry for him or if she was impressed at Caleb's nonverbal abilities.

'Do you have any idea what happened?' Caleb asked her.

'This is the first time I've seen my brother since arriving. I have no idea. But you know who does?'

She gestured to where Emma was standing. The Martin siblings' heads collectively turned, looking in that direction, as if they'd just realised she was still there. They all moved towards her, before Caleb stretched out an arm, stopping his siblings.

'At least one of us has to stay here.'

'Tate will,' Jada said.

At the same time Tate said, 'Jada.'

Caleb lifted a brow. They both sighed.

'Fine.'

'I can stay,' Piper offered, suddenly wanting to make herself useful.

The bond between the siblings was obvious, and it was making her nostalgic for something that had never been in her past. Or perhaps it had, after their mother had died and she and Liam had still sought comfort with one another.

'No,' Caleb said. 'They will. Help smooth everything over here, distract people. Pretend like what Liam did and everyone saw was part of the plan.'

'What should I do?' she asked in a small voice, emotion hammering into her like a battering ram. It broke down the defences she'd put in place, and she couldn't fight her instincts without them. Unfortunately, those instincts had been built and honed during her childhood. When she'd reverted to her father because he'd demanded she do so.

'Come with me,' Caleb said, interrupting her thoughts. 'You're his family. You deserve to know what happened.'

She didn't think she agreed with that, but she was touched by the sentiment. Enough that she obeyed, ignoring the whirlwind inside her. The war, really, between the part of her wondering if she was obeying because she wanted to or if it meant she was doing it again.

She'd ignored her feelings with Brad, had obeyed. Things had snowballed during their relationship. Two years later, she was still cold from being buried under the avalanche.

She wrapped her arms around herself, hoping to hide the shudder that had gone through her body. Caleb didn't seem to be paying attention to her though. His eyes were on Emma, her hunched-over frame keeping his focus. She glanced back at where she'd seen her brother disappear.

The boat was gone, the ocean calm, as if the turmoil of the last few minutes hadn't happened.

You'd better have a reason for running, Liam, Piper told him silently.

Emma went into his arms the moment they reached her. His heart ached and he tightened his hold before leaning back, keeping his hands on her arms.

'We saw what happened, but a lot of the guests didn't,' he said, knowing his sister needed him to take control. All of his siblings needed him to, in emergencies. 'I told Tate and Jada to pretend it was part of the evening's festivities. If you'd prefer we tell the truth, we'll do that. But I wanted to give you a moment to recover before you have people rushing to your side.'

Emma's lip wobbled but she nodded, stepping out of his embrace and straightening her shoulders. Pride filled him. He folded his arms to keep from reaching out to her anyway.

'What happened?' he asked after he'd given her a moment.

'He ran.'

'Yes, we know that. But you were fighting before. What about?'

She pursed her lips, taking a shaky breath. 'He has cold feet.'

Caleb barely kept himself from growling.

'We made an offer on a place back in Cape Town and the estate agent called to say they accepted the offer. It freaked him out.'

'So he ran?' Caleb asked, incredulous. He wanted to wring Liam's neck.

'Well, he started freaking out. Pacing. Breathing quick.' She dug a heel into the sand. 'It made me freak out and... and I told him something that made him run.'

'What?'

Her eyes met Piper's. Piper looked back steadily. For some reason, it made Emma's eyes fill. Before he could curse that he didn't have a tissue for her, Piper handed Emma one.

'Thanks,' she said, blowing her nose. She took a deep breath. 'He isn't ready for marriage.'

'What are you talking about?' Caleb demanded. 'He asked you to marry him. Hell, he asked *me* if he could marry you, which we both know takes guts.'

Piper blinked at him in surprise. He merely lifted his shoulders.

'He loves you, Emma,' Caleb said with a shake of his head. 'There's no way he doesn't want to marry you.'

If he didn't, Caleb would kill him. Then bring him back from the dead and force him to do right by Emma.

'It's true,' Piper said softly. It was the first thing she'd said since they'd arrived. He supposed he should be happy she'd contributed at all. He was particularly happy she'd contributed with this.

Emma breathing began to sound like sobs. Caleb angled his body to keep her from the guests' view. Piper did the same.

'He panicked,' Emma said. 'About the house and—' She broke off again.

'It's a big commitment,' Piper said. 'Especially for him.'

'I know. But I didn't force him to marry me. I didn't give him an ultimatum or anything. I didn't even tell him I wanted to buy a house.'

The more Emma spoke, the guiltier Caleb felt. He should have asked more questions. Done more than a credit check on Liam. He hadn't protected Emma, and now she was hurt. What kind of a brother did that make him? What kind of a father figure? He could almost hear his father's voice from the grave, asking him those questions. Hell, if his father had been here, this probably wouldn't have happened.

He quelled the guilt with anger.

'Did he force you to do this, Em?'

'What? No, no. No,' she said again. 'I wanted to do all this.'

'You signed the pre-nup, didn't you?'

'Caleb,' Emma said sharply, her first show of emotion apart from devastation, 'Liam wasn't doing this for the money.'

He didn't reply.

'Really.' Emma's voice softened. 'He ran because… because I'm pregnant, and it freaked him out. We never spoke about starting a family, and I think because of how he grew up…with your father,' she said to Piper, 'I think he's scared to be one. Or he doesn't know what kind of father he'll be. I don't know. I… I…'

She started crying in earnest now, and Caleb set aside his shock and admonishments—hadn't he had the sex talk with all his siblings; what didn't they understand about possible pregnancy and STDs?—and drew her into a hug. Her body shook in his arms. His heart shook along with it. And he got more and more upset. More determined that he should have protected her from a man who could be so careless with her heart. Guiltier that he hadn't acted like their father would have.

'Em,' Caleb said softly, running a hand over her hair. 'It's going to be okay.'

She said something, but it was muffled since she was crying into his chest. He looked at Piper, who was staring at them both a little helplessly. He knew it was irrational, but he was suddenly angry with her, too.

She should have warned Emma her brother would be so reckless. She should have warned *him* at the very least.

He could have warned Emma. Banned her from seeing Liam. Anything to keep this moment from happening.

Then she met his eyes and his heart flipped at the pain he saw there. At the extent of that helplessness. Something about it made him want to reach out and take her into his arms, too. Involuntarily, his muscles spasmed. Emma drew back and looked at them both. Her make-up was still flawless. He was glad that ridiculously priced make-up artist they'd hired was worth the money.

'You have to find him,' she said, blinking up at him. 'Please. He's scared, and I'm worried he'll do something dangerous.' She looked at Piper. 'You know why he did this. He needs you to bring him back.'

'He... I...' Piper stammered. She gave a quick shake of her head. 'No, Emma. He doesn't need me.'

'He might,' Emma said softly. 'He definitely needs me. He just doesn't know it yet.'

Caleb admired his sister's quiet resolve. He didn't appreciate that it was days before her wedding, and it came courtesy of a runaway groom.

'Emma—'

'Please,' his sister interrupted, aiming the full force of her puppy dog eyes at Piper. He silently wished Piper luck. He hadn't been able to resist that look since...ever. 'Please bring him back.'

'I... Okay,' Piper said hesitantly.

'Thank you,' Emma said, hugging Piper. Then she broke away from Piper and drew him into a hug. 'Thank you, Caleb.'

'Why are you thanking me?' he asked, though he patted Emma's back.

She aimed the puppy dog eyes at him now. 'Because you're going with Piper. You're going to help her find Liam.'

CHAPTER FIVE

'THIS EVENING DID not go like I thought it would,' Piper said.

It was after everything had ended at the rehearsal dinner. Jada and Tate had woven an elaborate tale about Liam going hunting for the perfect wedding gift on one of the Greek islands. Caleb and Piper had returned without Emma, assuring her they'd make something up about her disappearance, too.

They'd stumbled through an excuse. Something about her joining Liam on his excursion. He didn't think many people believed them—some of them had seen the argument and, of course, rumours had spread—but then the entertainment had arrived and they'd been distracted.

The dinner had gone on as planned without the bride and groom. He and Piper had sat at the designated seats to make their emptiness less conspicuous. It had only succeeded in making *him* feel more conspicuous. He was certain it had nothing to do with how it made it look as if he and Piper were getting married.

'You can say that again,' he said, lowering to join her on the planks. He'd grabbed two bottles from the bar on his way there, and only now saw what they were. 'I have a cider and beer. I'm not sure which one you want.'

'Cider,' she said. She waited for him to open it. 'Nice of you to think of me.'

'It's been a long night. Figured we needed it.'

She clinked her bottle against his. They drank in silence for a few minutes.

'Do you think Emma's going to be okay?'

'What do you think?' he asked, a little too harshly.

'This isn't my fault, you know,' she said after a beat. 'Liam is his own person. He makes his own decisions. I had nothing to do with him leaving.'

She was right, and he was desperately trying to figure out why he was holding her accountable for her brother's actions. Was it because that was what he'd done his entire life? He'd taken responsibility for his siblings' actions even though he had no control over what they did?

But that was family, he thought. That was what his father had taught him about being part of a family. Long before his mother had left, overwhelmed by the responsibilities of being a parent of four when his siblings had come in quick succession, his father had taught them they were a unit. They looked out for one another.

When his father had died in a freak accident inspecting a property under construction, Caleb had felt that responsibility more than ever. It didn't matter that he hadn't felt capable of parenting three kids. He'd barely been an adult himself; had just finished school. But he'd stepped up. He knew it was what his father would have wanted. And there was no way he was going to let his siblings go into the system.

He only hoped it made up for how he hadn't taken his father's teachings seriously when the man had been alive.

'I know,' he answered, taking a long drag from his beer.

'Do you?' she asked. 'I feel like you're judging me. Or treating me like I told Liam to run away instead of face his responsibilities.'

Something in her tone made him look at her. Something on her face confirmed his suspicions.

'He's done this before, hasn't he?'

She took a deep breath, set aside the cider. It was barely touched. For a long time she didn't speak. The only sounds were the staff clearing up around them. A few people lingered, but not close to them. Instead, they chose to explore the beach further down. Lights flickered in the distance, the faint sound of music vibrating through the air.

'He hasn't run from his responsibilities,' she said. 'I'm not his responsibility.'

'He ran from you?'

'Didn't you hear what I said?' she asked quietly. 'I'm not his responsibility so, technically, he didn't run from me.'

'Since when do technicalities matter when it comes to family?'

She angled her head, as if accepting his words. She didn't verbalise the acceptance.

'I will say that he runs from hard things,' she said after a moment. 'I imagine this experience has been hard for him. Then finding out he's about to become a father...'

She fell silent.

'You don't run away from hard things,' Caleb said firmly. 'Not from family or responsibilities. You face them.'

'*You* do, maybe. It's not as easy for the rest of us.'

He looked at her. 'What are you running away from, Piper?'

There was a beat. 'I wasn't talking about me. I was talking about Liam.'

He didn't call her out on her lie. Figured she'd told it to him for a reason. The same went for when he'd carried her down that path that afternoon. He was still dying to know what had happened then. But Piper didn't offer information for the sake of it. At least not about herself.

'Piper—'

'Look!' she interrupted him, jumping up and pointing into the distance. He could only hear the motoring of a boat, but when he stood he could see one that looked familiar.

'How did you know—?'

He cut himself off when he saw her lowering to take off the shoes she'd refused to remove earlier. Then she was running. Sprinting, actually, towards the dock.

A variety of scenarios went through his head. One was that if Liam had come back on that boat, Caleb would kill him. Two was that he couldn't let Piper go down there alone. They had no idea what they would face, or who would be there. And they were in a foreign country, for heaven's sake. One where they didn't speak English as their first language. Cursing, he ran after her.

She was already speaking to a guy on the dock by the time he arrived.

'I'm sorry, I don't know who you're talking about.'

The guy's English was perfect, though he had a slight Greek accent.

Caleb stepped forward. 'You're sure you didn't take a tourist anywhere today?'

The man shook his head. Caleb sighed, took out his wallet and a stack of euros.

'I'll give you all this if you tell me where he is.'

The stranger considered it for all of twenty seconds, before taking the cash from Caleb, counting it and pocketing it.

'I dropped him off at the other end of the island.'

'This island?' Caleb asked. 'He's still on the island?'

'He said he needed some things.'

Caleb turned to Piper. 'There's no way he went back to the villa.'

'Why not?' Piper asked, though mutedly, he thought. 'Everyone would have been at the party. We were comforting Emma for a long time. He could have come and gone and no one would be any the wiser.'

'But where would he go?'

'He asked about ferries when I dropped him,' the guy offered. 'I saw him walking to the ticket counter.'

Caleb studied the man, hoping his gaze would show how unimpressed he was that he'd only been given that information now.

'So he bought a ticket.'

'Where to?' Piper asked.

'That's the question,' Caleb said. He wondered how the hell he was going to tell Emma her fiancé had bought a ticket off the island. He shook his head. It wasn't an option.

He formulated a plan, thanked the man and walked a few metres before waiting for Piper to join him.

'We should go talk to the person at the ticket stall.'

'Good idea,' she said. 'You should do that.'

'Great,' he said, relieved she'd agreed. He'd been prepared for a fight. Then his brain caught up. 'Wait—did you say *I* should do that?'

'Yes.' Her gaze didn't waver. 'You've taken charge of this whole thing anyway. Giving instructions, asking the questions.'

'What are you talking about?'

'Don't do that,' she said with a shake of her head. 'Don't pretend like this is in my head. It isn't. I know what you're doing. I'm telling you what you're doing.'

'I wasn't doing that either.'

'No?' she asked. 'So being in control of your sister's relationship by *allowing* my brother to marry her, or telling us what to do after Liam left, or instructing me to follow you to speak with Emma, or now, when you took over a conversation I was having—you're saying none of that shows how you're controlling things?'

He opened his mouth to reply, but he started thinking about what she'd said and closed it again. He wasn't doing anything out of the ordinary. Taking charge, taking control was what he did. It was what he'd had to do since his father's death. It was what his siblings *needed* him to do. It had helped them all through unimaginable grief. So why was someone he'd just met making him feel guilty about it?

'Fine,' he said, his patience snapping. 'I'll do it alone. Because I don't run when things get hard. I take my responsibilities seriously and do what needs to be done.'

She hadn't been able to fall asleep, not until so late the sky had started lightening. When she'd woken up an hour later, she'd realised breakfast had started and she probably needed to be up. It would be a day of looking for her brother. And trying not to think about the night before.

Wonderful.

She took a quick shower, did her best with her make-up since her face gave away that she hadn't slept much. She didn't know what had kept her up. Was she anticipating a knock on the door? Either from Liam, coming to tell her he needed to talk, or from Caleb, coming to update her?

Or perhaps it was the concern that she'd overreacted at the dock? The persistent thought that she should apologise to Caleb and tell him *why* she'd overreacted? It was true that he was taking control. She was more sensitive to it than most. Every time something like that happened, her body stiffened. Since her muscles had been tight and achy almost the entire day, she knew she wasn't making it up.

But she didn't know if taking it out on him was fair. A pesky voice in her brain insisted it wasn't, and pointed out all the good things he'd done the day before as proof. Things that told her he wasn't like the men in her past. That he didn't deserve to be painted with the same brush. At the same time, he still triggered that…that *fear* inside her. She didn't know the cause of it entirely, but it was as good a reason as any to make sure things between them remained cordial.

She resisted the involuntary snort.

Thirty minutes later, she was locking up and walking to breakfast. She didn't have to walk very far. Breakfast had been set up next to the pool in the centre of Pleasure Villas. One long table had a breakfast bar with food. Servers stood behind it, ready with spoons, a steady stream of others replacing empty containers. Another table had been set up as a coffee station. A short distance away from that, a long table decorated with fruits and flowers stood where people sat and ate.

Piper found Caleb almost immediately. Relief slid through her. Until that moment, she didn't realise how worried she was that he'd found something at the ticket stall last night and left without her. Not that she wanted to be involved with this mess. She was still planning on killing Liam when they found him. But he was still her brother. Plus, she was sure that if Caleb found him first, Liam's death wouldn't be as merciful as she intended on making it.

She didn't go to Caleb like she wanted to. Didn't demand any answers either. Instead, she headed for the coffee station, poured herself a cup, then leisurely made her way back to the table. She sat across from Caleb, Jada and Tate, the latter of whom were looking at her with a glower. It must run in the family. Caleb, however, watched her coolly. She returned the favour, bringing her cup to her lips.

She wasn't sure how long they sat like that, staring at one another. It was only when Jada released an irritated breath that Piper looked over.

'You're still upset with me,' she said.

'Yes.'

'Jada,' Caleb warned, but Piper waved a hand.

'It's fine. I get it.' She directed her attention to the younger Martin siblings. 'I'm sorry. I didn't know this would happen. There's no excuse for his behaviour.'

They blinked. Jada looked around. No one seemed to be interested in them. She turned back to Piper.

'It sucks.'

'It does.'

She looked deflated. 'I'm sorry we're taking this out on you. It's not your fault.'

Piper gave her a sympathetic smile. 'I understand.'

Jada and Tate exchanged a look, before both looking at Caleb. Something wordless passed between the three of them. Piper felt an inexplicable turn of jealousy in her stomach. No, not inexplicable—she knew the reason for it. She wished she could have had such a bond with her family. She would have settled for Liam, but she was still upset with him. Partly because he'd left her to deal with this. Another part was that she could see how upset Emma's family was. Knowing how upset Emma had been the day before, too, Piper was most upset that Liam had hurt Emma.

He was repeating their father's mistakes. Hurting the people he loved. Because, despite all this, Piper knew Liam loved Emma. But moving forward meant leaving the past behind. He'd managed some of that, untainted by their father, in the way his relationship with Emma had been before he'd run. If he wanted a future with her, he'd need to learn to stop running completely. She felt some responsibility for teaching him that. She might no longer have hope for herself to be unscathed by the past, but she did for Liam.

She looked up in surprise when Tate and Jada got up and, with murmured goodbyes, left.

'Did you chase them away?' she asked lightly, only then noticing that somehow they were alone at the end of the table. The closest guests were sitting four seats away.

'I didn't say anything to them.'

'Oh, you said something. Not verbally, but you told them something.'

Caleb's mouth pulled up at the side. 'You're perceptive.'

'When you're raised not to have a voice, you learn how to pay attention to what isn't said pretty well.'

Now his eyebrows pulled up. It took that for her to realise she'd said something revealing.

'Did you find anything last night?' she asked, changing the subject.

There was a moment of silence as he adjusted.

'You know,' he said slowly. 'One of these days, you're going to tell me what happened instead of alluding to it.' She barely had a chance to snort at the arrogance—or to register the thrill it brought—before he was continuing. 'And yes, I did. Liam bought a ticket to Santorini last night. He left on a ferry an hour before we caught up.'

'Santorini?' she repeated. 'What would he be doing there?'

'I don't know.' Caleb paused. 'I'd like to say he needs time to process, but he could do that here.'

'Except Liam likes to process away from the problem. As far away as he can get, actually.' She frowned. 'Santorini isn't that far, is it?' she asked. Caleb shook his head. 'Okay, so he intends on coming back.'

'You sound sure of that.'

'I'm not,' she said with a little laugh. 'But, based on what I know…' She trailed off when she considered she didn't know that much. Not really. 'When Liam runs, it's clear when he's not coming back. If he wasn't planning on coming back now, he would have gone back to Cape Town. Probably,' she added, because she wasn't sure. 'Point is, there's a chance he'll be here for the wedding.'

'Do you want to take that chance?' he asked, his voice distant. 'There are only three days left.'

She frowned. 'It's not like we can go around Santorini trying to find him.'

'Why not? We did it here.'

'Because this island is small, and we knew what his steps were.'

'We know what his next step was. That's good enough for me.'

She exhaled, trying not to overreact again. *Cordial, Piper,* she reminded herself. With another breath, she nodded.

'I'm trying to help my sister,' he said after a moment. He'd been watching her. And he must have seen accusation on her face despite her attempt to school it if he was defending himself. 'I spent the entire night with her, waiting for her to wake up. When she did, I held her as she cried.' His jaw clenched. 'So—will you be coming with me?'

When she didn't answer immediately, he made a move to leave. Her hand shot out, startling both of them when it settled over the hand he had on the table. She ignored the heat of it, how it felt as if it were searing through her body from that small point of contact.

'Don't go,' she said softly. 'For one, you'll make a scene. You already have.' She smiled at him for the sake of the watching eyes, as if she were placating him somehow. 'The last thing Emma needs is for her guests to suspect something's wrong.'

His face settled into a blank expression—a smile was too much to ask for, apparently—but she could still see his anger in the way the corner of his mouth twitched.

Oh, why had she looked at his mouth? Despite the turmoil of feelings and tension happening inside and around her, that small gesture had her wondering what it would be like to kiss him. Would he be as demanding a kisser as he was as a man? Would his tongue ask her things and expect her to obey? Would she protest?

Startled by the intensity of her thoughts, she snatched her hand away. Midway through, she realised people were probably still watching and ran a hand down her ponytail instead. There was little chance of it looking natural, but at least she'd tried.

'What would you like them to think instead?' Caleb asked casually. He leaned back, watched her with interest.

It should have had alarms ringing in her head. It didn't. And it worried her. Worried her that she couldn't resist that look when she knew she should be able to.

'That we're having an argument?' he continued. 'Two lovers having a tiff?'

She fought to keep herself as calm as he appeared to be. 'We can be having an argument. I doubt anyone here would believe the nature of it to be romantic though.'

'Why not?'

'They're your friends and family,' she said simply. 'They know you.'

She left it at that, offering him a satisfied smile as she went to get herself some breakfast.

CHAPTER SIX

HE'D NEVER HAD these issues before. Perhaps he had been presumptuous, but he'd believed growing up with two sisters had taught him how to be around women. His history of successful dating stood testament to that. His interactions with Piper? Not so much.

The problem might have been that the dating didn't last too long. Sometimes, it carried on over weeks. A few months, in rare instances. But it always ended mutually, with each party satisfied.

Are you sure? Piper's voice asked in his head. He almost grunted, but then the real her—sitting across from him on the ferry, looking out the window—would have heard. She probably would have guessed he was talking to phantom Piper, too.

Yes, I am sure, he told that voice. *We both agreed things had gone as far as they could.*

Both of you? it asked. *Or did you simply make the decision for her, and she had no choice but to go along with you?*

He didn't answer that. It had nothing to do with the fact that a voice in his head had asked the question.

Most relationships aren't considered successful if they end, the voice spoke again.

Enough, he thought, clamping down on its freedom. Trying not to think about why he was having a conversation with himself in his head. Or why it felt as though he was having the conversation with the woman opposite him.

It felt like support for the fact that he'd never experienced this kind of animosity before. Animosity might have been too harsh a word, but what Piper radiated around him—and only him, he thought, remembering her interactions with his family—wasn't exactly positive.

He wondered what advice his father would have given him in the situation. Chad Martin never had problems speaking with people, no matter who they were. He could talk himself out of anything, and he'd been able to talk anyone *into* anything, too. When Caleb had taken over his father's business, he'd discovered he shared that with his father. It had connected them, had eased some of Caleb's grief as he worked to figure out how to be a property mogul in his late teens. Sometimes, Caleb wished he'd appreciated what he and his father had in common before Chad had died.

All of the time, he wished he'd just appreciated his father before Chad had died.

Caleb had been one of those annoying, sullen children. Fought his father at every opportunity. In Caleb's final year at school, Chad had urged him to get his real estate qualification. He'd refused, settling on studying towards a business degree for the sole purpose of annoying Chad. In the end, he'd followed his father's wishes—later, in his twenties, when he'd had a handle on being a businessperson and raising a family. Chad had handled the two roles easily. Caleb knew first-hand how hard it was, but Chad had never once shown it.

Maybe that was why Caleb felt the need to take care of everything for his siblings. To make sure they didn't have to worry, just like his father had once ensured for them. For *him*, Caleb corrected, something churning inside him. His siblings had been too young when Chad died to remember it.

'It'll be okay,' Piper said suddenly.

He frowned as his brain caught up to the present. She was staring at him, concerned.

'I'm sure it will be.'

'Are you?' she asked. 'You should tell that to your face.'

He grimaced, and she laughed. It was a happy sound, as if it had been hard fought for and was now finally free. The image made no sense and yet it made perfect sense. Which was yet another sign of what this woman was doing to his sanity.

'I wasn't thinking about this.'

'I'd like to ask you what you were thinking about, but I don't know if I should.'

'Me neither,' he agreed easily. 'You don't seem to like me much, so I doubt you'd want to know the inner workings of my mind.'

Her eyes went serious. He braced himself for a tongue-lashing.

'I don't know how I feel about you,' she said, in a tone similar to her expression. 'Despite that, I want to know what you were thinking about.'

It wasn't exactly a peace offering. Perhaps a temporary truce.

'I was thinking about my father,' he said, offering his own olive branch. 'I've been thinking about him a lot these days. It must be the wedding.'

'He passed away, right?'

'Yeah. Years ago—more than a decade.'

He looked out at the water splashing against the large windows of the ferry.

'But sometimes it still feels fresh?' she enquired gently.

He frowned, before remembering her father had passed away, too. 'It does. Do you feel that way?'

She blinked. Laughed without amusement. 'No.' The word was said curtly. 'Not about my dad. But I do sometimes feel that way about my mother. I think about how she'd react at big events in my life.' She chewed her bottom lip. 'I wonder about whether my life would be different if she hadn't died when we were so young.'

The unguardedness in her voice made him want to give her the same.

'I do that, too. Like now, I'm thinking about how he's missing out on all this. But maybe that's a good thing.' He shook his head as he said it. 'No, it's not. I don't know why I said that.'

'Because you feel it?' Her voice was soft. 'Maybe it's both a good *and* bad thing.' She shrugged at him. 'Human beings have complicated emotions. We don't always have to pick one thing over the other. We can let them be complicated, if they are.'

'Like your feelings for me?'

She stared at him, laughed with a shake of her head. 'I certainly have *strong* feelings about what I'd like to say to you now, yes.'

Caleb smiled, enjoying the lightness on her face. She was wearing her hair up again, with a cute summer dress and cute trainers. He wasn't sure if the cuteness came because that was what he found her to be, or if the items themselves were cute.

'Is this your first time in Greece?' he asked.

He wanted to know more about her. The sneak peek he'd got into her past now—that she missed her mother, but not her father—didn't seem to be enough. The strength of his desire to know surprised him.

'Yes.'

'The upside of Liam doing this then is that you'll get to see a little more of it.'

Her lips curved. Not enough for him to call it a smile, but enough to make his stomach ache with pleasure. He hadn't known that could happen until now.

'There are very few upsides to this, but I suppose that

could be one, yes. Another,' she continued, 'is that we found out we'll be getting a new member of our family.'

He frowned. Somehow, he'd forgotten about that. Not entirely—it was likely somewhere at the back of his head. But with worrying about Emma and thinking about Piper, and trying *not* to think about Piper... No, he hadn't processed he was about to become an uncle.

He took a breath. 'Yeah, I guess we are.'

'What do you mean, you "guess"?' she asked, incredulous. 'Emma told us she was pregnant.'

'I'm...still struggling to believe it, I think.'

Piper studied him, then nodded slowly. 'Oh, I see. You're having trouble picturing your sister having sex.'

He reared back. He could feel his entire face crease in disgust. 'What is wrong with you?'

'Nothing's wrong with me. Sex is natural.' Then—thankfully—she had mercy on him. 'Does this mean you're not happy about it?'

'Oh, it's not that. I've taken care of kids before. I can do it again if push comes to shove.' She gave him a look that made him realise how his words had sounded. 'I didn't mean—' He broke off, realising he *did* mean what he was about to say he didn't. 'I'm...worried, I suppose.'

'You shouldn't be.'

'The father of the baby ran off,' he said darkly. 'Why shouldn't I be?'

'He'll come back.'

'I thought you weren't confident about that.'

There was a moment before she answered. 'Fake it until you make it is a popular saying, I believe.' She sniffed.

He didn't know how or why it made him smile, but it did. Or how or why, when their gazes caught, he couldn't look away. Her eyes really were striking, her cheekbones so damn defined. He wanted to lift a hand and caress her cheek. Feel the skin that looked like satin, brush a thumb over her lips shortly after.

Speaking of…

He looked at those lips, saw them part under his perusal. It made him want to lean forward and kiss her. Slip his tongue through that parting and tease her until they forgot about their responsibilities—

Their responsibilities.

'I don't know if we can fake a groom on the wedding day,' he said gruffly, looking out of the window again. Wishing that the water could collapse over him and cool the tingling in his body.

'We won't have to.' Her voice was hoarse, too. It made him feel better. 'We'll find him, and I'll remind him of that.'

He looked at her now. 'Why does he need reminding?'

'How much do you know about my family, Caleb?' she asked seconds later.

'Not much more than you've told me,' he replied. 'Your parents passed away.'

She nodded. 'My dad only died five years ago, so he raised us.' She paused. 'He wasn't winning any Father of the Year awards. Most things in life we had to learn from books or TV. Things like responsibility.' Her fingers tightened in her lap. 'Liam is clearly still struggling with that.'

'How can he be? If your dad wasn't a good father, Liam must have looked out for you. That takes responsibility.'

She smiled at him. It reminded him of the day before, after he'd carried her, and she'd gone sad.

'I like that you think that,' she said softly. 'Almost enough to let you think all brothers look out for their younger siblings.'

He frowned. Thought about his sisters and brother. How lost they'd seemed after their father's death. How they'd needed love and protection. They'd needed *him,* and he'd given himself to them because he was their older brother. But young Piper apparently hadn't had that.

'Liam didn't look out for you.'

'No.' Her eyes flickered to him. 'It's not a reflection on his abilities to be a husband and a father.'

'Just a reflection on how poor a brother he is,' he said. 'Except you're still defending him.'

'Family is a hell of a thing,' she replied with a smile. 'Which is why you took care of your siblings after your father died. Why you still are.'

The way she said that last part niggled at him. He shrugged it off.

'My dad died when I was eighteen. Emma was the second oldest at eleven. It wasn't exactly a choice as much as a necessity.' He waited a beat. 'You know my mom left long before that.'

'I do. I'm sorry.'

'It is what it is.'

It was a facade of unaffectedness. Not so much about his mother—that part did make him feel rather unaffected. But his father's death at such a young age—how young his siblings had been when it happened—all of what his siblings hadn't got to experience because of it... Those were things that bothered him when he couldn't sleep. When his brain turned on and he couldn't switch it off again.

It happened more often than he wanted to admit. He'd learnt to live with it, to cope with it, by working or working out. But sometimes his mind and his body were too tired for that. Not for the thoughts though. Or for the guilt.

Who in the universe had decided *he* should benefit from having his father around for eighteen years when his siblings hadn't?

'I remember,' Piper said, her eyes sharp when he

looked at her, 'when I was around fifteen and Liam was seventeen, he was going through a…phase.'

'A phase?'

'He asked my father about it.'

'Wait—what exactly are we talking about here?'

'His body was changing.'

'At seventeen?' Caleb dropped his head, amusement shimmering through him. 'He was a late bloomer?'

She laughed, bright and sparkling like the water around them. 'Oh, I don't know. I think things might have already *bloomed* and he just wanted to do something about it then. He had a girlfriend. Carmen, I think. Or Camilla. I can never remember.'

He groaned. 'This is almost as bad as thinking about my sister having sex.'

'Which you shouldn't do.'

'Yeah, of course not.' He shifted in his seat. Stopped at the amusement on her face. She wanted him to squirm. He shouldn't enjoy it, but he did.

'Anyway, he asked my father about condoms or something and there was this moment of silence. You could hear a pin drop.' Her face went thoughtful. 'I wanted to laugh, but not because I found the moment funny. That's changed now, of course,' she told him. 'But then, it was because it was…awkward. Really, really awkward.'

His heart stalled at the look on her face. The way it had gone from teasing to something harder. More painful. More vulnerable.

'My father said, "no", and walked away.'

'He didn't answer the question.'

'No.' She met his eyes. 'It must have been hard for Liam to reach out to our father. But he was trying. I guess I'm trying with him now.'

'Hmm.' He took a few seconds before he continued. 'I hope he starts trying with you, too.'

She hadn't intended on telling him that story about her father. Or she had, but it wasn't meant to illustrate what a bad father hers had been. Or to imply that Liam needed to try and reach out to her. She'd only wanted to cheer Caleb up. Distract him from the obvious pain he felt about his own father.

But she couldn't stop thinking about it. Not even when they arrived in Santorini. At least not until something more pressing presented itself.

'I'm sorry—you want me to *what*?'

'Climb on the donkey,' Caleb said, as if it were a reasonable request. 'There are a lot of steps up to the village.'

'And riding a donkey up them is going to change that?'

'It'll make things a lot easier. We also get there quicker.'

'Except I'd be sacrificing my life in the process. Would speed and convenience make that worth it?' she asked him. 'Would you be happy if I died, but you got to the top of the island quickly and easily?'

'Do you always exaggerate this much?' he asked, narrowing his eyes. At least she assumed. He was wearing his sunglasses again. She didn't mind it as much now that she knew what was beneath it.

'I'm not exaggerating,' she told him. 'Look at that.'

She pointed at the area where the donkeys waited. They stared at her blandly. One flicked its tail, another stamped its hooves. The men waiting for them to decide muttered impatiently. Caleb sighed next to her.

'You're right. They're killing machines.'

'Why can't we stay here?' she asked, turning her back to the donkeys. 'It's gorgeous.'

The ocean twinkled in various shades of blue, the sun

gleaming off it. It was midday, hot, though the sea breeze offered some relief. There were rocks in the distance, tall and rugged and brown. Boats navigated through them easily, stopped at the port regularly. There was chatter from tourists, from salespeople at the kiosks at the port, but it didn't change the beauty of the place.

'We can't stay here because these men say your brother went into the city.'

'They could be lying.'

'I offered them enough incentive to be truthful,' he said dryly.

'Doesn't mean they're telling the truth. If you were offering me money to ask if I'd seen some guy, I'd do exactly what they did.'

'No, you wouldn't.'

'No, I wouldn't.' Should it bother her that he knew that about her? 'I'm still not getting on that donkey. Not even if you pay me for it.'

She walked past the animals, barely sparing a glance for them, though her heart beat painfully in her chest. She'd had one experience with donkeys on a school trip when she was twelve. She'd been scarred by it. She still remembered how they rode in a circle in an enclosed track. The donkey had gone faster than it was supposed to, spooked by something no one had been able to disclose to her. At no point had she been unsafe, but she'd learnt her lesson about the unpredictability of the animal. She couldn't imagine what would happen if a donkey got unpredictable on a flight of steps.

By the tenth step, she knew she would pay for this decision. By the twentieth, she was breathing hard, and she was barely a quarter of the way up. At the thirty-fifth she stopped, put her hands on her waist and panted.

'Regretting this decision now?'

She whirled around. When the movement made her unsteady, she pressed her back against the mountain. It was cooler there, and she closed her eyes on an exhale. When she opened her eyes again, Caleb was still there, watching her, as unruffled as ever.

'I didn't realise you were climbing with me,' she said, her voice breathy.

'Did you think I'd climb on a donkey and wait for you at the top?' he asked sarcastically. She almost made a sarcastic reply in return before she realised it would take energy she didn't have. Which annoyed her because not only was he not breathing hard, but he had the energy to be sarcastic with her, too.

'I would have been able to suffer in silence then,' she breathed, closing her eyes again.

'Your wish is my command.'

After a moment, she wished he hadn't listened to her. Or that she'd said something about him watching her as well. Though she couldn't see him do it, she could feel him. She opened her eyes, caught him. Then found herself caught, just as she had been on the boat.

He'd taken off his sunglasses, giving her direct access to his gaze. It was…intense. Being its focus made her feel as if she wanted to curl up in front of him, purr. She didn't get the chance to be embarrassed by the thought when emotion flickered across his face.

'What?' she asked, pulling her ponytail over her shoulder when it made her feel self-conscious.

'I was going to ask you the same thing,' he replied. 'What were you thinking about now?'

'I…wasn't… I mean, I…'

'Piper,' he said when she stopped stammering. When she gave up on trying to form a full sentence. 'You're charming when you're embarrassed. Has anyone ever told you that before?'

Her cheeks flushed, but she shook her head. A donkey rattled past them, then two more. Caleb moved closer to her to get out of the way. It brought him very much into *her* way. She lifted her chin to meet his eyes, though heaven only knew why she would. She shouldn't look at him when this…this strange *thing* was happening between them. When she still wanted to purr, but now, with his body centimetres away from her, wanted him to pet her, too.

Stroke a hand down the curve of her spine…have his hand settle on her lower back… He'd pull her even closer, until there was no space between them. Lower his lips to hers, so she could taste that contrary mouth of his. She would feel what she knew would be a hard, firm body against her softness. She might even be tempted into hooking a leg around his waist so that—

Her mouth opened and she drew in air. She couldn't breathe, and it had nothing to do with her climbing up the steep steps to the village of Oia. It was because she'd just thought about Caleb *petting* her. Her brother's future brother-in-law. A man she would share a family member with when Emma gave birth. Not only that—though the entire idea of being petted spoke wonders about her sanity—it had nothing to do with petting at all. She wanted to make out with him. To taste him and feel him. To indulge that faint buzz inside her that told her their connection wasn't only physical attraction. To pretend that was the most important thing she had to do.

But it wasn't. She had to think. Her brain had helped her survive the years of her father's control. Obeying him had been better than the alternative: fights and punishments, the latter getting crueller as she grew older.

He'd be late on payment for school fees, so she'd have

to take a letter home or not get her report card when everyone else did. He wouldn't fetch her after school, or he'd make her wait. He wouldn't help her apply for university. He certainly didn't help apply for funding.

But she'd survived it—only to find someone else who'd treated her exactly the same.

She couldn't make those same mistakes now. Oh, Caleb might seem different, but what if he wasn't? What if he *allowed* her to do things? Or took over, and made her think she couldn't do things herself?

It had happened before. It could happen again.

She couldn't be wooed by this man. She had to break through whatever spell he'd woven over her...

'They're done,' she said quietly. Dipped her head. No more eye contact. 'I'm ready to climb again.'

She did exactly that, not stopping again even when her lungs started to burn and her legs felt sore and heavy. They were halfway now, then three-quarters of the way up. Still, she didn't stop. Her legs were burning now, too. There was a stitch in her side.

Good, she thought. She'd punish herself for whatever had happened with them at that step. It would be a reminder that she shouldn't have been in that position. She should have been protecting herself. She couldn't entertain the idea of a make-out session with this man. It would no doubt bring her the emotional equivalent of the physical pain she was currently feeling.

'Piper,' came a voice from beside her. It was joined by a gentle but firm grasp around her arm. She refused the pleasure of its warmth. Pulled away.

'What?'

'You're pushing yourself too hard.'

'I'm...climbing,' she said between huffs. Now that she

was standing still, her body was berating her for doing exactly as Caleb said.

'Yeah, but you're not taking breaks.'

'Neither…are you.'

'I don't need them.'

'Oh, right,' she said, rolling her eyes. 'Because…you're a perfect…male specimen.'

The biting tone of the words was undermined by the breathiness.

'I'm only saying if you need a break, take one.'

She narrowed her eyes at him. He grunted. Then made another sound that was strangled.

'How about if I go ahead? Would you feel more comfortable with stopping, going at your own pace then?'

No.

'Yes,' she replied, out of spite.

His eyes swept over her face. He gave her a curt nod.

'I'll wait for you at the top.'

He began to climb the steps, and her gaze immediately dipped to the muscular calves, the strong legs, the fine butt. There was that spell again, she thought. It pointed out how rude she was being when he'd been perfectly kind to her, despite how inconvenient she'd made this climb for him.

But perhaps this was good. Perhaps he should be annoyed with her. Angry, even. That way, he wouldn't be tempted to give into that pull she knew he felt, too. If he didn't, it would give her another layer of protection. He didn't pursue her; she didn't fall for him. Easy.

Her eyes found him climbing the steps again, admired him within seconds.

Hmm. Not so easy, then.

CHAPTER SEVEN

HE WAS GOING to get a crick in his neck from turning around so often. Not that it mattered, since he'd probably die from falling down the steep steps he was climbing first. It wasn't a good idea to keep checking on Piper. He needed to focus, to climb, to get to the top of this damn island. But the arguments were useless. The fact that he turned once again, looked for her frame, proved it.

She gave him a headache. Everything about her was annoying, contrary, and so *appealing*. He wanted to know why him taking charge bothered her so much. Why she had such a problem with his suggestions. He wanted to know why there was that moment after he'd make a suggestion. She'd blink, tilt her head slightly, then look directly into his eyes and give him an answer. Her brain was obviously working, and he wanted to know what it was doing.

But she infuriated him almost as much as she intrigued him. The more it happened, the more it irritated him. He was trying to help her. Especially since it seemed she wouldn't help herself.

When he'd pointed out that she was pushing herself, she'd seemed surprised. He couldn't tell if that surprise was because she hadn't noticed, or because he had. Surely the latter. She must have known she was pushing herself too hard. Her face was pink, her breathing laboured. He'd wanted to stop her earlier, but thought she would herself, as she had the first time. It was only when he'd heard her gasp for air—a literal gasp—that he'd intervened.

He didn't think she'd noticed she'd done it.

It was tempting to take up the offer of one of the waiters peering out of their restaurants. Cold drinks, a meal? It sounded like heaven. But it would waste unnecessary time. He needed to remember why he'd come here, which was to find his sister's fiancé. He couldn't go into a restaurant, enjoy a cold beer when—

Wait. There was something there.

He stopped, getting what he imagined was a curse word from the man behind him. It was in a foreign language, one he didn't recognise, but he knew it nevertheless. He'd used the same tone countless times before. In fact, because of it, he turned back and apologised, before asking the nearest waitress if she could speak English.

'Of course,' she said without skipping a beat. 'Would you like a table, sir? For how many? One? Two?'

'Neither. I was hoping you could help me with something.'

Her face changed. Another thing he'd seen many times before, particularly from people who were propositioned regularly. Her expression became guarded. Her eyes hooded. To her credit, or perhaps to the shame of the tourists who'd flirted with her, her smile didn't fade.

'How can I help?'

'I'm looking for a man.'

Her brow furrowed. 'A man?'

'Yes. He's about my height, brown hair, brown skin. I think brown eyes.'

'Sir, you are describing many people.'

'Sure,' he said. He looked down, wondering how far behind Piper was. She had a photo of Liam on her phone, which would probably be quite useful.

She was still climbing, giving way to a few tourists who were pushing behind her. She looked frazzled, her face no less pink than earlier, her breathing no less laboured. He thought her beautiful. Breathtaking, actually, since he was struggling to get air into his lungs watching her.

'Sir?' When he turned, the waitress was regarding him with amusement. The traces of hostility on her face had disappeared. 'Your wife is very beautiful.'

'My... That woman over there?' he asked. Unnecessarily, since they both knew who she was talking about. 'She's not my wife.'

'Oh,' the waitress replied, disappointed. 'I am sorry. Your girlfriend? Fiancée?'

'We're not in a relationship.'

'But—' She cut herself off with a knowing smile. 'Ah, you pine. Do not worry,' she said, patting his arm. 'If it is meant to be, it will be.'

He didn't comment on that, too offended by her assumption to even—

Oh, who was he kidding? There was absolutely a part of him that pined—in a way he never had before. The annoyance, the frustration were merely excuses not to face it. Facing it would be a distraction. He had proof of that, didn't he? He'd already considered abandoning his search for Liam the night before because of her. But he couldn't. He needed to do this for Emma. His father would have wanted him to.

A familiar weight settled on his shoulders. They ached at the strain, but reminded him the weight hadn't *settled*. That implied it had gone, even for a moment. It hadn't. It never did. It was simply heavier now. More acute because Emma needed him and he was afraid of letting her down.

That fear was almost crippling. It made him think terrible things. Things that made him feel even guiltier than usual. Like how he wished, for once, his siblings could take care of themselves. That he could be free of the weight—of it all.

He shook his head. The fear wouldn't cripple him. And he wouldn't indulge such terrible thoughts. His family needed him. There would be no pining. No distractions. There was only finding Liam.

'Waiting for me?' Piper asked from the step below him.

'Yes.' His voice was curt. He had to stop himself from telling her it wasn't about her when he caught the quick flash of hurt on her face before she hid it. 'I'm not doing a good job of explaining how Liam looks.'

Piper looked at the waitress. 'Did he tell you the man had brown hair and brown skin?'

The woman smirked. 'Yes.'

Piper shook her head. 'How did you describe him to whoever was at the ticket stall last night?'

'Exactly like that. The man found it sufficient.'

'Ah, the man.' Piper looked at the waitress again, digging out her phone from her bag. 'See how he's implying the ability to describe someone is gendered?' She shook her head. 'Men.'

The waitress laughed, looked him straight in the eye and smiled. 'I see why you pine, sir. She is marvellous.'

Oh, that uncomfortable comment had been worth the look on Caleb's face.

She was still trying to figure out why the waitress had said it an hour later. Not that she should have been thinking about that. The woman hadn't seen Liam, nor had the other waiters from the restaurants on the steps to Oia. They hadn't had much luck with the shops in the immediate vicinity either.

Now they were both exhausted, hungry, with no clear route to follow.

'Do we give up?' Piper asked, leaning against the railing on top of a wall that stood between restaurants. She imagined it was to keep people from falling over, although she couldn't imagine anyone doing so.

Then again, the view *was* spectacular enough for accidents to happen.

The endless stretch of sea was idyllic in its vastness, a reminder of how tiny human beings truly were. Oia was known for its sunsets, and Piper could only imagine what an experience that must be. Seeing the light go from yellow to orange to pink in the blue sky. Watching the sun disappear behind the dark blue ocean. She nearly sighed at the picture it made in her imagination. Badly wanted to be able to look at it in reality.

'We can't give up,' Caleb said from beside her. He was watching her, not the view. She was suddenly reminded of the waitress's words, and felt her face flush.

'What do we do next, then?' she asked, looking back at the ocean. 'We have no leads. We can't keep going around asking people if they've seen Liam.'

'We can. We should.'

'Caleb,' she said on a sigh, 'that idea is impractical. There are too many pathways, too many shops, too many people here. The chances of us—'

'We have to try,' he interrupted. 'I can't go back to Emma without news.'

'What if he's already gone?' she asked, intrigued by his intense reaction.

'Where would he go? He'd have to take a bus to the airport or ferry... We should go to the bus station,' Caleb said, straightening. 'Or go back down to the port. Ask them if Liam came back. We didn't think about that, Piper. We should have thought about that.'

'Caleb,' she said again. This time she put a hand on his arm. Unsurprisingly, the swell of his biceps was firm and large beneath her fingers. 'You sound like you're spiralling.' At his blank expression, she elaborated. 'Out of control.'

'What?' he asked, head jerking back. 'No. I'm in control. I'm always in control.'

For some reason, the statement didn't repel her as it should have. Again, she worried about it, but the feeling was overwhelmed by a different worry. Not for her missing brother or the wedding he was running from. But for Caleb. He seemed...untethered. He must have felt it, too, which clearly bothered him.

She tried not to think about why she cared. Why a man losing control, when other men had exerted it over her, affected her so much.

'Okay, you're in control.' She dropped her hand. It might make him feel more comfortable. 'How about we take a moment to think things through? We'll get some lunch, something cool to drink. Think about our strategy.'

He protested—of course he protested—but eventually she wore him down. They walked to the closest restaurant, checked out the menu. Piper winced as she did the currency conversion in her head, thinking that a single meal cost as much as an entire day's food back home.

She'd always been careful with money. For one, because she'd rarely had any growing up. Because of that, she recognised it as the commodity it was. Recognised all the things it could bring her.

Perhaps that was why she'd fallen for Brad. He'd come from money. It was never an issue for him, so he swept her up and away and she could have whatever the hell she liked. Except it hadn't been the freedom she'd thought it was. Certainly not with him. Each expensive meal, each expensive gift, had come at a cost. A party she couldn't attend. A dinner she had to go to. After that she'd realised it wasn't money that was the commodity; it was having her own. Not depending on anyone else.

She'd started working long before that realisation had settled, despite her father's protests. It was her first real—and only—act of rebellion. It had come at sixteen, after Liam had left for university. It had barely been legal to work then, but it had taken her out of the house. She'd had to give half of her salary to her father, but she'd saved the rest. Used it to buy textbooks for her degree in education when her funding didn't cover it and her father had refused to help.

He'd died before she'd started dating Brad, a man who'd wanted to spend money on her. But, just as her father had kept money from her to control her, Brad had spent money on her to control her. When she'd broken up with him, he'd taken back everything he'd given her. She saw it as a lesson, and appreciated it. Now, she bought what she wanted when she wanted to, and all for herself.

That didn't mean she could justify spending an entire day's budget on one meal. Especially since she'd already had the unexpected cost of the ferry.

'We don't have to eat here.'

'What?' she asked, blinked back into the present. 'Oh, no, it's fine. I was just...thinking about what I'd be eating back home.'

'What?'

'A chicken sandwich.'

'A chicken sandwich,' he repeated. Shook his head. 'You are not having a chicken sandwich in Greece, Piper. Come on.'

He walked towards a different restaurant, one he seemed to know, before stopping and coming back to where she stood. She hadn't moved to follow him.

'I'm sorry. That was a bit...bulldozing of me.' He

frowned at the words, as if he couldn't believe they'd come from his mouth. 'I'd like to take you to a restaurant I've been to before. It has some authentic Greek food I would love for you to try.' He paused. 'If you'd like to come.'

Her lips twitched. He was frowning too deeply to notice.

She schooled her face. 'What if I don't?'

He opened his mouth, closed it. The frown got deeper, though she had no idea how that was possible. 'We can go somewhere that'll give you a damn chicken sandwich.'

'Together?' she asked, her voice more delighted than she'd given permission for it to be. 'Would you really?'

'If that's what you want.' He looked at her, expression pained, then it cleared. 'You're pulling my leg.'

'I was. But now I kind of want to go to some place that'll give you a chicken sandwich to see if you'd go through with it.'

'Isn't my admission enough?'

She tilted her head, felt warmth spread through her. 'Yeah, it is. Come on, let's go.'

He grinned, and the warmth that had initially been innocent turned into something dangerously lusty.

'Thanks. You'll love this place. It gets great reviews. I went with a friend years back when I first came to Greece and we ate like kings.'

'Sounds expensive.' She hated saying it. Hated how small her voice sounded.

'Yeah, but it's worth—' He broke off. 'Yes, it is. I'm sorry.'

'Why are you apologising?'

'It was presumptuous of me.'

She stiffened. 'I can pay for expensive meals if I want to.'

'Of course,' he said with a frown. 'I was talking about

how it's presumptuous of me to assume you'd let me pay. It's not a date or anything,' he clarified quickly. 'It's the least I can do, with everything you've done for Emma. She told me how kind you've been to her. That helped her with the plans for the wedding.'

'I didn't,' she said, shaking her head.

'You made the gifts, didn't you?'

'Yes, but they're stupid little crafts. Flowers.' She shrugged. 'Nothing to write home about.'

'Except it made her happy. She was so pleased you were contributing.' He waited. 'Will you let me pay for lunch?'

'Like you've paid for the accommodation? And the flights? And all the meals while we're here?'

'That was for all the wedding guests, not only you.'

She studied him, then rolled her eyes. 'Fine. But just this once.'

He grinned again. *Oh,* her insides sighed.

She was going to have to figure out some kind of protection against the potency of it.

'You've made me a happy man, Piper.'

'Must be all that pining,' she replied easily, smiling at the mortification on his face.

CHAPTER EIGHT

'Wow, THIS IS...'

Piper didn't finish her sentence, only stared out of the window next to the table they'd been seated at. He loved watching her take in the Greek experience. Her joy and astonishment were genuine. There was a purity in it that reminded him his travels had desensitised him to beauty.

No, he thought immediately, eyes flickering over Piper's face. He could still appreciate beauty. He supposed it depended on the form it came in then.

'You should see it at sunset,' he told her, thanking the waiter as the man filled their glasses with water. 'It's one of the best views in the city.'

'I can imagine,' she said, eyes big. Pure.

'I'll show you some time.'

She didn't speak, only gave him a small smile that reminded him she wouldn't be there long enough for him to show her. Suddenly he wanted nothing more than to ask her to stay. He'd take some more time off work—hell, he'd been working non-stop for the last thirteen years; a month wouldn't matter—and he'd show her the world.

He'd start with Greece, with sunsets in Oia, then he'd take her on a boat trip to visit all the islands. They'd fly to Italy—to Venice, where he'd take her on a gondola ride and watch her as she was serenaded. They'd go to Scotland so she could appreciate the countryside; to Bora Bora so she could relax in the sun.

And all the while he would enjoy her. Enjoy experiencing these countries he'd gone to before but never appreciated, through her eyes.

The intensity of his fantasy startled him. No, not the

fantasy: the emotion accompanying it. The deep desire. The *yes, please* his heart sighed at the prospect.

Maybe he was losing his mind. Perhaps he *had* fallen down the steps when he'd been checking for her earlier. This was a dream he was having while unconscious—or possibly dead. But when Piper looked out of the window again, her eyes softening, appreciation lighting up her entire face, he knew he couldn't be dead. If he was, he was in heaven. Considering how ungrateful he'd been before his father's death, he wasn't sure he'd end up in heaven. At least not until he balanced the scales. Until he made his father proud by being the kind of family man Chad had been.

Why did that feel like more of a hardship when he was with Piper?

'What are you thinking about?' she asked him, her eyes no longer on the view but on him.

For how long? What had she seen?

'You ask me that a lot.'

'If I recall, you've asked me the same thing,' she retorted. Quirked a brow. 'So, are you going to tell me?'

He considered for a short moment. 'I was thinking that I'd like to show you the sunset.'

'Oh.' Colour lightly stained her cheeks. She frowned. 'You were upset by that?'

'The prospect didn't...not please me.'

'Your expression showed more than a lack of pleasure.' She cocked her head. 'Then again, you have resting annoyed face, so perhaps I'm reading too much into this.'

'Resting annoyed face?' he asked, amused. 'That's a thing?'

'With you it is.'

'Yours isn't much better.'

She fluttered her lashes. 'Are you sure? I've been told I have resting sunshine face.'

'By whom?'

'My students. Their parents.'

'You're a teacher?'

'Yes,' she said, the teasing tone leaving her voice. 'You didn't know?'

'How would I have known that?'

'You didn't do research? Make sure you knew the family your sister was marrying into?'

'I...'

He hesitated, embarrassed that he had. That, in fact, he did know she was a teacher; he just hadn't remembered. It was different when the information he'd read was abstract. Liam had a younger sister. She was a teacher. But now that he knew Piper, knew it was her the information was describing... Part of him wished he could go back and read it again. But that didn't help him now.

'So you did know,' Piper said with a curve of her lips that wasn't a smile. 'Why am I not surprised?'

'I was looking out for Emma.'

'Of course,' she said smoothly. 'What else did you find out?'

'Only what you've already told me about your parents.'

'I don't suppose the research told you I miss the idea of my mother more than I do the memory of her?'

A trap, he thought. He didn't reply.

'Or that I don't miss my father at all?' Her eyes went cold. 'I'm only sorry he didn't die sooner.'

Silence followed. A horrifying, awkward, stunned silence. Out of the corner of Caleb's eye, he saw the waiter walk towards them, take in the scene, pause, then turn to another table, pretending they'd called him. Caleb couldn't blame the man. He didn't understand why he wanted to comfort Piper instead of fleeing then. He wanted to pull her in his arms, soothe her until the ice in her eyes defrosted and the shame permeating off her as her skin turned red subsided.

She let out a harsh breath.

'I'm sorry. That was…' She trailed off. Looked at him. 'Uncomfortable, wasn't it?'

'I'm sorry you feel that way.' He was sorrier that his actions had prompted her to rehash it. 'I didn't mean to pry. I only wanted Emma to be safe.'

'What did you think you'd find?' she asked, going for light-heartedness, he thought, but not quite succeeding. 'Links to a prominent South African gang?'

'Maybe.' Wanting to give her some relief from it, he said, 'I was disappointed to find nothing scandalous, I admit.'

She smiled. It went from relieved to curious in seconds.

'You're protective of them, aren't you?' she asked. 'Emma and Jada and Tate?'

'Unreasonably so.'

'Why?'

'Why?' he repeated with a small smile. 'They're my siblings. My younger siblings. Whom I raised.'

'Ah. *That's* why you feel protective of them.'

'I think generally siblings are protective of one another.'

'So they're protective of you, too?'

He frowned. 'I… I don't know.'

'That makes me feel better about my relationship with Liam,' she commented after a brief pause.

'You're looking for him now. That must come from being protective.'

'I suppose,' she said thoughtfully. 'Maybe he just isn't protective of me.' She laughed, but it was strangled.

'He seemed protective when he called me at the airport yesterday,' he pointed out. 'He sounded worried.'

Something passed over her face. A mixture of hope and resignation.

'I don't know what to tell you,' she replied. 'We had a hard childhood. As soon as Liam could leave, he left. Except he left me alone with that hardness. We really only reconnected after my dad died. More so when Emma came into the picture.' She smiled. 'She definitely had something to do with that. I think she shares your view on siblings.'

It should have soothed the unsettledness her question about how his siblings felt about him had evoked. It didn't.

'Maybe you do, too. You're here,' he said again. 'You obviously care about him.'

'That's part of the problem.' Her smile turned sad. 'I can't seem to stop caring about him. There's a...loyalty I feel for him that he doesn't feel for me.'

'He loves you.'

'What does love mean if there's no action?' she asked. With a quick shimmy of her shoulders and a now shaky smile, she reached for her menu. 'I should probably get something more interesting than water to drink.'

She perused the list, giving it more attention than selecting a drink deserved. He understood. There was a part of him that was tempted into doing the same. Finding something trivial to distract him. But he couldn't. Her words kept echoing in his head.

What does love mean if there's no action?

She was right. Love was *doing* something, not merely saying it. He knew it because his mother had told him she loved him, but she'd still left.

Susan Martin had been a present mother for the first twelve years of Caleb's life. She'd got pregnant in university, dropped out to take care of him while his father built his business, and then went back three years later to get her degree. It had taken her longer than most, but she'd graduated. She must have still been happy at that point because they'd decided to have another child...and another...and another. He suspected his youngest brother and sister weren't as planned as Emma had been. Suspected it because his mother had left when Tate was one, claiming her life had got away from her.

He'd been twelve when she'd told him that. He remembered the day clearly. There had been shouting in the living room between her and his father. Tears when she'd come into the room, kissed his siblings goodnight, stopped with him. She'd leaned in, said those words, apologised, then told him she loved him. He hadn't believed her.

He wasn't angry that she didn't care for the demands of being a mother or wife. He believed that she had the right to do whatever she wanted. She could find her value in contributing to a family or to a company. In doing both. Neither. Honestly, he didn't care. What he did care about was *when* she'd figured that out. After she'd already been married for twelve years, with four children, three of them aged five or younger.

His mother had been the perfect example of how love didn't matter without action. Which was why he'd acted after his father's death. Part of it had been to make up for being a terrible teenager, yes. But a bigger part was to live up to his father's legacy. To give his siblings the space to make mistakes and learn, like his father had done for him. Like his father would have done for them if he hadn't died.

But when does it stop?

A piercing sound prevented him from pondering the disturbing thought. Piper dug into the handbag that had been hanging over her chair. When she saw the display, she looked at him with wide eyes.

'It's Liam.'

'Let me talk to him,' Caleb said immediately.

'No,' Piper said, disappointment coursing through her. *Protect yourself,* it seemed to say, highlighting how commanding Caleb's tone had sounded. *Stop falling for him. It'll only lead to heartache.*

She took a steadying breath. 'If he wanted to talk to you, he would have called you.'

Caleb swore. She ignored him.

'Hello?'

'Pie?' Liam said.

'Yeah, of course. Who else would it be?'

'You could have given your phone to one of the Martins.'

'Why would I do that?'

'You wouldn't. Of course you wouldn't.'

Liam sounded relieved. As if he'd really worried one of the Martins would be listening in on the conversation.

Well, that was half true. But Liam didn't have to know that.

'Where are you?'

'In Santorini.'

'Santorini?' Piper repeated, straightening. 'You're still here?'

'What do you mean, still? And here?'

'I…er…' She pulled her face at Caleb, who was watching attentively. He made a *go on* gesture with his hands. Easy for him to say. 'I meant you're still here in Greece. We were sure you'd left.'

'We?' he asked. 'So you are working with the Martins?'

'I've been forced into co-operating with them since I'm your only relative at this wedding. They were wondering why you'd run away from a woman you clearly care about. They thought I'd have answers. Heaven only knows why.'

'I'm sorry,' he said. To his credit, he sounded sincere. 'I…panicked. I needed some time to breathe.'

'You couldn't have chosen some other time? Maybe some other place, too? Like back home, not four days before your wedding in a different country?'

'There's some new information—' He broke off, released a huff of air. 'Look, I called for a favour. I need you to stall.'

'I will not.'

'Pie, please. I can't come back, and I'm surprised Caleb hasn't hired a private investigator to find me.'

'Yet,' she said darkly.

'Exactly. Buy me some time. Tell them I'm safe in Santorini. I need a moment to get my head right.'

'How long is that moment going to be?'

'Not long,' he promised. 'I'll be back for the wedding.'

'Yeah?' she asked, not believing him. 'So you want me to tell your fiancée that you need time but you'll be back for the wedding?'

'Please.'

'Liam, you're being ridiculous.'

'You don't understand—'

'So make me. Where are you staying?'

'What?'

'I'll come to the island and we can have a conversation about what you're going through. That's the only way I'll stall for you.' She met Caleb's eyes. He was fuming, but he didn't say anything.

At least he exerted control over himself, too.

After a moment of hesitation, Liam named a hotel.

'I'll see you in an hour.'

'What?' he said, surprise in his voice. 'It isn't going to take an hour for you to get to Santorini from Mykonos.'

'As luck would have it,' she said dryly, 'I'm already on my way. Good thing I thought today would be a good day for exploring Greece.'

CHAPTER NINE

'LET'S GO,' SAID Caleb as soon as she put down the phone.

'If I show up there now, he'll think I was lying to him.'

'You are lying to him,' Caleb pointed out. 'I'm also wondering why you said *I,* as if you're the only one going to meet him.'

'I am.'

'Really?' Caleb said casually. Dangerously. 'We're not in this together then, are we?'

'Of course we are,' she replied a little irritably.

Although she was more irritated at herself. She would have been annoyed if he'd assumed she wouldn't go with him if the roles were reversed. But she didn't like that he'd assumed. Didn't like that it felt as if she was giving in when, logically, she knew she wasn't.

Oh, her father and Brad had messed up her brain. Given her complexes. Complicated the way she interacted with people. With men. Even those who seemed safe.

Safe?

'Explain to me how this is going to work?' Caleb asked before she could explore where that word had come from.

'You'll go with me to the hotel. Stay out of sight while I try to talk some sense into Liam.' She was tired of the tension now. 'Once I do, you're free to make yourself known. Just don't scare him off.'

'If he's that easily scared, he doesn't deserve Emma.'

'Yes,' she agreed. 'But she still wants him, which is more important, isn't it?' She lifted a hand, calling for the waiter. 'Now, I figure we have about thirty minutes before we have to wrap things up here. Why don't we order something that'll sate our stomachs, then get going?'

He studied her, then picked up his menu, asked her opinion on some options that would be quick. By the time the waiter arrived, they'd selected three appetisers to share, including at least two different forms of carbs. Piper ordered an iced tea to go with it, though a glass of wine would have gone down smoother. Anything, really, with alcohol in it. But she needed her wits about her, and drowning her sorrows in wine had never got her anywhere.

Unfortunately.

'Look,' Caleb said when the waiter left, 'I don't mean to come across as though I'm…taking control.' He said the phrase with such distaste she had to hide her smile. 'But I need to make sure this goes right for Emma.'

'Okay.'

'Okay?' he asked, blinking. 'I thought you were going to give me a tongue-lashing for sure.'

'The fact that you know that means I don't need to.' Which was interesting. Was that why she suddenly thought him *safe*? 'Anyway, I'm too tired to fight. We've already argued today and—' she leaned forward '—my legs are *aching*. Did you know there are over a hundred steps up to this city? *A hundred.* I stopped counting after that and we were barely past halfway.'

He chuckled. 'They should look into building a lift.'

She regarded him carefully. 'You're a millionaire, aren't you? *You* should look into that.'

His laugh was louder, bolder now. Full of life and happiness. It bloomed inside her like flowers in the spring. Made her feel fresh and new in a way she hadn't experienced before.

He was trouble, she thought. The more time she spent with him, the deeper she fell into the trouble. She could tell not only by the fact that her body liked his, but that her mind liked his. And that they could go from squabbling and annoying one another to making one another laugh within minutes.

She thought back to how considerate he'd been with her when she'd been prickly on the steps. How he apologised for making assumptions. How he seemed to have taken her accusation of him taking control and engaged with it. Apologised for it. How he was adapting to it. How he was protective of his siblings. How outraged he'd been on her behalf when she'd told him Liam wasn't protective of her.

She liked all of it. She liked…she liked him.

Oh, he was *definitely* trouble.

'He's gone,' Piper said when she came out of the hotel.

At first, Caleb thought he'd heard wrong. Liam couldn't be *gone*.

'What do you mean?' he asked. 'Are we meant to meet him somewhere else?'

She gave him a strange look. 'No. The man at reception told me I missed him. By minutes, apparently.'

'Piper,' he said after a moment, 'are you telling me that if we'd got here earlier, we might have seen Liam?'

She lifted her chin. 'Maybe. But he left a note to say he'd like to meet me here tomorrow instead.' She showed him the note, which had the name of a restaurant on the opposite side of the island. 'He wants to meet at lunchtime.'

'Because he's clearly demonstrated how well he keeps his appointments,' Caleb said sarcastically. 'This is terrible.'

'It's not,' she said. 'We know where he'll be.'

'If he shows up.'

'He will.'

'Really? You're defending him.'

'Absolutely not. But he had the decency to leave a note. He made another appointment. I'm going to give him the benefit of the doubt. Maybe he needed more time, like he said.'

'This is the definition of defending him.'

'Yeah, well, we've already established I'm a fool.'

She gave him a smile that broke his heart. Damn it, he couldn't be angry any more.

'I'm sorry he disappointed you.'

'I'm sorry he's disappointing Emma.'

'Emma.' Caleb groaned. 'She asked me to call her with an update.'

'So call her and tell her what we know.'

'Which is what?'

'We're seeing him tomorrow.'

'How am I supposed to explain that he'll be gone from her another day?'

'You don't have to, Caleb,' she said gently. 'He will, when they see one another again.' She reached out, squeezed his forearm. 'I'll give you some privacy.'

He watched as she walked up the narrow path to the top of the island. Her legs were beautiful, toned, almost golden. They were also entirely inappropriate to look at when he was supposed to be calling his sister with bad news.

With a twisted stomach, he called Emma. He kept the conversation short, trying hard not to feel guilty when she quietly started crying. He did end up feeling like a coward though, when he said goodbye at the first possible moment. When he joined Piper again, he thought he had the emotion of it under control. One look told him he hadn't succeeded.

'That bad, huh?'

'She was crying,' he said. 'I think that qualifies as being bad.'

'It does.'

She reached out, squeezed his arm again. He was getting used to it as a show of comfort. The action, not the explosion of warmth that went through his body every time she touched him.

'There isn't anything I can do about it except hope that he shows tomorrow.' Caleb sighed. Then realised they needed to make plans. 'What are we going to do?'

'What do you mean?'

'Are we going to wait here? Go back to Mykonos?'

'That's over seven hours of travelling in two days.' She sighed. 'I suppose we'll have to.'

'Or we could stay here.'

'How?'

'I have a place on the other end of the island. Close to where Liam wants to meet, actually.' He wondered why he was so nervous making the offer. 'We could watch the sunset here, get a car and stay over there for the night.'

'It wouldn't be...imposing?'

'Not at all. I usually hire out the place during the peak season but, with Em's wedding, I thought we might need it.'

'Always prepared, aren't you?'

He smiled. 'I try to be.'

'What are the chances you prepared for this, though?' she asked. 'Toiletries, a fresh set of clothing?'

'We can buy that.'

Her face tightened. 'It's not in my budget.'

'It is in mine. Millionaire, remember?' he teased lightly. 'Come on, we barely ate at that restaurant. See this as a continued thank you.'

'No,' she said softly. 'I know what this is. You're being—' she hesitated '—kind. Hospitable.'

'Yes,' he replied, relieved.

'I'll pay you back.'

'Piper—'

'I need to,' she interrupted firmly, but gently. 'It's important to me to be able to pay my way.'

'Of course,' he said. 'Fine, you can pay me back.'

She nodded. 'Great. Now, what should we take care of first?'

They sorted out a plan, first going to the supermarket near the bus station to buy the essentials. Caleb packed in anything he thought she might want, claiming it was for himself. He didn't want her to pay him back, but he understood the principle of her wanting to. Respected it, too.

Perhaps it was wrong of him to want to buy things that he thought she might want, but he was okay with being wrong then. He wanted to make her happy, especially since he'd forced her into this. Well, Emma had, but he hadn't stopped it. In which case, this really was a thank you.

As they walked back up to the city, he stopped at one of the shops and bought a backpack. While he was at it, he bought a fresh set of clothes and swimming trunks. She chose a swimsuit for herself when he told her he expected her to join him in the pool back at the house. He wanted her to get the full Greek experience, which meant straight exhaustion after a day of exploring.

They didn't buy anything after that, but Piper stopped at almost every shop, gushing over trinkets and ornaments, sometimes over clothes. She spoke with the shopkeepers about the history of the island, about what they sold in their shop, and listened, even when their English was broken.

When they finally made it through the line of shops and were on their way to where Caleb wanted to watch the sunset, some stray dogs trotted towards them. He had to stop Piper when she immediately lowered to pet the dogs.

'They're street dogs.'

'Okay.' She looked at him with innocent eyes. 'What's wrong with me wanting to pet street dogs?'

'They live on the street.'

She blinked at him.

'No one takes care of them, Piper.'

'And that means they don't deserve love?' she asked. 'That's terrible. Shame on you.'

'That's not what I meant,' he said. 'They're dirty, unvaccinated and carry all kinds of diseases.' He softened his voice. 'It's not a good idea, Piper.'

Her face fell. It was adorable, damn it. Damn her.

'I hope you'll never find out what it's like to be alone and dirty and without love.'

'Me, too,' he said dryly.

She sighed. 'What if I just touch them with my—?'

'Piper.'

She glared at him, gave the dogs a longing look before sighing. 'Take me away from here, then.'

He smiled, leading her to another restaurant Adrian had taken him to when he'd first visited Greece.

'This is terrible,' she said when they sat down. 'Someone should take care of those dogs.'

'The government does, to an extent. There's food and water all around.'

'But what about shelters? Vaccines? Cleaning them?'

'You're an animal lover, I take it.'

She gave him a look. 'Yes. But I also have compassion. Why are you smiling? This is not amusing.'

'No, it's not,' he said after a moment, the smile fading.

It wasn't amusing at all that somehow, during this conversation, he'd decided he would look into setting up shelters for stray dogs in Greece.

CHAPTER TEN

Who knew watching a sunset with an incredibly attractive man could be so romantic?

Okay, she did.

In theory, it had seemed fine. Two acquaintances watching the sun set. But they weren't acquaintances. They were something more. Something that had become blurred as they'd spent time together. Like when Caleb had threaded his fingers through hers as the sun had set. Contentment had washed over her and she hadn't pulled away. Hadn't wanted to. Then there was the delicious dinner, the laughing, the sharing... Maybe that had added to the romance of it, too.

She could almost forget she was enjoying him when she shouldn't be.

She continued to forget it when they arrived at his place. It was, he told her, old Santorini architecture. The building was at the end of a road—no, she thought. It wasn't at the end of a road. The narrow track they'd driven along had essentially been an uncovered tunnel. There were, in fact, holes that looked like tunnels burrowed into the peak of the island, which apparently was a volcano.

'Are you telling me,' she said as he slowly drove down the ridiculous track to where he lived, 'that I am currently on an active volcano?'

'I am telling you that,' he said with a smirk. 'The island is what remained after a volcano erupted in the first place.'

'I'm still trying to wrap my head around the fact that it's an active volcano. Who the hell thought it was a good idea to turn it into a tourist destination?'

'I imagine the people who live here. Perhaps they saw

the sunsets and figured people from around the world would want to see it.'

'It's a pretty great sunset,' she conceded. 'Although I'd rather be alive to see other sunsets than risk my life for one particular sunset. But that's just me, I guess.'

He chuckled, and again warmth ballooned inside her. She was getting too used to this. To hearing him laugh and seeing him smile. This after only a day. She could only imagine what would happen to her mind if she spent more time with him.

And she didn't only want to imagine it; she wanted to experience it.

The house offered a welcome distraction when he pulled up in front of it. It was a double storey, although the first storey wasn't level with the ground. They had to take steps down to get inside, though the second storey was above ground, making the design unique.

She walked into cool darkness. Caleb put on the lights, revealing concrete floors, modern appliances and décor, though the windows—round and high—looked old. A comfortable set of couches filled the living room, along with a TV and dining table. There were two bedrooms, one off the living room that had a king-sized bed and slid-ing doors that led out to the pool; another was upstairs, which was, when she followed Caleb up, essentially an entire apartment.

'You can stay here,' he told her, before explaining that the housekeeper had been round and Piper would have everything she needed. 'Shout if there is anything else though, and I'll try to organise it for you.'

'Thanks.'

'I'll see you at the pool in an hour?'

She smiled. 'Sure.'

He smiled back. It turned into a long moment of them

simply smiling at one another, before Caleb awkwardly took a step back and missed falling down the stairs because of quick reflexes.

'I'll see you later,' he said, face flushing. He didn't wait for her to reply this time, only hurried down the stairs.

She was still smiling after her shower. To be fair, that had just as much to do with his silliness as it did the fact that she could wash off the day and finally unwind. She had about forty minutes before she was supposed to meet Caleb, and she made the mistake of slipping into her sleepwear. She wanted to wait before putting on her swimming costume so she could be comfortable, but it meant that she was *comfortable*. The cool cotton bedding felt incredible. So did closing her eyes...

She woke up with a start, the inky darkness informing her she'd slept for much too long. Not that she'd intended to sleep at all. A quick glance at her phone told her it was midnight and she straightened, wondering how the hell she'd slept for four hours.

The house was quiet, which gave her plenty of opportunity to hear the voice in her head pointing out how poorly she'd slept for the last few weeks. She'd wondered if she should come to the wedding, had gone back and forth about it. But, as she'd told Caleb, she had no excuses. None, yet she'd kept trying to think of one. Deep into the night. For as long as two weeks before she'd flown. Longer, even. Every time she thought she didn't want to go, she saw Emma's disappointed expression, Liam's resigned one. Now she was here, looking for her brother, and she still wasn't sleeping well.

That was how she'd slept for four hours.

She padded into the kitchen, stopping when she saw a note on the table with her name on it. She picked it up.

Piper,
I want to say I'm mad about you falling asleep, but I
get it. If you wake up before morning you'll proba-
bly be hungry. I left something for you in the fridge.
Caleb

Curious, she went over to the fridge. She took out the
brown packaging, unwrapped the foil and gave a much
too loud laugh when she saw what was inside.

A chicken sandwich.

When she was done laughing, she stared at the sandwich in her hand. Her chest felt funny. Warm. It took her
a moment to realise it was because he'd done this for her.
This…considerate, kind thing. Such actions always meant
more to her because of the way she'd grown up. She knew
that consideration and kindness shouldn't be taken for
granted. She'd learnt that with Brad, too.

But Caleb… Caleb was both of those things. And he
didn't have any qualms about displaying them with her.
Towards her. Plus, she thought with a smile, he had a
sense of humour. She rubbed her chest absently as she
got a drink from the fridge. By the time she went outside
to eat, she was almost used to the comfort of the warmth
there. Which dissipated as soon as she noticed a figure
sprawled in a lounger.

She made a tiny noise, before seeing it was Caleb. She
managed to clamp down on any other sound when she
realised he was sleeping. A voice in the back of her head
told her she should walk away. Nothing good could come
of watching him sleep. She'd notice he had fewer lines on
his face, his body relaxed in a way she hadn't seen before.
She'd see the smooth expanse of his chest, the muscular
ridges since he lay there without his shirt on. His hair was

untidy, a towel draped over his lap, and she assumed he'd gone for a swim without her.

So it hadn't only been a line to see her in her underwear.

Slowly, quietly, despite her warnings to herself, she lowered to another lounger and began eating her sandwich as quietly as possible. She was about to start her second half when he opened his eyes, started at seeing her, then straightened, rubbing a hand over the back of his neck.

'What time is it?'

'After twelve.'

'Midnight?' he said, shock wiping the sleepiness from his face. A pity. 'I've been sleeping here for two hours?'

'You went for a swim at ten?' She reached for her drink, gulping down some of it though she kept her eyes on him. 'You realise that's not normal?'

'I was hot.'

'Didn't you tell me there's air-conditioning?'

'Yeah, but it makes a loud buzzing noise. If you're not used to it, it might wake you up.'

The warmth returned to her chest, fiercer than before.

'Are you saying,' she said carefully, wanting to get it right, 'that you didn't put on the air-conditioning because you were afraid of waking me up?'

'Yeah,' he said, shifting in his lounger and running a hand over his hair now. 'You wouldn't have fallen asleep if you weren't tired,' he added. 'I figured you needed as much of it as you could get.'

She nodded, still processing.

'And you left me a chicken sandwich in case I woke up.'

'I thought you might be hungry.'

'Hmm.'

She studied him—his bare chest, his mussed hair. It made her realise the warmth she was feeling was attraction just as much as everything else. And the everything else was significant on its own.

It was responsible for that pull. The one she'd first felt when they'd been climbing the steps to Oia. Only it was stronger now. It tempted her to get up, slide her hands into his hair and rest her lips on his.

She cleared her throat. 'That was nice of you.'

'I can be nice,' he said good-naturedly. 'Are you going to eat the rest of that?'

She looked down, only then realising she hadn't finished her sandwich. She shook her head, lifted her plate in a *you can have it* gesture. He got up, lowered next to her on her lounger. It became a little harder to breathe.

'It's pretty good,' he said after his first bite. He took a second before she could answer.

'Yeah,' she said, her voice strangled.

'Why does your expression make me think you're lying?'

'It's not the sandwich.'

He took the last bite with a frown. Finished chewing before he asked, 'Then what is it?'

'Nothing.'

Involuntarily, her eyes lowered to his lips, before she shifted her gaze. What was happening to her? A day in the presence of this man and she was losing all the progress she'd made after Brad.

Except this, him? It felt like progress. He might have been controlling, but it didn't have the same malice Brad had. Brad wouldn't have cared if she was sleeping; he'd still have made noise. He wouldn't have considered she might be hungry if she woke up. He certainly wouldn't have been looking for her brother when Liam was the one in the wrong...

Or was she making excuses? Was she ignoring the

alarm bells with Caleb because of the attraction they shared? Not only the attraction: the connection. That pull.

'I have… I need to…'

She didn't finish her sentence, only moved forward and tried to stand. But Caleb stood at the same time, and her urgency to get away from him—to escape the thoughts and the *feelings*—propelled her against his chest. Against his bare chest.

'Piper.'

His voice was soft. Gruff. It sent shivers down her spine.

'What?' she whispered, forcing herself not to look at his lips.

'What's wrong?'

'Nothing.'

'Piper.' He said her name on a sigh this time. 'You don't have to lie to me.'

'No, I do,' she said urgently. 'If I lie to you, maybe I can lie to myself.'

'About what?'

He brushed a strand of hair from her face. She closed her eyes, resisted—barely—leaning into his hand.

'This,' she said, looking at him. 'I want to lie about whatever this is.'

Caleb's expression didn't change, but it was only then that she realised what his expression was. A tenderness that soothed her heart. Her fears. A desire that sent another shiver down her spine.

'Don't lie,' he said softly. 'This doesn't have to be anything you don't want it to be.'

'That's the problem.' She slid her arms around his waist, rested her head against his chest. 'I want it to be.'

She didn't have to clarify the 'it'. The word, the hope, sat heavy between them. After a moment, Caleb's arms folded around her waist, and it happened again. That wave of contentment. That feeling of safety. She wasn't sure how it happened, but she didn't want it to end. So when she pulled back, she didn't lift her eyes to his. She let them linger on his lips. They were full, sensual. And when they lowered to hers, she gave a murmur of assent.

The touching of their lips was soft, though there was no tentativeness about it. She felt a vibration go through her, realised a second later it was Caleb's groan. She understood his reaction. That soft touching of their lips had sparked a wild desire inside her, too.

It shifted things. Made the kiss become more urgent than exploratory. It made everything more...*more*.

His tongue slid into her mouth; she felt an answering flicker of heat low in her belly. She cupped his neck with her hand, drawing him closer, giving herself more access. The world rumbled beneath them. She wondered if the volcano island had erupted after all. Strangely, now, she wasn't as concerned about dying.

His hands were on her skin, creating paths, trails she'd retrace when this was over and she was clinging to the memory. For now, she had the fire of it. An almost lazy one that burnt while the rest of her simmered. A juxtaposition that made no sense: the temperature was rising inside her with each sweep of his tongue, his hands responsible for the outside of her body recreating the supernova.

It was intoxicating, this man's talent. He knew how to kiss, how to caress. She was surprised she hadn't fallen prey to his charms earlier since he was clearly an expert at seduction. Now that he was aiming it at her, she was content in a way she'd never been before. Riled up in that way, too.

She didn't think about the firsts of it. Instead, she tentatively put her hands on his torso. The muscles beneath her fingers clenched. Trembled. It had desire quaking through her, the power of it impossible to ignore.

She was doing this. She was making this attractive, confident man tremble.

She pressed closer to him, lifting her hands to cup his face. It shifted the tone again, this time from seductive to emotional. From eager to grateful.

The movement of their tongues slowed. His hands stilled. And though she was aching she was able to catch her breath. Only for him to make her lose it again when he pulled back and rested his forehead on hers.

'This is…' he said, his voice husky. She felt pride tingle inside her.

'I know.'

'Are you okay with it?'

'Don't I seem okay?'

His eyes searched her face. 'I need you to say it.'

Softening, she said, 'I'm more than okay. This is more than I could have imagined.'

He smiled at her. 'Good. Because I wasn't done.'

She laughed. 'Me neither. I—'

She shut up when he picked her up.

His gaze flickered down to her. 'Objections?'

'None,' she said, voice shaky. Then she realised how close she was to him and began to trace the lines of his face. 'You don't look annoyed with me.'

'You want me to be annoyed with you?' he asked, amusement dancing in his expression. 'I'm sure that'll come. Keep talking. That's one way to get me there, for sure.'

'Hmm.' She narrowed her eyes. 'Maybe *I* should be annoyed with you. You do seem to have a gift for annoying me.'

He smiled, lowering his head to nip at her lips. 'Later. There are more important things now.'

He carried her through the sliding doors to his bedroom. Gently lowered her to his bed. Her heart pounded at the prospect of what might happen until he lay on the bed beside her and only looked at her.

'This is more important?'

He put a warm hand on her waist. 'It is.'

Warmth spread through her body, but not in the achy way kissing him had caused. No, this was different. Soothing. Gentle. She knew it was just as dangerous.

'I won't lie,' she said, shifting closer to him. 'I thought there would be more action.'

'There's time for action.'

'Really? When?'

'Now,' he replied. 'Ten minutes from now. In an hour. Tomorrow.'

'I'm not sure tomorrow's a possibility.'

'Why not?'

'I might have come to my senses by then.'

'Or maybe this *is* you coming to your senses.'

She stared at him, laughed quietly. 'You're good.'

He smiled. 'I know.'

'Cocky though.'

'You say that like it's a bad thing.'

'It might be,' she said, remembering.

Popping the bubble.

She cursed silently and turned onto her back, facing the ceiling. There was a fan there. She had no idea why, when there was air-conditioning. Perhaps it was for moments like this, when the doors were open. Or when a man didn't want to put on the air-conditioning because he was afraid to wake his grumpy companion.

Damn it. The thought of it sent another wave of pleasure through her. And it was probably why she was lying on her brother's future brother-in-law's bed, thinking about the men in her past.

'I'm sorry,' Caleb said suddenly, sitting up. 'I shouldn't have brought you inside here. You're uncomfortable.' He let out a breath. 'I'm messing things up.'

'No, you're not,' she said, pushing up on her hands. 'I am. I mean, I did. I hope not to any more.'

'You want to stay?'

'I want to stay,' she said simply.

After a long moment of silence where he studied her, he nodded and lowered back to the bed. She noticed that his body was tense now, that he'd moved away from her slightly. She sighed, lowering to her back again, resting her hands on her belly.

'My father,' she started, thinking the only way to make things easier was to explain, 'was…a challenge to live with.'

She felt him turn, face her again. But he didn't speak, and she had to commend him for giving her the space to figure it out.

'You know that already. And that my mother died when Liam and I were young. I… I don't think my father knew what to do with us. Or maybe it was simply that he didn't want us.' Her stomach twisted. She pushed on. 'He was very controlling. He'd punish us if we stepped outside of what he wanted us to do. It was like living on the top of a very narrow mountain. One wrong step and we'd fall long and hard to the ground.'

'He hurt you?' Caleb's voice was dangerously devoid of emotion.

She turned her head. 'You mean physically?' she asked. He nodded. 'No, he never hit us.' She looked up again. Wished the fan was on so she'd have something to look at. Something to distract her from the memories. 'We never had physical bruises.'

'Only emotional ones.'

She'd implied it, but it pleased her that he'd seen it. 'Yes.'

'How did you survive it?'

'I didn't take any steps,' she replied. 'I stayed on one spot on the mountain.' She paused. 'I used to walk around, but it wasn't worth the fall.'

'Was staying worth it?'

She angled her head. 'I don't... I don't know. I suppose I survived it, which is important. But I carry it with me, and it's so heavy sometimes.' She fell silent. 'I eventually moved. Fell.' Another pause. 'He didn't want me to go to university. He wanted me to stay home and take care of him.' She shook her head. 'I couldn't. When Liam left and didn't come back, I realised I was the only person who could get myself out of that situation. So I got a job, fought to leave, tried to find independence.'

'Did you?'

She thought about Brad. 'Not quite.'

'What happened?'

'I made a mistake.' She looked at him. 'I spent the entirety of my degree alone. Then my father died, and I didn't want to be alone any more. It was like...like his death gave me permission to...I don't know, date?' She rolled her eyes at the stupidity of it. 'But I dated the wrong man. Turns out, having a crappy male role model your entire life gives you a pretty skewed view of yourself and the people you should date.'

His brow knitted, and she could almost see him applying it to his situation.

'That didn't happen with your sisters,' she told him.

'No, but sometimes I wonder if I gave them other issues.'

'Like what?'

'I don't know.' He went quiet. 'I've spoilt them. And now they can't do things by themselves.'

'It's not too late.'

He gave her a dark look. 'I'm here looking for my sister's fiancé.'

'So am I,' she pointed out. 'Not my sister's fi— Oh, you know what I mean.'

He laughed softly. 'I do.'

'Why did you spoil them?'

'My father died.'

'And you thought it would help with their grief?'

'Yeah.'

'Did it?'

She gave him time to think about it when she saw his expression. The pain there. The confusion. Guilt, too, if she wasn't mistaken. All of it gave her a new understanding of Caleb. Of what he was doing for his siblings.

She'd been judging him according to her frame of reference, according to her past, but perhaps it was time to use his frame of reference. He'd had to parent his siblings. His father had died more than a decade ago; he probably hadn't been that old when that responsibility had come his way.

What if his control was a coping mechanism? What if he'd had to control things, to be a parent when he'd barely been an adult?

'I don't know,' he finally answered.

'And you feel guilty about it.'

He looked at her, his expression unguarded. 'I feel guilty. But not because of that.'

CHAPTER ELEVEN

SHE SAW RIGHT through him. He wanted to ask her how, but he didn't know if he'd like the answer. They were in a bubble. It had started inflating the moment they'd had dinner at sunset. Perhaps even before then. But everything had felt easy and significant, in a way he couldn't describe.

It wouldn't end well.

He should have known it when he'd walked into her bedroom after waiting ten minutes at the pool. He'd seen her curled into a ball in the middle of the sheets. She wore a soft blue sleep shirt and, with her gorgeous brown skin, made a picture on the white bedding. But it was her face that got him. The barriers had been lowered—the scowl she always wore gone, the carefulness in her eyes not visible. It had kicked him in the gut. Made him want to take care of her.

He'd only ever had that feeling with his siblings. Feeling it for a stranger…was weird. Especially now, when it was more intense after he'd heard what her father— her *brother*—had done to her. No wonder he was feeling vulnerable.

Not that he was running away from it. In fact, he was embracing it. The bubble was that powerful.

'You don't have to feel guilty, you know,' she said. 'I don't think their grief is keeping them from doing anything in their lives. I have no doubt that's because of you.'

'That's not it,' he said slowly.

'What then?'

'Having my dad.'

There was a stunned pause. He used it to figure out

how he'd just told her the thing he'd never been able to say out loud.

'What do you mean?'

He took a breath. 'I mean I feel guilty for having him for eighteen years of my life, and they didn't get nearly as many.'

'That wasn't your fault.'

'I know.' Another breath. This was harder than he'd anticipated. 'He was such a great dad, Piper. He was strict, but supportive. He was patient, and when he got things wrong, he'd say so.' He relaxed the fingers that had clenched the sheets. 'He wasn't perfect, but he tried. And Em, Jada and Tate should have someone who tries, too.'

'Is that why you're looking for Liam?' she asked. 'Why you're so involved with this wedding? Why you picked me up?'

'Yeah, I guess so.'

'Sounds...tough. Trying to be your father, I mean.'

'No. Just trying.'

'Okay.'

He didn't reply. Knew she knew her comment had already done what it was meant to. Facing it brought more guilt. But this was the bubble, wasn't it? Maybe he could finally say what he'd been feeling...

'It's exhausting,' he admitted, relief crashing into him. 'I don't think I can be him. But I still think I should try, because they deserve that. But look what they turned into. Adults who rely on their brother for everything. I know I did that, and I wish I hadn't. I wish...'

Shame kept him from continuing. But a warm hand closed over his, squeezing gently. He turned to see a non-judgemental expression on Piper's face. One that made him feel safe, despite his shame.

'I wish they didn't need me so much,' he whispered.

She cupped his cheek. 'You've taken on so much responsibility, haven't you?'

'My mother left when the kids were young. My dad died. What was I supposed to do?'

'Be a little selfish?'

'That's not an option.' He shook his head. 'My dad stepped up when my mother died. I had to do the same when he died.'

'And you did.' Her thumb brushed his cheek. 'Maybe it's time you let them step up, too.'

'This is scary,' he said, his voice ragged. From the realisations, the hope—he wasn't sure.

'Yeah.' There was a pause. 'I've never told anyone about what happened with my father. Or my brother.'

'He should have been there for you,' Caleb said, because he needed to.

She smiled. 'I'm here for him now. Hopefully that will change things.'

'You're here for a reconciliation?'

'Heavens, no.' She shook her head for good measure. 'I didn't want to come, remember? A reconciliation didn't even occur to me before this point.'

'Why did it now?'

'You,' she said simply. 'Your love for your siblings is… I guess it's something I'd like in my life, too.' She shrugged. 'You have to be willing to give before you can get, and all that.'

He turned to face her, shifting closer.

'I don't know how you feel about being here any more,' he said softly, 'but I'm very happy you are.'

'Right now,' she whispered back, shifting closer to him, too, 'so am I.'

Their lips touching this time was more of a sigh than a shout. It was tender, affectionate. Full of what they couldn't say to one another. Or perhaps full of what they had said to one another.

He put his hand back on the waist he'd had a brief feel of earlier. Now that she was lying, he could memorise the dip of it. That valley between her breasts and her hips. It was the perfect place to stop, to appreciate; he did neither. Instead, he ran his hand over the curve of her. The entirety of her side, from her shoulder down to her hand. Back up, over the side of her chest, her waist, her hips.

She shook beneath his caresses, and damn if he didn't think making her shake was the most important thing he'd ever done in his life. Her hands were on his chest, his bare skin absorbing the heat of it, sending it in pulses of pleasure into his body. He thanked the heavens that he'd fallen asleep after his swim. That he hadn't been able to cover himself.

If he hadn't he wasn't sure he'd have the pleasure of her skin on his. He didn't want to push her, wouldn't have wanted to remove his shirt because of it. It would have been a travesty not to know. Fortunately, he did know.

He cherished the tentative strokes of her hands against his skin. Cherished it as humans might have cherished fire when it had first been discovered. The feel of it was hot and dangerous, but he couldn't move away. He didn't want to move away. So he would stay even though he knew eventually he would burn. It would be worth it.

A groan slipped from his lips when her hands went around his waist and she pulled him closer. Their bodies were flush against one another. There was no hiding how he felt about what they were doing. How he felt about her, since this wasn't just another night with another woman— it was *this* night.

With her.

'I don't think I'm ready to sleep with you yet,' she said,

pulling away from him. Her chest was moving quickly against his. She wasn't wearing a bra, which meant he could feel… He could *feel*.

Suddenly he was clinging to that *yet* more than any grown man should.

'Okay,' he said, his voice sounding foreign to him. 'We don't have to.'

'But maybe we could do some other stuff.'

'Stuff,' he repeated, his brain malfunctioning.

She laughed, a hoarse, sexy sound that had his senses scrambling while his body said *yes*.

The morning after was always awkward. Or so the movies she watched told her. They were not accurate in this case.

Sure, she and Caleb hadn't had sex. But they'd done… *stuff*, which was as intimate. At least for her, since this wasn't the kind of thing she did. Outside of Brad, she'd had no romantic relationships. No romantic liaisons either. It had been her choice, one made from fear, yes, but also power.

For the first time in her life she could choose what she wanted and who she wanted to be around. It was fantastic. Her evening with Caleb seemed to prove it.

So did the morning.

She woke up to find him still there, sprawled under the sheet they'd pulled over themselves in the early morning. The clock told her they'd had about five hours of sleep. It was nowhere near enough, but she felt rested. More relaxed than she'd ever been. There was a brief moment when she thought about Liam and their meeting, but that was still hours away. She shoved it to the back of her mind. She'd deal with it when she had to. For now, she had a gorgeous man to stare at.

She'd managed all of two minutes before he woke up, smiled at her and pulled her into his arms.

'Breakfast,' he said in a gravelly voice that sounded way too sexy for first thing in the morning.

'Yes,' she told him with a quiet chuckle. 'I'll make something.'

'No,' he said when she moved to leave his arms.

She relaxed against his chest. 'We have to get up some time. Considering you're hungry and all.'

'I know.' He pressed a kiss into her hair. She winced. 'What?' he asked.

'It needs to be washed.'

'Would you like to do that?'

'Yes, very much so.'

'Okay, we'll shower. But only because I want to kiss your hair some more and I don't want you wincing every time I do. Plus, there's that food thing.'

'Did you say *we'll* shower?' she asked carefully.

He smiled. 'In our two different showers, yes. Unless…'

'It's going to be harder than that to get me to do your bidding,' she said, moving out of the arms he'd slackened. She widened her eyes as she climbed out of the bed. 'And to think I wasn't even trying to make a dirty joke with that. It just…worked.'

She missed the pillow he threw at her by leaping out of the way at the last second, and went to her room laughing.

'We'll go out for breakfast,' he called out. 'Wear something nice.'

Since she only had one option of clothing, she didn't respond. Her body sang as the hot water heated it, her head thanking her when she dipped it under the steam and rinsed out the coconut oil. She silently thanked Caleb for insisting she bought the things she needed for her hair when they were out shopping. She'd tried to save money, and a sulphate-free shampoo and conditioner seemed like an unnecessary expense when she had full bottles back at the villa.

'I'll use it when you're done,' Caleb had said, plucking the bottle from the shelf.

She'd eyed his close-cut hairstyle. 'You're going to use it on—what? Your scalp?'

'Sulphate dries my scalp out, so yeah, I guess so.'

Thoroughly chastised, she hadn't argued.

She didn't like wearing her hair loose when it was curly. It was long and thick, which meant her curls went everywhere when it wasn't blow-dried straight. She did her best to tame it with the conditioner, then, when that took too long, she put a band over her wrist and hurried down to Caleb.

She missed him already, which made no sense, but she didn't question it. She wasn't questioning anything until she met her brother and everything changed. Tension pulled at her stomach but she stomped down on it. She smiled when she went onto the patio and found Caleb waiting for her.

'Hey,' she said. 'I know you said *nice,* which I think this is since we both decided on— What?' she asked, when his eyes went wide as he looked at her. 'What's wrong?'

'Your hair.'

'Oh.' Self-consciously, she lifted a hand to it. 'I was about to tie it up,' she said, gathering the curls.

'No,' he said, moving forward. 'Don't.'

She stopped, lowering her hands awkwardly.

'This is what your hair looks like wet?'

'When it's not blow-dried, yeah.'

'It's…'

She held her breath.

'Beautiful. Breathtaking, actually. That's what I was trying to say. I was hoping for something more eloquent.'

'That was plenty eloquent,' she said in a small voice as pleasure filled her. It cleared her brain, told her that that expression she'd first seen on Caleb's face had been awe, not disgust.

'Did you think I'd say something else?' he asked, drawing her in with an arm around her waist. With his free hand, he played with the curls. There was a joy on his face that healed a wound she hadn't known was inside her.

'No,' she lied.

Caleb's expression changed. It was so slight that she couldn't be sure, especially when he quickly smiled. When he pressed a soft kiss to her lips. 'It's extraordinary. You're extraordinary.'

'So,' she said, stepping back as the warmth did its thing in her chest. 'What's for breakfast?'

'You'll see,' he said with a grin.

They drove the complicated road to the beach in silence. It was easy, companionable, and allowed her to enjoy the sight of the sand stretched in front of the dark blue sea. The sea crashed into the mountain on its left, and a row of restaurants and beach recliners sat on its right.

'This is beautiful,' she said when they sat down. Caleb had headed straight to this restaurant and she'd followed, because she assumed he'd brought her there for a reason.

'Isn't it?'

He smiled at her and picked up the menu, reading his recommendations to her. They ordered, and when the waiter left Caleb took her hand.

'You lied to me earlier,' he said softly.

'What?' she asked, warmth quickly freezing in her chest.

'When I asked you about your hair. You were lying about what you thought my reaction would be.'

'Oh.' She took a breath. 'Well, yes, but we were having such a nice time. I didn't want to—'

'You don't have to lie about your past,' he interrupted.

'Oh.' It was strange being with someone who said things she needed to hear. Or who made her feel comfortable enough that she didn't feel ashamed when he chided her. 'I'm sorry I lied. I didn't want to spoil the moment.'

'Tell me now.'

She hesitated. Sighed. 'My father, my ex-boyfriend… They disapproved of me wearing my hair curly.'

'Your ex-boyfriend… You dated someone like your father?'

Though she'd been expecting it, hearing the words hurt her. They were an accusation, even though he hadn't meant them to be. This was why she didn't want to think about her past. She knew she would be reminded of her mistakes. Her stupidity.

'Yes,' she said, as unaffectedly as she could manage. 'I told you I had some relationship trouble.'

'You didn't say it was this kind of trouble.'

She studied him. 'You're wondering why I would date someone like my father.'

The waiter brought their drinks. When he left, Piper began to trace patterns into the menu.

'You don't have to answer if you don't want to.'

Caleb's eyes were warm. Supportive.

So she gave him an answer.

'I didn't see it. He wasn't exactly like my father. Especially not at first.'

'He lied to you?'

'He manipulated me,' she replied, though they were two sides of the same coin. 'It was easy to do. He was the first man to pay attention to me when I had my freedom. When I could actually do something about it, I mean,' she added. 'We went out a few months before the suggestions started. And they *were* suggestions at first.' She took a breath. 'Well, he gave me choices, which I suppose isn't the same thing.'

She flipped the menu, smoothing out the lamination. Not that it was necessary.

'But those choices felt like suggestions. That...that felt like freedom. To someone who didn't have choices growing up, choosing felt like freedom. Even when the options were predetermined.' She felt faintly sick about it, even now. 'It was years before I realised that. And who he was.' She shook out her shoulders. 'It's done now, and I'm over it.'

He smiled. It was an indulgent smile, and it told her he didn't believe her. She couldn't even blame him. She *wasn't* over it. Not when the fear of repeating those mistakes still haunted every decision she made.

'You know,' she said after a moment, 'I probably shouldn't have told you this. Not when you're having an existential crisis of your own.'

'I'm not—' He broke off. Scowled at her. 'Is it too late to stay in bed?'

'Afraid so.'

CHAPTER TWELVE

HE DIDN'T SHOW.

Caleb tried not to be annoyed with Liam, considering what Piper had told him about their childhood. He could see that feeling trapped might be a problem for Liam. Could see that his fiancée telling him they had a house and would soon have a baby could make him feel trapped.

He tried, but he didn't succeed.

'I wonder if he's made a will. If he has, I hope he left something to you. Most of it should go to Emma,' he said, 'but you should get some, too. After I kill him, I mean.'

'Some of what?' Piper asked dully. 'The profits of his failed businesses? Or his debts? With my luck, that would be the only thing he's left me.' She blew out a breath. 'This is getting tedious now.'

'You're telling me.'

'It should mean something that he's pitching up, though?' she asked, holding the note Liam had left. This one just said, *Sorry, I'll be in touch soon.* 'Yes, I know I'm clutching at straws,' she said in response to the look he shot her. 'I'm trying to stay positive. It's getting harder. The wedding's two days away.'

'And there are festivities.'

'Festivities?' she repeated.

'Yes.' He grimaced. 'Emma wanted a countdown party for every day until the wedding day. Three, two, one,' he clarified.

'Tonight's two?'

'Today's two,' he corrected. 'In a few hours, we're all supposed to meet at the lighthouse in Mykonos. A photoshoot followed by drinks on the dock until sunset. Dinner, then partying until day one.'

'What happened yesterday? Day three?' She didn't wait for him to answer. 'And what'll happen tomorrow?'

'Much of the same,' he said with a sigh. 'I should probably call her and tell her he's not here.'

'No,' she said. 'Let's wait until he gets in touch before we tell her anything.'

'She'll worry.'

'I know, but she's worried now anyway. At least if we wait, she'll have hope. And we might have something to tell her.'

'The news isn't becoming more positive.'

'It might.'

She said it so hopefully he gave in.

'Fine, but I have to call Jada to update her. She and Tate are in charge of the guests on the island—' He broke off with a wince. 'This is ugly.'

She patted his arm as he made the call. More comfort, although he wished he didn't need it. He didn't want to be calling any of his siblings with bad news. He'd done it when they'd lost their father, and that had been more than enough for his entire lifetime.

Or so he wanted to believe.

'Please tell me you have good news,' Jada said when she answered.

'No.'

She heaved a sigh. 'Figures. Otherwise you'd be calling Em, not me.'

'How is she?'

'How do you think?' Jada asked dryly. 'She's two months pregnant and her fiancé is MIA. He might not make it to the wedding.'

He could almost hear Jada rolling her eyes.

'I'm staying in Santorini for the day. We might have a lead, so we're waiting to see how it pans out. Is everything going okay with the countdown party?'

'You mean, besides the bride and groom being on an imaginary pre-wedding trip on their own? And also the bride's brother and the groom's sister being conspicuously missing? Yeah, it is.' There was a pause. 'You and Piper are getting along, then?'

Heat immediately curled around his neck. He angled his body away from Piper's.

'Yes.'

'Yes? That's it?'

'Yes.'

'Oh, I get it. She's nearby.'

'Yes.'

'So you're getting along, huh?'

'I already said yes to that.'

'How well?'

'If you've got everything sorted for tonight, I'll let you go annoy someone else.'

'*That* well? Wow, Caleb, you move really fast.'

'Goodbye, Jada.'

He put down the phone, though he could hear her still speaking. Piper gave him an amused look.

'So, she's teasing you about me?'

'How did you know?'

'You're blushing,' she said. 'You angled away from me when, I'm guessing, she started asking about me.'

He felt his colour deepen. Scowled because of it.

She patted his arm, though now it was condescending, not comforting.

'I'm a teacher, Caleb. I deal with this kind of thing all the time.'

'You don't have to be so self-satisfied about it.'

She laughed. It sounded delightful. He wouldn't show her that.

'I do enjoy using my skills outside the classroom. Makes me feel like my education wasn't wasted.' Her eyes glistened with amusement and, damn it, he couldn't resist smiling at her. Then her eyes shifted to behind him and she grinned. 'Ice cream! Let's go get some.'

He knew she was trying to distract him. Since he was currently eating butterscotch ice cream, he figured she'd succeeded. More so since she'd chosen her ice cream in a cone, and the movement of her tongue was mesmerising. He averted his eyes so he wouldn't embarrass himself.

'So what now?' he asked when his gaze slipped back to her.

'I don't know,' she said with a sigh. 'We have to stay in phone range. We probably also have to stay on the island since Liam might still be here.'

'Doesn't give us too many options.'

'True.'

They both went silent.

'What if we go back to the beach and wait it out there?' she asked. 'I mean, there could be worse things.'

His brow knitted. 'Did you see the stones on that beach? It's not swimmer-friendly.'

'You're comparing it to Cape Town beaches,' she scolded him. 'Those rocks are part of the experience here.'

'I'm not cutting my foot on a rock for the experience.'

'This from the person who wanted a donkey to take us up more than a hundred steps.'

'That was safe. Have you ever heard of death by donkey in Greece?' he asked at her lifted eyebrows.

'No, but I haven't looked. I'm sure I'll find it.'

'I'm still not swimming with rocks.'

'How did you create such a successful business when you're so risk averse?'

'I take risks,' he defended himself. 'They're a lot easier to take when it's business.'

Or when your livelihood and sanity depend on it.

He didn't say it. She didn't need to know how the business had been a blessing and curse after his father's death. It had given him something else to focus on, but it had reminded him of his father. And of his new responsibilities, since if he messed up at work his siblings wouldn't live the life he'd been lucky enough to live when his father had still been alive.

He released a breath. He needed to move on from this. And though he had no doubt it would be hard, he thought letting his siblings stand on their own might be the place to start. Even the thought of it gave him anxiety.

He was relieved that Piper didn't notice his turmoil. As they drove back to the beach, she chattered about this and that, making astute if irrelevant observations about the island.

'Can you imagine learning to drive here?' she asked when a car pulled in front of them without warning. 'No rules, no laws. Each person for themselves.'

'This isn't the Wild West, Piper,' he said with a laugh. 'There are rules.'

'Really?' Her voice dripped with sarcasm. 'Please do tell me what they are as I cannot for the life of me see order in this. There aren't even robots here.'

'I think they'd call it traffic lights.'

'Yes, but what does it matter, since they don't have them?'

He laughed again, and the tension he'd felt earlier faded. He should probably start putting distance between him and Piper. Stop enjoying her company so much. Stop letting her make him feel better. As soon as they got back to Mykonos, their bubble would pop. And they would fall— hard, he had no doubt. But maybe if he pulled away now... If he guarded himself against the inevitability of it...

Then Piper said something that made her laugh, and he knew he couldn't do it. How could he resist that bright and happy laugh? How could he resist someone who made *themselves* laugh in that way? He was too far gone to be guarded. She'd already crept under the barriers. Ones he'd only now realised he'd erected.

The discovery drew him into his thoughts. Piper must have realised he'd stopped listening because she stopped talking, too. The silence that followed wasn't uncomfortable. It felt pregnant, as though one of them might break it at any moment. Neither of them did. By the time they got to the beach, Caleb worried he'd broken something by not talking. Until he looked over and saw Piper was sleeping.

She'd woken up before him that morning, and he hadn't got the opportunity to see her like this. Up close. It was probably why he hadn't minded that she'd been watching him sleep. When he'd woken up and seen her looking at him, he'd immediately understood. He would have done the same thing if he could.

Because he could now, he did. She took his breath away. Awake, more so, because he could add the light in her eyes when she was teasing him, the quirk of her eyebrow when she was challenging him. It lit a fire inside him—one fuelled by annoyance and attraction and desire. More dangerous than the fire was the fierce wave of protectiveness that extinguished it in moments he least expected it to.

When she'd come out of the house that morning with her long thick curls forming a curtain around her face, her shoulders, she'd taken his breath away. The fire had raged, this time entirely from attraction, desire. Of course, that was partly due to how they'd spent the night before. To how waking up with her in the morning had felt.

But then she'd lost all her confidence and spark when she'd asked him about it. Her reasons—her past—made him angry. He didn't know what to do with that anger. It crackled whenever he thought about the emotional abuse she'd endured. She hadn't said it was that, but what she'd told him was a clear example of it. He wished he could go back and protect her from it. Which had the anger blazing again when he realised she *had* someone who could have protected her. He simply chose not to.

These last two days had not been good for his opinion of his future brother-in-law. Though at this point Caleb was hesitant to call Liam even that.

'Piper,' he said, his voice hoarse. He cleared his throat. 'Piper,' he said again.

Her eyes opened, softened when they saw him. It did him in and he leaned forward, kissing her. She made a soft noise before lifting her hands and cupping his face. The meeting of their tongues felt meaningful, more than the night before. He wasn't sure how that was possible, but he embraced it. Channelled all the confusion about what he felt for her into the movement of their mouths.

When he pulled back she smiled at him. It was a shy smile, a happy smile. His heart filled with pleasure.

'What was that for?' she asked.

'You're beautiful.'

Joy burst from her face, flooding her cheeks with colour. 'You're not too bad yourself.'

He smiled. 'Good to know.'

'Out of all your siblings, you're at least in the top two handsome men.'

He laughed. 'You certainly know how to put a man in his place, don't you?'

'Not any man,' she said serenely. 'Only you. Since I've met you, I've wanted to do nothing else.'

He rolled his eyes, but he didn't bother hiding his smile. He would enjoy her. Time was running out on how long he could.

She felt bad. Mostly because she knew what was happening back on the island of Mykonos. Tate and Jada were desperately trying to keep the guests from finding out her brother had run away from his pregnant fiancée. Emma was heartbroken. Not to mention that Liam was somewhere out there, trying to wrap his head around what his life would become.

She, on the other hand? She was enjoying an ice-cold cocktail with the most attractive man she'd ever seen. On the beach. Under an umbrella that kept her out of direct sunlight but didn't keep her from the heat of the sun.

She sighed in pleasure—and guilt—and turned her head to Caleb.

'This is wrong. We should be doing something more than this to find Liam.'

'Is your phone on?' he replied.

'Yeah.'

'Do you have signal?'

She checked. 'Yes.'

'Battery?'

'Yes.'

'What could we do besides that?'

His chest rose and fell with his breath. He'd taken off his shirt, and she got distracted by the muscles before answering his question.

'I don't know, but I feel like the answer should be more than this.'

He took her hand, brought it to his lips. He enjoyed doing

that; she enjoyed having him do it. No—she loved that he did it. She loved the easy affection. It was a new experience for her. Brad hadn't believed in PDA, even small ones like this. She'd dated him for years and not once had they held hands in public. How had she not seen that as a red flag?

'I know this is strange, considering everything. Believe me, there's nothing more I want to do than to find Liam and get some answers. But our best bet is waiting for that phone call. I don't want to waste my time running around the island, only to discover he's not here.'

'So you'd rather waste your time on the beach with me?'

'There's no one I'd rather waste my time with,' he replied with a smile.

She shook her head. 'You need to work on how amusing you think you are.'

'You need to work on your sense of humour.'

He winked at her before putting his sunglasses back on and slipping down on the beach chair. She didn't laugh, didn't smile, though she did both on the inside. She complimented her self-control, right until the moment she stuck her tongue out at him.

'I saw that,' he said lazily.

'You were supposed to.'

He laughed, and she lowered onto her own beach chair, letting the heat soothe her body. They stayed like that for hours, sipping drinks, ordering food. When it got too hot, they walked down to the beach front shops and bought another pair of swimsuits. Piper didn't complain this time. She didn't want to spoil their afternoon.

She did protest at the costume Caleb selected for her though. A piece of string, essentially, that she gave her opinion on with a single look. He laughed, tried again with an equally revealing bikini. She ignored him and chose something she was more comfortable with. They changed and went for the swim. She didn't even mention Caleb's fear of hurting himself on the rocks...

Oh, who was she kidding? She mentioned it several times, particularly when she swam towards him, wrapping her legs around his waist.

'I should leave you here to fend for yourself,' he said when she teased him yet again. They were in deep waters, Caleb easily keeping them up with his strokes.

'By all means,' she said. 'I'm sure there'll be at least one gentleman who'd be interested in picking up where you left off.' She pretended to look around. 'Maybe that one over there? Sir,' she called loudly. 'Sir, would you be interested in—'

He cut her off with a kiss, and she giggled into his mouth, a free sound she'd never heard come from herself before.

'Keep going,' Caleb said, his eyes hot. 'I would love to keep you from talking some more.'

'Your suggestion has been noted,' she said lightly. 'Alternative suggestion. How about we just keep making out? No excuses.'

'I like the way you think.'

Their lips met again, and they kissed until Caleb forgot he was keeping them up and they both slipped under the water. Laughing, they left the ocean. It was sunset by then, the start of the evening punctuated by loud traditional Greek music.

Night fell as they were having dinner. Locals and tourists alike filled the road between the restaurants and the beach. There was laughter and breaking plates. Loud chattering, dancing, fun. It was the kind of scene shown in movies, and Piper felt incredibly happy to witness it in real life. More so to witness it with Caleb.

Then her phone rang.

'Liam,' she answered immediately, ignoring the tension that grabbed her entire body. 'Where are you?'

'Hello?' came a voice. 'Pie? I can't hear you.'

She gestured to the crowd for Caleb's sake, stood and left the restaurant. She manoeuvred through the people until she could find a quiet spot. It was some metres away, and she told Liam to stay on the line.

'Hey,' she said once she finally found a quiet place. 'Sorry about that. It's loud out here tonight.'

'You're at the countdown party?' he asked.

'Um,' she said, only just remembering that he didn't know where she was. 'No. I'm still in Santorini. I thought I'd wait in case you're still here. Are you?'

'Yeah.'

'Okay.' There was a pause. 'Can we meet up?'

'You're not alone, are you?'

She sighed. 'No. Emma wanted Caleb to come with me.'

There was a long stretch of silence. The only way she knew he was still on the phone was because she could hear his breathing.

'He's mad, huh?'

'Why are you worrying about him, Liam? Your fiancée is not only mad, she's heartbroken. You left her after she told you she was going to have your baby.'

'She told you?'

'Of course. She thought I might have some answers about why you left. I didn't,' she told him. 'But I'm still here looking for you, letting you mess me around with your phony meet-up times, because family is supposed to show up for one another.'

She was out of breath when she was done. Surprised, too. She hadn't expected all of that to come out of her mouth. She knew it was there, but it had always been there. What was different now, that she'd finally said it?

'So you're mad, too.'

'It doesn't matter,' Piper said, fighting for control. 'You need to get your head right with your priorities, man. You're about to become a father.'

'I know,' he said. 'I know. I… I'm scared, Pie. Dad was a terrible father. What if I am, too? I'm already a terrible brother. I'm a terrible fiancé. If the pattern continues, I'll end up being a terrible father.'

Piper exhaled. She knew she should comfort him. Reassure him. But she couldn't do either. Her mind spun around his admission that he'd been a bad brother. That he *knew.* It was the first time he'd ever acknowledged it. She wasn't sure what to do with it.

It inspired her to ask, 'What are you going to do about it, Liam?'

'What do you mean?'

'You have a choice. You choose who you want to be. You don't have to be terrible if you don't want to be.'

'Easy for you to say.'

'No,' she said quietly. 'It's not. It's hard, actually.' She took a breath, hoping the air would settle her. 'Brad was like Dad, Liam. I didn't know it until it was too late. By then, the damage was already done.'

'Pie.'

It was all Liam said, his voice strained. It was oddly comforting.

'I managed to break up with him, and I vowed never to let anyone treat me that way again.' Her heart thudded, her mind stirring. She didn't pay attention to why. 'I chose not to let the past repeat itself. You can, too. If Emma is at all important to you, if your unborn child is, you *should*.'

He didn't respond immediately.

'Tomorrow. Same arrangements as today. I promise I'll be there.' He paused. 'Come alone, Pie. We need to talk.'

CHAPTER THIRTEEN

'WE MEET TOMORROW. Same time and place as he wanted to meet today.'

That was all Piper said when she returned to the restaurant. Caleb hadn't been able to follow her—their plates were full, and he still needed to pay. He'd weighed it up, figured their conversation couldn't be that long, based on past experience. She'd been gone for about ten minutes; he'd been getting ready to go after her when she finally came back.

And that was all she said.

He waited for her to say more. Through the dinner they finished though it was slightly cold. Through the trip back to the house. But she was silent. When he tried to ask her about it, she was reticent.

She walked straight to her room when they got to the house, not giving him a chance to ask her anything. He let her go. What choice did he have? He'd asked her about it. He'd been straightforward. If she didn't want to tell him, that was her decision. Damn the fact that they'd spent two incredible days together. The night they'd shared didn't seem to matter either. Once again, they were two strangers who didn't share their thoughts and feelings.

He managed to resist for the entirety of his shower. The moment he was in his clothes again, he marched up the stairs.

'What the hell?' she asked when she saw him.

She was standing in the doorway of her bathroom, a towel wrapped around her body. Her magnificent hair was piled on top of her head. Water trickled down from it over her face.

'You're wet,' he said.

'Thanks for pointing that out.'

She gave him a look of disdain before grabbing a bottle from the vanity and going back into the bathroom. She shut the door for good measure.

He deserved it.

He was a complete idiot for storming into her room. She deserved privacy. He had no right to be in her space without asking. He left her to it, disgust at himself taking him to the kitchen. He poured himself a shot of whisky, hissing at the burn of it in his throat. Then he went outside, back to the deck where she'd come to him the night before. She found him there again twenty minutes later.

'That wasn't—'

'I'm sorry,' he interrupted. 'I know what you're going to say. I shouldn't have come up there and I'm sorry.'

She searched his face. 'As long as you know you were crossing a line.'

'I'm apologising for it.'

'You are.'

She angled her head in what he assumed was acceptance of his apology. Then she sat down on the lounger opposite his. She took the long plait she'd braided her hair into and rested it over her shoulder.

'Liam wants me to see him alone tomorrow.' Her eyes met his. 'I think I should.'

He yanked the *no* from the tip of his tongue, knowing he'd stop the conversation before it even started if he said it. He resisted the urge to curl his hands into fists. Refused to sit on them either when that seemed like less effort. The strain of controlling himself so precisely made his heart thud. He thought it would be worth it if he could have a conversation with Piper where he'd convince her not to go alone to see her brother.

'Why?'

It was the only word the control would allow him to say.

'He…he's scared,' she said slowly. 'I think he wants to talk with me about our family issues.' She lifted a shoulder. 'He needs this.'

'Him or you?'

She blinked. 'Excuse me?'

'Does he need to talk about the family issues, or do you?'

'I'm not sure how you came to that conclusion,' she said, her brow furrowing. 'I have no horse in this race. He's the one who ran away from his wedding.'

'You have no horse in this race,' he repeated. 'So shutting me out earlier had nothing to do with you worrying about what's happening between us?'

He wasn't offended by the surprise in Piper's eyes. How could he be when the question came from nowhere for him, too? His control had apparently snapped and words were hurtling out unchecked. Now that they were in the open, Caleb had no choice but to realise that his anger had flared again when Piper hadn't opened up to him about that phone call. It wasn't logical, and it told him that he was worrying about what was happening between them, too.

All the *we have this moment* stuff he'd been telling himself over the last day had been hiding the fact that he was scared. He didn't like the feeling. It reminded him too much of how he'd been after his father died. Terrified of letting his family down. Of letting his father down.

Was that what was happening here, too? Was he scared of what would happen with his siblings once he got back to Mykonos? Was he scared of letting them down? Was he scared of letting Piper down?

'I think,' Piper said, standing up, 'that we should save

this conversation for when our emotions aren't so close to the surface.'

'You mean, when you're not this scared?' he asked recklessly. Hell, the control was already gone. He might as well lean in.

Her eyes went cool. 'Goodnight, Caleb.'

'No, Piper, please,' he said, standing. 'I'm sorry. I shouldn't have—' He broke off when he realised he would be lying if he said he shouldn't have said that. 'I need to know.'

'Why?'

'Because something's happening here. I need to know I'm not the only one freaked out about it.'

There was a flicker of emotion on her face before it cleared. He didn't know what she was thinking or feeling. It was torture.

'You're not,' she said when the silence stretched so long he thought she wouldn't answer. Then she turned on her heel and left him with his thoughts.

He watched her leave before he went back to his room. He closed the doors and the blinds. It was utterly dark, the only light coming from the moon shining through the window high above the doors. His housekeeper had replaced the sheets, so he wasn't sure why, when he lay on the bed, he could still smell Piper.

He left the air-conditioning off, turned the fan on instead. Then he lay and watched it spin. His eyes adjusted, his body sank into the bed. It didn't help him fall asleep. His thoughts were a mess of regret and guilt from the past and the present. In some illogical twist of time, he thought it came from the future, too.

This moment felt significant. As if his actions now would affect the rest of his life. His happiness. No wonder he couldn't sleep.

* * *

The tension between her and Caleb was her fault. She knew it and, despite the fact that she longed for things to be different—she wanted to go back to Piper and Caleb on the beach, in the ocean, at dinner, in his room—it couldn't be. At least not until she saw her brother.

'I was thinking about it last night,' Caleb said during breakfast.

Piper had woken up to hear his housekeeper in the kitchen, cooking. Though she would have liked to cook breakfast herself, that urge was overwhelmed by the relief that she didn't have to be alone with Caleb.

'Yes?'

'You should see Liam alone. But I'd like to take you, and wait nearby in case you need me.'

She wanted to protest. Looked into his eyes, saw the desperation and the defiance there. This was the best he was willing to offer. She didn't have the energy to argue. She gave herself a moment to think about whether that was because of her tendency to let people control things, or because she was picking her battles. Was she being naïve, or was she being smart?

She'd lost her ability to discern between the two at some point during her time with Caleb. She'd gone from doubting everything he said to doubting nothing. She'd told him she was terrified the night before, and this was why. Because she didn't know if she was losing herself as she lost her heart to him.

Oh, no. She was losing her heart to him.

'That's fine,' she said in a thin voice. 'You'll need to give us some space, but that's fine.'

'You won't see me, I promise.'

The politeness they were treating one another with would have bothered her more if she weren't so concerned by the revelation that she was falling for him. Of course she had known. On some level. Otherwise the fact that she'd told her brother she was choosing a different life wouldn't have bothered her so much.

But here now, actually admitting it to herself? It sent wave after wave of panic through her. She could barely finish the fruit bowl she'd made herself. She didn't touch the croissant she'd put on her plate as an afterthought to have with her coffee. Her stomach was tightening, her heart pulsating heavily against her chest. All because she was starting to feel something for Caleb—and because she knew who she was.

The same Piper. Beneath her progress and her determination to choose a different life, there was the same old Piper. That Piper would talk herself into believing that Caleb's controlling tendencies wouldn't affect her. She understood them now and couldn't judge him for it, but that didn't mean she wouldn't find herself back to where she'd been with Brad. Or did it? She didn't know. And that uncertainty was why she couldn't fall for this man.

She excused herself from the table, not bothering to give Caleb an explanation. In her room, she packed up her things. Things he'd bought her, for heaven's sake! She pushed at the thought—she'd pay him back, even if it meant not making rent for a month—and went downstairs. He was standing at the foot of the staircase.

'You want to leave after meeting Liam?' he said, taking one look from her bag to her face.

'Yes.'

He nodded. Shoved his hands into his pockets. 'Okay. Should we buy tickets online?'

'We?'

'Yeah,' he said. 'Regardless of whether Liam pitches, I've been away from Emma too long. She needs me. And it isn't fair of me to expect Tate and Jada to take all the responsibility for the guests.'

All the aching inside her stopped for a moment. She looked at him, at the sincerity of his expression, and couldn't be upset that the warning signs of her body had taken a break. The care this man had for his family was admirable. It was part of why she liked him so much.

The judgement she'd had for her feelings eased. Because when she looked at him like this, when she heard his concerns about his siblings, she could almost imagine she wouldn't lose herself with him.

'Of course,' she said when the moment caught up with her. 'We can do it right now.'

They bought the tickets, packed up and left the house much earlier than they needed to. But what were they going to do there? Lounge around the pool, ignoring one another? Take a swim, not speaking? It was torture not being friends. Well, not friends, since she didn't think that was what they were, but *friendly*. Especially when she knew what it was like.

When they reached the place she was supposed to meet Liam, it was an hour too early. They got out of the car, then stared at one another.

'What do you want to do?' he asked.

'I'm not sure.' She looked around, saw only buses and shops. Then a man in a red shirt passed them, a crowd following behind him. Piper looked at Caleb. 'What do you think they're doing?'

'A tour, probably.'

'A walking tour?'

'I assume.'

Piper narrowed her eyes as she stared after the crowd. 'Twenty minutes. We walk with them for twenty minutes and then we come back. It'll give us twenty minutes to spare before Liam gets here.'

'Are you sure?' he asked mildly.

'Yes.'

Anything to escape the tension.

She didn't wait to see if he was following her; she knew he would be. Soon they were walking along a narrow path surrounded by white buildings. They stopped in front of a whitewashed church, where she and Caleb hung back far enough from the group that the guide didn't notice them. They got some of the history, but Piper was more interested in the architecture. The church had a blue dome on top of it, a signature of Santorini architecture, and a bell beneath the roof.

The group began walking again, but they didn't follow, since the guide had said their next stop would be in twenty minutes.

'We should have done this yesterday,' she told him with a sigh. 'I would have loved to see the wine estate they're going to next.'

'I'm sorry.'

She waved a hand. 'It isn't your fault. I suggested the beach.'

There was a beat. 'I don't regret yesterday.'

She turned at the emotion in his voice. Caught her breath at the emotion on his face.

'Most of it, anyway,' he said with a small smile. 'Should we get going?'

'I don't regret it either,' she replied, ignoring his question. 'I didn't mean it in a "I wish we could go back and replace the day with something else" kind of way. Or with someone else.'

'I wish I could go back and change whatever happened that made things so awkward between us.'

'Would you like to change me?' she asked playfully, desperate not to think about the way her heart cracked at his question.

'Never.' He took a step closer. Cupped her face. 'I wouldn't change you for the world, Piper. You're perfect the way you are.'

He lowered his head, but not enough for their lips to touch. He did so purposely, she knew. Wondered why the action had the judgement of her feelings for him going down another notch.

But she didn't spend much time dwelling on it. Instead, she closed the distance between them, moaning when the contact banished the doubt inside her. When it was replaced with a certainty that this was supposed to be happening. This kiss had an urgency that none of the others had. Even when they'd been deep in exploring one another the other night, it hadn't felt like this. Desperation spurred the movement of their tongues. Passion directed their hands.

Vaguely Piper thought about the fact that they were in public. Less vague was the thought that no one was around. The walking tour group had left a while ago. Caleb had her against the wall, angling her so that they were obscured from the main path.

She let herself sink into it. The urgency, the desperation, the passion. She loved the taste of him. Mint and the faintest hint of coffee. Her hands memorised the shape of him. The ripples of his abs, the curves of his chest, his biceps. Her head dropped back when he moved his lips from her mouth to her neck. Moaned when his tongue brushed over the sensitive skin in the nape of her neck, when his teeth gently nibbled on her. Pleasure meshed with pain and she gasped, putting a hand on her chest in protest.

In thanks.

He pulled away, his chest heaving, his eyes glazed with pleasure.

'I...got carried away.'

She scraped her nails down his chest, over his abdomen. 'We both did.'

He took a breath. 'You're dangerous.'

'So are you.'

His mouth lowered to take hers again, softer this time. She melted against him, marvelling at his skill, his intuition. She didn't care that those things must have come from practice. She only cared that he was using them on her. Making heat pool in the pit of her stomach. Making her ache with a longing she'd never felt. Didn't think she'd wanted to until now.

When he pulled away from her he smiled, brushed her hair back. Tentatively placed a kiss on her lips. Then he looked her directly in the eyes.

'I'm scared, Piper. Terrified.' He tilted her chin with his fingers. 'You're not alone.'

CHAPTER FOURTEEN

PIPER ONLY REALISED she'd been holding her breath when Liam walked into the restaurant and the air gushed from her lungs. It took her a moment to find it again, as if her lungs had forgotten how to function. Once she reminded them by going through the motions of breathing carefully, she raised a hand and got his attention.

The first thing she thought was that he looked terrible. There were bags under his eyes, his skin looked ragged, and he walked as if the world was on his shoulders. The second thing she thought was that he needed help. So when he reached the table she stood and pulled him into a hug.

His body was stiff at first, then slowly he relaxed and folded his arms around her. They stood like that for longer than they had hugged before—though this wasn't a feat. They hadn't really hugged before. The only memories she had were before he'd left for university, and after their father had died. When they'd realised they were finally free.

She stepped back, patted him awkwardly on the shoulder, and they sat. She waited for him to speak.

'Thank you for coming,' he said eventually. He took the glass of what she'd ordered, drank as if he'd come from the desert. 'I know you didn't have to.'

'I did,' she said. 'Not only because your fiancée asked me to, but because you're my brother.' She let it sit. 'But the first might not matter any more if you have no intention of marrying Emma.'

He gaped at her. 'What? Of course I'm still going to marry Emma.'

'You should probably let her know that, then.'

'She doesn't?'

'You ran away the night she told you she was carrying your baby. What do you think she's thinking right now?'

'Good riddance,' he said bitterly.

Piper sighed. 'You need to get over this, Liam.'

'Over what?'

'Your self-pity.' She didn't mince her words. Had neither the patience nor compassion to do so. She did have empathy though, which meant that she knew what her brother needed. Tough love. 'You've made this all about you. You feel sorry for yourself.'

'It is about me.'

'Oh, are *you* pregnant?' she asked. 'Carrying a baby, are you? It's wreaking havoc on your body and your emotions and your fiancée's just left you after you told her you're expecting?'

There was a silence before he mumbled, 'You're supposed to be on my side.'

'There is no "supposed to" when it comes to us, Liam,' she said, careful when his words hit a nerve. 'We were supposed to be a family with Dad. You were supposed to be my big brother.' She waited a beat. 'No one in their right mind would have called you, me and Dad a family. And big brothers... Well, they're not supposed to leave their baby sisters to fend for themselves against controlling fathers.'

He blanched at that. She didn't try to make him feel better. Didn't try to make herself feel better either. She accepted the pain of it, let it wash over her so that one day she'd know when it washed through her.

At some point during the silence Liam's entire demeanour changed. He straightened his spine, drew his shoulders back. He pushed the wild curls of his hair back—they shared at least that familial connection—and looked her straight in the eyes.

'You're right.'

She was holding her breath again. It took those two words for her to realise it, but they were enough. Again, she found herself focusing on her breathing. Then he was talking and she forgot to focus on anything besides his words.

'I wasn't there for you. I should have been.'

She swallowed. 'Thank you.'

'Don't thank me, Pie,' he said with a humourless smile. 'You have every right to be angry with me. Just like Emma does.' His voice dropped at that, his brow lowering. He shook his head. 'I was a bad brother. I'd... I'd like to change that.'

Her heart swelled. When Liam reached out to cover her hand with his, it burst. She gasped in air, then realised her breathing had turned shallow and took a deep breath, then another. Liam didn't look amused or concerned. He only waited for her. She gave him the go-ahead with a slight nod.

'I couldn't stop thinking about what you said last night about choosing to be better.' He ran a hand over his face. 'I got in here a few minutes ago and I still didn't know why...I was still whining.' He gave her an embarrassed smile. 'I blamed the world for what Dad did to us. Asked *Why me?* too many times to count.'

'I did, too,' she said softly. 'Especially after the whole thing with Brad. I couldn't believe I'd gone down that path. That I'd chosen it. I blamed—' She broke off before she could say *myself*. Not because it wasn't true. Because she didn't want to admit it out loud. 'The world,' she finished lamely. 'I blamed the world, too.'

Liam squeezed her hand, then folded his arms.

'You know, I never liked Brad.'

'What?' she said, dropping her head. When he smiled at her, she laughed a little. 'Would have been nice of you to tell me that sooner.'

'Would have,' he agreed. 'I should have stepped in. Not

to tell you what to do, but to warn you so you could make the decision for yourself.' He exhaled. 'We're a mess, kid. Now I'm supposed to be a husband and a father as a mess.'

'Do you love her?'

'More than anything else.'

'Then you'll clean up. You'll step up.' She nodded at him. 'One, because she'll force you to. Emma's not going to allow you to be anything less than a good dad and husband.'

'I have her brother to thank for that.'

'Why?' she asked, curious despite the warning bells in her brain.

'She's never had to compromise on anything. She always had a good role model in him.' Liam blushed. 'I've always felt like I have to measure up.'

'You do,' Piper said. 'She deserves someone who loves and treats her like Caleb does. You have to do better. And you will.'

His lips curved. 'Was that the second thing?'

'What do you mean?'

'You said "one" when you told me I'd step up. What's two?'

'Oh.' She leaned forward. 'Two, you'll stop running.'

Panic fluttered over his face. 'I don't want to run. I just... I worry that I'm going to let her down like I let you down.'

'You only let me down because you ran, Liam.' She let the realisation move around in her mind. 'It was kind of okay, what Dad did to us, because we were together. It wasn't that he was doing it to me, it was that he was doing it to us, and that seemed less personal.' She took a breath. 'When you left...'

'It was like he was doing it to you.'

'Yes.'

He reached over, linked their hands. 'I'm sorry, Piper. I should have come back. I didn't because—'

'I know why you didn't,' she interrupted, thinking about all the times she'd wished she could run away. When she'd had the opportunity to leave, she hadn't come back either. Until her father had died, she hadn't gone back to that house.

What would she have done if she'd left a sibling behind?

She almost laughed out loud when she realised she wouldn't have done what Liam had done. Her presence in this small Greek café proved that. Liam hadn't done anything to earn her loyalty, and yet she was there, trying to help him. There was no way she would have done what he did. Hell, she was more likely to have sacrificed her own life, like Caleb had, than do what Liam had done.

But she understood the impulse. Understood that someone who had different priorities might not have come back. Liam hadn't.

It made her like Caleb even more, which was a problem with the way things currently were between them.

She exhaled. 'It's not about what you did, Liam. It's about what you'll do.' She paused. 'What are you going to do?'

The panic that had been on his face was replaced with determination. 'I'm going to stop running.'

'You let him leave?' Caleb asked, indignant. He looked at the café behind Piper, hoping to spot Liam. Hoping that what she'd told him wasn't true.

'He'll be at the wedding,' she assured him.

'And I'm supposed to believe that?'

'That's what he said. I believe him.'

'Why?' he asked. 'He's done plenty of things that mean he won't keep his word.'

'He also pitched up today.' She was being infuriatingly calm. Unmoved. As if the entire wedding didn't depend on a man who had already proven he was unreliable. 'He'll do it again.'

'That's naïve,' he said through clenched teeth. 'Especially after everything he did to you.'

Her eyes went cool, his only warning that he'd overstepped the mark.

'I didn't tell you about my past so that you can throw it in my face. Especially when, when we started this, *you* were using my relationship to him as a reason I should go with you.'

'That was Emma's idea. Besides, I didn't know about what he did then.' He sighed. 'I'm sorry. I'm a bit…stressed.'

'I can see that,' she said dryly. 'Let me guess—you spoke to one of your family members while you were waiting for us.'

'Emma. She's not doing well.'

'That's understandable.'

'I wanted to give her good news when we got back.'

'Again, understandable.'

'You also understand then why you telling me you let him go to do whatever the hell he wants to frustrates me.'

'Caleb,' she said, again in that irritatingly calm voice, 'this isn't your responsibility.'

He gritted his teeth. 'So you don't understand.'

She studied him, looked at her watch. 'We've got to get down to the port. Our boat leaves in ninety minutes.'

The gritting became grinding. He couldn't stop it when it was clear she would no longer entertain his questions.

'I can't go without him,' Caleb said when they reached the car.

'Then you're going to miss the wedding, Caleb.' She paused. 'Liam will be there. And if he's not, the only thing you can do for Emma is support her. It won't be your fault that he doesn't show up.'

'Why are you being so…so—'

'Reasonable?' she asked with a quirk of her brow. 'Because I'm removing my emotion from the situation.'

'It's that easy for you?'

'No, but it's necessary for my sanity.' She put a hand on the roof of the car. 'Does this mean I have to call for a cab, or are you going with me?'

He took a long time to make the decision. When he started driving he was surprised his teeth hadn't become ash, the way he was working them. He forced himself to stop, which allowed him to feel how uncomfortably his heart was beating. As if he had something important to do but didn't know what.

It *was* uncomfortable. The feeling, and the fact that he always knew what to do. Doing nothing wasn't an option. It was never an option. Damn it. He should be looking for Liam. He should hire a private detective. Maybe he could—

A warm hand on his thigh stopped his thoughts. He looked down, felt the warmth spread, then looked up and thanked the heavens nothing unexpected had happened or he might have caused the car to crash.

'Was that really worth your life?' he muttered, taking the turn that would lead them to the port.

'It stopped the downward spiral of your thoughts, didn't it?' she asked, unperturbed.

He didn't answer immediately.

'This is a departure from your initial thoughts on my driving.'

'I suppose I've learnt to trust you.'

The simple sentence became more meaningful with the squeeze of her hand. He opened his mouth. Shut it when he realised he didn't know what to say. Part of him wanted to ask her why she was pulling away from him. If she trusted him, why was she curling into herself, away from him and what they'd shared?

Another part of him thought it was for the best. There was no future for them once they reached Mykonos. That hadn't changed since the last time he'd thought it. And it was a good thing. With the mess he was anticipating with the wedding, Emma would need him more than ever. Then there'd be a baby, and he'd have to help with that. It would be what his father would have done. It was what he wanted to do.

Except he wasn't sure of that any more. He didn't know if he wanted to keep trying to be like his father. He didn't know *what* he wanted. In taking responsibility for his siblings, he'd lost the ability to discern what *he* wanted. It had taken wanting something so badly, and being torn between his family and that thing, for him to realise it.

He was distracted from his thoughts when Piper pulled her hand away and he felt as if he'd lost a limb. It reaffirmed that her pulling away was for the best. In fact, he probably should have done it first. He shouldn't be kissing her in front of churches. Shouldn't be telling her he was scared of falling for her.

Because you already have.

He grunted at the inner voice.

'What?' she asked, looking at him as they boarded the ferry.

'I didn't say anything.'

'You grunted.'

'That's not speaking.'

She sighed, as if he were an elderly person who required patience. Or simply someone who'd admitted to having feelings for a woman when he couldn't afford to. Either worked.

CHAPTER FIFTEEN

HE FELT CURIOUSLY numb when they arrived in Mykonos. An overload of emotion and realisations had put him in a mood he barely recognised in himself. It probably explained his reaction when Jada stormed to his side the moment they reached the villa.

'Done playing Romeo now, have you?'

'Is that really what you think I've been doing these last few days?' he asked. '"Playing Romeo"?'

Jada blinked. 'Well, you've been gone and—'

'I've been looking for Liam, Jada.' His tone sounded... passionate, though for the life of him he couldn't figure out where it was coming from. 'I've been spending my time trying to fix things for one of you, as I tend to do. The least *you* can do is acknowledge that, and not pretend like I'd abandoned you to romance Piper.'

He had, of course, been romancing Piper, but that wasn't why they'd been away. Besides, he'd realised he'd have to be firmer if he wanted his siblings not to need him as much. He didn't know how to reconcile that desire with living up to his father's legacy. Perhaps that helplessness was where the passion had come from.

When he looked at Piper and saw pride in her eyes, pleasure rushed into his system. He wondered if that had contributed to the passion, too...

'I'm sorry,' Jada said sincerely. It didn't hide the confusion but, since that was warranted, Caleb didn't doubt she meant the apology. 'It's just that... The guests are suspicious. They haven't seen Emma or Liam in the last two days, nor you and Piper. They're wondering whether something's going on.'

'Have you seen Emma?'

'Of course. *I* know this last-minute trip thing with Liam isn't real.' Jada bit her nails, a clear sign of her stress levels. 'But we told her she needs to stay in her room.'

'She was okay with that?'

'She doesn't exactly want to be around people, so yeah.'

'So you handled it.' Pride and satisfaction mingled inside him, soothing some of his earlier uncertainty about how ready his siblings were for independence. 'Where are the guests now?'

'Beginning Day One of the Countdown party.' When he only dropped his head in question, Jada sighed. 'They're getting ready to leave for the sunset cruise.'

'That buys us some time.'

'But does not help to lull suspicions. Tate's with them,' Jada said. 'He begins to dance every time someone asks him about Emma or Liam or you two.' Her face turned pleading. 'It's been terrible.'

He tried not to laugh at Jada's expression. Or at the idea that Tate was dancing his way through awkward questions. His brother was a terrible dancer, the only one in the family who hadn't inherited that gene. Only Jada had the courage to tell him that though. Since she made fun of almost everything he did, Tate hadn't taken her seriously. Caleb wondered if he'd done something wrong by not being truthful. Then he pictured his brother dancing again and chuckled. Wrong, maybe. Entertaining though.

Thinking about all of it broke the tension he was feeling.

'This isn't funny.'

He sobered. 'No, it's not.' Cleared his throat. 'Okay, the cruise starts with drinks, doesn't it? On the beach.'

Jada nodded. 'That's why I could be here to talk to you.'

'To complain to me.'

'Yes.'

He smiled. 'When do they leave?'

'Twenty minutes.'

He wanted to ask Jada what she thought they should do next. It was a test, he could admit, to see if she could handle things again. But her expression was pleading and, since he hadn't done much while he was away, he gave in.

Surprise, surprise.

He turned to Piper, ignoring the taunting inner voice. 'How do you feel about going back on a boat?'

Her face paled slightly, but she nodded. 'Sure.'

'You're feeling sick?'

'No, I'm fine.' She straightened her shoulders.

'It would be easier for all of us if he just came back.'

'He is,' Piper said, shifting so she could see Jada better. 'He's coming back.'

Jada brightened. 'He is?' She must have remembered she was upset with him because she immediately scowled. 'When?'

'I'm not sure.'

'You're not sure?' Caleb said. 'He didn't tell you?'

'He said before the wedding.' She turned to Jada. 'He'll be back, and if that means I have to get back on the boat to help with the guests' perceptions, that's what I'll do.'

Caleb took a deep breath. Another when he wanted to ask her how the hell she'd let Liam go without an exact time of when he'd be back.

'Jada, go with Piper. Em and I'll be down before the boat leaves.'

'You *and* Em?'

'Yeah,' he said. 'We'll pretend like she's back early, but she shouldn't be alone any longer.'

He walked away before either of them could reply.

Got his emotions under control before he knocked on Emma's door.

There was no reply. He knocked again. Heard nothing again. There could have been a million reasons for that. She could be in the shower. Sleeping. She could have her earphones in, listening to music. Another time, he knew he'd give these options more than a cursory thought. Now, though, worry overtook logic. He had flashbacks to that time Emma had decided to drink an entire bottle of wine and he'd discovered her passed out near a puddle of her own puke.

He knew that wasn't a concern now—Emma would never put herself in danger like that again, or her baby— but he didn't know what else to do. He knocked again, called out, got nothing. So he kicked the door open.

The first thing he saw was the mess. The bed was un-made, blankets on the floor, clothes all over the place. The second thing was the open door to the small courtyard, which each of the rooms had. He was there in two sec-onds and as soon as he got there he turned around, regret reverberating in every part of his mind.

He shook his head—shook it again—then walked out of the door before realising he'd kicked it open and couldn't close it. Before he realised someone else could walk in and see what he'd just seen. Nausea rolled in his stomach. At the fact that he had seen what he'd seen and also at the prospect of seeing it again.

He took his phone out, messaged Jada and waited for her to arrive. He was effectively standing guard at the door. Jada would never let him live this down, but rather her than him. Rather *anyone* than him.

He didn't even blink when Piper arrived instead. To her credit, after she took everything in, she didn't comment.

'I believe you need reinforcements?'

He nodded.

'Why?'

He tilted his head back, towards what he'd left behind.

'I'm sorry,' she said pleasantly. 'I don't understand your non-verbal communication at the moment.'

He glowered at her. She smiled.

'Why do you need reinforcements, Caleb?'

'Emma.'

It was all he could manage. When she peered around him at the open door, he saw alarm in her eyes.

'Is she okay?'

'Fine.'

She narrowed her eyes. 'What's going on, Caleb?'

'Your brother.'

She lowered her head. Made a gesture for him to continue.

'He's in there, too.'

'Liam's in there?' She looked around him again. Obviously, she couldn't see anything. 'Is that why the door's broken? Because you saw him?' She exhaled irritably. 'Boundaries, Caleb. This is ridiculous. They're engaged, and if they—'

'I walked in on them…' He couldn't say it.

'You walked in— Oh. Oh,' she said again, scrunching her nose. 'Oh,' she said for the third time, her face comically arranged. He couldn't find the humour in it yet though.

'I don't think I'll ever…' He shook his head. 'I saw…'

Her eyes widened. Her lips pursed.

He narrowed his eyes. 'It's not funny.'

'Oh, no.'

'Seriously.'

She pressed her lips together so hard they turned white.

'Piper,' he rasped. 'It's not funny.'

A sound burst through her lips. She put a hand over her mouth.

'You don't get it. They're—'

She interrupted him by putting her free hand out.

'Please, don't.' She said it with a little gasp, as if she'd been holding her breath. 'I don't want to be traumatised.'

'Yes,' he exclaimed. 'That's it. I'm traumatised. I saw my baby sister—'

This time she stopped him by putting her hand over his mouth. 'I said *don't*. I get it. I really do.'

'Then why are you—?' He stopped when she pulled her hand away so he could speak clearly. Started again. 'Then why are you laughing?'

'I'm not. I didn't.' She fluttered her lashes at him innocently. 'Does this look like I'm laughing?'

There was a moment. One single beat where their eyes met, linked. The light of amusement in her eyes was so bright he was caught in it. In her. As if she were the sun and that amusement, that happiness that she still somehow had inside, despite everything she'd been through, were rays heating his cold heart.

In that moment, that beat, his breath caught. His world changed. And he realised, quite simply, that he was in love with her.

Rubbish, the logical part of his brain told him. He'd known her for three days. There was no way he could love her. There was no way he'd fallen for her.

A sound escaped her lips. Laughter. The joy of it went right to his soul, defying logic. And then they were laughing together. Laughing and laughing at his expense, at his trauma. It didn't matter since the bubble they'd been in on Santorini had somehow come back. Bigger, more impenetrable than before.

In his mind, he knew that wasn't true. Bubbles, by

nature, were meant to burst. They were easily shattered. There was no such thing as an impenetrable bubble. In his heart, he didn't care about any of it. His chest felt oddly full, oddly light at the same time. And he memorised this moment. Knew that he would need the memory of it when the spell he was under faded or the bubble floated away. Because, deep down, he knew it wouldn't burst.

That was what worried him.

Something had changed. She felt it before they started laughing, but the laughter had been rolling around in her chest, her stomach, for too long and demanded attention. But she felt it. Saw it. Knew that her life would never be the same because of it.

When Liam and Emma staggered through the door of their room, faces flushed—from pleasure *and* confusion, she imagined—it finally caught up with her. Rolled around in her like the laughter had been. Except this didn't have the comforting strokes of the laughter. It was tight and fluttery, like a butterfly stuck in a confined space trying to get out.

'What…um…?' Emma said, putting her hands behind her back when she saw the two of them there. 'What are you doing here? And why is the door broken?' She blinked as she took in the scene. 'Why is the door broken?' she asked again, her voice more concerned. 'Caleb?'

Caleb didn't look at her. He was still looking at Piper. And she was still looking at him. It took all of her strength to look away. She stepped back, as if that small distance would protect her.

'Caleb!'

He finally turned and looked at Emma. 'What?'

Emma frowned, suspicion clear in the creases between her eyes. 'I asked why the door's broken.'

'I was worried about you.'

'You were—' Her eyes widened, suspicion forgotten. 'Did you come inside?'

'No,' Caleb said immediately. Despite the tight feeling in her stomach, Piper's lips twitched.

'But—'

'He didn't see anything, Emma,' Piper offered, schooling her smile. 'Besides, I'm sure there was nothing to see.'

'No,' Liam agreed, though the flush on his face had long since morphed from what he and Emma had been doing into embarrassment. 'We were...talking.'

Piper raised a brow at her brother. His colour deepened.

'Well,' she said, amused. 'If you're done *talking*, your guests are all convinced the wedding is off.' She turned to Caleb now. 'That's why Jada sent me. She's trying to keep up the façade.' The amusement turned to a full-blown smile. 'She's taken to dancing, too.'

'*Jada?*' Caleb asked, his head dropping. 'My *sister* Jada?'

Piper only looked at him. Looked away when that felt too intimate. *Damn it.* What was it that had changed?

'Yes. Now,' she directed to Emma and Liam, 'you two better pitch up before Tate and Jada scare off all the guests.'

Emma and Liam exchanged a look, then rushed back into the room. Awkwardly, Piper and Caleb stood guard at the door, not speaking. The tension built with each passing second. By the time Liam and Emma emerged, looking fresh in matching outfits, Piper was trying hard not to shift her weight. She'd only managed due to her pride. Thank goodness Caleb caused that emotion to flare inside her.

She wasn't as happy about the rest of what Caleb caused to flare inside her.

Inadvertently, she lifted her hands to her l
bering the kiss from that morning. S

when she saw him watching her. When there was a glint in his eyes that told her he knew exactly what she'd been remembering.

Damn it.

Emma chattered happily the entire way to the beach, as if her fiancé hadn't left her three days earlier. Liam looked at her adoringly, and Piper could only sigh at the easiness of it. What she wouldn't give to be able to brush off and forgive as easily as Emma seemed to have. Yes, she'd made progress with Liam, but she wouldn't trust him until he proved he'd meant what he'd told her.

Yet you trust Caleb.

The feeling in her stomach tightened even more. She rubbed a hand there, hoping to ease the ache. She'd meant to comfort Caleb when she'd told him she trusted him. His mind had been burning out, she could see, and she'd wanted him to think of something else. But when she'd said the words—words she'd told herself she'd have to guard against after Brad—she'd found them to be true. Which meant she'd fallen for Caleb.

Her feet stumbled. A strong arm caught her before she could fall. She looked at Caleb in surprise. He hadn't always been walking next to her. Had she really been so caught up in her thoughts of him that she hadn't noticed him there? And why did it feel significant that he'd caught her before she could fall?

Piper.

She straightened, thanking him quietly before walking again, catching up with Liam and Emma, who'd been walking in front and hadn't noticed anything. Nothing could come of thoughts like that. Of the hope that joined them. There was only that fear. That dread. That certainty that this wouldn't end well for her. It never did.

When she'd fallen for Brad, she'd lost something of

herself. Trust, primarily, in her judgement. What if Caleb wasn't as good a guy as she thought? No, she couldn't let it happen again. She had too little left to lose. One more bad decision might be the end of her, *especially* with him. If she let herself be with Caleb and things went wrong, she might have nothing left.

'Liam.'

Emma's breathy tone was the only reason Piper knew something had happened. She stopped, only then noticing the white stones on the beach. They were shaped in a heart, with Emma and Liam's initials in them. Around the stones were candles, flickering like the promises Liam now seemed to be whispering in Emma's ear.

She walked away when she realised this was a private moment. Went to join the small crowd who hadn't yet departed. It was as much of a mystery that they were still there as the fact that Liam had managed to arrange a grand gesture. She supposed they were linked somehow, and nodded at Tate and Jada when they both gave her a thumbs-up. She and Liam were apparently forgiven for the turmoil of the last three days then.

She shrugged it off, turned and watched the romantic moment with the rest of the crowd. Caleb joined her and she tried not to stiffen.

'I guess this means they're getting married.'

'Guess so,' she murmured.

'Piper—'

'Oh, look,' she said, partly because she didn't want to hear what he said, and partly because she'd been distracted by her brother and Emma.

Liam had picked Emma up and was swinging her around. The sun had started going down behind them, casting a glowing yellow light over the couple. Emma laughed, wild and happy, something Piper didn't think she'd see from the bride after her groom had run away. Liam looked up at his fiancée tenderly.

Piper wished she had her phone with her so she could capture it. So some day she could show it to Liam and Emma's baby and tell the child that this was the moment she'd known their parents would have a happy marriage.

A lump grew in her throat. She sucked her lip in, bit down on it when the lump kept growing. Her eyes were burning, too. Any moment now she would start crying. Piper didn't know how or why watching her brother be happy made her emotional. The threads of it were weaving together in her mind, showing her a picture that made her hate herself.

She turned, hurried back to the villa. They didn't need her on the cruise any more. Emma and Liam were both there, happy, clearly in love and preparing to marry. There was no more need for pretence.

She wouldn't have been able to manage it anyway. She'd barely been able to hide her emotions, for crying out loud. A slight breeze blew over her; her cheeks felt extra cool, telling her the tears she'd been fighting were falling. She started to run, ignoring the sand pouring into her shoes and the rocks digging into her feet. When she got to her room she shut the door, locked it. She made it to her bedroom before the tears turned into sobs.

She knew why she was upset. Because she would never have what Liam and Emma had. Certainly not with the man she wanted to have it with.

CHAPTER SIXTEEN

HIS TOLERANCE FOR pointless conversations had thoroughly been tested this evening. Usually, he was quite good at it. The countless hours he'd spent networking after he'd taken over his father's business had taught him how. He knew when to pretend to be interested when he wasn't. He knew how to hide his annoyance at close-mindedness, or his irritation at having to be there at all. They were skills he was proud of. Tonight, he didn't use one of them.

He was beginning to think love wasn't all it was cracked up to be.

That was the only reason he could think had motivated his behaviour. He'd realised he was in love with Piper, and everything he'd known before that had gone to hell. Then, of course, there was how Piper had acted around him. Tense and skittish. As if she were afraid of him. When she'd run from the beach earlier, he'd wanted to go after her. To demand she tell him why she was acting that way. Or to tell him what was wrong. But Tate had cornered him before he could. His brother had wanted him to talk to the captain of the boat cruise, who wasn't as impressed by all the delays as the guests had been.

He'd been torn. For a full minute he'd stared after Piper, ignoring his brother's nudges. When he'd met Tate's eyes and seen his brother's desperation, he'd recognised it as an opportunity to test Tate's independence. So he'd sacrificed his immediate desire to determine whether he'd be able to prioritise himself in the future.

After some grumbling, his brother had succeeded in calming the captain down. It had been as much of a lesson for Caleb as for Tate. With two of his siblings proving more than capable, and a third getting married, Caleb wondered whether he simply wasn't giving his siblings enough credit. Perhaps they weren't giving themselves enough credit either because of it.

'Caleb!'

He turned, saw Emma coming his way. She seemed deliriously happy. If he didn't know that she hadn't been drinking, he might have thought that happiness artificial. But no. That spark on her face, the bright light in her eyes? Natural. From love. His brow furrowed at the difference between her experience of the emotion and his.

Then again, she had just had three days of awfulness because of it…

'What?' she asked when she reached him.

'*You* called me.'

'But you're frowning.'

He relaxed the muscles between his eyebrows. 'Better?'

'Much,' she said with a grin, before tilting her head. 'You're okay, right?'

'Fine.'

'Fine enough to make sure my door's fixed?' Her cheeks flushed, a reminder of what had happened that afternoon that neither of them wanted to speak about.

'Yeah, sure,' he said quickly. 'I think we might have to move you for the night.'

'I can stay in Liam's room.'

'You're getting married tomorrow, Em,' he protested. 'You can't spend tonight with your fiancé.'

'Yeah, well, I'm already pregnant,' she said, putting a fist on her hip. 'It's not like we're waiting or anything. And the worst thing's already happened to me.' Her face tightened. 'I thought I lost him. So there's no chance of more bad luck.'

He didn't think that logic was sound, but it had been a

long day. At random moments, his mind had offered him an image of Piper laughing, or teasing him, or looking up at him as if she felt something for him. Sometimes, he swore he could even taste her. Smell her perfume.

No, he wouldn't burst his sister's bubble. Especially since wanting her to be independent meant he needed to stop trying to control her actions. He wondered what Piper would say about that realisation.

'Fine.'

'You're the best, Caleb!' she said, smacking a kiss on his cheek. 'Take Liam with you and the two of you can move my bags.'

'I can do that by my—'

It was too late. Emma had already flounced off, the tail of her dress blowing in the wind as she made her way to Liam. Seconds later Liam was walking towards Caleb. He didn't pretend to be excited about it.

'You don't have to help me,' Caleb said, walking from the beach where they'd been since the end of the cruise. 'I can move a couple of bags by myself.'

'I've got the keys to my room,' Liam said, dangling them from his fingers. 'Besides, I think she wants us to talk.'

'What is there to talk about?' Caleb said dryly.

The next kilometre went by in silence.

'Look, I'm sorry about what happened these last three days,' Liam said eventually.

Caleb grunted.

'I know it makes me seem like a jerk. You're probably worried about what Emma's got herself into. But I promise you, I'm a good guy. I'll be good to her, too. I just needed a moment.'

'Are you going to need a moment when your kid does something wrong? Or when Emma annoys you into being a better man?' He shoved his hands into his pockets. Rather that than what he wanted to do with his fists. 'What about when something serious happens? She gets sick or you do or your kid. Are you going to need a moment then, too, Liam? Or are you going to be a good guy?'

'The…the last one.'

They'd reached the villa, which was a surprise to Caleb since he was sure they'd started walking seconds ago. Maybe the anger had fuelled him more than he'd realised.

'Really?'

'Yeah, really.' Liam ran a hand over his face, turned towards Caleb. 'I get why you're asking me this. But—'

'Do you, Liam?' Caleb asked, taking a step closer. He was taller than Liam; he was also the brother of the woman Liam loved. Not quite equal ground, but it worked for intimidation. 'Do you know what it's like to step up for the people you care about?'

'I'm here, aren't I?'

'You say that as if it's enough,' Caleb spat. 'Emma's memory of telling you she's pregnant will always be tainted by you running—literally. As will the memories of her wedding. Not to mention the fact that you don't know what being there for someone means.'

'We're working it out.'

'You better,' he growled. 'Because if I find out you treated my sister the way you treated yours—'

'Caleb.'

The quiet voice stopped him. Only then did he realise he was so close to Liam he could poke the man in the chest. That if he tried hard enough, that poke could force Liam into the pool behind them. The temptation was there, but the voice pulled him. As did the disappointment and warning in it.

He took a step back, turning to find Piper. His heart lifted, soared at the sight of her. She wore a sleep shirt. It was nothing like the one she'd worn in Santorini. That one had been cotton with a high neckline and sleeves that covered her shoulders and some of her arms. This one was silk, with thin straps, dipping between the valley of her breasts. She pulled on the jersey he only now noticed around her, over the magnificence of her. For the first time he saw the swelling around her eyes, the slight pink of it.

'Piper,' he said, taking a step forward. 'What's wrong?'

'For one, you threatening my brother.'

He stilled. He'd already forgotten about Liam, if he was being honest. He clenched his hands tighter in his pockets. It upset him that she was defending a man who couldn't bother to do the same for her.

'Can you give us a minute, Liam?' Piper asked, folding her arms now.

'Are you sure?'

Caleb turned, unamused that Liam was feeling protective *now,* when he didn't need to be. Liam didn't look at him, kept his eyes on his sister. Something about the steadiness of his gaze made Caleb respect him more. If he'd been in the mood, he might have even admitted it.

'Yes.'

Caleb turned back at Piper's answer, waited until they were alone before he spoke again.

'Are you okay?'

'Why would you think that was a good idea?' she asked instead of answering him.

'What?'

'All of it. Getting involved with Emma and Liam's business.'

He gave her a look. 'We've been very involved with Emma and Liam's business for the last few days. Why stop now?'

Her eyes cooled. 'Because they don't need our help any more.'

'You don't think they're going to need help again?'

'Sure. That's what family members do, isn't it? Help one another.' She shook her head. 'I don't get you, Caleb. You've spent all your adult life helping them and *now* you have a problem with it?'

'Maybe I'm tired of helping them,' he snapped. 'Maybe if I get involved now, I won't have to get involved in the future. Maybe I can finally live my own life.'

She studied him. 'You're trying to control the situation now so you won't have to in the future?'

'I can hear the judgement in your voice.'

'I'm not judging you. Or maybe I am.' Her arms went around her waist now. 'Look, I get the control thing was a coping mechanism after your dad died. But why do you still need it? And why do you need permission to live your own life?'

He couldn't answer her. Didn't know how to say the words.

'You're afraid of something,' she said into the silence.

'You're one to speak of fear,' he retorted when his heart thudded hard against his chest at how she'd seen through him. 'We both know you're terrified of what's happening between us.'

Her expression opened. It just opened, and he could see every emotion on her face. It hit him in the chest. Guilt burned with shame in his stomach, ravaging everything around it.

'You're right,' she said. 'I am afraid.' She shrugged. 'But at least I know what I'm afraid of.'

'And what's that?'

'This.' Though everything about her—her stance, her expression—screamed vulnerability, her eyes remained steady on his. 'I'm scared you're going to try and control me. I'm scared... I'm scared I'll let you.'

* * *

She'd known the moment would come for her to say it. She hadn't expected it to come so soon. Certainly not the night before Liam's wedding, and certainly not that Liam would be the reason for it. But when she'd heard Caleb's threats she couldn't watch any more. Couldn't let him use her as an excuse for what she now saw was ignoring his fears.

Her tears, her emotions in turmoil earlier that evening—minutes ago, really, until she'd heard voices outside and come out to investigate—had prepared her for this moment. They'd prepared her to say this.

It hadn't prepared her for his reaction.

'You think you'll let me control you?' he asked, his expression one of disbelief. 'You really believe that?'

'I have already.'

'When?'

She opened her mouth, ready to list off all the instances. She couldn't remember one. Not because they didn't exist—she knew they did—but because his disbelief was rattling around her head, bouncing off the examples and causing them to ricochet away.

'I'll wait,' he said, jaw clenched.

'You know you've done it.'

'Yes,' he agreed. 'You've also put me in my place every time I have. Hell, you've made me adjust my behaviour.' His brow knitted. 'I think about how to phrase things around you. I don't want you to think I expect you to do anything, so I ask instead of tell. I suggest instead of state. And not only around you.'

'Brad suggested, too,' she said. She couldn't think what else to say.

'Brad?' he repeated. 'Your ex?'

She nodded.

'You're comparing me to the man who told you how to wear your hair?' he asked. 'The man who probably told you what to say and when to say it, too.'

She didn't bother confirming. They both knew it was true.

'You know why I try to control things, Piper. And as soon as you told me how it made you feel, I stopped doing it. I made an effort not to do it. If it came out, it's because it's been a habit of mine for longer than the three days I've known you. It's how I deal with stressful situations, which the last three days have been.'

He rested one hand on his hip, the other on his head. Then he shook his shoulders and shoved both his hands in his pockets again. It seemed to be his stance whenever he didn't know what to do with his hands. That usually happened when he was frustrated. She knew this because it had happened a lot in the last ten minutes.

'You can't really think I'm like him,' he said softly. It broke her heart. Forced her to face the truth.

'No, you're not.'

He nodded. 'Okay.' Nodded again. 'Okay, we can work with that.'

'Can we?' she asked, her voice broken now, too. 'Because it's not really about you. It's about me. And whether I can do this.'

'You know,' he said after a while, 'it took me a long time to face that I wanted a life of my own. I couldn't even say that out loud. Until you.' His face was the picture of sincerity. 'You made me realise that Emma and Jada and Tate are grown-ups. They can do things on their own. But I've enabled them. Shielded them. Now they expect me to be there every time something goes wrong, and I feel like I'm constantly on call.'

'They'd hate knowing that.'

'Yeah.' He looked down, then at her again. 'You helped

me to figure all this out, Piper. Why won't you let me help you do the same?'

Her legs suddenly felt unsteady under her, and she went to sit on the bench under the veranda. It was more romantic than it should have been considering the serious discussion they were having. Pink flowers crawled over the wooden planks above them, moonlight shone between the gaps, reflecting in the pool in front of them, too.

She didn't speak until Caleb joined her.

'You like me, don't you?'

His eyes flickered. 'Yes.'

'So you're probably giving me more credit than I deserve.'

'I'm not. In fact, most of the time I tend to give people in my life too little credit.'

He didn't continue for a long while, which made her realise something.

'Including yourself?' she asked.

'What? No.'

'Do you believe that the reason Jada and Tate and Emma are capable is because of you?' she asked. He didn't reply. 'You were an amazing example to them. And you were there when they needed you. You've proven yourself. Give yourself credit for that.'

'But what if I haven't proven myself?' He said it so softly she almost didn't hear him.

'What do you mean?' she exclaimed. 'You've spent all your adult years giving them a life most people only dream of.'

'I'm not talking about them,' he said. 'I'm talking about my father.'

CHAPTER SEVENTEEN

PIPER'S HAND CURLED over his as soon as he said the words. He wasn't sure how he felt about it. Was it comfort or pity? Then he saw the expression on her face, the compassion, and realised it was both. When it came from her though, it didn't feel like a bad thing. It wasn't condescending. It was…caring.

'Why?'

'Remember when you said you sometimes wonder what your mom would have thought about your life?'

'I do,' she replied. 'Not so much about my life, but about what my father did to us, and how things might have been different if she'd been alive.' She shifted towards him. 'Did you mean like that?'

He looked down at their linked hands. Delicate, he thought. Her fingers were long and thin and delicate. He couldn't imagine why that was important now, but it felt as if it was.

'You know I was trying to be like my father since he died. Part of that was because I feel guilty that I had him and they didn't. Another part is that…' He took his time. 'I was a brat when I was a kid. A real brat, Piper,' he said. 'I didn't listen to my father, didn't help at home. Made him worry about me just about every chance I got.'

'So you were being a normal kid.'

'Normal kids don't *try* to upset their fathers. They do what they do because they're stupid and don't know any better. I wasn't like that. It was…deliberate. I was trying to be a brat.'

'You must have had a reason.'

'I didn't,' he said, hating the warmth her understanding spread inside him. 'Maybe I was acting out because he was there and my mother wasn't. Maybe I was trying to figure out what would get him to leave, too.'

'Like your mom.'

'Yeah.'

'So you had reasons.'

'Not good ones,' he said. 'He didn't deserve it. He was a—' He broke off, sucked in a breath. 'He was a good man. A good father. He did his best, and that was more than…'

He pulled his hand from hers, linking it with his own. He didn't deserve to have her care.

'Now you're trying to prove to him that you're a good man, too.'

'Yeah.' He squeezed his fingers so tight his knuckles turned white. 'Or I'm saying sorry,' he mumbled, 'for being such a brat.'

'He wouldn't have needed you to say you were sorry. He probably knew that you were going through stuff.'

'Doesn't make it any better. Actions are what matter. Mine weren't great.'

She was silent for a moment. 'You don't think he'd be proud of what you've done now? You've sacrificed your life to take care of your family. You took over the family business. You've done more than enough. You don't have to feel guilty for stepping back now and living the rest of your life.'

'No, I do.'

'Why are you making this so hard on yourself, Caleb?'

Anger stirred, hot and irrational.

'Why are you trying to make it so easy? It's not,' he told her before she could answer.

'You're still scared.'

'I'm not scared.'

'Why?' she asked, ignoring his answer. 'You don't have to be. Everything is going to be okay.'

'I'm *not* scared.'

'You don't have to tell me, Caleb, but you have to work it out for yourself.'

That was the problem; he already had. But it was still messing around with his mind. He needed time to sort through it.

'Is that what you're doing?' He stood now, began to pace. 'Figuring things out and using it as an excuse not to date me?'

'No,' she said, watching him from her spot on the bench. 'I've already figured them out. I can't date you because I'll lose myself with you.'

He stopped walking. 'Did you lose some of yourself these days we spent together?' She opened her mouth but nothing came out. He nodded. 'So you know this is all an excuse, then.'

'Both parties need to be in the right space for a relationship to work, Caleb. Neither of us are.'

'Don't use me as an excuse to not take a chance on us,' he said quietly. 'If you don't want to, that's fine. But it isn't because of me.'

'You're making this more difficult than it needs to be.'

Too late for that.

He didn't say it. If he had, she would know that he was already in love with her. It was as difficult as it could get.

Piper didn't get any sleep. She thanked the heavens for the gift of make-up and the fact that she wasn't a bridesmaid. Hopefully no one would notice the bags under her eyes. And no one would ask her questions that would remind her that she'd sat up all night, looking out of the window, Caleb's words floating around in her head.

She wore a simple red dress to the wedding. It wasn't flashy, and it would likely clash with the shades of blue of the wedding theme, but it was the first item of clothing she'd bought after she'd broken up with Brad. An act of defiance. She'd walked into the first shop she'd seen, gone right for the colour Brad had hated on her and bought the thing she'd liked the most. It brought her a lot of joy. Today, it gave her a confidence she didn't feel. She left her hair curly, for good measure. Though, honestly, she was still trying to figure out whether she liked it.

Too late to worry about that now, she told herself, checking the time as she finished her make-up. She looked...decent. Like someone who was going to a wedding, which was probably a good thing since she was. But there was something different about the person she saw in the mirror. It wasn't the bags under her eyes or the red dress or her hair. It was the fire she saw beneath it all. The...the *strength*.

She blinked, took a step back from her reflection. She had no idea how she thought that might help. Was she trying to distance herself from her thoughts? Of course not. They were in her head. She couldn't run from them. Surprise was obviously an intoxicating emotion. An illogical one. She'd been surprised by the version of herself she'd seen in the mirror, that was all.

But once it simmered down, once it faded, Piper wondered if that strength was a matter of will. Had she hoped she'd see it there and so saw it? Or was it that Caleb's words—his question of whether she'd allow him to control her—were still floating around in her head, tempting her with the picture they'd created of her?

A strong woman. Someone who could take care of herself. Who could move on with life without wondering when the next person would destroy it. She had that power, didn't she? She could take control of her own life and refuse to allow anyone else to make her feel as if she didn't deserve autonomy. Unless she couldn't.

And believing she could when she couldn't would destroy her even more than *knowing* she couldn't.

She took a shaky breath, grabbed her things and closed the door behind her, refusing to look in the mirror while she finished up. A sigh of relief gushed through her lips as she leaned against the door. She closed her eyes, told herself things would go back to normal soon. None of this would matter when she was back in Cape Town, teaching her kids and living her life.

Alone.

It had always been alone, she told that irritating inner voice. When she'd lived with her father, she and her brother had fought for their lives separately. Then Liam had left and she'd kept fighting. After her father had died she'd had to fight in her relationship with Brad. Alone still. She'd lost more than she'd won, but the most important thing was that she'd walked away. She'd been able to walk away. Alone.

So, stupid inner voice, shut up.

When she opened her eyes she found herself staring directly into Caleb's. Her breath tripped over itself as her heart tried to claw its way to him.

'Hi,' he said after a moment.

His hands were in his pockets again. Since his expression was closed, that was the only thing familiar to her. That stance that told her he wasn't as comfortable as his presence there made it seem. She clung to it. Desperately.

'Hello,' she said carefully. 'What are you doing here?'

'Emma asked me to escort you to the beach.'

She quirked her brow. 'Really? That's the excuse you're going with?'

'Not an excuse,' he said, the side of his mouth lifting. 'She didn't want you to be alone.'

Piper tried not to think about how she'd just had a conversation with herself about being alone. About how she was fine with it. Except with Caleb there she didn't feel alone. For once in her life she felt cared about. The fact that Emma had sent him, had thought to send him, had her insides untying from the knot they were in. And the fact that he was looking at her the way he had the first time he'd seen her with her hair curly made her realise exactly why she was wearing it that way.

How was it possible that he could make her feel so incredibly beautiful with the very thing the men before him had used against her?

Because he's different.

It sent her heart into a panic. Or was that thudding in her chest a result of being in Caleb's presence? He looked good. He was wearing tan pants and a white shirt with a blue blazer. It wasn't quite what she'd been expecting, but she couldn't fault it.

'Did Emma pick out this outfit for you?' she asked.

'Yes.' He sighed. 'I'm sorry you have to see me like this.'

It made her laugh. 'Don't be.' The laughter died when she hesitated. Then decided to go for it. 'I think you look good. Handsome.'

He smiled, though it didn't quite reach his eyes. 'Thanks.'

She took a breath—a reprieve from the awkwardness. 'Let's get going.'

She was so beautiful it made him ache. He couldn't stop looking at her. As they walked down to the beach, he kept sneaking glances her way. That red dress wasn't sin on her. It was too respectable, too simple for that. But it made him *want* to sin. It made him hope. For things she'd made clear she didn't want. Things he had, at some point during his sleepless night, told himself it was better not to have.

When the sun had sneaked into the sky, turning the hazy blue into a canvas of light, he'd convinced himself he didn't want them either. Then he'd seen her standing against her door, her eyes closed. Her skin was striking against the boldness of that red dress, her red lips. And the curls she'd left wild around her face, curls she'd been so hesitant about the day before—only then?—set off a longing so deep his heart composed a song for her. Then beat to the insistent rhythm of it.

'Oh.'

The word drew him from his gloomy thoughts. When he saw where they were, he smiled. Turned to her.

'Shall I?'

'Oh,' she said again, looking at the decline in the path. 'No. I can do this by myself. I did it yesterday.'

'You weren't wearing heels yesterday.'

She bit her lip, breaking the red of her lips with the white of her teeth. He desperately wanted to lean forward, to nip them. He took a deep breath instead.

'It's not a problem if you want to do this by yourself,' he said. 'I don't mind offering a hand instead of my arms?'

Her eyes met his, something deep and meaningful crossing them before she said, 'You can carry me. If you want to.'

He didn't answer that. It was a trap. If he said yes, he wanted to, she might hold it against him. Or realise how desperately he wanted to help her. Hold her in his arms.

'May I?' he asked before picking her up at her nod.

He walked down carefully, things somehow tenser be-tween them than the first time they'd done this. When they were on level ground again, he looked at her. Warm brown eyes blinked back at him. Red lips pursed as a blush spread over her cheeks.

'What?' she asked.

'One dance,' he said. This couldn't be the last time he had her in his arms. He wanted one more time. One he could prepare for and know it was goodbye. 'Give me a dance later and I'll do everything in my power to pretend that nothing happened between us for the rest of Liam and Emma's lives together.'

Her hands tightened around his neck before she relaxed.

'One dance at the end of the night,' she agreed. 'Now, put me down. We have a wedding to attend.'

CHAPTER EIGHTEEN

THE TEARS BEGAN when he saw Emma in her wedding dress.

They'd set up a small area on the beach for her to get ready while the guests got settled a few metres away. He'd thought it all impractical when he'd first arranged it, but seeing her in the small space obscured from the guests with the ocean behind her... Well, the photographer had it right when she said the scene was breathtaking.

'Don't cry,' Emma said when he wiped at the tear that had slid down his cheek.

'I'm not,' he said with a smile. 'It's allergies. Damn sand.'

'You're allergic to sand?' Emma laughed. 'I wish I'd known that before I planned a beach wedding.'

'Like that would have stopped you,' he replied, moving forward to kiss her forehead. He ignored the photographer capturing what he would have liked to be a private moment. He'd already accepted this day would force him to share more with people than he'd like. 'You look beautiful, Em. Liam is a lucky man.'

She smiled at him, bright and cheery like his Em had always been. 'Thanks.' The smile turned into something else. 'But I'm the lucky one, Caleb. I had Dad for eleven years of my life and you for the next thirteen. Good, strong men who loved me more than anything. You helped me to realise what I deserve.' She laughed at Caleb's expression. 'Liam's a good man. He needs to grow up, but he's willing to, you know? He accepts that he needs to change.' She shrugged. 'Besides, I love him. What can I do?'

Pretend love doesn't exist, like I am?

'Anyway, my point is that I was lucky to have you as my big brother.' She cupped his cheek. 'Now I get to move on with my future and forge ahead with life.' She stepped back.

'About that…' He took a deep breath. Prepared to say what he'd told himself he would the night before. 'You probably won't need me as much when you're married.'

Emma frowned. 'What do you mean? Of course I'll need you. You're my brother.'

'And I'll be here for you. As much as I can be.' He cleared his throat. 'But you have Liam now.'

'Yes, I suppose—'

'I think he means Liam should be your first stop, not him,' Jada said from behind him. He had no idea when she'd got there since she'd been outside, checking for the signal from Tate that all the guests had arrived. 'He'll probably be telling me and Tate we need to figure some things out for ourselves next.'

Caleb turned. 'I'm not…' He paused. 'You know how you dealt with all of this stuff while I was away? How you and Tate both did?'

'I know,' she said. 'We can handle things without you. I get it. Got it when you came back from Santorini.'

He nodded. She'd always been the most astute of his siblings. 'I'll still be there for you.'

'I know.' Her lips curved into a sad smile. 'But you deserve some space, too. You've done a lot for us and we… took advantage of it. At least I did.'

'Oh, no,' Emma said softly. 'I think I did, too.'

'Not a great feeling, is it?' Jada asked her.

'I'm not accusing you of anything,' he interrupted. 'I do need some space, but from doing things for you, not from you.' He looked from Emma to Jada. 'You understand that?'

'Of course.' Jada waited a beat. 'I won't even tell Emma what brought on this sudden change of heart.' Her eyes gleamed.

'There's nothing to tell.'

'Really?'

'What are you guys talking about?' Emma asked with a frown.

'Nothing,' Jada said brightly. 'Come on. They were ready ten minutes ago.'

'Ten minutes? Why didn't you tell me? Really, Jada, this is my wedding day and…'

Jada winked at him as Emma ranted, and he realised his youngest sister had distracted Emma on purpose. She mouthed, *I love you.* He smiled, felt warm inside, and wondered how the conversation he'd dreaded had gone more smoothly than he could have hoped.

'Caleb!'

He blinked. 'What?'

'I'm supposed to be getting married.' Emma reached over, grabbed his hand. 'You'll have time to brood later. Right now, you have to walk me down the aisle, big brother.'

If Piper had to describe the event, she would have said it was happy. Emma and Liam laughed their way through the ceremony and their joy spread out to their guests, who realised that the couple shared something special and were grateful to be a part of the moment.

Of course, Piper was, too. Except Emma and Liam's happiness had the opposite effect on her. She brooded on her unhappiness, the fact that she would never be able to celebrate anything like this for herself. It felt cruel. It also felt unnecessary. Was denying herself a relationship, love really the only way she could protect herself?

Or was it only baggage from the past? Heavy and slowing her down, keeping her in that place where her actions were still dictated by the men she'd vowed never to allow power over her again?

She didn't have answers. Until she did, she was doing no one any good by staying at the wedding. She'd done her part. She'd been there, watched her brother say his vows. She'd had a meal and heard the speeches. But it was over now. The night was ending, people were dancing, and Emma and Liam had already left. There was no more obligation. She could leave.

There's one more obligation.

She ignored the voice, pulling off her shoes and walking the path to the villa barefoot. She called the airport, found out there was a plane leaving in three hours. She threw her clothes into her bag, called a car and, without another look, left her room.

'Piper.'

She swore when she saw Caleb there.

'You have to stop doing this,' she told him, dragging her bag behind her and moving past him.

'Where are you going?'

'Home.'

'Home?' he asked, tone incredulous. 'Your flight isn't tonight.'

'Oh, I used all my savings to get myself on a flight tonight.'

'Why?'

'Because I don't want to be here any more,' she said. 'I don't want to be around your family and my brother and I definitely don't want to be around you.'

Her bag snagged on a step and she snarled at it when it refused to move, no matter how hard she pulled. Caleb got down, looked at her for permission. She gave it with a curt nod. He gently extricated the wheel from where it had been stuck and the bag came loose easily. It only made her more upset.

'It was nice knowing you, Caleb,' she said, walking to the front of the villa. Damn it, the taxi wasn't there yet. She'd called fifteen minutes ago.

They didn't speak as time passed. She exhaled after five minutes. Gritted her teeth after ten. What was it with her and having to wait for transport?

She aimed a suspicious look at Caleb. 'You aren't my ride to the airport, are you?'

He blinked, then understanding cleared his expression and he laughed. 'No, unfortunately not.'

'Unfortunately?'

His expression turned serious. 'I wouldn't have taken you. Not because I'm trying to control you or anything.' He faced her. 'Because I don't want you to go.'

This was it, he thought, heart hammering. He was making a grand gesture. That was what the movies called it, right? The moment the protagonist proclaimed their love? When his stomach leapt he wondered if it was necessary to do this. Maybe he could simply tell her he wanted her to stay. One look at her expression axed that idea.

'What was the point of that?' she demanded.

'I, er, I want you to stay?'

'Yes, but why would you say that? Obviously I don't want to stay if I'm leaving.'

'Yeah, I get that.' Why was this so hard? 'But I'd like you to stay.' He shoved his hands into his pockets. 'I want my dance.'

She studied him. Ruthlessly, he thought, making him shift his weight from one leg to the other.

'There's a reason I wanted to leave before that dance.'

'What is it?'

'I don't want to be reminded of what we could have.'

He stared. Pulled himself together. 'Why can't we have it?'

'I already told you why.'

'Piper,' he started after a breath, 'I've been…extracting myself from my siblings' lives tonight.'

'What does that mean?'

'I had conversations with all of them about boundaries.' To his surprise—although he wasn't sure why he was still surprised by his siblings—his conversation with Tate had gone as well as the one he'd had with Emma and Jada. 'It proved something I realised recently… I've been living my life for my siblings because it makes me feel closer to my dad. If they're proud of me, maybe he'd be, too.'

Her expression softened. 'Of course he'd be proud of you. I'm sure he is now, wherever he is.'

'Thanks.' He ran a hand over his hair. 'Along with everything else, I've been trying to make up for who I was when he was alive with who I am now. That's why I took charge.'

'I know,' she said with a sigh. 'And there's nothing wrong with that, Caleb. You've done so much for your family and you're a great brother. The best man I know.' She said it with a wry smile.

'Okay,' he said, hope blooming. 'Let's figure this out.'

'No.'

'Piper,' he said flatly, 'I asked my family for space partly so you and I can explore whatever this is.'

'I didn't ask you to do that.' Her expression tightened. 'I told you—it's not about you, Caleb.'

'So there's nothing I can do to change your mind?'

She shook her head, her expression one of torture. 'I'm sorry.'

He told himself to leave it. To set it aside and move on. She'd helped him to the next part of his life. He should thank her for that and go live that next part.

He couldn't.

'You're scared. You're running.'

'I am,' she told him helplessly. 'You know I'm terrified of what I feel for you. It's big and demanding and I'm scared I'll give in to the big demands.'

His heart broke. 'I wish you'd realise how strong you are. How you'd never let that happen.'

'But I have let it happen.'

'In the past. You got through it, and you're even stronger for it.'

The car came then, slowly descending the winding road. Time followed suit, slowing down so much that Caleb held his breath, wondering what her reply would be.

She said nothing.

The car stopped. She handed the driver her bag. When her eyes met his there was an apology there. 'I'll send Liam a message when I'm safe at home.'

And then she was gone.

CHAPTER NINETEEN

IT TOOK HER a month to come to a conclusion.

Some of that could be attributed to her brother and new sister-in-law. They'd knocked on her door ten days after their wedding, honeymoon completed. They did not wear the same happiness as the last time she'd seen them. This time they wore accusation.

'You rejected my brother?'

It was the first thing out of Emma's mouth. With a sigh, Piper stepped back and prepared herself for a conversation that had nothing to do with Liam or his wife. Thankfully, it was short. She first listened to Emma's rant about how her brother had lived for them and the fact that he'd allowed himself to have feelings for Piper was huge. Emma then said that Caleb deserved happiness and maybe Piper wasn't the one to give it to him but she should have at least given it a try.

'Are you done?' Piper asked. Emma nodded. 'Good. One, my business with your brother is private.' She held up her hand at the protest she knew would come from Emma. 'Knowing him, he didn't ask you to come here.' She waited for the affirmation. It came in the form of a nod. 'So there's no reason to get involved. Two—' she pointed at her brother '—why would you think this is a good idea?'

He lifted his hands. 'I'm stuck between a rock and a hard place here.'

'But you're still here.'

He winced. 'To offer support?'

'To whom?' she asked dryly.

Wisely, he didn't answer.

'Look, Emma,' Piper said, voice soft. 'Your brother and I would never work.'

'You mean two people who like and respect one another, who are both level-headed and strong-minded, wouldn't work in a relationship?' Emma narrowed her eyes. 'What are your other excuses?'

None that she'd wanted to share with Emma, considering her mood. Her brother thanked her for that when they left, and Piper thanked him for their concern. It was something, she supposed. A small thing that on the surface felt intrusive, but deep down showed her how her life had changed. Especially since Emma had hugged her afterwards, whispering into her ear that she only wanted them to be happy.

Emma's words stayed with her, as did Caleb's parting words to her. And her life changing? It felt as if it came from the strength both those Martins claimed she had. She had left her father when she'd had enough, same with Brad. Maybe that woman she'd seen in the mirror before the wedding *did* exist. Maybe she needed to trust herself more. Give herself more credit. Not allow her past to affect her any more. She'd made one real mistake— Brad—since her father hadn't been her fault. And was one mistake worth sacrificing a lifetime of unhappiness?

Her answer to that was the reason she'd asked Emma and Liam to help her get into Caleb's house. Why she'd decorated his backyard with flowers and candles and fairy lights. Why she had music playing when he got home. She'd concluded that she deserved to try with Caleb. And that she missed him. And that she *might* be in love with him.

She was definitely attracted to him, she thought when he walked into the yard. He wore a black suit, perfectly tailored, with a green shirt. Her mouth almost watered. Then his eyes rested on her and his eyebrow quirked.

'What are you doing here?'

'I owe you a dance, don't I?'

The next moments were slower than any other in her life. He studied her, then walked towards her, taking her into his arms and gently swaying to the beat.

'It's also payback,' she forced herself to say, though she wanted to rest her head on his chest and stay there for ever, 'for all those times I walked out of my room in Greece to find you there.'

He laughed softly. 'You're lucky Em and Liam waited outside to warn me someone was here.'

'They told you I was inside?'

'Not in so many words.'

She searched his face. 'You don't look upset.'

'Am I supposed to be?'

'Yes. I would be if you'd left me in Greece and pitched up a month later.'

He angled his head. 'I guess I've learnt to accept that some things are outside of my control.'

'Wow,' she said with a small smile. 'Growth.'

'That wasn't a jab at you,' he said gently. Laughed when she raised her eyebrows. 'Okay, fine, maybe it was, a little. But things have changed since Greece. I've changed.'

'Not too much, I hope.' When his eyes softened, her insides did the same. 'How have the changes been going?'

'I'm not sure.' His brow knitted. 'I have a lot more free time since the kids stopped calling me to fix their problems.'

'You're okay with that?'

'They are, which makes it okay with me.'

'Of course they are.' She squeezed the hand at her waist. 'You made sure of that.'

'I know.' He smiled at her surprise. 'I'm trying.'

She took a breath. 'Me, too.'

'What does that mean?'

'For one, I'm keeping overdue promises,' she said. His lips twitched. 'For another... I don't know. I guess I'm letting myself be okay that I've made mistakes in my past.' She bit her lip. 'I let that control me, too. The fear of what happened repeating itself, I mean.'

'But not any more,' he said softly.

She smiled. 'Not any more.'

It was hard for him to imagine Piper was there for any reason besides reconciliation. He wasn't sure what they were reconciling, for one, since they'd never had a relationship. But pesky things like facts didn't matter to hope. The emotion bloomed so large, so bright inside him that the last month of misery was almost worth it.

He didn't rely on it though. Not until he was sure.

'That morning of the wedding,' she said, speaking marginally louder than the wind that rustled through the trees around them, 'I saw a different woman in the mirror. I think the scales were falling from my eyes. Or I was seeing myself like you did.' She paused. 'Either way, I didn't recognise who that was and it scared me. Until I realised it was a good thing. I didn't see the old Piper. Just this one. Someone who believes in herself. Who wants to, anyway, starting with trusting myself.'

'Piper, that's amazing,' he said, squeezing her hand though what he really wanted to do was kiss her lips. She'd painted them a glorious pink that popped against the white dress she wore. Man, he'd missed looking at her.

'Thank you.' She gave him a shy smile. 'You helped, you know.'

'No,' he denied. 'It was all you.'

'No,' she said with a shake of her head. 'You helped. You forced me to see myself in a different light. To see myself like you see me.' Her eyes sparkled up at him. 'I didn't want to believe it at first. How could I possibly be the strong woman you described? Then I realised I needed you to help me see it. Because you're the right man. And I appreciate you.' She blew out a breath. 'I'm hoping I'll get more opportunities to prove that to you…'

The hope within him turned to her, its sun, opening up like a sunflower. 'What do you mean?'

There was a beat of silence.

'You helped me,' she said slowly, 'because my feelings for you forced me to be honest with myself. To weigh up whether my fears or my love for you was more important.'

'You're…you're in love with me?'

Her face flushed. 'Maybe. Like seventy per cent? We still have a way to go, but I think it'll reach a hundred pretty soon.'

'This is the weirdest love proclamation I've ever heard.'

'Aren't you lucky?'

He laughed, leaned his head on her forehead. 'You're amazing, you know that?'

'I'm getting there.'

'I'm already there,' he informed her. 'You keep me on my toes, Piper.'

'Same here.'

'You're stronger than anyone I know,' he whispered.

'And you're the best man I know,' she whispered back. 'I trust you. With my heart.'

'It'll be my greatest responsibility to take care of it,' he replied, and kissed her.

HIS WEDDING BEGAN with a crying woman. Fortunately it wasn't his soon-to-be wife, who, his youngest sister told him, was as calm as a therapist.

It was Jada's comparison, not his. He figured it had something to do with the fact that she was currently doing her postgraduate degree in psychology. He wondered if it wasn't Jada, then, who should be left the task of dealing with Emma's tears.

'You're…getting…married and you've done…so much for…the family…and…and the business and Dad would be…so proud,' Emma said between sobs.

He patted her on the back, made eye contact with his brother-in-law. 'What did you do to her?' he asked.

Liam grimaced. 'I think it's the hormones.'

'You can't keep bringing that up,' he said. 'Lacey's two.'

'Not Lacey.' Liam grinned. 'Baby number two.'

Caleb's eyebrows rose, then he laughed and drew his sister into a hug. 'Champ, you're going to have another one?'

'I know,' she wailed. 'What if I'm not ready?'

He let Liam deal with that when he intervened, drawing Emma out of Caleb's room and letting him enjoy his breakfast in peace. Tate was there, but the youngest of his siblings knew the value of quiet. It was part of the reason he was the best man. When Liam returned—his only groomsman—he was sans Emma.

'Sorry,' he said. 'We only found out a couple of days ago. She's processing.'

'Near my fiancée?' Caleb asked, worrying about what that energy would do to Piper.

'Yeah, but Piper's beyond relaxed. She managed to

calm Emma down and she and Jada are talking about how fun it would be to have another baby in the family.' Liam gave Caleb a suspicious look. 'Something you want to tell me?'

Caleb snorted. 'No.'

Disappointment crushed the suspicion. 'Damn it. For a second there I thought I wouldn't be the only one going through this.'

'There's an easy way to keep from going through this,' Tate commented in his quiet way. Caleb laughed while Liam scowled. It was that kind of easiness that took him to the altar.

He had no nerves as he stood waiting for Piper. More… anticipation. Relief that they'd finally be married. They'd taken it slow for three years, figuring out how they were going to try with one another. When they'd settled into it—when he was no longer worried about proving something to his father; when Piper didn't go quiet every time they disagreed on something—he'd proposed. Yeah, it had taken longer than he'd liked. But they'd worked for their love. Now, their marriage.

The music began to play. Piper appeared at the end of the aisle, and he knew he'd never worked for anything more important.

Later, after they'd said their vows and celebrated—when they were alone in their room, the sliding doors of the Santorini house they'd once stayed in open—Caleb drew Piper close in his arms.

'How did you like your wedding, Mrs Martin?' he asked, kissing her forehead.

She snuggled into him, looked up with a sleepy smile. 'It was the best day of my life. I especially liked your wedding gift.'

'The Piper Martin Dog Shelter?'

'A bit wordy, but I'm sure the dogs won't mind.'

He chuckled. 'To think I signed up for a lifetime of this.'

'You wouldn't want it any other way,' she said, kissing his chest. 'I love you, Mr Martin.'

'One hundred per cent now?' he teased.

She laughed. 'Maybe more. But since I have to keep you on your toes, you'll never know.'

He chuckled again, pressing a kiss into her hair. 'I love you.'

'Good.'

Caleb couldn't have agreed more. It was good. It was all good.

* * * * *

A MAN YOU
CAN TRUST

JO MCNALLY

This book, with a Genuine Good Guy as a hero, is dedicated to the memory of a Genuine Good Guy— my dad. He was quietly, yet fiercely, devoted to the people he loved.

I love and miss you, Dad.

Chapter One

The resort parking lot was quiet.

That was hardly surprising, since it was seven o'clock on a Monday morning.

But Cassandra Smith didn't take chances.

Ever.

She backed into her reserved spot but didn't turn the car off right away. She didn't even put it in Park. First, she looked around—checking the mirrors, making sure she was going to stay. Pete Carter was walking from his car toward the Gallant Lake Resort. He waved as he passed her, and she waved back, then pretended to look at something on the passenger seat as she turned off the ignition. Pete worked at the front desk, and he was a nice enough guy. He'd offer to walk her inside if she got out now. And maybe that would be a good idea. Or maybe not. How well did she really know him?

Her fingers tightened on the steering wheel. She was

being ridiculous—Pete was thirty years her senior and
happily married. But some habits were hard to shake,
and really—why take the chance? By the time she finished arguing with herself, Pete was gone.

She checked the mirrors one last time before getting
out of the car, threading the keys through her fingers in
a move as natural to her as breathing. As she closed the
door, a warm breeze brushed a tangle of auburn hair
across her face. She tucked it back behind her ear and
took a moment to appreciate the morning. Beyond the
sprawling 200-room fieldstone-and-timber resort where
Cassie worked, Gallant Lake shimmered like polished
blue steel. It was encircled by the Catskill Mountains,
which were just beginning to show a blush of green
in the trees. The air was brisk but smelled like spring,
earthy and fresh. It reminded her of new beginnings.

It had been six months since Aunt Cathy offered
her sanctuary in this small resort town nestled in the
Catskills. Gallant Lake was beginning to feel like
home, and she was grateful for it. The sound of car
tires crunching on the driveway behind her propelled
her out of her thoughts and into the building. Other employees were starting to arrive.

Cassie crossed the lobby, doing her best to avoid
making eye contact with the few guests wandering
around at this hour. As usual, she opted for the stairs
instead of dealing with the close confines of the elevator. The towering spiral staircase in the center of
the lobby looked like a giant tree growing up toward
the ceiling three stories above, complete with stylized
copper leaves draping from the ceiling. The offices of
Randall Resorts International were located on the second floor, overlooking the wide lawn that stretched to
the lakeshore. Cassie's desk was centered between four

small offices. Or rather, three smaller offices and one huge one, which belonged to the boss. That boss was in earlier than usual today.

"G'morning, Cassie! Once you get settled, stop in, okay?"

Ugh. No employee wanted to be called into the boss's office first thing on a Monday.

Blake Randall managed not only this resort from Gallant Lake, but half a dozen others around the world. It hadn't taken long for Cassie to understand that Blake was one of those rare—at least in her world—men who wore their honor like a mantle. He took pride in protecting the people he cared for. Tall, with a swath of black hair that was constantly falling across his forehead, the man was ridiculously good-looking. His wife, Amanda, really hit the jackpot with this guy, and he adored her and their children.

Blake was all business in the office, though. Focused and driven, he'd intimidated the daylights out of Cassie at first. Amanda teasingly called him Tall, Dark and Broody, and the nickname fit. But Cassie had come to appreciate his steady leadership. He had high expectations, and he frowned on drama in the workplace.

He'd offered her a job at the resort's front desk when she first arrived in Gallant Lake. It was a charity job—a favor to Cathy—and Cassie knew it. It took only one irate male guest venting at her during check-in for everyone to realize she wasn't ready to be working with an unpredictable public. She'd frozen like a deer in headlights. Once she moved up here to the private offices, she'd found her footing and had impressed Blake with her problem-solving skills. Because Blake hated problems.

She tossed her purse into the bottom drawer of her desk and checked her computer quickly to make sure there weren't any urgent issues to deal with. Then she made herself a cup of hot tea, loaded it with sugar and poured Blake a mug of black coffee before heading into his office.

He looked up from behind his massive desk and gave her a quick nod of thanks as she set his coffee down in front of him. Everyone knew to stay out of Blake's way until they saw a cup of coffee in his hand. He was well-known for not being a morning person. He took a sip and sighed.

"I was ready to book a flight to Barbados after hearing about the wedding disaster down there this weekend, but then I heard that apparently *I*—" he emphasized the one-letter word with air quotes "—already resolved everything by flying some photographer in to take wedding photos yesterday, along with discounting some rooms. Not at *our* resort, but at a *competitor*. I hear I'm quite the hero to the bride's mother, but I'll be damned if I remember doing any of it."

Blake's dark brows furrowed as he studied her over the rim of his coffee cup, but she could see a smile tugging at the corner of his mouth. The tension in her shoulders eased. Despite his tone, he wasn't really angry.

"The manager called Saturday looking for you," she explained. "Monique was in a panic, so I made a few calls. The bride's mother used the son of a 'dear family friend' to organize the wedding, instead of using our concierge service. The idiot didn't book the rooms until the last minute, and we didn't have enough available, which he neglected to mention to the bride's mom. Then he booked the photographer for the wrong date." She smiled at the look of horror on Blake's face. "We're talking wrong by a full month. It was quite a melodrama—none of which was our fault—but the bride is some internet fashion icon with half a million followers on Instagram. So we found rooms at the neighboring resort for the guests we couldn't handle, and convinced the wedding party to get back into their gowns and tuxes for a full photo shoot the day *after* the wedding, which was the fastest we could get the photographer there. Mom's happy. Bride's happy. Social media is flooded with great photos and stories with the resort as a backdrop. I assumed you'd approve."

Blake chuckled. "Approve? It was freaking brilliant, Cassie. That kind of problem-solving is more along the lines of a VP than an executive assistant. You should have an office of your own."

She still wasn't used to receiving compliments, and her cheeks warmed. When she'd first arrived, she'd barely been able to handle answering calls and emails, always afraid of doing something wrong, of disappointing someone. But as the months went by, she'd started to polish her rusty professional skills and found she was pretty good at getting things done, especially over the phone. Face-to-face confrontation was a different story.

This wasn't the first time Blake had mentioned a promotion, but she wasn't ready. Oh, she was plenty qualified, with a bachelor's degree in business admin. But if things went bad back in Milwaukee, she'd have to change her name again and vanish, so it didn't make sense to put down roots anywhere. She let Blake's comment hang in the air without responding. He finally shook his head.

"Fine. Keep whatever job title you want, but I need your help with something."

Cassie frowned when Blake hesitated. "What is it?"

"You know I hired a new director of security." Cassie nodded. She was going to miss Ken Taylor, who was retiring to the Carolinas with his wife, Dianne. Ken had taken the job on a temporary basis after Blake's last security guy left for a job in Boston. Ken was soft-spoken and kind, and he looked like Mr. Rogers, right down to the cardigan sweaters. He was aware of Cassie's situation, and he'd made every effort to make sure she felt safe here, including arranging her reserved parking space.

"Nick West starts today. I'd like you to work with him."

"Me? Why?" Cassie blurted the words without thinking. She laughed nervously. "I don't know anything about security!"

But she knew all about *needing* security.

Blake held up his hand. "Relax. I'm not putting you on the security team. He'll need help with putting data together and learning our processes. I need someone I can trust to make sure he has a smooth transition."

"So...I'm going to be *his* executive assistant instead of yours?" Her palms went clammy at the thought of working for a stranger.

"First, we've already established you're a hell of a lot more than my EA. And this is just temporary, to help him get settled in the office." Blake drained his coffee mug and set it down with a thunk, not noticing the way Cassie flinched at the sound. "He's a good guy. Talented. Educated. He's got a master's in criminal justice, and he was literally a hero cop in LA—recognized by the mayor, the whole deal."

A shiver traced its way down Cassie's spine. Her ex had been a "hero cop," too. Blake's next words barely registered.

"I'm a little worried about him making the shift from the hustle of LA to quiet Gallant Lake, but he says he's looking for a change of pace. His thesis was on predictive policing—using data to spot trouble before it reaches a critical point." That explained why Blake hired the guy. Blake was all about preventing problems before they happened. He did *not* like surprises. "It'll be interesting to see how he applies that to facility security. His approach requires a ton of data to build predictive models, and that's where you come in. You create reports faster than anyone else here."

Cassie loved crunching numbers and analyzing results. She started to relax. If Blake wanted her to do some research for the new guy, she could handle that.

"I also want you to mentor him a bit, help him get acclimated."

"Meaning…?"

"Amanda and I are headed to Vegas this week for that conference and a little vacation time. Nick's going to need someone to show him around, make introductions and answer any questions that come up. He just got to town this weekend, and he doesn't know anyone or anything in Gallant Lake."

"So what, I'm supposed to be his babysitter?"

Blake's brow rose at the uncharacteristically bold question.

"Uh, no. Just walk him around the resort so he's familiar with it, and be a friendly face for the guy." He leaned forward. "Look, I get why you might be anxious, but he's the director of security. That's about as safe as it gets."

Her emotions roiled around in her chest. She hated that her employer felt he had to constantly reassure her about her safety. Yes, the guy in charge of security *should* be safe. All men should be.

"Cassie? Is this going to be a problem?" The worry in Blake's eyes made her sit straighter in her chair. What was it Sun Tzu wrote in *The Art of War*? The latest in a long line of self-help books she'd picked up was based on quotes from the ancient Chinese tome.

Appear strong when you are weak...

"No, I'm sure it will be fine. And the data analysis sounds interesting. Does he know...?"

"About your situation? No. I wouldn't do that without your permission. I only told Ken because you'd just arrived and..."

She was hardly strong now, but she'd been a complete basket case back then.

"I understand. I don't think the new guy needs to know. I don't want to be treated differently."

Blake frowned. "I don't want that, either. But I do want you to feel safe here."

"I know, Blake. And thank you. If I change my mind, I'll tell him myself." She was getting tired of people having conversations about her as if she was a problem to be solved, no matter how well-meaning they were. "When will I meet him?"

"He's getting his rental house situated this morning, then he'll be in. I'm planning on having lunch with him, then giving him a quick tour. He dropped some boxes off yesterday. Can you make sure he has a functioning office? You know, computer, phone, internet access and all that? I told Brad to set it up, but you know how scattered that kid can be."

Two hours later, Cassie was finishing the last touches in West's office. The computer and voice mail were set up with temporary passwords. The security team had delivered his passes and key cards—his master key would open any door in the resort. Brad, their IT whiz, had been busy over the weekend, and a huge flat-screen hung on one wall. On it, twelve different feeds from the security surveillance room downstairs were scrolling in black and white. It looked like a scene straight out of some crime-fighter TV show.

A familiar voice rang out in the office. "Hel-lo? Damn, no one's here."

Cassie stepped to the doorway and waved to Blake's wife. "I'm here!"

Amanda Randall rushed to give Cassie a tight hug. Cassie *hated* hugs, but Amanda got a free pass. The woman simply couldn't help herself—she was a serial hugger. She was also Cassie's best friend in Gallant Lake. They'd bonded one night over a bottle of wine and the discovery they shared similar ghosts from their pasts. Other than that, the two women couldn't be any more different. Amanda was petite, with curves everywhere a woman wanted curves. Cassie was average height and definitely not curvy—her nervous energy left her with a lean build. Amanda had long golden curls, while Cassie's straight auburn hair was usually pulled back and under control. Amanda was a bouncing bundle of laughing, loving, hugging energy. Cassie was much more reserved, and sometimes found her friend's enthusiasm overwhelming.

"I brought chocolate chip cookies for everyone, but I guess you and I will have to eat them all." Amanda held up a basket that smelled like heaven.

"You won't have to twist my arm. Come on in and keep me company."

Amanda followed her into the new guy's office.

"Wow—this is some pretty high-tech stuff, huh?" Amanda walked over to the flat-screen and watched the video feeds change from camera to camera. One feed was from a camera in front of Blake and Amanda's stone mansion next door to the resort. The private drive was visible in the view from above their front door. "I really need to talk to Blake about those cameras. I don't like the feeds popping up in some stranger's office."

"Hasn't resort security always been responsible for the house, too?"

"I was never crazy about that, but Blake insisted. And it was different when it was Paul, whom I'd known from the first week I was here. And then Ken. I mean, he's like having a favorite uncle watching over the house. But some hotshot ex-cop from LA watching me and the kids coming and going?" Amanda shuddered. "I don't think so. Have you met him yet?"

"Who?"

"The new guy? Superhero cop coming to save us all? The one who has my husband drooling?"

"No, I haven't met him yet." Cassie set a stack of legal pads on the corner of the desk, opposite the corner Amanda now occupied as she devoured a cookie. "What do you know about him?"

"What *don't* I know? He's all Blake talked about this weekend. 'Nick is so brave!' 'Nick is so brilliant!' 'Oh, no! What if Nick doesn't like it here?' 'What if Nick leaves?'" Amanda acted out each comment dramatically, and Cassie couldn't help laughing. "But seriously, he *really* wants this guy to work out. You know Blake—he believes in preventing problems before they happen, and that wasn't Ken's strong suit. He's so anxious for this guy to be happy here that he actually suggested we skip our trip to Vegas so he could be here all week for *Nick*! That was a 'hell no' from me. We haven't been away together without the kids in ages." Amanda finished off the last of her cookie, licking her fingers. "And this girl is ready to par-tay in Vegas, baby! Whatcha doin'?"

"Blake said Nick dropped off these boxes. I'll unpack them, and he can organize later." Cassie pulled the top off one of the boxes on the credenza. It was filled with books on criminal science and forensics. She put them on the bookshelves in the order they were packed. Police work was usually a life's calling. What made this guy walk away from it?

She stopped after pulling the cover off the second box. It contained more books and binders, but sitting on top was a framed photo. She lifted it out and Amanda came around the desk to study it with her.

It was a wedding portrait. The tall man in the image looked damned fine in a tuxedo, like a real-life James Bond. His hair was dark and cropped short, military style. His features were angular and sharp, softened only by the affectionate smile he was giving the bride. Her skin was dark and her wedding gown was the color of champagne. Her close-cropped Afro highlighted her high cheekbones and long, graceful neck. She was looking up at the man proudly, exuding confidence and joy. Cassie felt a sting of regret. When was the last time anyone thought that about her?

"Wow—are those two gorgeous or what?" Amanda took the silver frame from Cassie and whistled softly. "I wonder who it is." She turned the frame over as if there might be an answer on the back.

"I'm assuming it's Nick West and his wife."

"No. Blake told me he's single."

"Maybe she's an ex?"

Amanda rolled her eyes. "Who keeps photos like this of their ex? Maybe it's not him at all—could be a brother or a friend. But if it is Nick, he's hot as hell, isn't he?"

Cassie took the picture back and set it on a shelf. "I hadn't noticed."

"Yeah, I call BS on that. There isn't a woman under the age of eighty who wouldn't notice how hot *that* guy is. You'd better be careful, especially now that you're living in the love shack."

"The *what*?"

"Nora's apartment—we call it the love shack. First it was her and Asher. Then Mel moved in there and met Shane. And now *you're* there, so..."

Cassie's aunt had sold her coffee shop in the village to Amanda's cousin Nora a few years ago but still worked there part-time. The apartment above the Gallant Brew had been a godsend when it came vacant shortly after Cassie's arrival. But a *love shack*?

"I don't believe in fairy tales. And even if Nora's place *did* have magic powers, they'd be wasted on me." She started to pull more books out of the box, but Amanda stopped her.

"Hey, I'm sorry. I don't mean to push you. Sometimes my mouth gets ahead of my brain. But someday you're going to find someone..."

Cassie shook her head abruptly. "That ship has sailed, Amanda. I have zero interest in any kind of...whatever." She glanced back to the photo and studied the man's dark eyes, sparkling with love for the bride. Her heart squeezed just a little, but she ignored it. "I can't take the chance. Not again."

"Not every guy is Don. In fact, there are millions of guys who *aren't* Don."

Amanda meant well, but they were straying onto thin and dangerous ice here. Cassie had wedding photos, too. They were packed away somewhere, and they showed a smiling couple just like this one. She'd been so inno-cent back then. And stupid. She was never going to be either again.

"Look, I have a ton of work to do, and this guy—my *coworker*—is going to be here any time now. No more talk about love shacks and hotness, okay?"

Amanda stared at her long and hard, her blue eyes

darkening in concern. But thankfully, she decided to let it go. She picked up the basket of cookies. "Fine. I have to finish packing for the trip anyway. I'll leave these out on the coffee counter." She started to walk away, then spun suddenly and threw her arms around Cassie in an attack hug. "We leave in the morning, but we'll be back next week. If you need anything at all—*anything*—you call Nora or Mel and they'll be there in a heartbeat."

Cassie bit back the surprising rebuke that sat on the tip of her tongue. She was fed up with everyone hovering and fretting, but she knew it was her own damn fault. How many times had she called Amanda those first few months, crying and terror-stricken because of a bad dream or some random noise she heard? Sure, she'd changed her name and moved about as far away from Milwaukee as she could get, but Don was an ex-cop with all the right connections. That's why she kept a "go-bag" packed and ready at her door. She took a deep breath, nodded and wished Amanda a safe and fun trip. But after she left, Cassie was too agitated to sit at her desk. She ended up back in Nick West's office, unpacking the last box.

A little flicker of anger flared deep inside. It had been nudging at her more and more lately, first as an occasional spark of frustration, but now it was turning into a steady flame. She wanted her life back. She wanted a life where she could rely on herself and stand up for herself. She looked at the wedding photo again. She wanted a life where she smiled more. Where she didn't jump every time someone…

A shadow filled the doorway.

"Hey! Whatcha doin' in here?"

Chapter Two

Nick West knew he'd startled the woman, but he was just trying to be funny. It was a *joke*. He figured the auburn-haired stranger would jump, then they'd both have a good laugh as he introduced himself. Humor was always a good icebreaker, right?

He never figured she'd send a stapler flying at his head.

He managed to swat it down before it connected with his face, but it ricocheted off the corner of his desk and smacked him in the shin.

"Ow!" He hopped on one leg. "Damn, woman! I was just kidding around." He rubbed his throbbing shin, unable to keep from laughing at the way his joke had backfired on him.

But the woman wasn't laughing. She was wide-eyed and pale, her chest rising and falling sharply. Her eyes were an interesting mix of green and gold. Her hair was a mix, too—not quite red, but more than just brown. It was pulled back off her face and into a low pony-tail. She was pretty, in a fresh-scrubbed, natural way. Then he noticed her hand, which was clutching a pair of scissors like she was getting ready to go all Norman Bates on him.

The desk was still between them, but he raised his hands as if she was holding a loaded gun. He'd already seen how good her aim was.

"Whoa, there! Let's dial it back a notch, okay? I'm Nick West and this is my office...I think. Am I in the wrong place?" The thought didn't occur to him until he said it out loud. Shit. Had he just burst into some woman's office and scared the bejesus out of her? What if this was the boss's wife? He'd heard Randall's wife was involved in the resorts somehow. Even if it wasn't her, traumatizing a coworker wasn't a good way to start his first day here.

The hand holding the scissors lowered and color came back to her previously white knuckles. She lifted her chin, but it trembled, and there was genuine fear in her eyes. It made him feel like a jerk.

"Look, I'm sorry. I was kidding around. I do that sometimes."

"You scared the hell out of me, and you did it on purpose!" Those green-gold eyes flashed in anger. "Is that how you plan on introducing yourself to everyone here? Because I've got news for you—it won't go over well." She reached up to push her hair behind her ear and took a steadying breath. "This *is* your office, Mr. West. I'm Cassie...um...Smith, and I'll be working with you. I was setting up your desk."

Great. He'd never had a secretary before, and he'd just traumatized the first one he got. *Smooth move, West.*

He grunted out a short laugh, rubbing the back of his neck as he tried to figure out how to fix this mess.

"Let's rewind and start over, okay? You're my first secretary." He stopped when her eyes narrowed. "What? What'd I say wrong now?"

"I am *not* your secretary. I'm Mr. Randall's executive assistant, and I'll be supporting you with some of your projects. I'll provide data. I'll run reports. But I don't take dictation and I won't be fetching your damned coffee."

Well, well, well. The jumpy lady had a backbone after all. Nick knew how to be a good cop. He had no damned clue how to be a good executive.

"Not a secretary. Got it. Like I said, I'm new at this corporate thing. In LA, I had a dispatcher and a desk sergeant. Something tells me you'll be closer to the latter." He nodded down to her hand. "I'd be a lot happier if you'd put those down."

Cassie looked down and appeared surprised to see the scissors still in her hand. She dropped them to the desk like they were burning her.

"Sorry," she mumbled. She continued to look down, lost in thought.

Her body language was all over the place, causing his cop's sixth sense to kick in. First she was jumpy and defensive. Then proud and outspoken. And now, as she apologized, she visibly shrank. He didn't like timid women. They reminded him of victims, and he'd had his fill of victims. But then again, victims didn't fling staplers at people's heads.

"Don't apologize," he said. "That was a juvenile thing for me to do. I gotta remember I'm not in a police precinct anymore." And he'd never be in one again. He rubbed his thigh absently. Shoving that thought aside, he flashed her a rueful grin. "I'll probably need your help monitoring my corporate behavior."

She nodded, not returning the smile, but straightening a bit. "I don't like practical jokes, but I'm sure you'll do fine here. It's a good group of people, and they like to have fun."

Interesting. She said *they* like to have fun, not *we*. He looked around the office. He'd barely noticed it yesterday, just dropping off his boxes and checking in to his room to crash after the long cross-country drive. The view of Gallant Lake was sweet. The giant flat-screen on the wall with all the changing camera feeds was even sweeter. He saw the photo on the bookshelf and blinked. Jada. It was her death that chased him out of LA and into this new life. The picture was a reminder of how quickly good things could go bad.

A large hand clamped down on his shoulder from behind, and Nick restrained himself from spinning around swinging. Old habits were hard to break. In this case, it would have been especially bad, since it was his new boss.

"Sorry I missed your arrival, Nick. We had a guest giving the desk staff a hard time about the five movies on his room bill. Turns out his ten-year-old has a thing for superheroes and didn't realize movies are fifteen bucks a pop." There weren't many men who could make Nick tip his head back and look up, but Blake Randall was one of them. He was a few years older than Nick, but he had no doubt Randall could hold his own in a physical challenge. Blake spotted Cassie on the other side of the desk. "Oh, good, you've met Cassie. You're going to want to treat this girl right because she's the one who can make or break you, man."

Nick met Cassie's gaze. Her moods were as changeable as her eyes. Now that Blake was here, she was clearly more relaxed.

...*she's the one who can make or break you*...

Even after Blake's warning, Nick couldn't resist teasing her.

"Oh, don't worry, Blake. Cassie's made quite an impression already." Her eyes narrowed in suspicion. "She's already throwing things...I mean...*ideas*...at me." Her hands clenched into fists, and he was surprised his skin wasn't blistering under the heat of her glare. "She even took a stab at trying to define her job responsibilities."

Blake was oblivious to the tension buzzing in the room. "Trust me, there is no way to define her job duties. Cassie's always surprising you by doing more than expected." Nick's smirk grew into a wide smile.

"Yeah, she's full of surprises. Oh, look, the stapler fell off the desk." He bent over to pick it up from where it had landed earlier. He couldn't help wondering if exposing his back to the woman, with scissors still nearby, was a good idea. "We don't want the boss to think you were throwing things at me, now, do we?"

"No, we don't." She watched as he set the stapler on the desk. Her voice was cold as ice. "But Blake knows me well enough to know I'd never launch an unprovoked attack."

Nick looked up in surprise. *Touché.* She was playing along. He winked at her, and a little crease appeared between her brows.

Blake chuckled behind him. "I can't imagine Cassie throwing things at anyone." Her cheeks went pink, but Blake didn't seem to notice. "Come on, Nick, let's grab lunch and I'll make some introductions. Would you like to join us, Cass?"

"No, thanks. I have work to do. You and Mr. West go ahead and…"

"Mr. West?" Blake looked at Nick and frowned. "We're on a first-name basis up here, Nick."

"No problem. Cassie and I were joking around earlier and she's just trying to get a rise out of me." Now it was her turn to be surprised. She looked at him and her mouth opened, but she didn't speak.

For the first time, Blake seemed to pick up on the undercurrent of…something…that was swirling around them.

"Really?" He looked at Cassie with clear surprise. Apparently she wasn't known for cracking jokes. She gave Blake a quick nod and smiled. It was the first smile Nick had seen from her, and it was worth waiting for, even if it was aimed at someone else. Her whole face softened, and her eyes went more green than gold.

"You two go on to lunch, and let me get back to work, okay?"

His curiosity was definitely piqued. Cassie Smith had a story.

On Thursday morning, Cassie was still trying to put a finger on her riled-up emotions. It started before Nick West's arrival, so she couldn't place all the blame on him for this low rumble of frustration and anger that simmered in her. In no mood to deal with her tangled hair, she pulled it into a messy knot on top of her head and frowned at the mirror. Simple khakis, sensible shoes and a dark green Gallant Lake polo shirt. Practical attire for a busy day. She was giving Nick a tour of the grounds today and wanted to be able to keep up with his long strides.

The man was always in motion, leaving her constantly on edge. He paced when he talked and bounced when he sat. He had a foam basketball that he tossed around his office when he was alone in there, and it drove her crazy. Yesterday she'd moved her computer so her back was to his door, trying to avoid the distraction of the ball flying through the air. Nick started laughing the minute he walked into the office and saw the new arrangement, and laughed every time he walked by. *Jerk.*

She went downstairs in the loft apartment and poured herself a cup of tea, adding three spoonfuls of sugar. She usually joined Nora in the coffee shop before heading to the resort, but Nora had her hands full watching Amanda and Blake's teenaged son and toddler daughter this week. Mel might be down in the shop, but it was more likely Amanda's other cousin would be enjoying her coffee with her fiancé on the deck of their waterfront home. So Cassie fixed herself a bagel and sat at the kitchen island, feeling almost as restless as Nick West.

Ugh! She'd known the man only three days, and he was in her head constantly. His big laugh when he was kidding around with employees—who all seemed to adore both him and his practical jokes. The way he started every conversation with a booming "Hey! Whatcha doing?" The way he rapped the corner of everyone's desk sharply with his knuckles every time he passed it. Except hers. After the first time he did it and she'd squeaked in surprise, he'd left her desk alone.

But she hadn't managed to stop his infuriating running joke of putting her stapler—the bright blue one she'd flung at him on their first meeting—in a different place every day. Monday afternoon she'd found it on her chair. Tuesday, it was next to the coffee maker. And yesterday, when she attended a meeting in the surveillance room with Nick and the entire security staff, the blue stapler was sitting on the circular console that faced the wall of monitors. She spotted it immediately and turned to glare at him, only to find him laughing at her. *Ass.*

Sure enough, when she walked into the office later that morning, the stapler was sitting next to a small vase of daffodils on her desk. Wait. Where did the daffodils come from? The sunny flowers were in a simple vase, which on closer inspection turned out to be a water glass.

"They reminded me of you, slugger."

Nick West was leaning against the doorway to his office. He'd taken his jacket and tie off and rolled up the sleeves of his dress shirt. That was his usual uniform during the day. He always looked ready for action.

"Excuse me?"

"You know—sunny and bright and happy?" He was baiting her. Yesterday, he'd asked her why she was so serious all the time. Deciding the misogynistic question didn't deserve an answer, she'd walked away, but she should have known he wouldn't drop it. She dropped her purse into a drawer and clarified her comment.

"I was referring to the 'slugger' part."

"Well, you've got pretty good aim with that arm of yours, and you're a fighter. Slugger seems to fit you."

Cassie's breath caught in her throat. He thought she was a *fighter*?

"And what should I call *you*? Ducky, for how fast you dodged the stapler?" He gave her an odd look, somewhere between surprise and admiration. Then his face scrunched up.

"Ducky is a hard pass. Let's stick with Nick."

She looked at the flowers. "Please tell me the director of security didn't *steal* these flowers from the garden in front of the resort."

Nick winked at her. He was a big winker. She did her best to tell herself those twinkling brown eyes of his had no effect on her. "They actually haven't left the property, so at best, the director of security has just *misappropriated* them. I think they look nice there, don't you?" She rolled her eyes.

"I'm sure a cheating accountant thinks misappropriated funds look *nice* in his bank account, too, but that doesn't make it any less a crime."

He barked out a loud laugh. "And here I thought I left all the attorneys back in LA. You missed your calling." He turned back to his office, but stopped cold when she called out.

"Oh, Mr. West?" His exaggerated slow turn almost made her laugh out loud, and she hadn't done that in a long time. He admittedly had a goofy charm. "Don't forget the stapler. You seem to prefer mine to the one you have in your office, so maybe we should switch." She picked it up and tossed it gently in his direction, surprised at her own moxie. He was equally surprised, catching the stapler with one hand. She nodded at the daffodils. "And thank you for the stolen goods."

He gave her a crooked grin. "Just following orders. Blake told me to treat you right, remember?"

Cassie rolled her eyes again and turned away, ignoring his chuckle behind her.

A couple hours later, Nick was surprisingly all business during their tour of the grounds, jotting notes on his tablet and snapping pictures. It was a gorgeous early May day, warming dramatically from earlier in the week. A breeze raised gentle waves on the lake, which were shushing against the shoreline.

They started by walking around the exterior of Blake and Amanda's home, a rambling stone castle named Halcyon, then worked their way down the hill past the resort, all the way to the golf course that hugged the shoreline. The entire complex, including the residence, covered over one hundred acres, and by lunchtime, Cassie felt as though they'd walked every one of them.

She rattled off anecdotes as they walked. Nick's security staff had been showing him around all week, but Blake instructed her, in his absence, to give Nick a tour that included the *stories* behind the business. This place, with lots of help from Amanda, had changed Blake's life. He wanted his employees to understand its importance. Nick listened and nodded, busy with his notes.

She told him the history of Halcyon and how close the mansion had come to being destroyed, along with the resort. The rebirth of the resort, thanks to Amanda's designer eye and Blake's hotel fortune. The coinciding growth of the town of Gallant Lake, where most of the employees lived and many guests shopped and dined. The upscale weddings the resort specialized in, often for well-heeled Manhattanites. And the new championship golf course, already home to several prominent charity tournaments.

He glanced at her several times as they headed back from the golf course, but she was careful not to make eye contact. His chocolate eyes had a way of knocking her thoughts off track. The waves were larger now that the wind had picked up. Above them was the sprawling clubhouse, a stunning blend of glass and timber, with a slate tile roof.

"Where's the best place to launch a kayak around here?"

"What?"

"I want to get my kayak in the water this weekend, and my rental doesn't have a dock yet. Does the resort have a launch site?"

Cassie stopped walking and looked at him, brushing away the stray strands of hair that blew across her face. She knew her mouth had fallen open, but it took her a moment to actually speak.

"You're asking *me* about kayaking?"

"You live in a mountain town. You must do *something* outdoors. Are there mountain bike trails here? Places to rock climb?"

Her chest jumped and it startled her so much she put her hand over her heart. That had been dangerously close to a laugh. She shook her head. "You are definitely asking the wrong person. I'm sure those things exist around here, but I don't know anything about them. You should ask Terry at the front desk—he's outdoorsy."

"Outdoorsy?" His shoulders straightened. "I'm not 'outdoorsy.' I enjoy outdoor activities. There's a difference."

"And that difference would be?"

Nick stuttered for a minute, then rubbed the back of his neck. "I don't know. But it's different, trust me. You've never kayaked here?"

"Uh…no. My idea of a good time is curling up with a book and a cup of tea."

He shook his head. "Well, that's just sad. I'll think of you tomorrow night when I'm out on the water taking in the scenery and you're stuck at home reading some boring book."

She turned away and started walking. "I'm working tomorrow night."

"Yeah? On a Friday night?"

"There's a big wedding this weekend, and the rehearsal dinner is tomorrow. One of our events people is on vacation, so I'm helping our manager make sure everything runs smoothly."

"The manager is Julie, right? I spent yesterday afternoon with her. She seems on top of things." Cassie nodded. Julie Brown was nice. If Cassie was sure she'd be staying in Gallant Lake, they'd probably be better friends. But she couldn't afford to get too comfortable. Nick, walking at her side, shook his head with a smile. "Blake wasn't kidding when he said you don't have a defined job description—you're everywhere."

"I'm wherever I'm needed. *That's* my job description."

He studied her intently, then shrugged.

"Hey, if you'd rather work than join me on the water, that's your loss."

This laughing whirlwind of a man was making her crazy. Because for just a moment, she wondered if it really *would* be her loss if she didn't go kayaking with him.

She quickly dismissed the thought. Her in a kayak with Nick West? Not happening.

Chapter Three

Nick leaned back in his office chair, turning away from the security feeds to watch Cassie through the open door. She was on the phone with someone, typing furiously and glancing at the schedule on the tablet propped up on the desk by her computer. The woman could seriously multitask. Was she the calm, cool professional he saw right now? Or was she the meek woman who'd flinched when he'd dropped a pile of papers on her desk this morning? Was she the woman who got uptight if there were more than a couple people in a room? Or was she the woman he saw yesterday, giving him a tour of the property with pride and confidence?

He'd checked her employee file—a perk of his job title. The information was pretty thin. She'd been here only a few months. She'd managed an insurance office in Milwaukee for a while but had been unemployed for over a year before moving here six months ago. Not exactly a red flag. She could have been going to school or job hunting or whatever. She'd clearly won Blake Randall's confidence, but she didn't give off a sense of having a lot of confidence in herself. Instead, Cassie seemed all twisted up with anxiety. Unless she was busy. Then she was cool and...controlled. It was as if being productive was her comfort zone.

She hung up the phone, then immediately dialed someone else. Her back was to him, ramrod straight. Her auburn hair was gathered in a knot at the base of her slender neck. He wondered what she'd look like if she ever let that hair loose. She was dressed in dark trousers and a pale blue sweater. Sensible. Practical. Almost calculatedly so. He grimaced. This was what happened when you spent eight years as a detective—you started profiling everyone you met.

"Margo? It's Cassandra Smith, Mr. Randall's assistant. Did you see the email I sent you last week? I didn't receive a reply and thought perhaps you missed it..."

Nick's eyes narrowed. There was an edge to Cassie's voice he hadn't heard until now. She was a whole new person. Again. He picked up his foam basketball and started bouncing it off the wall by the doorway. He smirked when Cassie stiffened—the fact that she hated his throwing the ball around was half the fun of doing it.

"Yes... Well, if Mr. Randall saw these numbers, he'd definitely be concerned... Right. And if Mr. Randall is concerned, he might be on the next flight to Miami for a conversation... Exactly. The restaurant is consistently selling less alcohol than they're ordering every week. That inventory has to be going somewhere... What's that?... Oh, I see. The bartender had his own family restaurant and was ordering a little extra for himself? I'm assuming he's no longer employed with us?" She was scribbling furiously on a notepad on her desk. "You know, Margo, you have access to the same reports I do, so you may want to start reading them more closely... I'm sure you will. I'm glad we had a chance to talk... Yes, you, too. Have a great weekend."

Nick moved to the doorway while she talked, working her diplomatic magic with the Miami manager. As she hung up, he leaned against the doorjamb and started to clap slowly. Being Cassie, she just about jumped out of her skin, spinning in her chair with a squeak of alarm. He really was going to have to be more careful around her.

"Sorry, I couldn't help but overhear. Those were some good people skills, Cassie. I'm impressed, but since I'm responsible for loss management, I'm also concerned. Do we have a problem in Miami?"

Color returned to her cheeks and her chin lifted. "Not anymore. I saw the discrepancy last week. It was only a case or two here and there, but it's something the hotel manager should have spotted herself. She won't be ignoring any more of the reports I send out."

"And you really weren't going to tell Blake? Or me?" That might be taking her job responsibility a step too far. She stuttered for a moment, then met his gaze with the slightest of smiles, causing his chest to tighten in an odd way.

"It happened before *you* arrived, and I told Blake the minute I saw it."

Nick replayed the conversation in his head. Cassie let Margo believe Blake wasn't aware, but she hadn't actually stated that. Clever girl.

"Bravo, Miss Smith." She shrugged off the compliment, as usual. "Are you still planning on working the rehearsal dinner tonight?"

"Yes. It will probably run like clockwork as usual,

but with Blake out of town and one of our managers off this week, Julie doesn't want anyone thinking they can slack off." She checked the time on her phone. "I should probably get down there. Have fun kayaking."

Nick nodded and wished her a good evening, not bothering to tell her he wouldn't be paddling on the water tonight after all. He'd be sitting in the surveillance room with Brad, learning how everything worked in there. Turned out Brad was in IT and also worked security on the weekends.

Three hours later, his head was spinning with all the information Brad was throwing at him. Nick was comfortable with technology, but remembering which control moved the images from the smaller monitors up to the large wall monitors mounted around the room, which control sped up or reversed the feeds, how to copy a feed to the permanent drive rather than the temporary one that saved them for only fourteen days... It was enough to make his head hurt. And to have it rattled off to him by some geeky kid barely out of college didn't help his mood any.

There were digital cameras all over the resort, both in the public areas as well as in all the employee passageways and the kitchen. He'd spotted Cassie repeatedly. She seemed to be everywhere behind the scenes tonight, clipboard in hand, watching all the action. She'd changed into a crisp white shirt and dark slacks to match the rest of the staff. She didn't interact with a lot of people. He saw her speaking with the manager, Julie. Then she'd been with Dario, the head chef, gesturing toward the plates being prepared.

He'd seen that pattern with her before—if she knew and trusted someone, she was relaxed and looked them straight in the eye when she spoke. But if she wasn't comfortable with someone, her body language was completely different. She avoided both eye contact *and* conversation. She kept her body turned at a slight angle instead of facing them directly. Was she just painfully shy, or had something happened in her past to make her this way? Nick leaned back in his chair, chewing on the cap of his pen and scanning the monitors.

He spotted her a little while later, heading across the lobby toward the side door, purse slung over her shoulder. She was heading home. He frowned and checked the time. It was after ten o'clock and she was alone. They had cameras in the lots, but he'd noticed most of them were trained on customer parking, not the employee lot. He stood and shook Brad's hand.

"This has been a great session, man. Thanks. But I think I'll call it a night." He looked around and frowned. "You're on your own tonight?" Brad was a good kid, but he looked like a younger version of Paul Blart, the mall cop. Nick had doubts about Brad's ability to handle the type of situations that could come up when a wedding crowd got to drinking. "You've got my mobile number, right?"

Brad laughed. "I'm not alone. Tim's on vacation, but Bill's out doing the first night check on doors and gates." The team made the rounds to all exterior access points to the buildings three times every night. Nick nodded and left the room, waiting until he got to the hallway before closing his eyes in frustration.

Bill Chesnutt was even older than Ken Taylor had been. The guy was a retired marine, but he'd retired a *long* time ago. So basically they had Paul Blart and Andy Griffith watching over the resort on a Friday night. Perfect. He was going to need to make some changes here, but he didn't want to rock the boat too early. He'd have a sit-down with Blake when he returned and discuss the options—better training, better people or both. He headed out the side door toward the employee parking lot.

Cassie was walking in the next row over from him, head down and looking tired. There were nowhere near enough lights in this damn lot. Nick headed in her direction, making a mental note to talk to the employees about using a buddy system to walk to their cars after dark until he could get more lights out here. This might not be the streets of LA, but there were bad guys everywhere.

Nick walked up behind Cassie, not happy that he was able to get this close without her noticing. She should be more aware of her surroundings. He was only a few feet away and she didn't even know...

In the blink of an eye, Cassie spun and swung her fist at him. He dodged just in time, and something glinted in the light. Her car keys were sticking out between her fingers. That would have left a mark if she'd connected. She was digging in her purse with her other hand.

He barely had time to register what was happening before the pepper spray hit him in the face.

Chapter Four

"Agh! Son of a *bitch*! What the hell is wrong with you? God *damn* it, that hurts!"

Cassie watched in horror as Nick West covered the side of his face and doubled over, yelling in pain and letting out a string of curse words.

"Oh, my God. I didn't know it was you!" She stepped forward to help, but her lungs started to burn and she couldn't get a good breath. She started coughing, her chest burning. Still hunched over, Nick grabbed her arm, spinning her around and shoving her away with a hand to her back.

"What are you...?"

"Get away from me!" Nick's growl was rough and loud. "Get away!"

He was angry. He *pushed* her. She immediately fell back on a practiced reaction.

"I'm sorry..."

That wasn't what she was thinking. She was thinking Nick was an idiot to frighten her like that. But before she could take back her apology, coughing overtook her. Tears ran down her face.

"Damn it!" Nick's hand wrapped around her wrist and he dragged her to the grass along the dark edge of the lot. Then he propelled her even farther away from the cars, sending her stumbling. He was bent over, looking up at her with one eye tightly closed, like the Hunchback of Notre Dame. Rage burned in that one open eye. His voice was tightly controlled. Almost calm.

"Stay back. You inhaled some of your own pepper spray. Hell, Cassie…" He dropped to his knees, raising his hands to his face but not touching them to his skin. "Water…"

She dived back into her bag and pulled out a water bottle. She started to hand it to him, then realized he couldn't see her. "Turn your face up toward me, Nick. I'll pour the water."

He tilted his head. "Just the left side…" She poured the water slowly over the side of his face, and he took a deep, ragged breath. She did the same, noticing her lungs didn't feel like they were in spasms any more.

"What were you thinking, sneaking up on me like that? I thought you were kayaking." He didn't answer, just sat on the grass, his head between his knees, both eyes tightly closed. A low, steady groan was the only sound he made. She sat next to him. "I was only defending myself…"

Sun Tzu said it perfectly. *Invincibility lies in defense.*

His whole body went rigid and he raised his head, glaring at her with his right eye. The left side of his face and neck were bright red in the glow of the parking lot light, his left eye tightly closed.

"*Defending* yourself? I could write an entire training manual on what *not* to do from your performance just now." He closed his good eye and grimaced. "Damn, that hurts."

Cassie was caught between sympathy and anger. Anger seemed easier. "A training manual, huh? Since you're doubled over in pain right now, I'd say I did a pretty good job of rendering you harmless."

Before she could blink, Nick's hand snaked out and grabbed her wrist, yanking her almost onto his lap. His face was so close to hers that she could smell the pepper spray on his skin. She was too stunned to scream, but her heart felt like it was going to leap straight out of her chest.

"Do I look *harmless* to you right now, Cassie? If I'd been an attacker, you'd be dead, or worse. I could have forced you into your car and…" He growled to himself and released her with another curse, driving his fist into the ground at his side. "You did *everything* wrong. You let me get too close. You used the keys first when you should have used the spray. The keys-in-the-fingers trick only works when you're in close hand-to-hand combat, which should be your *last* resort. You took so long getting the pepper spray that I would have had your purse away from you before you could reach it."

Nick picked up the water bottle and poured what was left down the side of his face and neck. "You gave me time to turn away, so you didn't completely incapacitate me. And then, instead of running when you had the chance, you stepped forward, right into your own cloud of pepper spray, and nearly incapacitated *yourself*." He turned to focus his good eye on her. "So, yes. A whole training manual. On what *not* to do."

Cassie stared at the dark ground, focused on bringing her pulse under control. Nick had been careful not to hurt her when he'd grabbed her, but he'd still frightened her. On purpose. She'd hate him for it if it weren't for the truth of what he'd said. If he had been some random attacker—if he'd been *Don*—she would have been a victim. Again.

"Why are you armed with pepper spray? Did something happen to you?"

She didn't look up.

"Yes. Something happened."

"Here?"

She shook her head, her body trembling so badly she didn't trust her voice. The only sound was his wheezing breath. He finally cleared his throat.

"Okay. Something happened. Somewhere." His voice was gravelly from the pepper spray, but it was calmer than it had been a few minutes ago. "And you wanted to protect yourself. That's smart. But you need to do it *right*. I'll teach you."

Her head snapped up. He was doing his best to look at her, even though his left eye was still closed.

"What are you talking about?"

"I'll teach you self-defense, Cassie. The kind that actually works."

"Are you talking karate or something? I thought the pepper spray…"

"It's a tool, but you need more than that. If some guy's amped up on drugs, he'll just be temporarily blind and *really* ticked off." He picked up the pepper spray canister from the grass at her side. "This stuff will spray up to ten feet away. You never should have let me get so close before using it."

"I didn't know that."

"Exactly." He grimaced and swore again. "I need to

get home and dunk my face in a bowl full of ice water."
He stood and reached a hand down to help her up. She
hesitated, then took it.

"Are you okay to drive, Nick? Do you want me to…"

"I'm fine. I'm only a couple miles from here, and I
have one functioning eye. How about you?"

She was rattled to the core and definitely wouldn't get
any sleep tonight, but one of her favorite things about
Nora's place was that there were few places for anyone
to hide in the wide-open loft. She always parked her
car right next to the metal stairs that led to the back entrance. "I'm good. Don't worry about me."

Nick walked slowly to his Jeep, still cradling the side
of his face with one hand. She felt bad that he was suf-
fering, but she also felt a tiny spark of pride. Maybe she
hadn't fought back successfully, but she'd *fought*. That
was something, right?

Nick went into the office for a few hours on Saturday morning, but there was no sign of Cassie. He
should have been relieved, considering she about killed
him with that damn pepper spray the night before. Instead, he felt a nudge of disappointment, and more than
a nudge of concern.

Something happened.

One of the reasons he wasn't a cop anymore was
that he'd run out of patience with victims. He looked at
Jada's wedding photo on his shelf. No, that wasn't completely true. He'd run out of patience with victims who
didn't help themselves. Who willingly *allowed* themselves to be victims. That's why his partner was dead.
If Beth Washington hadn't gone back to her husband,
Jada would still be alive.

But Cassie had armed herself with pepper spray and

she hadn't hesitated to use it. She'd used it *badly*, but she'd used it. It was a good thing she was so bad with the stuff—at least she'd blinded him in only one eye.

He slid his notes from his time with Brad into a manila folder and put it on the corner of his desk to review on Monday. Blake Randall would be back in the office, and Nick's orientation period would come to an end. He looked forward to getting down to business. But first, he needed to finish unpacking and get himself settled in the small house he'd rented on Gallant Lake. He was getting sick of living out of cardboard boxes.

It was weird not seeing Cassie sitting at her desk when he left the office. He wondered if she'd take him up on his offer to teach her self-defense. She didn't need to become a Krav Maga expert to protect herself. But she was so damn jumpy and twitchy about everything. She'd have to lose that spookiness to be effective at self-defense, which was all about outthinking the enemy. Nick frowned. He didn't like the thought of the quiet brunette having enemies. Especially the kind who drove her to have such a quick trigger finger on a canister of pepper spray.

The heavy blue stapler sat on the corner of her desk, just begging to be hidden somewhere. Maybe he should leave her alone, especially with the boss coming back next week. But what was the fun in that? He set the stapler on the windowsill, tucking it behind the curtains that were pulled back to show the view of Gallant Lake and the surrounding mountains. Maybe he'd get out in the kayak tomorrow if the nice weather held.

But he woke the next morning to the sound of rain pounding on the metal roof. Kayaking was out of the question. He slid out of bed and opened the blinds on the window facing the water. Looked like a good day to do some shopping for the basics he needed to fill his pantry and refrigerator. He liked to cook healthy meals, but this transition week had seen him settling for far too many pizzas and frozen dinners. Time to get back on track. But first, there was an interesting-looking little coffee shop in Gallant Lake that he'd been meaning to try, and this was a hot-coffee sort of morning.

Apparently lots of people felt the same way, because the Gallant Brew was busy. As he stood in line, he studied the local artwork that lined the brick walls. A large bulletin board was filled with fliers about local events— a quilt show at the library, a spring concert at the elementary school, a senior travel group meeting at one of the churches. Slices of a small-town life he had no idea how to navigate.

His rising sense of panic settled when he saw the notice from the Rebel Rockers climbing club. The group was advertising a spring multipitch climb at the Gunks. The famous Shawangunk Ridge was known to be one of the best rock-climbing sites in the country, and a group climb like this would be a great way for him to learn his way around the cliffs. He'd get to know some local climbers, too. He tore off one of the paper strips with a phone number on it. Maybe this wouldn't be such a bad place after all.

There was a collective burst of female laughter from the back of the shop, and one of the voices sounded oddly familiar. There were two women bustling behind the counter, trying to serve the large group ahead of Nick. One was older and tall, with a long braid of pewter-colored hair. The other was petite, with dark hair and a bright smile. She said something over her shoulder toward the hallway that disappeared into the back of the shop. That's where Cassie Smith stood, juggling a large cardboard box in her arms.

The shorter brunette was filling a metal pitcher with frothy steamed milk, her voice rising over the hiss of the high-tech espresso maker. "Just set those mugs in the kitchen, Cass. I had no idea how low we'd gotten. You're a lifesaver!"

"No problem. I'll go get the second box for you." Cassie, dressed in snug jeans and a short pink sweater that teased a bit of skin at her waist, turned away. Hot damn, her auburn hair was swinging free this morning, falling past her shoulders thick and straight. The box struck the corner hard as she turned. Her grip slipped, and she threw a knee up to keep the box from hitting the floor as she tried to regain control.

Nick was there in three long strides, grabbing the box away from her. To his surprise, both women at the counter rounded on him like he'd gone after Cassie with a machete.

"What the hell do you think you're doing?" The older one slammed the cash register shut, ignoring the protest of her customer and heading his way with fury in her eyes. The petite one was less confrontational.

"Sir, you can't be back here…"

"Nick?" When Cassie spoke his name, both women stopped.

"You *know* this guy?" The taller woman looked him up and down, clearly unimpressed with what she saw. "I've never seen him in here before."

"He works at the resort, Aunt Cathy. He's okay." She reached for the box. "I'll take that."

Nick shook his head. "It's heavy. Tell me where you want it."

She opened her mouth as if to argue, then reconsidered, pointing to the kitchen. "Anywhere in there. Thanks." He set the box down on the stainless steel counter in the tiny kitchen, then turned to face her.

"That's too heavy for you to be carrying."

"Apparently not, since I managed to carry it down a long flight of stairs just fine. I didn't steer very well, that's all." She turned away and headed down the hallway, then looked over her shoulder at him in confusion when he followed. "What are you doing?"

"You said there was a second box. I'll get it."

She turned slowly, her right brow rising.

"No. You won't."

Nick shook his head in frustration. "We can stand here and argue about it as long as you'd like, but I *am* going to carry the other box down. If you'd bumped that one into the wall on the stairs, you could have fallen and broken your neck. Do you care anything at all about your own safety?"

"Seriously? I pepper-sprayed you in the face Friday night. I think that shows how much I care about my safety."

"Yeah? You still haven't agreed to my offer to help you learn how to protect yourself. And you're fighting me about carrying a box of coffee mugs when you know damn well I'm right." His voice rose slightly on those last words, and she stepped back. Her voice, on the other hand, dropped so low he barely heard her.

"I'm sorry…" Her brows furrowed as soon as the words came out, as if she hadn't expected them.

"You don't have to be sorry, Cassie. Just be smart. And accept help when it's offered. Come on…" His hand touched her arm and she flinched. What the hell? Was she *afraid* of him? He dropped the "cop voice" Jada always used to give him hell for and raised his hands in innocence. "Hey, I'm trying to be a nice guy here. Leave the door open. Tell your aunt to call the cops if we're not back down here in five minutes. Do whatever you need to do, but I think you know in your heart you're safe with me. And Cassie?" He waited until she made eye contact with him, eyes full of uncertainty. "Bring some comfortable clothes to the office tomorrow. We're going to hit the workout room and you're *going* to learn some self-defense moves."

Chapter Five

I think you know in your heart you're safe with me...

It was Thursday, and Cassie couldn't stop rolling
Nick's words around in her head. There wasn't a man
in the world she considered safe. Maybe Blake Randall, but as her employer, he held an awful lot of power
over her. She trusted him, but he wasn't exactly "safe."
There was a difference.

She hadn't felt afraid when Nick stepped inside her
apartment Sunday morning to take the second box of
mugs from where Nora had them stored in the laundry
room. She'd felt…uneasy. On edge. His presence, with
his loud, confident, king-of-the-world attitude, seemed
to suck all the air out of the place. He was true to his
word, taking less than five minutes. He'd taken the mugs
downstairs, accepted a free to-go cup from Nora as
thanks, then left with barely a nod in her direction.

She pulled the office curtain aside and picked up the

hidden stapler. It was the second time this week Nick had used that hiding spot. He was slipping, probably distracted now that Blake was back from vacation and grilling him about his plans for this resort as well as setting up a travel schedule to visit the other Randall Resorts International properties during the next quarter.

But Nick hadn't forgotten his promise to teach her self-defense, no matter how many times she tried to tell him it wasn't necessary. On Monday, he'd pointed to his face and said "pepper spray" to remind her of her so-called failure. Today would be their second session, and he'd warned her things were going to get more challenging. On Monday, he'd basically lectured her about judging proximity—when to use pepper spray (six to ten feet), when to use car keys in the fingers (within a foot) and when to go for the crotch kick (only if there's body-to-body contact). He explained the thumbs-to-the-eyeballs trick for if the struggle was up close. She'd objected, doubting she could press on someone's eyeballs, and he said the move was for life-or-death situations. She'd been in that type of situation more than once with Don. Yeah, she'd have gladly put his eyes out if she could have.

She heard the elevator ping down the hall, followed immediately by the sound of male voices echoing loudly in the hallway. Nick was telling a story about some would-be thief they caught nude in a chimney in LA. She braced herself just as the door to the office suite flew open. Blake was in the lead, laughing and giving her a quick nod before heading to his office. Right on his heels were Brad from IT and Tim from security, and bringing up the rear and laughing the loudest was Nick. The onslaught of noisy men set off all of Cassie's alarms, but she'd taken a deep breath before their arrival and managed to flash them a smile. Brad and Tim waved and greeted her before following Blake, but Nick stopped at her desk, a furrow of concern appearing between his brows.

"Everything okay?"

"You mean other than being invaded by what sounded like the entire second fleet? Yeah, I'm fine." She thought she'd managed to hold on to her bright smile, but he clearly didn't buy it.

"Sorry about that. I wasn't thinking."

She wasn't sure what to do with his apology. It wasn't something she had a lot of experience with when it came to men. Before she could come up with a response, Blake stuck his head out of his office door.

"You coming, Nick?" He frowned when he saw Nick leaning over Cassie's desk. "What's going on?"

"I was just apologizing to Cassie for the racket we made. I've gotta grab my file on the lighting I was looking at for the parking lots, and I'll be right in." Nick headed into his office, but Blake stayed put.

"Did our noise really bother you?" he asked.

"No, no. Of course not." Her face warmed.

"Then why was Nick apologizing?"

She busied herself moving papers around on her desk. She didn't want Blake fretting about her.

"I have no idea. Honestly, everything's fine."

Blake watched her for another moment, then shrugged and turned away. Before she could relax, Nick strolled out of his office with a file in his hand. He slowed as he passed her, his voice low and just for her ears.

"Five o'clock in the gym?" Worried that Blake might still be listening, she nodded, not even looking up. Nick reached out and knocked over her stapler with his finger as he passed, causing her to jump.

She reached for the stapler with a roll of her eyes.

"West!" Blake shouted from his office. "Come on, man!"

Nick gave her a playful grin. "Later, slugger."

The door to Blake's office had barely closed when Amanda Randall arrived, tanned and smiling. She set a paper bag on the corner of Cassie's desk.

"I'm betting you haven't had lunch yet, right?"

Cassie reached for the bag eagerly. Amanda was a great cook, which had never been Cassie's strong point. "No, but something tells me I'm going to have lunch now."

Amanda sat in one of the chairs by the window. "Only if you like roast beef sandwiches with cheddar cheese and horseradish sauce. Hey, the girls and I are going to the Chalet tonight for pizza. Wanna join us?" As much as Cassie liked "the girls"—Amanda's cousins Nora, who owned the coffee shop, and Melanie, who owned a clothing boutique in town—she had another commitment tonight that she was oddly reluctant to cancel.

"I can't, but thanks anyway."

Amanda, for all her blond curls, baby blue eyes and bubbly demeanor, was a smart and intuitive woman. "Can't? Or won't? I don't like the thought of you sitting alone in that apartment all the time. Being a hermit isn't good for you."

Being a hermit kept her safe, but she didn't bother reminding her friend of that. Amanda's assumption that she was turning into a recluse, while true, still rankled.

"I actually have plans tonight." She regretted the words as soon as she said them. Now she was going to have to explain something she wasn't sure she even understood.

"I'm sorry… What? You have *plans*? What kind of plans?"

She stalled by taking a bite of the sandwich. "Oh, wow, this is delicious…"

"Yeah, yeah, I know." Amanda took the arm of Cassie's chair and turned it so they faced each other. "Now tell me about these 'plans' of yours."

She glanced at Blake's closed door and lowered her voice. "I'm…meeting with Nick West at five o'clock." She took another bite of the sandwich, watching the speculation in Amanda's eyes.

"Meeting him for…?"

"A training session of sorts." More sandwich. The heck with stalling. The sandwich was really just that good.

Amanda leaned back in her chair, crossing her legs and folding her arms.

"Honey, I have two children. One's a teenager and one's a toddler. They will both tell you that I always sniff out the truth no matter how long it takes, so you may as well spill it."

Cassie set the sandwich down on a napkin, nodding in surrender.

"He's teaching me self-defense."

Cassie's mouth and eyes went round simultaneously. "Nick West? Nick West, the hot security guy?"

"Shh! He's in Blake's office, for God's sake."

Amanda lowered her voice, but not her astonishment.

"Nick West is teaching you self-defense? As in, really teaching you? One-on-one? Or is this some class he's offering?"

"It's a…private class."

"Holy shit, what happened to you in the week I was gone? You're going to let a hot hunk of man show you self-defense moves? Let him touch you? Learn to throw him down on the floor? Of course, now that I've met the guy, I wouldn't mind throwing him down myself!"

"It's not like that. And you're married. To Nick's boss."

"Hey, just because I'm married to the sexiest man I know doesn't mean I'm *blind*. But I'm more interested in what *you* think. The guy just got here, and you've become such good friends that you're okay engaging in hand-to-hand combat with him? All sweaty, up close and personal? That's not the Cassie I left in Gallant Lake last week." Her smile faded. "Wait, did something happen? Are you doing this because Don did something?"

Cassie was so caught up in the thought of "up close and personal" that she almost didn't answer. And when she did, she once again shared more than she'd intended.

"I pepper-sprayed him."

"Who? *Don?*"

"Of course not! *Nick*. He startled me in the parking lot last Friday night and I hit him with pepper spray. He was somewhat critical of my technique."

Amanda's look of horror quickly slid into one of great amusement. "You pepper-sprayed the new head of security? Here at the resort? That's priceless! Does Blake know?"

"Not from me. And I doubt Nick's bragging about it, since it didn't end well for him."

"So you assaulted the man and he responded by generously offering to give you private self-defense lessons? Why?"

And that was just one of several hundred-thousand-dollar questions, wasn't it? Why was Nick offering to help her? Why had she agreed? And would there really be sweaty, up-close contact in the process? And how exactly did she feel about that?

* * *

Nick had been in the resort's third-floor workout room for a full fifteen minutes with no sign of Cassie. Looked like she was going to blow him off. He was half hoping she *would* quit. Offering private lessons was a bad idea on a couple of levels. It was probably considered unprofessional—it showed favoritism, or something. It could be taken the wrong way, for sure. Was it creepy? Forward? She didn't seem any more interested in him than he was in her, though. She was a looker, but he'd never been drawn to meek women.

He moved from the treadmill to the free weights. He should have told her to go take a class or read a book or a dozen other things besides offering to train her personally. After all, while she was at work, his security team would keep her safe. And when she wasn't at work, it was none of his business. If she didn't show up today, he'd urge her to go find a gym somewhere and relieve himself of the responsibility. He'd learned with Jada that getting involved in solving someone else's problems only led to heartache.

There was a movement near the door and he looked up to find Cassie watching him, her eyes dark and unreadable. Her hair was pulled back into her usual ponytail. She wore a baggy gray sweatshirt over black leggings, with a pair of sneakers that looked new. So she'd been paying attention on Monday when he told her those old canvas flats were not going to cut it for actual exercise. That was good. It meant that, despite her skepticism, she was taking this seriously. Which meant there was no good way to get out of teaching her what she needed to know.

He set the weights down quietly, conscious of her aversion to loud noises.

"You're late."

Her cheeks flushed pink. "I had a last-minute call, and then I had to change. I'm sorry…" Her brows furrowed that way they always did when she said those two words. As if they were acid on her lips. Her shoulders straightened. "But I'm here now, so we should get sweaty…I mean…busy."

He laughed at her stammered words. "Sweaty, huh? We can do sweaty if you want, but I think we should take it slow. I want to show you some basics today that you won't need a lot of strength for."

"You're the instructor."

"You know, it wouldn't hurt for you to get sweaty once in a while." Her eyes went big and he laughed again. "I meant you should start some strength training and maybe some running. The stronger you are, the more confident you'll feel, and the more effective you'll be."

She scoffed. "Running? You think I should start *running*? I don't think so."

"If not running, then find something you enjoy that will give you some cardio and strength. Go hiking, or mountain biking, or anything. I'm telling you, Cassie, the more you move, the better you'll understand your body, and the better you'll be at defending yourself. Not to mention it's just healthy to do."

She looked at him for a long moment before shaking her head. "I'm not looking to become some health nut or kickboxer. Let's stick to the plan. Teach me the basics."

"You need to warm up first. Give me fifteen minutes on the elliptical."

"Why?"

"As you said, I'm the instructor. And you're my little grasshopper, so hop on that machine and show me what you got."

She obeyed, but not happily. "I don't understand what this has to do with self-defense. I'm not going to be able to elliptic away from someone." After only a few minutes, she was puffing for air and grimacing. Her legs were probably already cramping. She was in worse shape than he'd thought. He grabbed a fresh bottle of water from his bag and handed it to her. She came to a stop.

"If you can't make it five minutes on this machine, you aren't going to be able to do diddly against an attacker. You think you can fight a man the size of me or bigger? When you're standing there wheezing at me after doing basically nothing?" He didn't let her reply, grabbing the bottle from her hands and gesturing to her to get moving. "Okay, new plan. You hit this room every morning, and you get on the elliptical and go until you can't go anymore. Eventually, you'll be going thirty minutes or more, and you'll thank me for how great you feel."

"Don't...hold your...breath..."

It was ironic, listening to her talk about breath when she didn't have any. He gave her a wide grin.

"Okay, let's review while you're warming up. I'm an attacker. I'm six feet away and coming at you. What do you do?"

"I...use the...pepper spray..." She huffed out the words between gasps for air.

He shook his head. "Do you have pepper spray in your hands right now?"

She shot him a glare. "No!"

"Then forget it. If the perp is within twenty feet and running at you, you don't have time to dig in your purse for pepper spray. Same with a gun. Unless it's in your hand at that point, it's useless."

"I don't…want a…gun."

He rubbed the left side of his face. "Yeah, you're dangerous enough with pepper spray. I hate to think what you'd have done the other night with a handgun. So what do you do?"

"Scream?"

He shrugged. "Meh. It's not a bad thing, but it's not going to save you unless you're lucky enough to have the dumbest bad guy in the world and he's attacking you in a public place. Try again."

"Hit…him?"

"Where? With what?"

"I don't… Oh, shit… I can't…do this." She stopped moving. "Okay, maybe you're right about my conditioning." A soft sheen of sweat covered her face. "I'd hit him with my fist."

"Yeah?" Nick folded his arms on his chest. "Show me a fist."

She did what so many inexperienced fighters do. She folded her fingers over her thumb and into a fist.

"Do you intend to hit me as hard as you can with that fist? Maybe right on my jaw?"

She looked at her fist, frowning, as if she knew this was a trick question. Finally she nodded, but without conviction.

"Cassie, if you hit me hard with your hand folded like that, you'll not only break your damn thumb, but you won't hurt me at all. Go ahead, get off the elliptical and take a swing in my direction. Punch at my hand." He saw the doubt in her eyes. "I won't let you hurt yourself. I'm just trying to show you how limited your motion is with your hand like that."

She took a swing, hitting the flat of his hand, but he didn't offer any resistance, letting his hand come away.

"Okay. Now make a fist with your thumb *outside* your fingers, like this." He clenched his hand in a fist, releasing it the minute he saw her skin go pale. Shit. She'd seen a man's fist before. He swallowed hard. "Show me."

She did as he asked. He took her hand and moved her thumb, then curled her wrist so her knuckles were forward. "Now hit my hand. And put some oomph behind it. Start with your body low and rise up into the punch."

Her first attempt wasn't half-bad. Her next few were better, as she started to grasp the concept of lowering her center of gravity and propelling upward with her body, not just her small fist. When she actually connected with his hand with enough force to send it snapping back, she flashed him a wide grin.

"I did it!"

"You did. But throwing a punch is going to be your last resort. You need to know how to do it, but honestly, unless you connect with the guy's nose, or maybe the center of his chest, you're not going to stop him. He'll return the punch and it'll be lights out for you unless it's an eighty-year-old mugger."

Her eyes narrowed in on him. "So I can't use pepper spray and I can't scream and I can't punch. What do I do, just stand there?"

His curiosity got the best of him.

"What happened to you, Cassie? Were you assaulted? Mugged?"

She stepped back and visibly shrank before his eyes, shoulders dropping, head lowered, gaze fixed on the floor by his feet.

"I don't want to talk about it." His chest tightened at some of the darker possibilities.

"I get that, but it would help me to know what's driving your fear."

She stared at the floor so long and so intently he wouldn't have been surprised if smoke started rising from near his feet. He'd done enough interrogations to know that it was human instinct to fill a silence with words. He *could* wait her out, but she wasn't a perp. He opened his mouth, but she beat him to it, painting a picture he was hoping not to see.

"I was in a parking garage. At night. He came from between two cars. I was checking my phone and he was on me before I knew it." Her voice was monotone, like a robot reciting a programmed recording. "That's all you need to know."

"That's why you're so vigilant now. And jumpy."

Her head snapped up. "I'm not that jumpy."

"Says the woman who threw a stapler at my head and pepper-sprayed me in the face."

A trace of a smile tugged at her mouth.

"Okay. I'm jumpy. And I hate it."

He nodded, considering the best way to come at this problem. The "problem" at hand being Cassie's fear. He'd deal with the problem of his physical reaction to her vulnerability—a trait he generally abhorred in women—when he was alone and could think more clearly.

"Look, if a guy is coming at you with the intent to do you harm, you need to fight. Show him you mean business. Plant your feet wide and solid, like this." He took up a fighter's stance, and she did her best to mimic it. "Get in his face. Make noise. Fight like hell, and fight dirty."

"You said not to scream."

"No, I said it probably wouldn't do any good. But I'm not talking about screaming. I'm talking about *noise*. Aggressive noise. Have you ever watched karate or judo or even tennis?" She nodded. "Did you notice how some players make loud noises as they're swinging? Even if they're just chopping a wooden board? That sound makes them feel more powerful. It's more like a roar than a scream, and you can learn to do that once your confidence gets better."

He stepped up in front of her, hating the way she shrank back, but not reacting to it. She was going to have to get used to this. "When the attacker is up close and personal, look to find a weak spot."

"You mean his balls?"

He barked out a laugh. "No, that's another lesson, when I'm wearing protection. Look at my face. What are my weak spots there?"

She studied him intently, and he did his best not to fidget under her examination. There was something about her gaze that made him energized and restless. Uncomfortable and excited at the same time. The sensation kicked him way outside his comfort zone.

"You told me about the eyes already."

"What else do you see that's vulnerable?"

"Your nose?"

"Right. But here's the key—don't swing at it from the side. Come at it from below, with the heel of your hand slamming up against it. Picture yourself driving his nose right into his skull. It'll hurt like hell, and it could give you a chance to break free. Like this." He took her hand and pressed it against the base of his own nose. And damned if he didn't have the crazy urge to kiss the palm of her hand. He shook it off and tried to stay focused. "But just like the punch, put your whole body into it. Think of every move as your only shot." She pressed against his nose and he grinned at her. "We won't be practicing that one. At least not on me. Now what else do you see that's vulnerable?"

Her eyes darkened when her gaze fell to his mouth. He did his best to ignore the stirring he felt below his waist. It was a normal response to a pretty woman studying his mouth, right?

"Yes, the mouth can be vulnerable. It's not the best place to start, but lips are tender. Pinch, bite or smack him with your elbow, like this." In slow motion, he swung his elbow out and stopped an inch from her mouth. "If you've got room to swing, use your elbow before you use your fist. It's harder and more likely to do harm without hurting yourself in the process. What else?"

"I don't know. That's about it, right?"

He moved his hands to each side of her face and gently tugged on her ears. Her eyes met his, and it took all his focus to stay on topic. "No one likes having their ears yanked. And if you really latch on and pull, the guy will be screaming. If you're in close contact and your hands are free, don't hesitate to pull on those ears as hard as you can." He released her ears, but his fingers lingered, brushing back her hair and stroking the tender skin of her neck... *What the hell?* He pulled his hands back and stepped away from Cassie. She looked as confused as he felt. But she hadn't stopped him. Interesting. He cleared his throat.

"Yeah...so...that's about it, I guess...for tonight... um..." Nick couldn't believe his own voice. He was babbling. Nick West, tough cop, was *babbling*. And all because he'd touched Cassie's warm, soft skin with the tips of his fingers.

Color flooded her cheeks as she blinked and looked away. "Yes. Of course. That gave me plenty to...um... think about... Thanks." She turned and grabbed the small canvas bag she'd dropped by the door.

He regained some composure once she turned her back on him. "Hey, don't forget about the elliptical in the morning."

She looked over her shoulder, her hand on the door handle. "Tomorrow's Friday."

"Yeah? And? No excuses, girl." He nodded toward the machine. "You need to make yourself stronger, Cass. Give yourself a fighting chance. You owe yourself that much."

Chapter Six

Cassie stood outside the door to the Chalet for a long time. A really long time.

Amanda had been relentless about Cassie getting out more, threatening to drop off a dozen cats at the apartment to complete her transition into a little old crazy cat lady. Amanda knew why Cassie was leery of going out, getting attached to people, exposing herself. But Cassie knew she had a point. When Julie Brown invited her to the weekly gathering of resort employees at the local bar tonight, as she did almost every week, she'd surprised them both by agreeing.

Maybe it was Nick's king-of-the-world attitude rubbing off on her. Her self-defense classes had morphed into strength and agility training over the past few weeks. He'd been horrified by her lack of conditioning and athleticism, which she'd never seen as a problem. But the time he forced... No, that wasn't fair... The time he *encouraged* her to spend on the elliptical had proved his point. She'd had no stamina at all. She absently rubbed her lower back. She was paying the price with a host of sore muscles, but she was also starting to feel a little more confident. A little stronger, both physically and mentally. He was challenging her, and surprisingly, she liked it.

She could hear the band playing country rock, and the hoots and hollers of the patrons inside. Some of them were her coworkers. Julie. Tim. Brad. Josie from the restaurant. It was the innocent sound of people having a fun Friday night in a small town. Nothing to worry about. But she hadn't thought there was anything to worry about in Milwaukee either, that night she went out to have fun with some coworkers and ended up in intensive care.

It was the anger of that memory that propelled her forward. This was *not* Milwaukee. She steeled herself and stepped inside. She could do this. She had to do this. She had to start living again.

Julie ran over, laughing in a high-pitched voice that suggested she'd already had more than a few drinks. "Cassie! Oh, my God, I'm so glad you came tonight! It's turned into quite a party." Julie waved her arm vaguely in the direction of the U-shaped bar. "It's one of those nights when everyone invited actually showed up, even *you*!"

Cassie recognized most of the people gathered on one side of the bar. Mostly front desk staff. And one tall, dark-haired man at the corner of the bar, watching her with a wry smile over the rim of his beer glass. Nick West. What was he doing here? Trying to prove he was one of the guys? She frowned. That wasn't fair. Maybe he was just trying to make friends in a new town.

Julie followed Cassie's gaze and nudged her shoulder. "I know, right? The girls have been practically killing each other to take that empty stool next to him, but he said he's saving it for a friend. We're all hoping that friend is as hot as Nick is, without the I'm-your-boss baggage."

"He's not my boss." Cassie said the words to herself, but Julie managed to hear them in the noisy bar. Maybe Julie read lips.

"That's right, you both report to Blake. Are you interested?"

"What?" Cassie forced herself to look away from Nick and met Julie's speculative gaze. "Interested? I'm not interested in any man. Been there. Done that."

Got the scars to show for it...

"One and done, huh? He must have been a doozy." Julie linked her arm through Cassie's. "Come on, let's get us some drinks."

Cassie did her best not to make eye contact with Nick when they walked past, but he made that impossible when he stood and greeted them.

"If you gals are looking for seats, you can have these two." He gestured to the bar stool he'd just vacated and the one beside it.

"I thought you were saving it for someone."

Nick looked directly at Cassie. "You're someone."

Julie looked back and forth between them with a grin. "Okay, then. Thanks!"

Having Nick here set her plans to *slowly* start a social life a little off balance. This was no longer a gathering of employees having fun. This was Nick West, and she was never on her best footing when he was around. For one thing, he made her snarkier than usual.

"Sitting at a bar seems a little tame for you, Mr. West. I'm surprised you're not out climbing a mountain or hunting wild boar with your bare hands."

His right brow arched high, making a direct hit on

her heart. "And I'm surprised you're not curled up in a bathrobe with a book of pretty poetry and cup of tea, Miss Smith."

He had no idea how tempting that idea was. "That actually sounds lovely. You might want to try it sometime."

He grinned. "Are you inviting me to a private poetry reading?"

She tried to picture the two of them sitting by the big windows in her loft, reading quietly and glancing at each other warmly as they sipped their tea. Her reaction to the vision was visceral, with her entire body heating and a shiver of some unknown emotion tracing down her spine. She forced herself to laugh lightly but wasn't sure if it sounded genuine at all. This was a game she wasn't used to playing.

"I think there's as much chance of that happening as there is of the two of us going mountain climbing together."

Julie chimed in, looking delighted. "Oh, my God, you two are adorable together!"

She and Nick both looked at her in surprise, speaking in unison.

"We're not together!"

Julie waved her hand dismissively. "Whatever. You're both so serious at work, but here you are being all teasing and flirty and it's… It's cute. That's all."

Nick glanced around, and it burned Cassie to realize he might be wondering if any other employees thought he was being "cute." Probably not a trait the head of security wanted to be known for. And she'd started it all with her sarcastic comment.

"I'm…I'm sorry." She closed her eyes, furious with herself for saying those two words so often. "I should probably…" She started to slide off her seat, but Nick stopped her with a hand on her hip. He moved his hand away as soon as she stopped, but she could still feel the warmth of it.

"No, don't go. And stop with the damn apologizing." His voice dropped for her ears only. "You do that way too much." His gaze locked on hers, and she swallowed hard. Yes, she apologized too much. It was a survival tool she hadn't managed to shake. His eyes softened. He leaned against the bar, his chest only inches from her back, his breath blowing across her neck as he spoke. "What'll you have to drink, ladies?"

Julie held up her glass. "Chardonnay for me, thanks."

Cassie managed to nod and speak without stuttering. "Sounds good. I'll have the same."

Nick caught the bartender's attention and placed the order, chatting with the guy as he filled their glasses. That was Nick. Outgoing. Full of life and laughs. Her total and complete opposite. Their drinks were delivered, and Nick moved on down the bar to talk to Tim. Cassie was relieved. She didn't want to be rude to the guy, but she also didn't want to hang out at a bar with a man who made her body tingle in dangerous ways.

Everyone started to mingle back and forth, and within an hour, there was a cluster of resort employees standing around Julie and her. People were laughing and jostling each other, and some even took to the dance floor when the music started. Cassie couldn't relax completely, but she did her best, laughing along with everyone else at the stories being told. She didn't have any funny stories of her own to share, but no one pressed her. Most gave her a quick look of surprise when they saw her, but no one made a big deal of her first outing with them.

Julie was telling a story about the woman who tried to tell her the rottweiler she had stuffed into her wheeled dog carrier was within the resort's fifteen-pound limit for pets. Cassie excused herself for the ladies' room, located beyond the dance floor and down a darkened hall. The back of her neck prickled as she stepped into the hall, and her hand automatically reached for her bag. Damn it. She'd left the bag, and her pepper spray, on her chair. She pulled her shoulders back and scolded herself for being paranoid. She couldn't live the rest of her days afraid of being around people. As Nick said, there were ways of being smart that would keep her safe without needing weapons or an armed guard. She just had to focus on her surroundings and be prepared. She locked the bathroom door quickly.

She saw the man as soon as she stepped back out into the shadowy hall. He was behind her, near the men's room. Waiting. He smiled when she glanced his way. She was in a small-town bar with friends. It wasn't likely he was an actual threat. But being alone with him in this hall with the music blaring so loudly that no one would hear her scream was not a wise thing. And self-protection was all about acting wisely. Cassie straightened.

Never look like a victim.

Nick had repeated those words a dozen times in the past few weeks. *If you look like a victim, you're a temptation someone might not be able to resist.* It wasn't about dressing or looking a certain way. He was trying to make the point that a distracted, weak-looking woman was exactly what bad guys were looking for. A smart bad guy would think twice about approaching an alert woman with a bold stride and a don't-mess-with-me expression, even if she was faking it. As Sun Tzu said, *all warfare is based on deception.*

She gave a quick, polite grin to let the man know she saw him and turned toward the dance floor, acting far more unconcerned than she felt. Then she felt his hand on her arm. She swallowed her panic and tried to pull away, but he didn't release her.

"I saw you laughing with your friends at the bar. You're pretty. Wanna dance?" His words rolled into each other just enough to tell her he was drunk. As much as her heart was screaming *Danger! Danger!* her brain told her there was no threat to his words. He wasn't out to hurt her. He was a drunk guy on a Friday night looking for a dance. All the same, she curled her hand into a proper fist, just in case. She struggled to come up with an appropriately noncommittal smile.

"Thanks, but no. Now if you'll excuse me…" She tried again to tug her arm away from him, but he wasn't giving up. The booze had clearly given him a shot of confidence in his ability to woo a woman in the bathroom hallway. *Damn it, please give up!*

"Aw, come on, babe. Just one dance. And after that, you can walk away if you want…"

Her spine went rigid with defiance. She was so tired of being ordered around. Of being told what she could and could not do. There was no attempt to smile this time around.

"Actually, I can walk away from you right now, *without* dancing. And that's what I'm going to do." She planted her feet firmly, imagining herself lowering her center of gravity as Nick taught her to do. Then she pressed the heel of her hand against the guy's chest and pushed, pulling her arm free. He stumbled back a step, eyes wide in surprise.

"Okay. Okay. You're one of those independent women. I dig it. But, honey…"

He reached for her, but before she could decide how much pain this drunk deserved to feel, he was gone in a blur of dark color that came from behind her. She heard the thump of the guy's back hitting the wall, and the whoosh of air that escaped him at impact.

"You want to walk out of here under your own power?" Nick West growled the words through clenched teeth as he leaned on his forearm, which was braced against the guy's chest. "If so, I suggest you keep your grabby-ass hands in your pockets and find an exit *now*."

The drunk nodded quickly, and Nick stepped back. The man scooted past Cassie without even glancing in her direction. Leaving Cassie alone in the dark hallway. With Nick. Which suddenly felt far more dangerous than before.

"What do you think you're doing?" She was surprised at the edge of anger to her voice, and Nick seemed to be, too.

"I *think* I'm saving your ass from the drunk dude who just ran off." Nick frowned. "Did he hurt you?"

"No! I didn't need your help, Nick. I had it under control."

"He had you by the arm. Out of sight in a dead-end hallway. I swear to God, woman, you seem determined to put yourself in harm's way…"

"I freed my own damn arm, and he was just a drunk." She lifted her chin. "And now I'm in that lonely hallway with *you*, so what's the difference?"

"The difference is you know *I'm* not going to drag you into one of these closets and hurt you. You didn't know that about him. But you're right—you did free your own arm. Without me." The corner of his mouth quirked up into a crooked grin. "Wonder where you learned that trick?"

He was fishing for compliments. When she didn't answer right away, he rubbed the back of his neck, glancing over his shoulder at the crowded dance floor, where people were stomping along to a line dance. Her sense of fairness finally kicked in.

"Yes, I'm a good little student." She looked around, chagrined to realize she hadn't noticed the other doors in the hall, one labeled "office" and the other labeled for "employees only." The drunk *could* have pulled her into one of those rooms and no one would have known. Except Nick, who'd apparently followed her. Looked out for her. She lost more of her anger. "Now you know why I stay home and read books. I don't have to fight my way to and from the restroom when I'm home by myself."

Nick stepped closer, and her back brushed the wall as she tried to retreat.

"Maybe not, but sitting around alone, doing nothing, is no way to live." He shuddered. "I'd go stir-crazy."

She couldn't help smiling at the thought of always-restless Nick sitting in an easy chair with a book in his hand. "Maybe we both live the lives best suited for us. You charge after adventure, and I read about it."

The timbre of his voice changed, lowering in volume and increasing in intensity.

"Maybe the proper balance is somewhere between our two extremes."

She nodded. "You might be right. Maybe we could help each other out with that."

There was something about this guy that made her blurt out her thoughts before she had a chance to digest them.

"What are you proposing?"

"What? Oh…um…nothing. It was just a random thought. An observation more than an invitation."

She needed to get out of here. She wasn't used to this type of banter with a man, and she wasn't good at it. All this push and pull, advance and retreat, was a mysterious dance she'd never done before. After all, Don always made sure there were no obstacles to her being attracted to him. He'd paved the way and groomed her to rely on him. But Nick didn't do that. Nick kept her guessing, left her wondering if he wanted to be around her or if she was nothing more than a pest. She started to turn away but stopped when Julie walked into the hallway, carrying Cassie's purse.

"There you are! I thought you left and forgot this… Oh…" Julie noticed Nick's presence and her eyes went wide. "What's going on, guys?"

Nick moved a bit farther from Cassie, but his eyes never left hers. "We were just talking about helping each other out with a few things."

Julie looked speculative. "Out *with* or out *of* a few things?"

"Oh, my God, don't be ridiculous!" Cassie felt her cheeks warming. "We just bumped into each other, and now I'm leaving." She grabbed her bag from Julie. Nick took her arm.

"I'll walk you to your car." Of course he would, and it would be a waste of time to argue. Julie winked as they walked past her. Cassie and Nick would probably be gossip fodder at the resort Monday morning.

The employees were still at the bar, laughing and drinking. A few waved at them, and a few more watched with interest. Cassie didn't like people talking. Too much talk was why she'd had to leave Cleveland. That's how Don found her there. That's why her last name was now Smith. Nick nodded good-night to the group, then opened the door and held it for her to go out.

"You can go join the guys, Nick. I'll be…"

He looked down at her and continued to hold the door, his expression saying it all.

"Right. You're going to walk me to my car whether I need it or not."

"Now you're getting it." He followed her across the dark lot, and she tried to define the emotions swirling around inside her. It wasn't fear—she knew what fear felt like. But the jolt of adrenaline wasn't dissimilar. She was on edge. Anticipating, but anticipating what? That Nick would touch her again? Or that he wouldn't?

She resolved that question when she almost walked right past her car. She stopped so quickly that Nick bumped against her back, his hand resting on her waist to steady them both. But she didn't feel steady. He was usually quick to remove his hands from her, ever since that second training session when he let his fingers linger on her neck. But his hand wasn't moving now. In fact, she could almost swear his grip tightened just a little. And damn if she didn't lean into him.

"Cassie…" Nick cleared his throat, his grip loosening but not releasing her. "Isn't this your car?"

"Oh…yes. Sorry." She stepped away, proud of herself for being able to do it calmly and thanking the heavens for the dimly lit lot. He wouldn't be able to see her confusion. She reached in her bag for her keys.

"You aren't going to pepper-spray me again are you?" She welcomed the wry humor in his voice. This was the Nick she knew how to deal with.

"No, you're too close for it to be effective." His brow rose in admiration, and she grinned. "At this range, I'd probably try running first, or maybe throwing something at you and screaming, since we're in a public place." She glanced around, trying to remember her lessons. "If you came any closer…" He stepped toward her, stopping just short of brushing against her chest. He was testing her, and she was ready. "Now it's heel time. I'd stomp on the bridge of your foot with my heel while simultaneously jamming the heel of my hand into the bottom of your nose." She mimicked the moves as she spoke.

Nick gave a short laugh. "You really are a good little student."

Cassie felt an unexpected burst of pride. It had been only a few weeks, but she was stronger. And smarter. She gave him what he was looking for, because he deserved it.

"I've had a good teacher."

"You have. But you also listened and followed through. That'll come in handy when we go rock climbing tomorrow."

Cassie stepped back, bumping into the car. "Excuse me?"

"Wasn't that the deal you suggested? I teach you to have a life, and you try to teach me how to sit still and read a book?"

"No, I wasn't serious…that was just… No. We're not doing that. I am *not* hanging from some cliff by a rope!"

He folded his arms across his chest.

"Fair enough. How about a simple hike up Gallant Mountain? There's a trail. We'll stop before the rock climbing part." His head tilted. "Let's see how all that elliptical work has helped your stamina."

A rough laugh escaped her. "That's a hard *no*. Not happening."

It was as if she hadn't spoken. "Blake has a conference call scheduled with the Barbados resort at two, so I'll pick you up after that. We'll still have enough daylight. It'll get chilly as the sun gets lower, so bring a sweatshirt or jacket. And good walking shoes."

"Did you hear me? Not. Happening."

"It's a lot of walking—wear thick socks or double up so you don't blister."

"Nick! I'm not doing that." What part of *not happening* did he not understand?

He reached behind her to open her car door. "Come on, get in. I want to make sure you get out of here safely. Text me when you're in your apartment."

"I don't have your number…"

He handed her his phone. "Send a text to yourself. Then you'll have it."

She stared at Nick's phone in her hand.

"Yeah, and you'll have mine." A total of four people knew her current mobile number. Amanda. Blake. Her mom. And an assistant district attorney in Milwaukee. Everyone else had the landline number at the apartment.

…*I think you know in your heart you're safe with me*…

She typed her number in and sent a short text, knowing he'd read it.

Not happening.

She handed the phone back. He read it but didn't react.

"Text me when you're inside, or I'll be driving over to check on you."

"Don't give that number to anyone."

Nick's head snapped up. This was a matter of life and death for her.

"I won't, Cass. You have my word." She thought about all the promises Don broke in the past. But Nick wasn't Don. At least, he didn't seem to be. It was too late to take the number back, so she finally nodded. What was done was done.

She kept her eyes on Nick in the rearview mirror as she drove out of the lot, his expression troubled in the glow of her taillights. He had questions. And she wasn't about to answer them.

Chapter Seven

Nick had never been the type to go after viral social media fame. But the look on Cassie's face when she opened the back door to her apartment Saturday afternoon was so priceless he regretted not capturing it with his phone. She clearly wasn't expecting him, judging from the unicorn leggings and oversize T-shirt she was wearing. Her hair was pulled up into some kind of messy twist on top of her head. Her feet were bare, showing off surprisingly bright blue toenails.

But her expression? That was the prizewinner. Her green-gold eyes were wide, and her mouth formed a perfect, pink-lined O. She seemed frozen there, her hand clutching the edge of the door. Cassie slowly took him in, and once again, her lingering gaze had the power to make his blood heat. She started with his well-worn hiking shoes, then on up to his cargo shorts and rugby shirt before her gaze finally reached his face.

"What are you doing here?"

"Uh… We're going hiking, remember?"

Her head went back and forth emphatically. "What I remember is telling you that I was *not* going hiking. So thanks for stopping, but you're on your own." She started to push the door closed, but Nick's hand shot out to stop it.

"Have you even stepped outside today?" He gestured behind him to the bright blue May sky and the maples leafing out on the other side of the parking lot. The air was fresh and rain-washed from the showers they'd had that morning. "You haven't, have you? You've been cooped up in this place all damn day." She opened her mouth to protest, but it was obvious he was right. "Come on. Go change, and we'll take a pleasant stroll on the mountainside—nothing challenging. You need to get some sun and exercise, and you'll love the views from up there." She still hesitated, so he offered a trade-off. "Look, you go for a hike with me today, and I promise to give you a day doing whatever you want. Including reading and sipping tea, if you insist."

Her eyes narrowed, but the corner of her mouth betrayed her amusement.

"Whatever I want?"

Nick had the sinking feeling he was getting the losing end of this bargain, but it was too late to back out now.

"Whatever you want." He held back a groan at her obvious pleasure with his concession. "But it's late and it's gonna get cool as the sun gets low, so hurry up."

There was another moment of indecision before Cassie nodded. "Fine. Give me ten minutes. And this had better be a nice 'stroll' because I am not climbing any cliffs. Got it?"

"Yes, ma'am." He remembered how tense she'd been

a few weeks ago when he went into her apartment to carry that box of mugs. "I'll wait for you in the Jeep." He tapped his watch. "Ten minutes."

The drive to the trailhead wasn't long, but it sure seemed that way with the silence hanging over the vehicle. Cassie had changed clothes in a flash, but she'd also withdrawn into Nick's least favorite of her personas—the quiet mouse. She was answering his questions about her day in single syllables, staring out the window instead of at him, huddled against the passenger door as if ready to open it at any second and throw herself out of the moving vehicle. He finally had enough and pulled off on the side of the mountain road.

"Tell me what's going on."

Her cheeks flamed, then paled. "Wh-what do you mean?"

"I know I coerced you into joining me on this hike, but the idea is for you to enjoy it. And you are definitely not enjoying yourself right now. Why?"

The color came back to her face and she straightened a little at his brusque question. "You can't just order me to have fun, Nick. I told you last night I didn't want to hike a mountain with you."

"And yet you changed your clothes and hopped into the Jeep with me when I showed up at your door. What's happening? Do you want to go back?"

A slideshow of emotions played across her face. As a cop, he'd always been good at reading people, but this woman defeated him every time. He had no idea what she was feeling, and he had a hunch she didn't know, either. But the primary emotion he picked up from her body language was...fear.

"Are you *afraid* of me?" Her silence spoke volumes. "You have got to be freaking kidding me..."

He slammed the Jeep into gear and did a U-turn. He wasn't kidnapping the woman, for God's sake. He was only trying to help her get out more. Had she really been too intimidated to refuse him? The thought gave him pause. How many times had Jada warned him about his "steamroller" approach when he thought he was right? Was that what he'd done to Cassie? He'd driven only a mile or two back toward town when Cassie sat up straight and spoke.

"Stop, Nick. Turn around. I don't want to go home."

This woman gave him emotional whiplash.

"Are you sure?" She nodded, and he pulled into the next driveway and turned back up the mountain. "Are you going to tell me what the problem is?"

She chewed on her lip for a moment, then turned to face him, her words coming out in a rush.

"I haven't been alone in a car with a man in a long time..." When her words trailed off, he took his eyes off the winding road just in time to see a single tear spill over. Damn. He hated when women cried. She hadn't told him much of her story since that day in the gym. She'd been attacked in a parking garage. Maybe the guy dragged her into a vehicle? *Shit.*

"When you were attacked..."

"No, not then." Her hands twisted in her lap. "I just haven't been alone in a car with a man driving in a really long time, and it freaked me out more than I thought it would." He turned away to focus on driving, and was thankful when she continued. "I tried to work through it in my head, but I couldn't get past it. I thought I'd be relieved when you turned the car around, but I wasn't. It felt like surrendering, and I don't want to do that."

"You're a fighter." His words were low, almost unintentional, but she heard him and gave a soft snort of laughter.

"You've said that before, but I'm *not*. I'm a mess." She gave a gasp of surprise when he turned off the pavement and started up the steep dirt track. "Where are we going?"

Nick was thankful for the change in subject. "We're going up the mountain. In the Jeep for as far as we can. Unless you'd rather walk?" The truck rocked as it hit a dip on the path. She grabbed the door, but she no longer looked like she wanted to escape. In fact, she was smiling and leaning forward, watching the brush sweep the sides of the truck. She laughed when the wheels spun in the mud from last night's rain, finally catching hold of solid ground and catapulting the vehicle forward.

He had his hands full with the driving, but he soaked in the sound of Cassie's laughter and held it in his heart like the precious thing it was. He couldn't help stealing a glance at her, and her smile had him letting up on the gas pedal and nearly driving into a tree.

It was the first *real* smile he'd seen on her. Oh, he'd seen her smile. The warm-but-professional smile she had for Blake Randall. The conspiratorial smile of friendship she shared with Amanda or Julie. The cool, polished smile she used with employees and visitors. And the involuntary smile of frustrated amusement she occasionally sent his way when he'd been teasing her over something.

But this smile… He glanced over again, and she laughed, one hand on the door and one braced on the dashboard as they climbed the rutted path… *This* smile was really something. It was…uninhibited. Genuine. Uncensored. Unguarded. All of Cassie's protective shields had come down, and he was seeing his new, most favorite version of her ever. He was seeing Cassie unfiltered.

"Is this what they call four-wheeling?"

They reached the small clearing where the path leveled off. A wooden gate with a no-trespassing sign blocked their way. Nick turned off the truck, glad to be able to face her now without putting their lives at risk.

"Not exactly. Four-wheeling is usually done on four-wheelers, but I guess sometimes it's with trucks. And that was actually a pretty decent track to drive up—not exactly off-roading..." Nick stopped abruptly. He was babbling like a nervous schoolboy. And Cassie was still smiling at him. In fact, she may have even giggled—something he wouldn't have thought possible before now.

"That was fun! I'm so glad we turned around!" Yeah, so was he. She looked around at the thick woods surrounding them. "Will you have room to turn here?"

"Eventually, sure. But first, we hike."

She looked at the gate and the posted sign and arched her brow. "You want me to go trespassing with you to take a hike I didn't want to take in the first place? I don't think so."

He grinned at her last-ditch attempt to avoid hiking and opened his door. "It's not trespassing if you have permission from the owner. And Blake Randall told me it's just fine."

Cassie was pretty sure her calf muscles were tearing apart. The burning pain had her wincing as she followed Nick up the steep path. She wondered if she'd ever walk without pain again. A "nice stroll," huh? This was more like climbing Kilimanjaro with no training.

A few weeks on the elliptical were no match for Gallant Mountain. She could ask Nick to stop, but she'd just asked for a break a few minutes ago, and that was the third one. She hadn't missed his amusement or his sigh of impatience when he'd glanced up the trail. She vowed not to stop again. Surely they'd be stopping soon. He'd *promised* her there would be no rock climbing, and she could see a wall of rugged gray getting closer.

Too bad her legs would be destroyed beyond repair by the time they got there.

Nick glanced over his shoulder and slowed. She knew he was already taking this hike much slower than he usually would, so she gave him the brightest smile she could muster.

He frowned. "You okay?"

No, I'm dying. Literally dying.

"I'm fine! Great!"

I'm in agony, and you know it, you bastard.

His brow rose. "Really? You're feeling great?"

How much longer are you going to torture me?

"Sure, great! Absolutely!"

He shook his head, and she was pretty sure he was laughing at her, but she couldn't prove it, since he was climbing up the trail again. She stuck her tongue out at his back and bit back a groan of pain as she followed. If only they'd stopped their little adventure after the truck drive up the mountain. That was fun.

She'd never done anything like it, with the engine growling, the tires searching for traction and the Jeep rocking back and forth like some amusement park ride. She'd been so inside her head when they left the apartment, fighting off her unease at being alone with a man who was literally in control of the vehicle and, therefore, her. But once Nick confronted her silence, and then was willing to take her *home* rather than make her uncomfortable, she'd finally set her fear aside. Nick was right—it was a gorgeous day and she'd been missing it, sitting inside with her book.

When he'd turned the truck onto the steep dirt road—all rutted and muddy—she was so surprised that all she could do was laugh. Never in a million years had she ever pictured herself bouncing around in a Jeep going up a mountain. And it was...*fun*. She couldn't remember the last time she'd had actual fun doing something. Not that she hadn't had moments of happiness or laughter since leaving Milwaukee, but to *do* something that was fun, instead of just laughing along while someone else did something... Yeah, she hadn't done that in years.

Even this hike, with all its pain—and she was in serious pain—was almost fun in a weird way. She was so far outside her normal comfort zone that she was pretty amazed at herself. And proud. She slowed for a moment, thinking about that last word. She was *proud* of herself. Pride was that odd, unrecognizable sensation she'd felt over the past few weeks as she pushed herself to become stronger. As she started taking responsibility for protecting herself. For standing her ground.

She tried to remember the last time she'd felt proud of herself. High school? She'd always had good grades, but reading and studying had come easy for her, so it wasn't a big challenge. College? Her social awkwardness as an introvert made it hard to fit in with any of the cliques and clubs, but she had worked hard to stay on the dean's list every semester. That was something to be proud of, right?

"Cass? Seriously, are you okay?" Nick was right in front of her now, snapping her out of her thoughts and back into the present. The present where her legs were in flames. She blew out a long, slow breath and tried to keep her face as neutral as possible.

"I'm great, Nick. Don't stop for me."

He gave her a crooked smile. "I didn't stop for you. I stopped because we're here."

She looked around in surprise. They'd reached a small, grassy clearing. To her right, a giant boulder—the size of a city bus—sat at the base of the rocky summit far above. To her left was a view of Gallant Lake that took her breath away.

The mountains around the lake glowed with the bright green of new growth. The clear blue sky above was reflected in the calm waters of the lake, creating a palette that screamed, "Spring!" Cassie walked toward the rocky drop-off, mesmerized by the view. Nick gently stopped her with a hand on her shoulder, releasing her as quickly as he'd touched her.

"After yesterday's rain, let's not chance the slip-factor on this cliff, okay?"

She didn't respond right away, staring at the view. Then she spun to face him.

"We did it! We made it to the top of the mountain! And my legs aren't cramping anymore... Well, not as much, anyway..."

His quick flash of amusement vanished. "Your legs were cramping? Here, drink some water." He reached around and pulled a metal water container out of the small canvas pack he had slung over his shoulder. "You're probably dehydrated. You didn't say you were getting leg cramps—that's nothing to mess around with."

She took the water and drank deep. It was cold and refreshing. Then she handed it back with a wide grin. "Thanks." She gestured toward the view. "This made it worth it. I can't believe I climbed to the top of a mountain!"

He chuckled, his laughter warm and deep. "You didn't 'climb' a mountain. You hiked up a mountain path after I drove halfway up here. And we're not at the top." He looked over his shoulder. "But I can get you a little closer to it. Come on." He took her hand and gave a gentle tug. It felt oddly right to have her hand in his. He led her to the bus-sized boulder and she discovered there was a little path to the side that allowed her, with minimal climbing skills, to scramble to the top of the rock.

"Here," Nick said, tugging her back to the cliff wall. "From back here if you look out, it's like you're standing at the edge of the cliff with nothing below you. Without the risk of falling a few hundred feet down the mountain."

He was right. If she put her back to the rocks, the boulder was wide enough that it hid the grassy opening and trail, showing nothing but the lake and mountains.

"It's like flying." She barely whispered the words, but Nick nodded in agreement.

"That's what it's like when you climb a peak. You're on top of the world, and it feels like no one has ever been there before you."

There was something magical about standing here, sharing this moment with him.

"You've only been here a month—how did you find this amazing little secret up here?"

"It's not exactly a secret. Blake said it's a pretty popular spot for the locals, because it's such an easy walk..." She huffed out a laugh and he grinned. "Easy for the kids who like to climb up here, anyway. They call it the Kissing Rock."

She didn't answer right away. Gallant Lake seemed to inspire a lot of romantic names for places. Amanda called Cassie's apartment a love shack, and now she was standing on the Kissing Rock.

"It's a stone with a view," she said. "What makes it a Kissing Rock?"

Nick shrugged, and the movement caused his arm to rub the length of hers, pointing out how close they were standing. She could step away. But she didn't.

"I guess it's been called that for generations. People came up here with picnic lunches, and maybe the view, um…*inspired* them. Or maybe they came up in the evenings and watched the sun setting, like it's starting to do now, and they were alone at the edge of the world like this…" He looked down at her, his eyes dark and his emotions hidden. Was he pressing more tightly against her? Or was that her leaning in? "And I imagine a young couple might feel their inhibitions disappearing up here. No one would see them. No one would know if they stole a kiss or two."

They were facing each other now. She wasn't sure how that happened, but they'd both turned, so it was mutual. The sun was warm. A soft breeze rustled the young leaves in the trees that lined the view toward the lake. There were birds singing, but it felt like silence. Like a warm, safe cocoon of silence and…safety.

…you know in your heart you're safe with me…

They were so close she could feel the vibration in his chest when he spoke.

"It's a little like Vegas, I guess. What happens on Kissing Rock stays on Kissing Rock."

His hands were resting on her waist. How had that happened? And hers were on his biceps. His strong, hard biceps. This was an afternoon for new sensations.

First was fun. Then pride. And now? Now she was feeling something she hadn't felt in…maybe forever. Sure, Don made her want to be with him. He'd paved the way to make it feel inevitable. But she'd never felt this pool of warmth deep in her belly as she flexed her fingers against Nick's arms and saw his nostrils flare in response. She'd never felt the tingle of excitement that had moved her so close her pelvis brushed across the zipper of his shorts, earning a low, strangled sound from him as his grip tightened on her.

He turned, putting her back to the rocks. Blocking the sun. Blocking everything but this new kind of burn. Not one of pain, but one of need. She whispered his name, and he closed his eyes, holding them tightly closed as if having a battle with himself. She said his name again, and he shook his head. His eyes didn't open until he started to speak in a voice filled with gravel and deep with emotion.

"This isn't why I brought you here. I didn't plan this…" He cupped her cheek with his hand. "There are a hundred ways this can go wrong…"

She rested her hand over his on the side of her face. "I can't believe you're the one being timid right now. *You.*" He smiled at that, but he didn't make a move. Oh, God, why wasn't he making a move?

He closed his eyes again, shaking his head slowly. "This is a mistake." He stepped back, moving his hand away from her face and running it through his own hair. "We're coworkers. We hardly know each other. We've both got baggage. You're not…"

A chill ran through her veins. Nick didn't want Cassie. Of course he didn't. He was a cool, confident ladies' man, and she wasn't his type. She was a timid bookworm who jumped and flinched at everything, and big, bold Nick West, hero cop, didn't want someone like her. Nick wanted a fearless woman who swung from cliffs and rode a mountain bike. A woman who didn't need self-defense lessons. She straightened and moved out from between him and the rock face.

"Of course. You're right. I'm sorry." Damn it to hell, there she went, apologizing again. Apologizing for this *mistake*. Apologizing for being who she was.

Nick reached for her, but she tugged free, moving to the spot where they'd climbed up onto this stupid Kissing Rock. The sun was getting lower, and they really should get back to the Jeep and back to reality. The reality where she understood her place and knew her limits. She took hold of a small tree and put her foot on a root that had acted like a ladder rung on the way up here. But her heel couldn't grip that damp, round root the way her toes had earlier. Before she knew it, she was falling, her butt hitting the rock hard and catapulting her forward on her hands and knees on the ground. The fall, and abrupt halt, stunned her into silence. But it had the opposite effect on Nick, who was scrambling down while calling her name and cursing.

"Cassie! Are you okay? Damn it, Cass, say something!" He hit his knees next to her just as she sat back and rubbed the palms of her hands on her jeans, wincing a little. The mud softened her landing, but her wrists were still sore. And her knees. And her butt.

Nick's hands were running down her arms now, and then her back, before running up her neck and holding her face from each side. "Are you hurt?"

"Other than my pride? I don't think so." She gently pushed his hands away, not ready to fall into that temptation trap again. She stood, and he rose with her, one arm around her waist to steady her. The pain in her hip, where she slammed into the rock, made her grimace. "I'm such a klutz. I bet you've never seen your mountain climbing buddies do that move. As you know, my hand-eye coordination is subpar at best…"

"Cass, I once missed a cleat on a rock face and fell twenty feet before the rope caught me. But my harness was too loose and I ended up hanging upside down fifty feet in the air, swinging back and forth like a pendulum, with my ass exposed to the whole world."

She couldn't help a short laugh. "I would have liked to have seen that."

"Oh, you can. My buddy caught it all on his phone, and it briefly went viral on the rock climbing forums." His hand ran down her back, stopping at her hip when she flinched. "Yeah, I thought I saw you bounce off the rock right there. You'll have a hell of a bruise. Do you think it's any more than that?"

She took a few steps. She was sore, but that was probably as much from the climb up as from the fall. "I'm good. We should get back before it starts getting dark." He nodded, but he didn't head for the trail. Instead, he walked straight to her. She put her hands up and he stopped, his chest brushing against hers. "Wh-what are you doing?"

He stared at her hard, then slid his arms around her. She didn't resist when he pulled her up tight to him. "I'm doing what I should have done up on that damn Kissing Rock. Or maybe what I shouldn't have done. I don't know. I only know there's no way in hell I'm leaving this mountain before I've kissed you." Her fingers twisted into his shirt, just to make sure he didn't change his mind again. He didn't move, waiting for her consent.

She tugged on his shirt and lifted her chin.

"Well, what are you waiting for?"

And just like that, his lips were on hers. His kiss was firm and commanding. In control without making her feel overpowered. And skilled. Oh, so skilled. She parted her mouth and his tongue was inside her in a flash. She melted against him, trusting him to hold her upright, and he did, with a low growl of approval. Their mouths moved as one, in a dance as seductive as a tango. He took and she gave, then she rose on her toes and took from him, and his fingers gripped her waist and held her there. Her hands were eager to be part of the game and slid up so she could clutch the back of his head. Their teeth clicked together and apart and together again, and it wasn't enough for her. She wanted more, and she stretched even taller to meet him. To have a moment of control all for herself. As if knowing what she needed, Nick bent his knees, then lifted her up so her head was above his. The kiss never broke, but now she was the one being demanding. She was the one taking over. Her hands cupped his face. He stared up at her with a fire that mirrored hers. Startled, she pulled back.

Nick let her slide slowly down to her feet, his eyes never leaving hers. He kissed her again, but this kiss was different. This wasn't the experienced player using his skills to leave her legless. This was a kiss with more uncertainty in it, as if he was exploring some new territory where he'd never been before. Tender, cautious and slow. He drifted from her lips to her chin, then down her neck and up to the tender skin below her ear, then back to her lips. She was drunk on him. Drunk on Nick West. And she was hopelessly dependent. Craving her next fix before this one even ended.

Then his lips were gone from hers. He'd set her at

arm's length from him, staring at her in bewilderment, then turning away.

"Holy shit, Cass." He shook himself as if to shake off whatever spell had come over them both. "What the hell was that?"

"Uh...a kiss?"

"Baby, that was a lot more than just a kiss."

Baby? Cassie did her best to ignore the endearment. It didn't seem as if Nick was using it that way anyhow.

He stared at the ground, then looked out to the lake, and the sun lowering beyond it. He kept his back to her.

"We should get back to the truck before it gets dark. Can you walk?"

What just happened? That kiss had seemed *electric...* until Nick flipped off the switch and pushed her away. But then again, Don always told her she was a boring lover.

"I'm sorry..." Every time she said those words, it burned her. But this time they felt appropriate. Clearly, she'd had a different experience than Nick had. "I'm not very good at that stuff. Kissing. Sex. All of it...none of it...whatever..."

Chapter Eight

Nick stared at Cassie in confusion. What the hell was she apologizing for? She'd just rocked his world with a kiss that would forever raise the bar on any future kisses that came his way. And did she say she wasn't good at *sex*? No way did he believe that. Not after a kiss that had him turning away to hide the erection tenting his shorts. If he didn't get her off this mountain, they'd be joining the decades-long list of couples who'd consummated their relationships on the Kissing Rock. And as much as his body wanted that to happen—*right now*—Nick knew Cassie deserved better. This wasn't where or how he wanted it to happen. *If* it happened. And it probably shouldn't happen. But *damn*...

She turned away, her head hung low. He had to fix this, and fast.

"Cassie, I don't know who the idiot was who told you that you weren't—" he raised his fingers into air quotes

"—'good at this,' but he was wrong. Like, *really* wrong. Like, he couldn't have been *more* wrong." He walked toward her. "Did you not feel how great that was?" How could she not have felt that?

Her cheeks flamed. "I did think it was pretty...great. But then you stopped..."

He chuckled softly. "Uh...I had no choice. It was either put some space between us or embarrass myself like some middle school teen. You had me thinking some very impure thoughts, Cass, and if we'd stayed that close, you would have felt just how strong those thoughts were."

Her brows furrowed, then rose in surprise.

"Oh..."

Nick wouldn't have thought it possible, but the color in her cheeks deepened even further.

"Oh!" Her mouth lifted into a slightly proud smile. *Damn straight, girl.* "Oh. I thought..."

"You thought, once again, that you'd done something wrong. That's always your first response, isn't it? Why is that?"

Her smile vanished, and he kicked himself for speaking his thoughts out loud. But instead of avoiding the subject, she looked at him and nodded.

"It's generally my go-to. I...I had a lot of years of someone telling me I was doing everything wrong. Apologizing becomes habit after a while." She ran her fingers through her dark hair, smoothing the ponytail that had been mussed from her fall, and then from their kiss. "And you seemed to be...fighting it. Up there..." She glanced up to the top of the rock. "We were so close, and you started listing all the reasons we shouldn't..."

Nick couldn't help laughing. "That little speech up there? The list of all the reasons kissing you was a mis-

take? That was me giving myself a verbal cold shower."
He ran his hands down her arms and caught her hands.
"Being that close to you had my blood rushing to places
it had no business rushing to. Not in the middle of the
day on the side of a mountain. Rattling off that list
cooled me down enough to step away and gather my
wits."

He squeezed her hands. "But when you got upset and
tumbled down the side of the rock trying to get away
from me, I knew 'space' wasn't what I needed. Or at
least, it wasn't what I wanted. But if I thought being
close to you was a turn-on, *kissing* you was... Well,
like I said. That was more than chemistry. That was a
whole damn laboratory fire going on."

She held his gaze, and he could see her mind racing
and stalling and crashing. Yeah, he should have just
kissed her again before she had a chance to overthink
things. She swallowed hard.

"But you weren't wrong... It's a mistake. We *do* work
together. And we *do* have baggage. And we *don't* know
each other that well..."

He let her pull away, sensing her rising panic.

"*Now* who's taking the cold shower?" He grinned, and
she did her best not to grin back, but failed. He shook
his head. "First—I think we know each other pretty
well. I'd like to think we're friends, even. We may not
have shared our life stories yet, but that can be rem-
edied over dinner some night. Second—everyone has
baggage. That's an empty excuse. And third—yeah, we
work together. But I'm not aware of any rules against
fraternization at Randall Resorts International. I'm not
your boss, and we didn't kiss in the office." He shrugged.
"Honestly, so far all we've done is have a stellar kissing
session at the Kissing Rock. I'd like to have *another* stel-

lar kissing session with you somewhere else, but that's your call, Cassie."

"I... I'm not good at this..." She held up her hand to stop his objection to the way she always put herself down. "That's not self-pity, Nick. I mean I'm not...experienced...at dating, or relationships, or kissing guys on mountains. I don't know how to navigate what happens next."

"Okay. Executive decision time." He took her hand and tucked it in the crook of his arm. They headed for the trail. "Let's stop worrying and get away from this damn rock. What happens at the rock, stays at the rock and all that." Cassie snorted in laughter. He liked all her laughs, even the snorting ones, so he kept lying to her. "No, really. No one has to know, and our friendship doesn't have to change. On Monday, we'll have a normal day at work, and a normal gym session afterward, like today never happened. And if one of us decides we need to pursue this—whatever this is—we'll discuss it like adults. Deal?"

She glanced his way quickly, careful to also watch where she was stepping as they went down the trail. He wasn't fooling anyone. Nothing would be the same between them, and the thought made him sad. He'd enjoyed the teasing and fun they'd shared. Watching Cassie gain new confidence and strength as they worked out together. He didn't want to lose that. As tempting as it was to pursue more kisses, or perhaps more than just kissing, he didn't like the thought of anything changing their existing relationship.

"Of course. That makes sense." She was playing along. "Nothing needs to change... Oh!" She stumbled on the trail, but Nick caught her waist and kept her upright, resisting the sudden and unexpected urge to pull her into his arms, bury his hands in her hair and kiss her senseless.

Bad idea… Too complicated…baggage…coworker…

"Exactly. Nothing needs to change. Nothing at all."

"Cassie-girl, where *are* you this morning? Nora called your name three times to tell you your cappuccino is ready."

Cathy set the foam-topped mug in front of Cassie on the window table inside the Gallant Brew. "Is everything okay? You haven't heard from Don…?"

"No, Aunt Cathy. It's not that. I'm just tired. I overdid things a bit yesterday."

That was the understatement of the century. She'd not only agreed to hike Gallant Mountain with Nick West, she'd also *kissed* the man. More than once. And she'd *liked* it. A lot. Definitely overdone.

"What'd you do, honey? Is Blake working you too hard up there at the resort?"

"Uh…no. He's not." Amanda Randall walked in. "Why would you ask that?"

Nora walked over with a plate of ginger cookies and a sly smile. Over the past few weeks, Cassie had given in to Amanda's pestering about becoming a hermit and started joining the cousins and Aunt Cathy for their before-the-Sunday-rush coffee in Nora's shop.

Nora set the cookies on the table and grabbed a chair. "Cassie said she overdid things yesterday and Cathy was worried. But I don't think it was Blake who kept her busy." Nora winked at Cassie, and she felt a sense of dread. "I think Nick West might be the one 'overworking' her these days."

Amanda sat quickly, putting her elbows on the table and her chin in her hands. "*Really?* Do tell, Nora!"

Cathy's eyes narrowed. "Nick West? That guy who was in the shop a few weeks ago and followed you upstairs? Cassie, what's going on?"

Amanda laughed. "I *told* you that apartment was a love shack! Come on, Nora, spill what you know."

"Hey, wait!" The last of the cousins, Melanie Lowery, rushed into the shop, smoothing her hair with her hand and looking flustered. "No spilling anything until I get some espresso and join in. I'm always missing the good stuff!"

Nora sighed and went behind the counter to make Melanie's coffee. "Maybe if you weren't always late to the party, Mel, you wouldn't miss everything."

The tall brunette waved a dismissive hand. "Honey, my fiancé's been on the West Coast for a week. By the time his flight landed, we had a lot of…um…catching up to do, if you get my drift." She took a cookie and sighed as she took a bite. "Oh, I love my gingers."

"Got it, Mel. Sweet ginger cookies. Hot ginger fiancé." Amanda fixed her gaze back on Nora as she rejoined them, delivering Mel's espresso with a flourish. "Spill it, girl."

Nora glanced out toward the empty sidewalk, making sure there were no customers heading their way, then leaned forward, lowering her voice dramatically.

"Well, I just happened to set some trash outside the back door yesterday afternoon to keep it from stinking up the kitchen. I always clean out the fridge and the display on Saturday afternoons to make way for the fresh Sunday baked goods…"

Amanda rolled her eyes. "Yes, yes, we know you're the queen of organization. Get to the good stuff."

"Seriously?" Cassie interrupted, glaring at Amanda. "Is this the 'magic of having girlfriends' you told me

I needed?" No one paid any attention, all eyes fixed on Nora.

"Well," Nora said. "Imagine my surprise when I saw Nick sitting in his Jeep out in the parking lot. Before I could set the trash down and wave, I heard footsteps on the back stairs, and there was Cassie—" all four heads swiveled in Cassie's direction "—trotting down the stairs and over to the Jeep and hopping right in. Then they drove off together. On a Saturday afternoon. Almost like a date or something."

Three sets of eyebrows rose, but Cathy was scowling. "Cassie, you don't know this guy. Don't you think it's a little soon to jump right back into a relationship?"

Being the center of attention put Cassie on the defensive. "One kiss doesn't make it a relationship."

Oh, damn her filter-free mouth when she was nervous...

There was a collective gasp of delight from the cousins. Melanie rested her hand on Cassie's arm.

"You *kissed* Nick West?"

She bit her lip, upset that she'd blurted that out, but also wanting the advice of women she trusted and admired. She hadn't lied yesterday when she told Nick she had little experience at this. After college, Don had pretty much been her only relationship, and that was hardly the measuring stick she wanted to use for future ones.

Amanda's voice softened. "Hey, guys, it's a big deal to move on after what Cassie's been through. If she doesn't want to talk about it..."

"Actually, I think I *do* want to talk about it."

"Oh, thank God! Tell us everything!" Amanda's laugh made Cassie smile.

She gave the women a summary of the Nick-and-

Cassie story. Their disastrous first meeting when she threw the stapler at him. Pepper-spraying him. Agreeing to let him help her with self-defense and fitness training. The playful teasing they did at work, with him hiding her stapler and her scattering reports across his desk in an untidy array that annoyed him every time. The bar Friday night, where she told him she would *not* go hiking with him. Nick showing up at her door anyway. The hike she thought would kill her. The kiss that nearly did. And finally, her and Nick's agreement to not allow it to change anything. There was silence for a moment when she finished, then Amanda spoke.

"So you think you and Nick might be friends, and you don't want to screw that up."

She thought about that. She looked forward to going to work when Nick was there. She never knew what she'd find on her desk or where her stapler might be. He always dropped some off-the-cuff comment that made her smile. He drove her crazy with that stupid foam basketball. He also did his best to make sure she felt secure, while pushing her to try new things. She'd never had a big brother, but if she had, she had a feeling that's what their relationship would be like.

She nodded at Amanda's guess. "I like Nick. I mean, like him like a friend. A fun coworker. He's a good guy who annoys me to no end, but he's also..."

"He's also someone you want to climb like a tree?" Melanie lifted her coffee mug in a toast. "I think we've all been there, right, ladies?"

The three cousins laughed and agreed, but Cathy wasn't amused.

"Keep it in the friend zone, honey. If you get attached and have to..."

Cassie nodded. The go-bag sitting by her door upstairs was a constant reminder that she could end up running again. Changing her name again. Starting over again. It hadn't been that hard to leave Cleveland, but leaving Gallant Lake? This move was going to hurt if it ever came. And getting involved with Nick West would make it that much more complicated. He didn't strike her as the kind of guy to just let her leave. He'd want to rescue her, and the thought of him going up against someone as flat-out evil as Don made her shudder.

"It's not easy to do." Amanda sighed. "Blake and I were friends, and I worked for him, but after that first kiss… Well, as hard as we tried, the friend zone was toast." Nora and Mel nodded in agreement, dreamy-eyed and smiling.

Cassie finished her coffee, trying to block the memory of yesterday's kisses. Going down that path would only lead to heartbreak.

"Aunt Cathy's right. I can't let this change things. Yesterday was a surprise. And yes—" she rolled her eyes at Amanda's snicker "—it was a nice surprise. It's nice to know I can still feel desire for a man, and that a man might desire me. That I could melt like that…" And there she went, oversharing again. She needed to get better at this girlfriend thing. Nora stood as a group of customers walked in, dressed in their Sunday church clothes.

"I gotta run," Nora said. "But if that man made you 'melt,' you should think twice before passing him up."

Chapter Nine

"Man, that climb was turbocharged today, Nick! Was there a race that I didn't know about?" Terrance Hudson took a long drink from his water bottle, then poured some on the edge of his shirt and wiped the sweat from his face. Nick, Terrance and the rest of the Rebel Rockers climbing club were sitting atop the Arrow Wall at the Shawangunk cliffs, known locally as the Gunks. "Shit, man. For someone who's never climbed this sucker, you were on fire. I ain't never seen a guy go up this wall that fast!"

Nick took a swig from his own water, pouring the rest of it over his head. The sun was high and hot today. He nodded to his climbing partner, whom he'd met only a week ago at his first meeting of the Rebel Rockers at the Chalet in Gallant Lake.

"Sorry for the pace. I tend to climb quick. That last part of the climb—what do they call it, Modern Times? That was pretty intense for a 5.8 rating. I just wanted to get it over with and get up here to relax." Also, he was running from the memories of yesterday's kisses with the not-so-shy-after-all Cassandra Smith. But Terrance didn't need to know that.

"Yeah, that last stretch is a challenge, but man, the views, right?" Terrance nodded toward the valley that stretched out hundreds of feet below them. It was impressive, but it had nothing on yesterday's view of Gallant Lake reflected in Cassie's golden eyes right before his lips touched hers. He shook off the memory. So many reasons not to do that again. And so many nerve endings humming in his body, begging for more.

Terrance turned and started chatting with another climber—Sam something—leaving Nick to consider all the options with Cassie. As much as he'd dismissed the coworker issue, he knew how messy workplace flings could be. He'd seen the damage done at the precinct back in LA when two of his fellow detectives had a quick affair. She'd ended it, but the guy didn't want to take no for an answer. Things got so ugly they ended up transferring the woman across town, which never sat right with Nick. She wasn't the one causing problems.

And he and Cassie would probably end up being a quick affair. They had nothing in common, other than driving each other crazy with office pranks. He was still finding new places to hide that blue stapler every morning. He'd even snuck into the ladies' room to set it on the sink in there. And ever since he told her how much he valued organized files, she'd started coming into his office and shuffling his folders or scattering them all over his desk.

But other than the office high jinks, what did they have? Well...hot chemistry, for sure. But besides that, what was there? He was restless and liked to be physically active. He hated sitting around, and that was her favorite thing to do—sit with her tea and a book. As much as she was improving her strength and fighting skills in their gym sessions, she was still jumpy and quick to take on blame. Always apologizing. He tucked his water bottle back in his pack.

She was a victim. He thought about Beth Washington going back to her brute of a husband over and over, until Nick shot the man dead. After Earl Washington had murdered his partner. Beth's refusal to leave the man, to protect herself, had directly led to Jada's death.

The fire of his physical attraction to Cassie started to cool as common sense prevailed. If she was one of those perpetual victims, then she wasn't right for him long-term, and short-term wasn't really an option when they worked in the same damn office. Problem solved. Sharing any more kisses was a no go.

"You ready for the return trip? Got your lines ready?" Terrance stood, his dark skin shining with sweat. He was sure-footed and relaxed, just inches from the cliff edge. Good climbers respected the mountain but were never intimidated by it. Nick stood and checked his gear.

"I'm ready if you are."

"Cool. Let's not race this time, okay? We won't be back here until next month, so try to enjoy it, man."

Nick nodded. His little self-talk had him settled down now where he could focus. From this point forward, he and Cassie were friends, and that kiss was an aberration that wouldn't be happening again.

"Nick, I swear to God, you're driving me crazy! I need my stapler!" Cassie slammed her desk drawer closed. She'd checked her desk twice and Blake's desk once. She'd looked on the coffee counter and the storage cabinets and the empty office by the door. She'd pulled the curtains completely open, and checked under the air-conditioning unit. She'd gone through Nick's office once while he was meeting with Tim in the surveillance room and was ready to toss it again, whether Nick was in there or not. And he was. Smirking at her from his desk chair, twirling his pen innocently.

She stood in the doorway and folded her arms, glaring at him. He'd upped his prank game this week to whole new levels. The stapler, of course. But, with Blake out of town and just the two of them sharing the office suite, he'd gone all out. Her desk phone went missing on Monday, hidden behind the drapes. On Tuesday her tape *and* the stapler *and* her notebook were sitting on Blake's desk. Her wireless keyboard was tucked behind the coffeepot on Wednesday. Yesterday the stapler was *inside* the empty coffeepot. And today, when he knew damn well she had to put together presentation packets for Blake's investor meeting this weekend, the stapler was nowhere to be found.

"Is there a problem?"

"Yes. A big, stupid problem who needs to get a life. Where. Is. My. Stapler?"

He tossed his pen in the air and caught it. That devilish grin made her heart jump. Damn, he was sexy. And annoying, she reminded herself. An annoying friend and coworker who was like a big brother and she wasn't attracted to him at all. Nope. Not one bit. She hadn't been attracted to him yesterday in the gym when he taught her how to use her elbows to break free from being grabbed from behind. Which meant he'd had to grab her over and over again, insisting that she get it right. Nope. Not attracted at all.

He'd been cool as a cucumber all week. He'd brought

up the kiss first thing Monday morning, assuring her that it wasn't going to be a problem between them, and they should forget it ever happened. It was nothing more than a Kissing Rock spell that had been broken as soon as they left the mountain. She'd felt a sting of disappointment that he could set it aside so easily after telling her he'd had a hard-on after kissing her, but his actions seemed to support his words. He'd been the same Nick he'd been the weeks before—joking, teasing, playing basketball with the foam ball, teaching her, clowning around with the staff.

It seemed Nick had moved on from their kiss with nothing more to show for it than a renewed enthusiasm for his job. And driving her crazy. He tossed his pen again, almost to the ceiling, and had to lean back to snatch it out of the air when it came down. She bit back a sigh of frustration. He'd wait her out until the offices closed if he had to.

"Where is it, Nick?"

"Where have you looked?"

Her eyes narrowed on him. She was done playing. She reached for his desk and tried to take his cell phone, but he was too quick for her. He held it over his head and laughed.

"Seriously? You thought you'd outmaneuver a cop?"

"You're not a cop anymore, Nick. You're just the jackass who won't give me my stapler."

A frown flickered across his face. He didn't talk about his days on the LA police force. Amanda told Cassie last week she'd learned the beautiful woman in the wedding gown in the photo behind Nick was his former partner. And that she was dead.

He summoned a fresh smile and shook off whatever

he'd been thinking about. "Check the coat closet. You might have to work for it this time."

"Wonderful. As if I'm not already working." She turned and went to the closet. She didn't see it at first. She looked up and saw the edge of the stapler barely peeking over the top shelf. She called over her shoulder as she rolled a desk chair to the closet. "Nice job, Nick. There's only an eighty percent probability this thing will bonk me on the head when I try to get it."

She was just putting her foot on the chair and praying it would stay put when she felt Nick's arm around her waist, pulling her back. "Are you actively trying to kill yourself? You can't stand on a chair with wheels." He sent the chair rolling back to the empty desk. "I'll get it. I didn't think about it hitting you, but you're right..." He stretched and worked the stapler off the shelf with his fingertips, while still holding her waist with his other arm. Her skin was tingling, but he seemed unaffected. "If it was going to happen to anyone, it'd happen to you. Here." He handed her the stapler, then rubbed his knuckles in her hair. Like she was his kid sister. Like she was a puppy. Like he had no desire for her whatsoever. And it ticked her off.

She swatted his hand away. "Here's an idea—stop hiding the damn thing! You're not a twelve-year-old, Nick, and this isn't grade school. What's next? Putting gum in my hair? This is an *office*. You said you wanted to keep things professional between us, so why don't you surprise me and actually *act* professional for once?"

"Whoa...easy!" Nick held up both hands in surrender. "What just happened?"

It was a fair question, but she wasn't in the mood to answer it.

"Nothing. I've just got actual work to do, Nick. And

I'm pretty sure you do, too." She brushed past him and went back to sit at her desk. He closed the closet door and studied her, but she refused to make eye contact. She didn't trust her feelings right now, especially with the traitor tears threatening to spill over. What was *wrong* with her? Hadn't she decided that being friends was better than trying to follow up on that kissing business and possibly ruining everything? Wasn't that exactly what she'd agreed to on Monday—pretend the kiss didn't happen? Nick not being attracted to her was the best possible scenario. Besides, apparently the kiss really *had* been just a fluke for him, and that whole "chemistry lab on fire" that made him want a cold shower was a momentary phenomenon that had clearly passed. She was no longer the woman whose kisses made him hot and bothered. She was just a girl he liked to tease, whose hair he liked to noogie.

Nick walked over and sat on the corner of her desk, facing her. "Come on, kiddo, what's going..."

Kiddo?

She was on her feet in a flash.

"I'm not your *kiddo* or your *grasshopper* or anything else." And that was the truth. She wasn't anything else to him. And that was a *good* thing, damn it.

"What the hell is wrong with you today?" He took her arm, but she pulled away. She was losing it. She needed to get away from him before she burst into tears or threw herself into his arms. Either one would be a huge mistake.

"I need to go." She looked at the clock on the wall. "I'm taking an early lunch."

"Early lunch? It's not even eleven..." She glared at him and he stepped back, shaking his head. "Okay! Early lunch. Maybe we can talk this out later."

She nodded mutely, grabbed her purse and headed out the door.

Chapter Ten

Cassie headed for the lakeside path, hoping to avoid other humans for a while. It felt like something had just snapped inside her back in the office. Something that had been simmering since Saturday when she and Nick kissed up on the mountain that now rose above her, reflected in the water. When he slid his arm around her waist by the closet, everything she'd felt on Gallant Mountain had come rushing back. The heat, the liquid desire, the way his lips felt on hers, the sensation when he lifted her into the air and she'd looked down into his eyes, with the lake beyond him.

How could Nick deny what happened up there? How could he just continue to tease and taunt and touch her as if nothing had changed, when she knew she'd be forever changed? If nothing else, she'd learned she was capable of feeling not just desire, but as if *she* was *desirable*. Not a trophy on a shelf like Don treated her. But a woman who could appeal to a man like Nick West. Could make him want her. And damn it, she *knew* she'd made him want her, even if only for that moment.

To her, the sensation had been new and transformative. But Nick had kissed plenty of women in his life. She'd probably just been one more on a long list of fun little interludes he could easily forget. She slowed her pace, pausing to stare out over the water.

If that was the case, then it wasn't fair to be angry with him. He'd moved on because he'd had practice at moving on. And if he could do it, so could she. It would just take her a little longer. Like forever. She laughed softly to herself. *Stop being melodramatic.*

She was getting stronger. Smarter. Tougher. And Nick was the guy who'd helped her get there. Even when he didn't mean to. Sure, he taught her self-defense. But he also gave her noogies and hurt her feelings and kissed her senseless and hid her damn stapler. It seemed that *everything* Nick did made her stronger. And she couldn't be mad about that. She turned to head back to the resort. All she needed to figure out now was how to explain her little meltdown to Nick so they could continue as… friends. Wise, experienced, worldly friends who kissed one afternoon and were strong enough to move on without causing a ripple in their relationship.

Nick was gone when she walked into the office. Her stapler sat in the center of her desk, next to a vase filled with hydrangeas. They looked suspiciously similar to the blue hydrangeas near the back veranda of the resort. Stolen daffodils had gone out of season. She picked up the note he'd left, in his usual hurried scribble that made it seem the words were ready to dash right off the page.

Your stapler looked sad, so I thought it might like some "borrowed" company. I forgot I have that meet-

*ing with the staffing firm in White Plains this afternoon.
Let's start fresh tomorrow, and I'll give you a proper
apology? —Nick*

She smiled. He was a hard man to stay mad at. She'd
forgotten all about the meeting in White Plains. They
used temporary staff for large events, and Nick was
training the company on proper security procedures.
He'd be there all afternoon. Maybe it was for the best
that they were going to have a little time apart. It would
give her a chance to get her mind straight and put Nick
firmly in the friend zone again. If he could move on
from that kiss, well, then, so could she.

"Hey, Cassie! I'm so glad you're here." Julie came
into the office. "Blake called a little while ago, but you
and Nick were both gone." Julie gave her a pointed look,
and Cassie rushed to set her straight.

"Nick's on his way to a meeting. I took an early lunch."
She should have made sure the office was staffed. It
wasn't like her to forget such a basic thing as making
sure calls were handled. "I'm sorry. I should have let you
know I was stepping out. What did Blake need?"

Julie looked flustered. "His flight is delayed, so he
won't be here until almost midnight, and the welcome
reception for the investors is tonight. Amanda offered
to play hostess for dinner, but he wanted us to help her
out for a few hours. He figured the group would go party
on their own at the bar after that. Can you join us?"

Cassie frowned. A party with a bunch of powerful
people she didn't know was not her idea of a good time.
But she owed it to her friends and her boss to do her best.
Besides this was new, improved Cassie—she was strong
enough to do this. She put her hand on Julie's arm.

"I'll run home later and change into something
dressy, and I'll be back in time for dinner."

Julie grinned. "You're a champ, Cassie! And after dinner, maybe you and Amanda and I can have a few Friday night cocktails together."

"Yeah, maybe." She had no intention of doing that, but Julie seemed so excited at the idea that Cassie didn't want to burst her bubble. She was sure she'd be so exhausted from pretending to be an extrovert and entertaining important investors over dinner that she'd beg off later with an excuse and head home.

But it ended up being a more relaxing evening than she'd anticipated. The four representatives from the investment firm were older, extremely professional and actually pretty interesting. The one woman in the group, Margaret Ackerman, was a book lover like Cassie, and they ended up discussing their favorite women's fiction while Amanda and Julie talked sports and travel with the three gentlemen. It made for an enjoyable meal. When the dessert plates had been cleared and the investors had gone off to their rooms to rest up for the early round of golf Blake had arranged for them, Cassie found herself with no viable excuse not to join the other women at the bar. After all, that's what girlfriends did, right?

Besides, she was eager to shake off her emotional morning with Nick. As happy as she was with her new plan to follow his example and just be buddies, there was a restlessness humming inside her. Her senses were on high alert, sending images of Nick's intense dark eyes through her mind. She could hear the breeze rustling through the trees up on Gallant Mountain, and the low growl in Nick's chest as he kissed her. She could feel his hands on her waist, lifting her into the air without breaking their kiss. She could smell the pines...

"Can I have another?" She blurted out the words as the bartender, Josie, passed by.

"Easy, girl! You're already on your second Gallant Lake Sunset." Amanda laughed.

Cassie shrugged. "Hey, it's just orange juice, right? And a little honey liqueur?"

Julie held her empty wineglass up to let Josie know she needed a refill. "And vodka. Don't forget the vodka that's in there. But don't worry, I can drive you home later."

Amanda looked at Julie's wineglass. "Isn't it customary for the designated driver to abstain from alcohol? Cass, there's always a room open at Halcyon, and it's right next door." Amanda and Blake lived in an actual castle, built on the lake over a hundred years ago. The place had at least ten bedrooms. But she didn't feel drunk at all. She checked her phone.

"It's only nine thirty, ladies, and this drink isn't that strong. I'll stop at three drinks and be done. Now, Julie, finish telling us about this old farmhouse you bought." Julie was more than happy to oblige, describing the adventures she'd already had with the old house outside town. Cassie sat back and sipped her drink. This was part of the girlfriend game that she could get used to. Listening to women laugh and share their joys and frustrations together. It was much nicer when *she* wasn't the topic of conversation.

She was halfway through her fourth Sunset by the time the conversation started to wind down. The drinks were sweet and tasty and proved very effective at helping her forget all that earlier confusion about…what's-his-name. They helped her be better at girl talk, too. She giggled at Julie's stories about the leaky roof and sagging floors at the old house she'd bought. She laughed at Amanda's description of her young daughter, Maddie, throwing a tantrum at preschool because their nap

time was on yoga mats, not "real" beds with lacy cano-
pies like she had at home.

"That's one of the reasons we wanted her in preschool
as early as possible," Amanda explained. "We're not *intentionally* spoiling her, but the kid lives in a castle, and
Blake and Zachary dote on her every whim."

"And you don't?" Cassie winked at Julie, who was
holding back laughter.

"No! I mean…not on purpose. But you guys, she's
so damn cute. And smart. Way too smart." Amanda
yawned. "And that busy brain likes to wake up early, so
I'd better get home. It'll be midnight by the time Blake
gets here from LaGuardia, and he won't want to get up
with her. Cassie, you're coming with me, right?"

They all stood, but Cassie was the only one who had
to reach out and grab the edge of the bar to steady herself. The room wasn't exactly spinning, but it wasn't
staying still, either.

Julie shook her head. "I tried to tell you mixed drinks
will get you every time. Stick to wine or beer, girl. I'll
drive her home, Amanda. I switched to water a while
ago." Amanda looked skeptical, but Julie closed her
eyes and touched her fingers to her nose while standing on one foot. She didn't stop until Amanda gave in.

"Fine! Text me once she's inside, since I don't think
she'll remember to do it."

Cassie frowned. Her face felt funny, almost like she
couldn't quite feel her own mouth moving. "*She* is standing right here between the two of you. I know I had too
much to be able to drive, but I'm not exactly wasted." She
turned and gave Amanda her most serious look, which,
for some reason, made Amanda giggle. "And I *will* remember to text you when I'm home. Mom."

"Yeah, yeah, laugh all you want at the responsible

adult trying to keep everyone safe. That's fine. I'm outta here." Amanda gave them each a quick, fierce hug and headed out of the bar. Halcyon was a short walk up the hill, and Cassie saw Bill Chesnutt heading toward the boss's wife to escort her up to their home. She'd be fine.

"I have to get my stuff from the back office," Julie said, "and hit the ladies' room. Meet you by the staircase in five minutes?" Julie side-eyed Cassie as they headed out into the lobby. "Are you going to throw up or anything? Because my car has leather seats, and..."

"I am *not* going to throw up! I'm not drunk. I'm... tipsy. And I'm very much enjoying this rare and precious little buzz, so you buzz on out of here and do whatever." She looked across the lobby. "Maybe I'll go get a cup of tea."

Nick watched the two women from the top of the lobby stairs. He couldn't believe it. Cassie Smith was *drunk*? No, not drunk. *Tipsy.* She called it a "precious little buzz." Cassie was damn cute when she was buzzed.

He'd spent the afternoon in meetings and training sessions, but she'd been on his mind the entire time. She'd been really upset with him that morning. Things had been so good all week, after they agreed to pretend that kiss on Saturday never happened. He might have been a little more of a pest than usual, but he was only trying to show her that nothing was going to be weird or awkward just because they'd slipped up and kissed a few times. By accident. When he'd given her that little noogie today, it was just to emphasize how totally cool they were. But something had set her off, and she'd hissed at him like she'd done that very first day, when she sent the stapler flying at his face. And then she'd...

well, he was pretty sure she'd almost…cried. Over *him*. It had bugged him all afternoon.

He tucked his planner under his arm and descended the staircase. The planner was more an excuse than anything else. It was a reason to paddle over to the resort tonight. Via the kayak he was thinking of buying.

The short, sturdy kayak he'd brought from California was designed for white water. And while there was some of that around, especially farther north in the Adirondacks, it wasn't the best for lake paddling. On lakes, the longer kayaks gave a faster, smoother ride. The only problem with this one, which the hardware store owner, Nate Thomas, was selling, was that it was a little *too* long. It was a two-person kayak, and Nick wasn't sure he wanted that, even if the extra seat could come in handy for carrying a cooler or other supplies. But he wasn't planning on paddling out on a three-day trip anywhere. And it wouldn't sit on the Jeep very well if he ever wanted to travel with it. He'd pretty much talked himself out of buying it before he put it in the water.

But the sleek vessel had cut through the water like a hot knife through butter tonight on the journey from his house to the resort, and was stable and easy to handle. He just never expected the trip to end with Cassie giggling and weaving across the lobby in front of him. At eleven o'clock at night. He frowned. How were these two women planning on getting home?

Her hair was pulled back, as usual, but tonight it was held in place with sparkly clips behind her ears. She was wearing a dress instead of her usual slacks and sweater. The dark gold dress, swirling above her knees, was loose and fluttery. The fabric followed her curves when she moved. Her smile was a little crooked, and a lot adorable, as she watched Julie walk away. She headed for the coffee bar—definitely a good idea in her condition—and swayed only a little.

She was so intent on opening her tea bag packet and actually getting the bag *inside* the cup that she jumped when he walked up behind her.

"Pulling an all-nighter, Miss Smith?"

"Nick! What are you doing here? And why are you dressed like…"

She gestured to his attire, which he'd forgotten about. Battered cargo shorts and a well-worn T-shirt from Yosemite. A ball cap sat backward on his head, and he quickly grabbed it off and ran his fingers through his hair, tucking the cap in his back pocket.

"I'm more interested in why you're so dressed up. What was the occasion?"

Her brows furrowed, then she looked down at her dress.

"Oh! This? Uh…Blake's flight was delayed and Amanda needed Julie and me to help entertain some investors who arrived today."

"And how exactly did you entertain them?" Had she been hanging out at the bar with sleazebag bankers all night?

She rolled her eyes. "We had *dinner* with them, Nick. No self-defense moves required. Then we decided we deserved a girls' night out and went to the bar. And I had my first Gallant Lake Sunset. Well…" She smiled and shrugged. "I had my first four Gallant Lake Sunsets."

"You had *four* drinks? And you think you're driving home?"

She turned away from him, finally managing to get the tea bag inside the cup. She filled it with hot water and added her usual three packets of sugar. Her voice turned prim. "That's not really your concern, is it? After all, we're just coworkers. Just friends. So go on and do whatever it is you're doing, and don't worry about me."

She said "just friends" as if it was an accusation. It was what they'd *both* agreed to Monday morning. Unless maybe she wanted more? That possibility had Nick once again reciting all the reasons they shouldn't. Coworkers. Baggage. And... What was the last one? The memory of how she felt in his arms was short-circuiting his ability to focus. He forced himself to be the responsible one.

"I heard somewhere that friends don't let friends drive drunk, so I have every right to ask how you're getting home."

She heaved a dramatic sigh. "Fine. If you must know, Julie's driving me."

Nick couldn't help laughing. "The same Julie who was drinking with you and Amanda? Where is Amanda, anyway?" The last thing he needed was for the boss's wife to get in trouble under his watch.

"She went home. And before you ask, no, she didn't drive, and yes, Bill walked her to Halcyon. There he is right now." She gestured toward the main entrance and took a sip of her tea.

Bill saw them and headed their way at the same time Julie did.

"What's up, boss? I just walked Mrs…"

"Yeah, I know. Thanks." Nick fixed his gaze on Julie. "Are you in any shape to drive?"

"Sure. I had water for the last round, so I should be good." She pushed her short brown hair behind her ear and gave him a confident smile.

"But the multiple rounds before that were not water, right?"

"Yeah, but it was only wine. I wasn't pounding the

cocktails like Little Miss Cassie here. That's why I'm driving her home."

Nick looked at Bill, who sighed and nodded in agreement with the unspoken request. He turned back to Julie. "No, you're not. Even if you feel sober, there's no way you'd pass a Breathalyzer, and Dan doesn't seem like the type of cop to let that slide." Nick had met the local sheriff's deputy, Dan Adams, for lunch last week to discuss security measures at the resort. The guy seemed like a stand-up cop who cared about his community, and the community returned the sentiment. Everyone called him Sheriff Dan. "Julie, Bill's gonna drive you home."

She opened her mouth to object, but thought better of it.

Cassie spoke up. "What about me?"

"I'll get you home." He didn't mention it would be via kayak, but once they got back to his place, he'd put her in the Jeep and drive her to her apartment. Just like any good friend would do.

It was a sign of how much alcohol she'd had that she followed him out the back door of the resort without question. It wasn't until they were halfway down the lawn that she realized where they were headed.

"Wait. This isn't the parking lot. Where are we going?"

"I came here by boat. It'll only take a few minutes to get to my place and the Jeep."

"Oh. Okay. A boat ride sounds fun."

It wasn't until they got to shore and he pointed her in the direction of the long kayak that she balked.

"That's not a boat, it's a canoe!"

"It's not a canoe, it's a kayak."

"It has no motor!"

"*I'm* the motor. Don't worry about it. You sit up front and I'll have us back to my place in no time."

"Will it hold both of us without sinking?"

"It won't sink, trust me."

"But it's pitch-black out there! No one will see us if we drown. Will it tip over?"

"Not if you behave yourself. Come on, slip your shoes off and I'll help you get in."

That effort was a little tricky between her dress and alcohol consumption, but he finally got her settled and pushed off the beach, hopping in behind her. She squealed when the kayak rocked, and made a move to jump out.

"Sit!" He barked out the word, and she froze. "Stay still and trust me, okay?"

She didn't answer, but she did settle back into her seat, tense but curious.

"So you've done this before? Kayaked in the dark?" She hesitated. "With a girl?"

"I've competed in white-water kayak races, and I've kayaked in four different countries. And yes, I have been out on some waters with just the light of the moon to guide me."

She turned so quickly he had to steady the craft with the paddle. "But have you been with a *girl* after dark?"

Was shy little Cassie *flirting* with him right now? He needed to get her tipsy more often.

"I've been with plenty of girls after dark."

"But in a *kayak*?"

"No, sweetie, you're my first."

She did a fist pump that had him resting the paddle in the water again to steady the vessel.

"Yes! I'm your first!" A weird something fluttered in his chest.

"Turn around and sit still, will you? I'm trying to keep this thing upright."

She turned as requested, dropping her hand to run her fingertips through the moonlit water. But she wasn't done being playful.

"Are you really worried you can't keep it upright, Nick?"

He swallowed hard and didn't answer. This woman would have no problem keeping him "upright." He was almost there now. He put a little more effort into paddling, and the kayak started slicing through the water. The light on the back of his rental house was glowing bright. He angled them toward shore.

Cassie sat back, looking up at the moon as her fingers traced in and out of the water. Her voice was low and soft, as if she was talking to herself.

"It's beautiful out here."

Another big swallow for Nick, his eyes never leaving her. "Yes, it is."

She was so quiet the rest of the way that he thought she might be nodding off. The alcohol was probably catching up to her. He wasn't prepared when, as he was nearing the shoreline, she sat up and moved to leave the kayak.

"Oh! We're here! I'll help pull the boat in…"

"No! Cassie!"

She didn't do a bad job of holding her body up and swinging her legs over the kayak before dropping into the water. The problem was, even though they were only fifteen feet offshore, the water was still over four feet deep. Cassie's eyes went wide as she kept going, not hitting bottom until the cold water was up to her chest. She grabbed at the kayak, tilting it wildly. He struggled for a moment to keep it steady, then realized he had no choice but to get wet if he was going to get her safely out of the water without flipping the boat. He emptied his pockets and dived in, grabbing the kayak line with one hand when he came up and Cassie with the other.

"Come on, you goofball. Out of the lake and inside the house."

She was sputtering and starting to shiver.

"I thought you were driving me home?"

"Yeah, well, that was before you decided to take us for a chilly swim. We both need to get warm and dry first." She didn't argue, the night air cold on their wet skin. He pulled the kayak up and onto the lawn, then took her arm and led her inside.

Chapter Eleven

Most of Cassie's alcohol-induced glow popped like a bubble when she hit the cold water of Gallant Lake. She'd watched Nick wade several yards offshore at the resort in knee-deep water. When she saw how close to shore they were at his place, she figured she'd be helpful—the level of her helpful ability probably inflated by cocktails—and bring the kayak in. It wasn't as much the cold as it was that moment of terror as she kept going and wondered if she'd ever hit bottom that sobered her up in a hurry. By the time her feet hit bottom, she was soaked up to her breasts, the gold dress clinging to her and turning nearly transparent.

She followed Nick up the steps to the deck behind his cute little rental house. As soon as they were inside, he grabbed a blanket from the back of the sofa and wrapped it tightly around her.

"Hang on and I'll get some towels." He saw her head-to-toe shiver and frowned. "On second thought, maybe you should go take a hot shower to warm up. I've got a shirt you can put on after, and some sweats."

She shook her head sharply. "I can shower at home."

"I know that." He took her shoulders and turned her toward the hall. "But you're cold and wet *now*, and we're not heading to your place right away because I am *also* cold and wet. Go on, and I'll bring you dry things. I'll shower in my room." He gave her a light push toward the bathroom door, reaching in front of her to turn on the light.

And just like that, she was alone in the bathroom. She waited for him to return with dry clothes before peeling off her cold dress, then locked the door and stepped into the shower. The blast of hot water killed any remaining intoxication, but she still felt…something. To be here in his house, naked, even if it was behind a locked door, felt exciting. Which was silly. But she couldn't deny what she felt. It was the same sensation she'd had on the mountain last weekend. It was desire. She moved the washcloth slowly over her skin, closing her eyes and pretending it was Nick's hands she felt. And really… What harm was there in that? She'd been without male company for a long time now, and her own fingers could do only so much. She was ready for more. And maybe a little sexy time with a player like Nick West was the solution. He'd just bragged about how many women he'd been with after dark. Why couldn't she be one of them? And then this itch would be scratched and maybe *then* they could be just friends.

She lost track of time as she let the hot steam seep into her skin. It was after midnight, but she felt wide awake. Maybe she could come up with a plan to keep Nick from taking her home tonight. Eventually she turned off the water and dried off. She slipped into Nick's sweats and shirt, both woefully too big on her, and stepped out of the bathroom. The house was quiet, and she had no sense of where Nick might be. She checked the kitchen and living area first, but it was empty. She headed farther down the hall, finding an empty guest bedroom and then Nick's room.

The only light was from the attached bathroom. Nick was on the bed, as if he'd stretched out there to wait for her. He'd showered, because his hair was rumpled and wet. He was sound asleep, one arm behind his head, the other resting on his bare chest, rising and falling in slow, deep breaths. She shook her head and sighed. So much for her big plans. He'd had a long day, and it had clearly caught up with him. She pulled his blanket up to cover him, but not before admiring his chest, cut with muscle and highlighted with a fine layer of dark hair that trailed down to vanish beneath his shorts. She wanted to reach out and touch him, but she was afraid of waking him, so she covered him and went to stretch out on the sofa to sleep.

Nick woke her two hours later. "Cass, what are you doing? Are you okay?"

"Uh...yeah. I was sleeping. Are *you* okay?"

He ran his fingers through his dark hair, leaving it standing even more on end than it was to start with. "Did I fall asleep while you were showering? Damn, I'm sorry. Why don't you use the spare room and I'll run you home in the morning. Or I can take you now if you want..."

Cassie shrugged off the blanket and stood. She'd been dreaming about Nick and now he was there in front of her. The hum she'd felt before was still moving under her skin. She put her hand on Nick's chest, sad that he'd slipped on a T-shirt before coming to find her. He sucked in a sharp breath.

"What are you doing?"

"What do you think I'm doing?" She moved closer, and his eyes darkened. "Let's face it, Nick. The whole 'just friends' thing isn't going to work if we're both wondering what we'd be like together. That kiss last Saturday promised some things that don't fit in the friend zone."

He set his hand over hers. "Cassie, you've been drinking, and…"

"That was hours ago, and the dunk in the cold lake pretty much took care of it. Any liquor left in my system after that was washed away in the shower. I'm perfectly sober." She was also tired, and steadfastly ignoring that ever-present "be careful" voice in her head. If she woke up too much…if she thought about this too much… She'd never go through with it. She pushed onto her toes and pressed her lips against his. He didn't react at first, but it wasn't long before he let out a low sound and slid his arm around her, pulling her tight as he took over the kiss, pushing his way into her mouth to let her know he was on board with this plan of hers.

"Are you sure?" he asked softly as he left her mouth and trailed kisses along her jawline.

She made a sound of some kind. It wasn't a word, really, but he understood it was her assent. He looked down at her with a crooked smile. "Here or in my bed?"

The sofa had been fine for sleeping, but she wanted something a little more special than a thirty-year-old pine-and-plaid sofa that had clearly been included in the lease. She took his hand and started down the hall with him obediently behind her. She could feel his amused smile, and who could blame him? It was pretty rare for her to take charge of anything, especially sex. After all, with Don...

She stopped so fast in the doorway that Nick brushed up against her, resting his hands on her shoulders. Her bravado was fading fast. If tonight was just an attempt to erase Don's hold on her, it wouldn't be fair to Nick. Could something ever be good if it was done for the wrong reason? Doubts started a whispering campaign in her head. What if it wasn't good at all? What if she couldn't please him?

Her mind was racing and blank all at the same time. This was it. The moment of truth. She focused on the electricity she felt through Nick's fingertips on the bare skin at the base of her neck and took a deep breath, still staring straight ahead.

"Nick, I want this. I really do. It's just that..." Her shoulders sagged as she felt her confidence waning. "I'm not exactly experienced... I mean, I've only been with two men in my whole life." She gave a short laugh. "The first was my college boyfriend, which was hardly memorable. The second was...well...memorable for all the wrong reasons... I'm not very good at this sex stuff. I don't want to disappoint you..."

Before she could continue, Nick kissed the back of her neck, setting her body on fire.

"My beautiful Cassandra..." She tensed at the name. Nick didn't know it wasn't really hers. There was so much he didn't know. He continued to softly kiss her neck and shoulders as he spoke. "I have two important things to say to you. First, nothing that's happened before tonight—before right this instant—matters at all. Second..." Nick's kisses moved up her neck and toward her left ear. Cassie tilted her head to expose more of her skin to his lips as he continued. "Second... We are very definitely *not* having 'sex stuff' tonight. That's what teenagers do the in the back seat of their dad's Buick. If you walk through that door, I am going to give you a night like you've never experienced before."

With that, Nick gently turned Cassie so they were facing each other. He rested his forehead on hers and spoke again, staring straight into her wide eyes. "But Cassie, you're going to have to walk through that door on your own."

She felt every cell in her body singing to her to make the move.

...nothing that's happened before tonight matters at all...

She smiled and turned, lifting her chin and stepping through the doorway with determination. She walked to the center of the room, near the foot of the bed, and turned to face Nick. He was still in the doorway, with his hands resting on each side of the door frame. His coffee-colored hair fell across his forehead. His gaze was intense, his eyes so dark they were nearly black. He looked so damned sexy she thought she'd swoon right then and there.

Cassie didn't flinch from the desire she saw in his eyes. When he stepped into the room, Cassie let out the breath she didn't realize she'd been holding. He walked to her slowly, and she didn't back away. She felt no fear, had no second thoughts. She wanted this.

He folded her into his arms and kissed her. She gave as good as she got, standing on tiptoe to push against him as their tongues teased and danced together. Nick reached down and lifted the hem of her borrowed sweatshirt. She stepped away to allow him to pull it over her head, shimmying out of the loose sweatpants at the same time.

Maybe she should have felt insecure as she stood naked before him for the first time, but...no. She felt self-assured. She felt beautiful. Nick made her feel beautiful, with his dark stare and the upward curve at the edge of his mouth. He was already making love to her with his eyes, and she reveled in it.

With one smooth motion, he peeled his shirt off over his head. Cassie was more than happy to have another chance to admire his broad shoulders and the sharply defined six-pack. He was one fine specimen of a man.

He lifted her into his arms. She embraced his neck and placed her lips on his. The kiss was full of lust and need. He laid her on top of the sheets, then stepped away to shed his shorts. Nick walked to the bed and placed one knee on the edge of the mattress. He looked into her eyes and she knew he was looking for permission. She granted it with a barely perceptible nod.

She could feel his gaze sweeping across her skin, and it made her blood burn with need. When his eyes reached hers, he fell on her like a starving man falls on an all-you-can-eat buffet.

They were consumed by the heat of their desire. Their hands ran over each other's bodies frantically. Nick's kisses began on her forehead and ran down her neck and chest. He paused along the way to trace her breasts with his lips, as light as a whisper, before he went across her abdomen, then ever lower. Cassie's nervous anticipation of everything that was to come had her writhing in excitement before he even reached his goal. His fingertips were tracing the same trail around her breasts that his lips had just followed. She moaned, her eyes closed as his mouth settled on her most private and sensitive place. She tried to resist letting herself go too soon, but failed. Loudly. He was too damned good at what he was doing, and she fell hard.

Now it was Nick's turn to moan as he continued, ignoring Cassie's pleas for mercy as she continued to move under his onslaught. He stopped only to tear open a condom wrapper grabbed from the nightstand, then he followed his own trail of kisses back up to her lips. Her legs curled around his torso, and she cried out his name when he entered her. She dug her fingernails into his back, causing him to grunt in response. His muscles rippled under her fingers.

They both felt a driving sense of urgency. The sheets wrapped around them as they moved across the bed. At one point, Nick grasped Cassie tightly and rolled so that she was astride him. She braced herself with her arms beside his shoulders. They stopped moving momentarily and she looked down at him. Her hair fell wildly around her face. She felt giddy with power.

Nick smiled up at her. "You seem pleased with yourself, ma'am."

Cassie gave a throaty laugh. "Oh, I am very pleased indeed. I'm even *more* pleased to see that I'm pleasing you."

"Oh, you are definitely doing that, babe."

They smiled slyly at each other as if they were both in on some very special secret. Nick put his hand securely on her back and rolled so that she was lying under him again, without breaking their bond. He kissed her gently and began to press into her at an increasing pace. Cassie felt the room spinning as her body responded yet again. She closed her eyes and arched her back. As she did, Nick slid his arm under her and lifted her lower body up into the air as he rose to his knees. And that was it for her. She cried out and let herself fly.

Nick shouted her name roughly and dropped her back to the bed, setting his teeth on the tender skin at the base of her throat as he drove on to his own release. His face dropped over her shoulder into the pillow beneath her. They lay in that position for several minutes, their deep breaths the only sound in the room.

As Nick's body weight pressed down on Cassie, she finally had to react. She tapped the front of his shoulder and softly said, "Nick, you have to move."

"No." He muttered it into her hair without flinching. "You destroyed me. I can't move."

"Yeah, well, I can't breathe, so you're going to have to move or listen to me suffocate."

Nick groaned loudly and rolled to lie at her side, with one arm draped over her ribs as he got rid of the condom with the other. Cassie put her hand on her chest and felt the sheen of sweat on her skin. Her heart was pounding.

Nick covered her hand with his. She turned away from him, pressing her back against his chest. He pulled her tight and kissed the base of her neck.

"I'm a shell of a man right now. I knew we had a physical attraction going on, but…damn, girl! That was some wickedly world-class sex."

Cassie smiled in contentment. "I didn't even know there *could* be sex like that, Nick. If this house were on fire right now, I wouldn't have the strength to move, much less stand or run."

Nick laughed softly, his mouth near her ear. "Then we'd burn together, babe, because I can't move, either. Now go to sleep. You're safe in my arms. Just go to sleep…" His voice was fading as he spoke.

When she woke, the digital clock on the side of the bed read 4:28 a.m. She'd rolled over onto her stomach in her sleep, and someone's fingers were lightly tracing up and down her spine. She lifted her head and Nick, propped up on one elbow, smiled down at her softly.

"So," he said, "it wasn't a dream."

Cassie stretched like a cat, turned on her side to face him and returned his smile. "Felt pretty dreamy to me."

He reached out and brushed Cassie's hair behind her ear. "There's only one problem. It left me wanting more."

"Really? I seem to have the same problem…"

Cassie leaned forward and kissed him, sliding her arm around his neck. Without saying another word, they made love again. But this time, it was less frantic, less desperate. They took things slow and easy. There was no crying out of names, only sighs and whispers and soft moans as they caressed each other, exploring each other's bodies with their fingers and lips. Eventually they brought each other to a sweet and tender release that left them both trembling. Cassie fell asleep clasped tightly in Nick's embrace, and she felt more secure and protected than she'd ever felt in her life.

It couldn't last, of course. She'd kept secrets from him. Big ones. They were just two grown-ups scratching an itch and all that.

But Cassie couldn't shake the illogical but powerful conviction that here, in Nick's arms, was exactly where she belonged.

Chapter Twelve

Nick slipped out of bed shortly after dawn. Cassie turned and murmured something unintelligible, then settled back to sleep. He watched her for a moment, then walked away. He needed to clear his head.

He thought maybe last night would be a resolution of their "chemistry" issue. But he'd been a fool to think one night with Cassie would ever be enough. He'd seen enough addicts on the street to know that for some, all it took was one time—one hit—and they were hooked. That's how he felt. Just one night with Cassie, and he was toast. Her kiss had ruined him for all other kisses, and making love with her had destroyed him for all other women.

What did it mean, though? Was there any chance in hell of them having a relationship that wouldn't make a mess of both their work life *and* their friendship? Was she even interested in a relationship? Or was last night enough for her? Maybe she'd explored their chemistry and found it wanting. Would that be a good thing? Or would it make the ache he felt in his chest just that much worse?

He took his cup from the coffee maker and gulped half of it, anxious to clear the fog in his head. He glanced around for his phone, then remembered he'd taken it out of his pocket before diving in the lake last night. Hopefully it was still in the kayak. He headed outside, where a gentle mist rolled across the smooth surface of the water.

The phone screen was lit up with messages, and something else was buzzing in the boat. Cassie's purse was still there, and her phone was going off, too. Had something happened at the resort? His phone chimed with an incoming call. Blake Randall. He frowned. *Something* was happening, that's for sure. Blake wouldn't call him this early on a Saturday morning otherwise.

"Blake? What's up?"

"I don't know, man. You tell me."

"I…what?"

Blake let out a sigh. "Just tell me if Cassie's with you, wherever you are."

"I… I'm home." Nick stalled. "Why are you asking about Cassie?"

"Julie said you were giving Cassie a ride home. But she's *not* home. Are you saying she's not with you?" Blake's tone sharpened with concern, and Nick had to come clean.

"She's here."

"Thank Christ." Blake's voice grew faint as he spoke away from the phone. "She's okay. She's with Nick." Amanda's voice was muffled in the background. Blake came back on the phone. "Did something happen? My wife's been texting and calling her all damn night. She was getting ready to call Dan Adams and report her missing. Was she scared to go home or something? She's not running, is she?"

"Running? Running where?" Nick grabbed Cassie's purse and headed back into the house, trying his best to catch up with this conversation.

"From Don. The asshole who almost killed her a couple years ago. Damn. She hasn't told you that yet, has she?" Blake paused. "Wait. If she wasn't scared to go home, then why is she at…?" Another pause. "Aw, hell. Are you two a *thing* now?"

Amanda's voice was much louder now. "I knew it!"

Blake shushed her. "So she's at your place because *why* exactly?"

Nick wasn't used to being grilled by his employer about whom he did or didn't sleep with.

"No offense, Blake, but I don't see how that's your concern. I'm sorry you two were worried, but Cassie's safely asleep and this won't affect our job performance on Monday."

Blake digested that for a minute, then agreed. "Fair enough, but I call BS on the job bit. It'll affect you at work, one way or the other." Amusement crept into his voice. "Just do your best to keep things cool, and don't hurt that woman or you'll have to deal with my wife *and* her cousins. Trust me when I say that won't be pretty."

"O-kay." This was one of those small-town things he'd have to get used to. People knew your business and took sides. In LA, they were too busy to care. Blake's voice dropped.

"Nick, now that my wife is out of the room, let me say one more thing. Cassie and Amanda have some stuff in common from their pasts, and you need to know about it before you go much further. If you're serious about her, you need to talk. If you're not serious about her, well… You're an idiot. She's a hell of a woman."

"Yeah. I know. Thanks."

After the call, Nick sat on the sofa and watched the lake wake up with Saturday action. At this hour, it was primarily local fishermen, drifting or trolling with their lines in the water, occasionally pulling in a fish. A blue heron strolled calmly along the shoreline, watching for minnows.

So Cassie had secrets. As a former cop, it bugged Nick that he didn't know that. Of course, he knew she'd been assaulted in a parking garage, and the incident made her hypervigilant. Maybe that's all Blake had been referring to. But Nick suspected there was a lot more to it than that. It was something Amanda had in common with her, but that information wasn't helpful, since Nick didn't know Amanda's past. Had she been a victim of some crime, too? Was everyone at the resort hiding some dark past, or was it simply overblown small-town drama?

"Good morning." He turned to see Cassie standing near the kitchen. She'd pulled on the sweatshirt he'd given her last night, and it fell off one shoulder to reveal a swath of white skin he suddenly hungered for. Secrets or not, he wanted her again.

"Good morning." He stood and headed into the kitchen to start breakfast. Keeping busy would settle his mind and make the situation less awkward. "Scrambled eggs and sausage okay?"

"Um, sure. Or I could go…"

"Do you want to go?"

She stared at the floor and shrugged. Insecure Cassie had returned. "I'll do whatever you prefer. I don't want to be in your way."

He'd learned that a blunt approach tended to snap Cassie out of this timid persona that always made him angry. Angry *for* her, not with her.

"What I'd prefer is you naked on the sofa while I cook, so I can enjoy the best view in town."

Her mouth dropped open and her face colored. Then she laughed, and he saw the spark of confidence return to her eyes.

"And what about *my* view? What would I get out of this deal?"

"I don't think nudity and frying pans go together very well, so you'll have to wait for your special view."

"Yeah, well—so will you. I'm going to go freshen up and see if my dress is salvageable. I left it hanging in the bathroom. I don't suppose you have any tea?"

"I think there's a box in the cupboard on the end."

Cassie found the green box and smiled. "English Breakfast. My favorite."

"I don't have a teapot."

"Don't need one. I'll run water through the coffee maker without putting a pod in there. That's how I do it at the office." She dropped the tea bag into a mug, pressing the button with a grin. "I'm very resourceful."

The conversation was neutral. Normal, even. They were just a couple of adults, standing in the kitchen together. He had no shirt. She had no pants. Making breakfast. It was nice.

A sizzle from the stove brought his attention back to cooking, and by the time he looked up again, she was gone. She returned as he was plating the food, wearing a wrinkled, but dry, dark yellow dress. Her hair was pulled back into her usual ponytail. Her skin was radiant. Nick frowned. *Radiant?* Since when did he start using words like that? She took her plate to the small table by the windows. Since he met a woman like Cassandra.

They were almost done eating breakfast before he thought to tell her that Blake had called.

"Oh, God, I was supposed to text Amanda last night! I completely forgot. Where's my purse?" She jumped up from the table.

"Relax. She knows you're here and you're okay." He carried the plates and utensils to the kitchen, nodding at her purse as he passed it.

"Amanda knows I'm *here*? Oh, no. That means they all know…"

"They?"

"The cousins. Amanda, Nora and Mel are basically one unit. What one knows, they all know." She groaned. "I hope Nora didn't tell Aunt Cathy…" She scrolled through her phone, then hurriedly typed a message. It chirped a minute later, and her shoulders relaxed. "Amanda said Cathy doesn't know and she's off today anyway. She also said I have lots of 'splaining to do. Tomorrow's coffee meeting should be fun."

"Coffee meeting?" This was the problem with having a casual breakfast conversation with someone you didn't know all that well. There were too many blanks to fill in. Which reminded him that he had a few blanks he needed filled in sooner rather than later.

"We have coffee early on Sunday at Nora's café, before the after-church crowd starts filling up the place. Amanda insisted I join them, because she thinks I need friends." She frowned, and he had a feeling she'd said more than she'd intended.

"You don't have friends?" Nick finished cleaning the cooking pans and put them away. Cassie shrugged, looking everywhere but at him. "Cass?"

"Well…I'm fairly new to town, and it's not always easy to make new friends. Especially when you're a homebody like me."

"What about your friends in Milwaukee?"

She stiffened. "There weren't many. Not *any* that lasted past me leaving town." She gave him a bright, tense smile. "Like I said, I'm a homebody. Give me tea and a book and I'm happy."

"But you had a job there. Didn't you make friends at work?"

Nick knew how to read body language, and hers was screaming that she didn't want to have this conversation. He moved closer and put his hands on her shoulders, tipping her chin up with his thumbs.

"Hey, it's me. The guy you had wild-and-crazy sex with last night." The corner of her mouth twitched toward a smile, but her eyes were clouded. He bent over and kissed her.

It was supposed to be a quick kiss to jolt her into trusting him, but as soon as his lips touched hers, he forgot all about his motivation. He wanted more. His hands slipped behind her head and he kissed her hard and long. And damn if she didn't kiss him right back, matching him beat for beat. Her fingers buried in his hair, and she pressed her hips against him, creating an instant response. He pushed her against the wall and dropped his hands to cup her behind and hold her against his now-aching body. She hooked a leg around his, as if afraid he'd move away. Not a snowball's chance in hell. He lifted her up and slipped his hand under her dress, quickly moving past the lacy underwear he encountered.

She moaned his name, long and slow and rough, and he slid his mouth down her neck to nip at her throat, all the while moving his fingers inside her. She was grinding against him, and he was ready to lose his mind. It was broad daylight. They'd just had breakfast. He was supposed to be taking her home because everyone was so concerned about them being together. It was a mistake to keep this going. They worked together. They had baggage. She was keeping secrets. The back of her head hit the wall with a thud as she arched her body against him. That cold-shower list of excuses didn't work anymore. He knew what sex with her was like now, and when she shuddered in his arms and cried out as she came for him, he knew where they were going to end up.

"I want you. In my bed. Right now."

She dropped her head to his shoulder and nodded against him. It was all he needed. He scooped her into his arms and carried her down the hall. There was a flurry of clothing hitting the floor. He was so desperate to be inside her that he almost forgot protection. She laughed when he swore at the foil package, which didn't open anywhere near as fast as he needed it to. And finally, *finally*, they were connected and moving as one. It was fast and hard and hot and they both made the same strangled sound of ecstasy when they reached their goal together. He stayed over her, unable to look away from the sight of her hair splayed out on the mattress beneath her like a flame.

She pinched his side. "You gonna stay there all day?"

He bent down and kissed her. "Would you mind if I did?"

Her smile lost some of its light. "Real life is going to catch up with us sooner or later."

He nodded. "Yeah, this was a very nice but unexpected detour on our morning." He reluctantly left her softness and slid off the bed. "I'm going to shower, then I'll take you home. After we talk about what comes next."

Chapter Thirteen

What comes next...

Cassie tried to sort out her poor, abused gold dress for the second time that morning, but it was hopeless. Somehow, it had been torn both near the neckline and under one arm. She couldn't blame Nick, because he hadn't undressed her. No, that was her, in a frenzy to get naked, who had torn the most expensive dress she owned. It was bad enough she'd be doing the walk of shame to her apartment in broad daylight, but to do it in a rumpled, water-stained and torn dress? With hopeless bed hair, kiss-swollen lips and a general haze of good-sex vibes in her eyes? Ugh. If the cousins saw her like this, she'd never hear the end of it.

...what comes next...

She glanced at the bedroom window. She could probably escape the upcoming conversation by climbing through it, but she had no idea how to get home from here. Like it or not, she was going to have to talk about "what comes next" with Nick. Sex last night was beyond her dreams. She'd thought she was going to have a night with a guy who kissed her senseless, and then she'd be able to move on. Easy-peasy. Sure, she'd expected it to be good. But being in bed—or against a wall—with Nick was more than good. It was…transformative. There wasn't a chance in hell either one of them would be able to pretend last night, or this morning, didn't happen.

So…what? A relationship? Bad idea. Despite her best efforts to pretend it wasn't the case, her life was a mess. At any moment she might have to pack up and run. If she and Nick were going to be more than just one night—and morning—he needed to know that. He needed to know everything.

She did her best to tame her hair back into a ponytail and found a clean black T-shirt in Nick's dresser. She pulled it over her dress and tied it into a knot at her hip. Not exactly a fashion statement, but it concealed the torn fabric and most of the wrinkles. She grinned at her reflection. If she pulled her ponytail over to the side of her head and teased it a little, she'd look like a flashback to *Flashdance.*

Nick apparently thought the same thing. He gave her a wide smile.

"Nice look. Are you off to the disco later?"

"I did the best I could. Maybe we should wait until after dark to take me home." It was bad enough the cousins knew she'd spent the night with Nick. The whole town would know it if she tried to sneak into her apartment in the center of town in an outfit straight out of the 1980s.

"That's your decision, babe. But first…" He patted

the sofa cushion next to him. "We need to talk, Miss Smith."

"That's not my name." Not exactly the way she wanted to start this conversation, but the words just blurted out. Nick leaned forward and frowned.

"Your last name isn't Smith?"

She twisted her fingers together. She was in it now, and Nick deserved to know the truth.

"My last name isn't Smith. It's Zetticci. And my first name isn't Cassandra. It's Cassidy."

"Your name is Cassidy Zetticci. For real." He started to smile, as if he thought she might be pulling his leg. When she didn't respond, he realized it was no joke. "How did you manage to get past the resort's background check?"

"Really? *That's* the first question you have?"

He stared at the floor for a moment, his foot tapping anxiously. "I looked at your employee file." He glanced up and noted her surprise. "I look at *everyone's* files, Cassie. It's my job. You picked the most common surname in America to make yourself harder to find. Who's looking? Don?"

Now it was her turn to be surprised. "How do you know about Don?"

"Well, I didn't hear about him from *you*." He stood and paced by the windows. Carefully avoiding her. "Blake mentioned the name this morning, and it's not that hard to put together. He's the one who assaulted you, right?"

On which occasion?

"Yes."

Nick stopped, his brows furrowed.

"And now he's stalking you?"

"Yes."

"You were in a relationship with him?"

He was in full cop mode now.

"He was my husband."

Blake didn't move, yet Cassie could feel him backing away. His eyes went icy cold. His hands curled into fists, then quickly released. His mouth slid into a disapproving frown.

"You stayed married to a guy who beat you." He was no longer asking questions. He was accusing. And she didn't like it.

"I said he *was* my husband. Past tense."

"Did you leave the first time he hit you?"

"Am I a suspect in some crime here, Officer?"

He rubbed the back of his neck, his jaw sawing back and forth. He turned away, staring out the window toward the lake. She waited, not willing to give him any more information until she knew what he was thinking. Of all the reactions she'd anticipated, anger with *her* hadn't been one of them. He shoved his hands in his pockets and let out a long breath.

"I wasn't ready to hear that you were a victim of domestic violence. I thought it was some stranger…"

"Does it matter?"

"It shouldn't."

"No kidding. But it obviously does." She shook her head. "In the interest of full disclosure, he was a police officer. A patrolman."

Nick turned. "He was a *cop*?"

"Yes, Nick. He was a cop. Believe it or not, cops do bad stuff, too. Or are you going to stand behind your 'blue line' bullshit and deny that?"

They'd completely traded places now. She was the angry one, while Nick seemed chagrined.

"The blue line is a brotherhood, not a blindfold. It doesn't protect criminals."

She scoffed at that, remembering the lost friendships and lack of support from the police in Milwaukee after Don was charged. The roadblocks that were thrown up time and again as the district attorney put the case together. The mishandling of evidence that led to the retrial now pending. While Don remained free.

Nick took a step toward her, and she tensed. He stopped, reaching out to take her hands gently.

"Okay, let me rephrase that. It *shouldn't* be used to protect bad guys. I'm sorry. I…I have some history with domestic abuse victims as a detective. Some bad history." He gave her hand a squeeze and she looked up to meet his gaze.

The coldness was gone. She was once again looking at the man who'd whispered kisses across her ear when he thought she was asleep last night. The man she trusted. The corner of his mouth lifted into a half smile.

"Last week we agreed we both had baggage, Cass. I brushed it off as no big deal. But I'm beginning to suspect the things that led each of us to be in Gallant Lake are a little more connected than we imagined." He lifted her hand and pressed a kiss to her knuckles. "We had a deal that if you went hiking with me, then I was going to owe you a day of sitting quietly. Today's that day. Let's sit and talk."

"Actually, I think you said you owed me a day of doing whatever I wanted, and you're crazy if you think I want to talk about this."

"You can have the rest of the day to boss me around. But right now we need to talk. No assumptions. No grilling for answers. Okay?"

Her voice dropped to almost a whisper. "It makes me feel weak. Vulnerable. Stupid."

"Hey." Nick tipped her chin up with his finger. "I saw from the first moment we met that you were a fighter. Not weak. Not vulnerable. And definitely not stupid. So get those words out of your vocabulary. That's *him* talking, and you need to kick that asshole out of your head. Now I understand why you apologize and doubt yourself all the time, and that needs to stop."

"It's not that easy."

He pressed a soft kiss on her lips, and she welcomed the warmth of it. "Nothing worthwhile ever is."

They settled onto the sofa. She sipped her fresh cup of tea, stalling for time. Nick waited patiently, and she finally had to fill the silence with something. So she started at the beginning.

She told him how she'd always been a shy kid. Her parents had a volatile marriage and an even more volatile divorce. To avoid their arguments as a child, she'd stayed in her room and lost herself in books. She was good with numbers and awkward with people. Don was the opposite—outgoing, with the ability to charm everyone he met, from children to little old ladies.

She was working at an insurance company when Don came in to discuss an accident investigation involving one of their clients. She'd been fascinated by the handsome, blue-eyed blond in uniform. He looked like a Nordic god, and he paid attention to *her*. He was ten years older and had the kind of calm confidence she'd craved. She couldn't believe it when he asked her out for coffee.

He made it easy to want to be with him. He took her mom to the ballet, and he took her dad fishing on Lake Michigan. He was the first thing in years that her parents agreed on—they adored him. He treated Cassie like a princess, and if he was a little controlling, he'd always explain that it was only because he loved her so much and wanted the best for her. And she'd believed him. She'd married him, ignoring the little warning signs leading up to the big day.

"What kind of warning signs?" Nick reached over and took her hand.

"He made *all* the decisions about the wedding. Where. When. What I'd wear. Whom we'd invite— which did *not* include any of my friends from school or my coworkers. He started distancing me from my former life, told me I was 'too mature for that crowd.' He pressured me to be like the other, older police wives. I was so eager for his approval that I threw myself into it, not noticing I was leaving my life behind for his." She took another sip of tea, delaying the words that made her cringe with shame. "We'd been married a year when he hit me for the first time. I had a flat tire one night. A coworker changed it for me, but I was late getting home. Don accused me of lying and told me I must be cheating on him. It was so ridiculous that I laughed, and he slapped me. Hard."

Nick didn't say a word, but his grip tightened on her hand as she told him the rest. About Don's tearful apology. That time, and the next time, and the next time after that. The way he subtly made everything her fault. If only she wouldn't "provoke" him, he wouldn't lose control. The episodes were sporadic at first, and she thought he really meant it every time he said he'd never hurt her again.

But when he was passed over for sergeant, things took a darker turn. It was all her fault, of course. She'd distracted him because he had to "keep an eye on her" all the time. She'd embarrassed him with her appearance, her words, her behavior. She was flirting with everyone. She didn't listen. She finally worked up the courage to walk away after he tried to push her down the stairs in their home one night. But leaving didn't make her safe.

"He's the one who assaulted you in the parking garage?"

She nodded. "I'd gone out with a bunch of people from work to celebrate my birthday. It felt so good to be with people my own age, relaxed and laughing. No one there to criticize my every move. It was the first night I'd felt *free* in ages. It was a new beginning. On the way back to my car, he jumped me and just started punching, over and over, telling me what a whore I was. He broke my cheekbone and five ribs. Punctured a lung. Slammed my head against the cement so hard that I was unconscious for two days."

"Jesus…" Nick's voice was thick with emotion.

"Yeah."

"So the bastard's in jail?"

"Not exactly." She shrugged. "He went to trial, but there was some mysterious mix-up with the evidence or procedure or something, and the judge declared a mistrial. His new trial is coming up. Meanwhile, he's on probation and isn't supposed to leave Milwaukee or contact me in any way. I moved to Cleveland to put some distance between us, but he tracked me down. Got my phone number. My address. Called the office where I worked. Started texting me with threats from a burner phone or something, telling me he was watching me. The DA's office said that wasn't possible, but it freaked me out. Don had never met Aunt Cathy, so I called her, changed my name and came to Gallant Lake."

Nick stared out at the water. She could tell he had a

lot of questions, but he was trapped by his promise not to grill her. He was tense. Angry. With her? He said he had a "bad history" with domestic violence victims, but she had no idea what that meant. Police went on a lot of those calls, of course. And they tended to be fraught with danger because they were so unpredictable. Did something happen? She reached out to touch his hand, but he flinched and she pulled back, hurt and confused. Never one to stay still for long, Nick got up and started pacing again. He rubbed his neck in agitation, coming to a stop but not making eye contact.

"I should probably get you back to your place." Her heart fell.

"That's all you have to say?"

He finally met her gaze, and she was shocked to see his eyes shining with...tears? She stood, and he blinked away from her as if he knew what she'd seen. This wasn't about her. This reaction of his may have been triggered by her story, but it wasn't about *her*. It was about someone else.

His voice was gruff. "I know I'm being a jackass right now, and I'm sorry. But I need a little time to digest this."

"Was it the woman in the photo? Your partner? Was she abused?"

Cassie knew his partner was dead. Had she been murdered by her spouse?

His mouth hardened. "Jada wasn't abused. She would never have put up with tha..." She did her best not to show how much that hurt.

Nick shook his head. "Shit, I don't mean it like that. I just..." He stared up at the ceiling. "Jada was killed on the job. By a guy who beat his wife."

Cassie sucked in a sharp breath.

...the things that brought each of us to Gallant Lake are a little more connected than we imagined...

"Nick, I'm so sorry."

He gave a short laugh, but there was no humor in it. "I haven't even said those words to you, have I? I didn't tell you how sorry I am for the hell you went through. That's how far in my own head I am right now. Look, I need to process this..."

They stood there for a few minutes, neither of them moving or speaking. He was wound so tight she thought he'd snap. She knew what that felt like. It was her normal. But Nick—this strong man who kept people safe for a living—didn't know how to deal with the fear of losing control. It wasn't until she saw a small shudder go through his body that she knew she had to help him. And she had a crazy idea that might snap him out of his melancholy.

"So the plan is for us to spend today doing what I want to do, right?"

Nick finally took his eyes off the ceiling and looked at her.

"I don't think that's a good idea, Cass. I'm feeling a little...raw...right now. I won't be good company. Let me just take you home, okay?" He walked to the sliding glass doors but froze when she placed her hand on his shoulder. She hated to see him in this kind of pain.

"What I have planned will help you relax. Come on."

He pulled the door open, still not looking back. "I don't think..."

"You don't have to think. You just have to do what I say. That was the deal, and you're a man of your word, right?"

She peeked around his shoulder to glimpse up at his face and saw the quick, reluctant smile.

"I'm a man of my word."

"I thought so. Get moving."

"Where are we going?"

"My place. I have everything we need there."

"Need for *what* exactly?"

She gave him a push to propel him through the door. "You'll see when you get there."

"That's wrong. I told you what we were doing last week."

She laughed. "You told me it was going to be a *stroll*. That was a hell of a lot more than a stroll."

He turned, his gaze heated. "Yeah, it was a lot more than a stroll."

She shoved him again, knowing he was referring to that red-hot kiss that ultimately led to them falling into bed together last night. "Go on. You climb rocks to unwind. I'm going to show you how I do it."

Chapter Fourteen

"You expect me to take a *bubble bath*?"

Nick stared, stupefied. No way in hell was he getting into that tub full of sweet-smelling foam, surrounded by candles. *Candles!*

"You expected me to climb a mountain, so yes, I expect you to take a bubble bath. It's decadent and a lot like being in a sensory-deprivation capsule. The world just falls away, and you can't help but relax." Cassie looked pretty proud of herself.

He never saw this coming. He'd tried to bail on her, but she had a stubborn streak a mile wide, and she was determined this was his Day to Obey. When they got to her place, they'd sat in the living room of her funky little loft above the coffee shop for a while. He didn't think anything of it when she excused herself, figuring she'd gone to change. She *had* changed, into a simple top and jeans, but she'd also created…this.

After she'd dropped that bombshell on him earlier about having a crazy ex-husband who nearly beat
her to death, he'd been having a hard time pulling his
thoughts into line. The story filled him with rage. Rage
that someone had hurt her. Put her on the run. Made her
feel like a lesser person.

He already had an endless slideshow running on a
loop in his head 24/7 from that night two years ago. Beth
Washington admitting she'd let Earl move back into her
house. His partner, Jada, who had always wanted children, carrying the Washingtons' baby down the hall to
put her to bed. The sound of a shotgun blast.

Now those familiar images were mixed with new
ones from his imagination. Cassie being slapped hard
across the face. Cassie at the top of a long flight of
stairs, fighting for her life. Cassie being brutally attacked in a deserted parking garage. Maybe he did need
the distraction of whatever silliness she was going to
subject him to. But a bubble bath?

"If you think I'm going into that tub, you don't know
me very well."

"I *don't* know you all that well, Nick. But I know
you're taking this bath, because you're a man of your
word, remember?"

"With the emphasis on *man*. I don't do bubble baths."

She was unimpressed.

He resorted to begging. "Come on, Cass. I don't want
to do this. It won't be relaxing, it'll be…embarrassing.
Annoying."

She folded her arms and arched a brow high.

"I distinctly remember telling you I did *not* want to
go hiking. It was hard, and exhausting, and I was embarrassed when you had to keep stopping for me. I was

pretty damn annoyed by the time we got to the top of the trail. And I was in pain."

He grabbed her waist and tugged her close. "Yeah, but look how much fun we had once we got up there. That made it all worth it, didn't it?"

The sound of her light laughter made his chest feel funny. "And who's to say you won't get a nice surprise later today..." She pushed away from him and reached for the door. "*After* you get in that tub." She gave him a wink. "Man of your word, remember?"

He groaned, knowing he'd been outplayed. She flipped off the lights and closed the door behind her, leaving him in the candlelit bathroom. It was a big tub, framed in large marble tiles. She'd told him Nora had remodeled the downstairs bathroom before Cassie moved in.

Cassie's voice called through the door. "I don't hear any splashing in there! Don't think you can bluff me, Nicholas West. I'm going to deliver a glass of wine in a little while, and you'd better be chin-deep in bubbles."

Nick shook his head. May as well get it over with. Besides, the idea of Cassie bringing wine sounded pretty damn good. Maybe he could convince her to join him after all, and restore his manly pride. He shed his clothes and stepped into the not-quite-scalding water. As he settled down into the tub, he tried to remember the last time he took an actual bath, other than soaking in some hotel hot tub. He had to have been a kid, and there were no bubbles involved that he could remember.

What was he supposed to do? Scrub behind his ears? Or just sit here and wait? He felt ridiculous. But Cassie was right—she'd hiked a mountain last weekend when she really didn't want to, and he'd made a deal. He finally leaned back and let himself settle into the water a bit. The warmth felt pretty good on his muscles, tired from a night of lovemaking, and the flickering yellow light of the candles was almost hypnotic. He closed his eyes. That hideous slideshow was still playing in his head, but the images started to shift as he inhaled the perfumed suds.

He saw Jada, but she was at her wedding now, kissing her wife, Shayla, under an arbor of ivory roses. Laughing in the car on a stakeout, teasing him about his "obsession" with healthy eating while she devoured a bacon double cheeseburger. He saw Cassie, but she was trimming the daffodils he'd given her, bending over her desk to inhale their scent and smiling to herself. She'd had no idea he'd been watching her, or she never would have let on how much she liked the stolen goods.

There was a soft tap on the door, and Cassie stepped in. Her eyes lit up when she saw him in the water, chin-deep as ordered. And the hell if he didn't feel relaxed and sated. He didn't even bother trying to deny it.

"I could do without the actual bubbles, but I gotta admit—this feels pretty good."

"Now you know another of my secrets, Nick. I do this a few times a week, just to relax and feel pampered." She handed him a glass of wine, and he was glad to see she'd brought one for herself. That meant she was staying. To her, bubble baths were about feeling pampered. *He* wanted to be the one to make her feel that way. He wanted to be the one who kept her safe and spoiled her rotten and made her forget anything bad that had ever happened to her.

She sat on the corner of the tub, her hair falling loose over one shoulder. The candlelight made her skin glow as if from within. She was the prettiest thing he'd ever seen.

He crooked his finger at her, ignoring the white bubbles that drifted away from the movement.

"Join me."

Her smile was playful. "That defeats the purpose of pampering *yourself.* You're supposed to be relaxing alone."

"And I was doing that…until you walked in. Which makes me think maybe you really want to join me in here before the water gets too cool."

Her mouth opened, then closed again and she stood. "Soak up a little more warmth and relaxation, and I'll see you in the kitchen when you're ready." She moved to walk past him, but he reached out and grabbed her hand. She was the only comfort he craved.

"Don't go, Cass. Being alone with my thoughts is not… It's not relaxing."

She sat again, this time behind his shoulder. "Why don't you tell me about it. Tell me what happened in LA."

"Not much to tell. My partner died because of me."

"I don't believe that." Her answer was quick and sure.

"It's true. I made a bad call, and she paid the price. Jada was shot. Killed. Because of *me.*" Her fingers traced patterns through his hair, her words barely a whisper.

"Tell me."

He told her about the night that replayed in his dreams over and over again. When he'd heard uniforms were called to Beth Washington's house earlier that night, he'd felt sick. He and Jada had been there a dozen times in previous years, but, with their encouragement, Beth had dumped her bastard of a husband. Nick and Jada had been there the day Earl moved out, to make sure there wasn't any trouble.

"Let me guess," Cassie said. "She took him back, because he promised he'd change?"

"She seemed like such an intelligent woman, but…" Nick glanced up at Cassie and grimaced. "Sorry, I didn't mean to say you aren't intelligent, but at least you left and didn't go back. I don't understand how someone can go back to a guy who does that. He broke her freakin' arm *twice*, and she still took him back."

Cassie sighed. "I had plenty of opportunities to leave before I finally did it. Abusers are very good at convincing you they'll change. They're the world's best apologizers. They play head games better than anyone else. They make you think *you* were the one who caused it, so if you just behave the way they want, things will be fine. But things never are."

Nick couldn't imagine forgiving someone for beating on him. But he'd heard all the science supporting what Cassie was saying. His head knew she was right, but his heart couldn't get past that night at Beth Washington's. Couldn't get past Jada paying the price.

"Jada and I drove by the house a few hours after the patrol unit responded to the call. The report said a neighbor had complained about a loud argument and crashing sounds next door. Of course, Earl gave them some BS story. He said they'd been watching a movie with the volume way up, and that was what the neighbor heard. His wife and kids backed him up, so the patrol told him to keep the volume down and left."

"But they weren't watching a movie, were they?" Cassie's fingers stopped moving. She knew what was coming next. Too bad *he* hadn't been smart enough to see it. It was only supposed to be a wellness call at the end of their shift. Jada had already taken her vest off. They'd argued about that constantly—she hated wearing a vest.

"We knocked on the door and Beth answered. I told her we were just checking on things, and she told us the same movie nonsense. But there was something about the look in her eyes. In the eyes of those kids lined up on the sofa. Jada took the youngest girl down to her room, and I asked Beth where her husband was. She said everything was fine. Kept saying we needed to go."

And just like that, Nick was back in that living room again. Nice house. Nice neighborhood. No sign of the horrors that had occurred. No warning of the horror to come. Jada returned from putting the baby to bed, stopping at the end of the hallway. Nick was lecturing Beth about how they couldn't protect her if she wouldn't protect herself. Beth looked up at him, tears and terror filling her eyes. That moment was his first clue that something was *wrong*. *Really* wrong. The hair on the back of his neck stood on end when she grabbed his shirt, hissing that Earl had a gun. He'd said he was going to kill them all, and if she couldn't get Nick and Jada to leave, he'd kill them, too.

"I looked up at Jada. We both reached for our weapons. There was a shotgun blast, and Jada…" Cassie stroked his head again. "When she fell, Earl was right there behind her, reloading the shotgun. I shot him in the chest, then grabbed the two kids and Beth and hustled them out the door. Everyone was screaming. I went around to the back door to get the baby from her room. The neighbor took a picture of me running out of the house with the screaming kid in my arms, and the media went nuts, making me out as some kind of hero cop. It was all bullshit." He swallowed hard. "I did everything wrong, and my partner…my friend…died in my arms. Because of me. My colleagues on the force knew it, too. I could see it in their eyes when the story hit the news. I could see it at the funeral. The way they looked at me. The way her wife, Shayla, looked at me. They all knew."

"Nick…" Cassie waited until he turned to look up at her. "Are you sure you weren't just projecting your own guilt into their eyes?"

Cassie watched Nick consider her words. He weighed them, almost gave in to the temptation of believing them, then dismissed them, opting to hang on to his pain.

"Good cops don't let their partners get shot in the back. That was on me."

"That's a lot of weight to carry around." He shrugged, staring at one of the candles that were burning low. She'd almost forgotten where they were. What a bizarre place to be having this conversation. "It's why you left LA."

"I was done being a cop. I didn't have the fire for it anymore. I started blaming the victims for putting themselves…"

Cassie nodded. "You blamed them for putting themselves in danger. For being victims." It certainly explained why he'd reacted so angrily to discovering her ex-husband had assaulted her.

Nick raked his fingers through his hair. "I know it's bad. It's wrong. And it sounds even *worse* when you say it out loud. But the fact is, if Beth hadn't taken Earl back, Jada would still be alive."

"So now you're saying it's Beth's fault that Jada is dead, not yours."

"Don't twist my words. It was *my* fault. I walked us right into the middle of a disaster."

"Did Jada not want to go? Do you think she had any idea what was going to happen when she took the baby and left you alone in the living room?"

"No, of course not."

"Then how is this all *your* fault? You both stopped at the house out of concern, and Jada agreed to it. Neither of you expected to run into a lunatic. Something terrible happened, but I don't see how you made any huge mistake that led to it." She tugged at his hair gently until he looked up at her, his dark eyes troubled with memories of a night too horrible to imagine, much less witness. She leaned forward, resting her forehead on his. "Nick, if you and Jada hadn't stopped that night, that whole family would be dead. Those innocent children would be dead."

He closed his eyes. He didn't *want* to feel better about it. He wanted to hurt.

"Shayla tried to tell me that, but it doesn't help."

"Because you don't want it to?"

He pulled away, looking at the bathtub with a flash of surprise, as if he'd forgotten he was in there. She didn't want to push him any further. They'd both shared a lot, and he was probably feeling as raw and wiped out as she was. She stood and handed him a towel.

"I imagine that water's pretty cold by now. I'll make some grilled cheese sandwiches and warm up some tomato soup, and we'll sit and relax for the rest of the afternoon. That will square us up on the deal we made."

He stared at the towel before reaching for it, avoiding eye contact with her.

"It might be better if I head home."

"And I think it would be better if we both had some food and took some time to recover from all the soul-baring that's gone on today. And since this is *my* day to call the shots, you don't get a vote."

He looked up, one brow arched, his mouth sliding into a devastating grin. And then he stood, glistening wet and completely naked. A small cluster of bubbles slid slowly down his chest, and she watched their journey in fascination. He sounded amused.

"I think I liked you better when you were timid. This bold-and-bossy Cassie makes me think I've created a monster."

Cassie licked her suddenly dry lips. Her mind was empty of coherent thought. The bubbles were below his ribs now, gliding towards...

"My eyes are up here, babe."

She blinked and looked away from him, which finally freed her tongue. "I know where your eyes are. They're right above your smart-ass mouth. Get dressed and..."

He stepped out of the tub. The combination of hard male body and floral-scented bubbles was frying her brain cells. Nick chuckled.

"Are you sure you want me to get dressed? Or did you mean to say you want me just like this?"

Oh, yes. She wanted him alright. Just like this. Just *exactly* like this. The crooked grin. The mischievous light in his eye. The vulnerability he'd shown earlier. The tenderness when he'd held her in his arms. The strength of those arms, the safety she felt when she was with him. It was all so new.

Nick was her friend. He was her safety net. The man she'd made love to. No—had sex with. No. Made *love* to. The man she was falling for. Freefalling for. She had no right to. She was a fool if she did. But it was too late. He was her everything. And she was falling in love with him.

The realization caught her by such surprise that a nervous giggle bubbled up. She covered her mouth to keep from blurting the words out loud, since this man always left her thoughts in chaos and her mouth with no filter whatsoever. She giggled again as she, for some reason, remembered a Sun Tzu quote from her self-help book.

In the midst of chaos, there is also opportunity...

Chapter Fifteen

Nick was standing naked and wet in a bathroom with a woman who was giggling at him.

It wasn't exactly great for his ego, but he tried not to take it personally. She seemed as surprised by it as he was, the way her hand came up and covered those soft lips. The way her eyes went wide. The way her cheeks flushed pink. He cleared his throat loudly.

"So the sight of me standing like this makes you laugh, huh?"

"I'm sorry. I really am. It's been such a…*day*… Hasn't it?" Her hands went wide. "I don't know what we're doing, Nick. I don't know what's happening, or what comes next, or how to…"

"Shh." He put his fingers over her lips this time. "Let's not overthink this, okay? One day at a time seems like a good place to start. Let's take it a day at a time, together, and we'll figure it out as we go."

Her eyes went more gold than green, her brows furrowed. "But shouldn't we have a plan?"

She'd been on the run for a year now, planning for all kinds of contingencies. All sorts of what-ifs, ready to flee in the middle of the night. Letting their relationship simply play out was clearly scaring the daylights out of her. But he needed time to sort through his own feelings, and he couldn't do that while laying out some master plan of how this might work. He decided to distract her.

He kissed her softly, his hand pushing her hair back from her face. She trembled when his lips touched hers. And that was it.

That little tremble was his moment of truth. He was falling for this woman. Not *because* she trembled at his touch. That was just his wake-up call. He was falling for her because she was strong and tough and kind and funny. Because she made him want to be a better man. Made him want to be her protector. Forever. He'd known lots of women. But only one made him think of forever. And it was this woman. Right here. Right now.

"You're naked." She said the words against his mouth, and he felt her smile. He'd gotten her to smile again. And it made him feel like a god. He grinned.

"I am. It's generally the way to bathe, or did I do the bubble bath thing wrong?"

She shook her head. "No. You did it just right, Nick." She was still smiling, but there was something else going on behind those eyes. Something deep. She blinked and straightened. "I'd like to think we can do more than hop in bed every five minutes, though. So let's eat and sit and have that quiet afternoon together, okay?"

He didn't want her thinking they were just bed bunnies. He knew now that he wanted more. He wanted all of her.

"This is your day and I'm at your command." He kissed the tip of her nose. "And I *know* that we can do more than hop in bed every five minutes, Cass. We're more than that."

She looked into his eyes intently. He wasn't sure what she was looking for, but she seemed to find it. She nodded and relaxed against him. Then, remembering his nakedness, she pulled back and gave a nervous giggle. Glancing down, she noted his physical response to their close proximity. It was pretty tough to hide while naked, and he didn't bother trying. The corners of her mouth tipped up. "Who knows? Maybe I'll decide on some bed hopping later."

"Whatever you want, babe."

The rest of the day passed in quiet, peaceful time together. They were both exhausted—emotionally from all the sharing they'd done, and physically from a night full of activity. Nick was shocked at how much he enjoyed settling onto the flowered sofa and having another glass of wine while he watched Cassie read her book in the armchair by the window. She'd explained that the furniture all belonged to her landlady, Nora, who owned the coffee shop downstairs. Much of the main floor of the apartment was open to the beamed ceilings two stories above. There were metal stairs leading to a loft where Cassie slept every night. He wanted to see that loft, but, surprisingly, he wasn't in a rush. It was nice to be here with her, each lost in their own thoughts, but together. And the together part felt really good.

He glanced toward the door and frowned at the duffel bag sitting there. The only dark spot of the afternoon had been when Cassie explained it was her "go-bag," packed and ready to grab if Don ever tracked her down here. Nick wanted to tell her to unpack that thing and forget about leaving, but he could sense the security it gave her to feel…prepared somehow. They'd discuss it some other time, when he'd convince her it was no longer needed, because she had *him* to protect her now. Now and forever.

Damn, that word kept moving through his thoughts. *Forever.* They'd had one night. One night, even one amazing night, couldn't possibly lead to a forever. Could it?

He dozed off for a while, and when he woke, the lake outside the windows was peach colored from the setting sun. Cassie had fallen asleep, too, her book open in her lap, her head back against the corner of the wing-back chair. He got up as quietly as he could and took the brightly colored throw from the back of the sofa, wrapping it around her. He figured he'd leave a note and slip out before she woke. They both needed the sleep. But as soon as he straightened, her eyes swept open and she stretched, yawning before smiling up at him.

"Whatcha doin', Nick?"

"I figured it's time for me to head to my own bed. We're both wiped out."

"Stay." It wasn't a question. Just one simple word that could lead to a whole lot of complications.

"Are you sure?"

"I'm sure I don't want to go to bed alone tonight. Do you?"

She had him there. He knew he'd be reaching for her in his dreams.

"No, I don't." He helped her to her feet. "But be sure, Cass. Because one night together is…one night. *Two* nights is a relationship. Even if it's not a long one, it's a relationship. It means something." This already meant something to him, but he wasn't certain where Cassie's head was. If they were doing this thing, they were doing it. All or…nothing? He didn't even want to think about what nothing might feel like.

Luckily, he didn't have to worry about it. Cassie took his hand and led him up the long flight of steps to where a huge iron bed sat, facing the arched windows on the top level of the loft. She turned to face him by that bed, repeating the only word he needed to hear.

"Stay."

Cassie smiled into her tea, staring at her computer screen, struggling to focus on work. She and Nick had settled into a happy routine over the past few weeks. Most of their free time was spent at Nick's house, to avoid the prying eyes of Nora and Aunt Cathy. Nora and the cousins were delighted over their being together. Amanda reminded Cassie that now the apartment really was an indisputable "love shack."

Aunt Cathy, on the other hand, was not delighted. She worried that Cassie was jumping into a serious relationship too soon. That Nick was "smothering" her by being around all the time. Cassie tried to explain that the difference between this and her former marriage was that she *wanted* Nick around. Cathy reminded her that Nick was a cop, just like Don. But that wasn't fair. There were thousands of honorable police officers out there, and Nick was one of them. Cathy had finally agreed to reserve judgment until she had a chance to get to know Nick better. Which would be happening that weekend.

Here at work, things were easier than she'd anticipated. They made a deal to stay focused on the job while at the resort, and, for the most part, it worked. Nick still hid her stapler every damn day, just like always. They continued to have sparring sessions in the gym like always. He continued to *borrow* flowers for her desk. Other than Blake, no one would ever know things had changed. Unless they saw Nick pull Cassie into his office for a lunchtime make-out session.

Blake wasn't exactly enthusiastic about the new office dynamic, but he didn't post any objections, either. Other than a quiet warning that first Monday to keep it professional and to save their personal life for their personal time, he'd stayed quiet.

A foam basketball went whizzing past her head, bouncing off the window and up into the air. She jumped and squeaked in surprise, then turned her chair to see Nick leaning against the door frame to his office, looking very pleased with himself.

She rolled her eyes. "Are you bored?"

"Hey, you're the one who said nothing should change at work. So this is me, not changing." He picked the ball up from the floor and flipped it into the air, catching it behind his back with a flourish. "I thought maybe we'd take the kayak out after dinner tonight, and watch the sunset from the water."

"You really think it's a good idea to put me back in a kayak?"

He bounced the foam ball off her desk, snatching it from midair in front of her face. She did her best not to flinch. He grinned, impressed.

"I don't know. You in a kayak worked out pretty well once before."

She tried to hold back her laughter, but failed. "Fair enough. I'll give it another try, and I'll try to stay inside the boat this time."

And she succeeded. Nick rowed them out toward the center of the lake that night, where they drifted on the calm water and watched the sun slide behind the mountains. Nick had come prepared, with cookies and wine. She teased him about drinking and rowing. But when she insisted on trying to row herself, they ended up going in circles, so she finally conceded and let him take them home. Neither of them got wet, but they still ended up in bed later, wrapping themselves up in each other after making love.

Aunt Cathy arrived for a cookout on Saturday wearing a healthy dose of skepticism. Nick laid on all of his charm, but Cathy was tough. She'd been through a lot of men back in her day, and most of them had been bad apples. But as the afternoon went on, and Nick presented flawless grilled steaks and veggies, sharing stories and treating Cassie like a queen the whole day, Cathy seemed to relax. Cassie thought maybe they'd won her over, so she was blindsided when her aunt leveled a look at Nick across the picnic table.

"So what are you going to do when Cassie has to pack up and leave Gallant Lake?"

There was a beat of silence. Nick looked at Cassie, then back to Cathy. His voice strong and sure.

"That won't happen."

"Really? Don found her once. What's to say he won't find her here?"

"Aunt Cathy…" Cassie didn't want to talk about this today. Especially after getting two hang-up calls this week from a Milwaukee number she didn't recognize. But that could have been anyone. She hadn't mentioned the calls, because talking about them gave them more weight than they probably deserved.

"No, it's okay, Cass." Nick looked her aunt right in the eyes. "I didn't say Don wouldn't find her. But that's not what you asked. You asked about Cassie leaving, and *that's* not going to happen. Because I'm here, and I'll keep her safe."

It wasn't the first time he'd said that this week, and it was beginning to grate on Cassie. She didn't want him thinking he had to protect her all the time. After all, that's why he'd taught her self-defense.

"I'll keep *myself* safe," she said. Nick and Cathy both turned to look at her in surprise. "One way or the other, I'll keep myself safe."

Cathy frowned. "Your go-bag is still packed and ready."

"And it'll stay that way." She cut off Nick's objection. "Until Don's in jail, I need to be ready to go. It's not just me he'll be looking to hurt. He'll go after anyone near me. I'm not saying he will find me. I've been careful. But he has connections. He's smart. And I've got to be ready, just in case."

Nick's jaw worked back and forth.

"Don't you leave me, Cassie. You call me, no matter what, and we'll face it together. Promise me you'll call me before you do anything." He reached out and took her hand. "Promise me, babe."

She hesitated, then nodded. "I promise." He stroked her hand with his fingers, the way he often did when they were sitting together, and they gave each other a warm smile.

Cathy looked back and forth between them.

"Well, I'll be dipped. There really is something going on between you two."

Cassie scrunched her brow. "Uh, yeah. That's why you're here, remember?"

Cathy waved her hand in dismissal. "I don't mean the shacking-up part. I wasn't crazy about you two playing with fire when you were in such a precarious position, honey. But you're not *playing* with the fire. You're already dancing in the flames, aren't you?"

Nick looked as confused as Cassie felt.

"Aunt Cathy, what are you saying?"

Her aunt sat back, pushing her pewter-colored braid over her shoulder. She looked at the two of them, then started to chuckle lowly.

"You don't even know it yet, do you? Okay." She stood, and Nick scrambled to his feet, reaching out to help Cassie extricate herself from the picnic table. Cathy shook her head. "I had my doubts about this, and it could still all go down like the *Titanic*, but one thing I know after today. Whatever's happening here is real. And real lo… I mean, real…well…you deserve a chance to make it. If you want my blessing, you have it. But remember one thing." She fixed one last glare on Nick. "I know where you live now. And if you hurt this girl, I will be paying you a visit. Got that?"

"Yes, ma'am."

After her aunt left, Cassie looked at Nick. "What on earth was she talking about?"

"Damned if I know. She's *your* aunt."

"Ugh. I need a cup of tea. You want anything?" These days, Nick's kitchen was fully stocked with tea, sugar and wine for Cassie, along with her favorite cereal and cookies. He'd teased her about her sweet tooth, but she shut him down fast when he suggested she try baked kale instead of a cookie. She didn't mind getting herself in better shape. She didn't mind the new curves and muscles she was developing, or the stamina she hoped would get her up Gallant Mountain tomorrow with less huffing and puffing than the last time. She didn't even mind cutting her carb intake a *little*. But trade cookies for kale? Nope.

Her phone buzzed in her pocket. She pulled it out, and a shadow fell on her happy afternoon. It was the Milwaukee area code again, but a different number this time. She quickly tucked it back into her shorts. If it was someone she knew, or someone from the DA's office there, they'd leave a message. If it was the random hang-up caller, there wouldn't be any message. Was it Don? One of his pals? But how would they have her number? Maybe it was just a fluke.

"Cass? Who was it?" Nick was frowning at her. "What's wrong?"

"Nothing. Just one of those telemarketing places that got my number somehow."

His forehead creased. "How would they get that number? I thought you said only a few people had it."

She shrugged, heading to the house. "Who knows? Probably on some random list out there. If I don't answer, they'll give up." She hoped. Especially since she knew, deep in her heart, that it was not a random call. It wasn't fair that, at a moment when happiness was finally staking a claim in her life, her past was trying to kick down the door.

The calls didn't stop. She received three more the next week. She answered one of them to see if the caller would speak, but they hung up immediately. The fourth call came the following Sunday, while she and Nick were coming home from the crazy-high cliffs he'd climbed with his buddies, called the Something-Gunks. She'd stayed at the base with a handful of nonclimbers, male and female, who agreed their respective significant others were insane for clambering up the sheer rock face. But when Nick came back down laughing with his pal Terrance a few hours later, he looked energized and happy. As long as he never expected *her* to do anything like that, she was cool with being an observer.

The call came just as Nick was driving down the hill into Gallant Lake. She looked at it, bit back a sigh and moved to put her phone away. But Nick grabbed it from her, glaring at the screen.

"Why didn't you answer? Who is it? Why do they keep calling?"

She bristled at his tone. "Don't use your cop voice with me. You know I don't like it."

His voice softened, but she could see from the set of his chin he was agitated. "Cass, you've been getting these calls for over a week now that I know of." She started to speak, but he cut her off. "And don't give me that telemarketer BS. What area code is that? Milwaukee? Is it Milwaukee? Is it Don?"

She didn't answer. She couldn't, not with him pressuring her like that. Firing off questions that sounded more like accusations. She shrank back in the seat, hating herself for feeling vulnerable right now. With the guy who was supposed to make her feel safe. Nick muttered something under his breath as he pulled into the parking lot behind the apartment. Even in his anger, he'd remembered she wanted to pick up some more clothes. He put the Jeep in Park and sat back against the seat with a sigh.

"I'm sorry. I don't mean to give you the third degree. But I'm worried. I see the expression on your face when those calls come in. The way your whole body goes tense. Something's going on, and you're keeping it a secret for some reason."

"Okay, okay. I've had a few calls from a Milwaukee area code. I don't recognize the numbers, and they're not always the same. They always hang up. Maybe it's just somebody with a wrong number."

"Somebody in *Milwaukee* with a wrong New York number? That's quite a coincidence, don't you think?"

Cassie shrugged. She didn't want to tell him that's how it started in Cleveland, too. Random hang-ups until one night it was Don's voice on the line. Nick thought she was a fighter. He'd given her the tools to take care of herself. She didn't want him thinking she was just another helpless victim.

He didn't ask about the calls again, but he started hovering more than usual over the next few weeks. He was hanging around if she worked late, even after she told him she'd meet him back at the lake house. He jumped to attention every time she looked at her phone, even if she was just checking the time. Maybe she should be more appreciative of his desire to protect her, but instead, she found it annoying. She didn't tell him about either of the two new calls that came in, for fear he'd overreact and start insisting on driving her everywhere like some damn bodyguard.

A few months ago, she'd have given anything to have a big, strong bodyguard. But that was before she learned to protect *herself*. Before Nick pushed her to be stronger, smarter, tougher. And now that she was finally seeing herself that way, he suddenly wasn't.

Chapter Sixteen

The final straw came when she and Julie went to lunch the following Wednesday at the Chalet to celebrate Julie's birthday. The place was crowded with noisy tourists and locals.

"You're different now," Julie said as she finished up her cheeseburger.

Cassie picked up her taco. "Different in what way?"

"I don't know." Julie studied her for a moment. "You're calmer these days, almost mellow, and it's not just because you're shagging Nick West."

Cassie coughed and sputtered, trying not to scatter taco crumbs everywhere. "What are you talking about? I'm not…"

"Oh, please, everyone in town knows you two are together." Julie waved her hand. "I know you're trying to be discreet at work, but no one can miss those sizzling looks going on between you two. But that's not why you're different. No…" Julie reached over and pinched Cassie's bicep, then nodded. "You're leaner. Stronger. You're not as jumpy and timid. You make eye contact with people. You even *walk* different, with that don't-mess-with-me vibe. It's a good look on you, girl. You came out of your shell."

They moved on to talk about the new proposal Blake was working on, trying to build vacation condos on the water. But Cassie kept rolling Julie's words around in her head. If other people were noticing how much she'd changed, why couldn't Nick?

When they walked out to Julie's car, Cassie couldn't believe her eyes. Nick's red Jeep was pulling out of the parking lot. She recognized the climbing sticker on the back door. Had he *followed* her? Her eyes narrowed. This wasn't a coincidence any more than the Milwaukee calls were a coincidence. He was following her, just like Don used to. Not for the same reason, of course. But it still ticked her off. She didn't say anything to Julie, but she was fired up when she got back to the resort.

Nick's head snapped up in surprise when she stomped into his office and closed the door sharply behind her. He quickly smiled and came to greet her.

"Hey, babe, what's up? Did you miss me…? Oof! What was *that* for?" He rubbed his upper arm, where she'd punched him. Hard.

"Did I *miss* you? How can I ever miss you when you never let me out of your sight?"

"What…?"

She held her hand up flat in front of his face. "Stop! Don't tell me you weren't at the Chalet just now. You probably know what I ordered, what I drank and what time I went to the ladies' room. I didn't get rid of one stalker just to pick up another!"

"Whoa. I am *not* stalking you, for Christ's sake. I know you're worried about those calls you refuse to talk about, and I want you to feel safe!"

"But isn't that what all the self-defense classes were for?"

"Well, yeah, in case you're alone and in trouble. But you don't have to be alone anymore. You've got me to protect you."

She dropped her head in frustration. He cared about her. In fact, there were times when she saw the spark of something in his eyes that looked a lot like how she felt for him. A lot like love. But she couldn't let this obsession keep going. She met his gaze. His expression was somewhere between amusement and worry. Damn the man for making her feel this way.

"Nick, I love…how much you care." Whew, that was close. This was no time to blurt out that she loved him. "But you have to trust me to handle myself. You've given me the tools. I've got the moves. Let me have a chance to use them."

He rested his hands on her shoulders. "Today was a fluke, I swear. I had to run up to the sports shop in Hunter. I drove by the Chalet, saw your car and remembered you were going to lunch with Julie. I knew there was that mountain biking event in town. I knew you were in there with a bunch of testosterone-loaded adrenaline junkies, so I figured I'd just…make sure…" His words trailed off, and he had the good sense to look embarrassed. "I don't want you to *have* to use those skills I taught you, Cass."

"I'm not saying I want to put myself at risk. But you can't always follow me around. What about when you're gone this fall to visit the other resorts? I'll be alone then, so why can't you let me be alone now?"

Nick scowled in thought, then gave her a begrudging nod. He cupped the side of her face with his hand and leaned in to kiss her.

"Be patient with me, babe. I'll try to do better. It's just...I tend to lose the people I care about... And I don't want to lose you."

Her eyes went to the photo of Jada on the bookcase, and her chest tightened. He was fretting because he cared. She had to remember that.

"Okay. You try to do better—and I mean *really* try. And I'll try to be patient. But you have to understand that having someone watch my every move brings back bad memories. We *both* have baggage, remember?"

Nick tugged her into a warm embrace, and she rested her head on his shoulder. He really was her safe place. They just had to figure out how to keep him from also being what she wanted to run away from.

A soft knock on the door forced them apart. Nick opened it, and Blake walked in, stopping short when he saw Cassie there.

"Oh...uh... Am I interrupting...?"

"No, we're done." Cassie blushed. "I mean, we're done *talking*. Just talking. And now... We're done."

Nick started to laugh. "Quit while you're ahead, Cassie." He pulled her in for a surprising kiss in front of their boss, and whispered into her ear. "I'll see you at home tonight, and you can show me some of those moves you've got."

She knew her face had to be flaming. She didn't answer, but she also couldn't keep a straight face when she passed Blake and went back to her desk, thinking about which self-defense moves would translate best to the bedroom.

Her muscles were still protesting her successful efforts the next day when she joined Nora and Cathy at the Gallant Brew to help them take inventory. The coffee shop was too busy on weekends to do it, so Blake had given her Thursday afternoon off to help her aunt.

"Hey, Cassie, should I start looking for a new tenant upstairs?" Nora winked at her. "You two don't seem to be spending much time there these past few weeks."

Cathy barked out a sharp laugh. "They prefer his place, where no one's watching their comings and goings. You must be moved in there by now, right?"

Cassie waved her clipboard with one of Nora's infamous checklists attached, and stared at the two women in mock exasperation.

"It's a little early for me to be permanently taking up residence there, and I still have clothes and a toothbrush upstairs, so don't evict me yet." She and Nick hadn't formally discussed their living arrangements, but it was true they seemed to be unofficially living together. And last night they'd managed to christen the few rooms they hadn't already made love in, including the shower in the master bath. Yeah, that was fun. She bit back a triumphant grin. "But I did not come here to be quizzed on my love life, ladies. I came here to help with inventory, remember?"

Cathy glanced at the only occupied table in the place and lowered her voice. "Closing time was half an hour ago. They've paid, but they don't seem interested in leaving. Should I say something?"

Cassie looked at the teens sitting near the window. They were involved in an intense discussion, or at least the shaggy-haired boy was. He was leaning forward, his blond hair hiding his face. But his head jerked as he spoke, his shoulders rigid. The girl couldn't be more than sixteen. She didn't do much talking, just nodded, her head down and shoulders rounded. She was closing in on herself, in a protective stance that Cassie recognized immediately. That girl was afraid of him.

"I'll take care of it." Nora and Cathy looked at each other and shrugged.

The girl startled when she saw Cassie approaching, then brushed her dark hair back over her shoulder and looked away. There was a yellowed bruise on her wrist. The boy sat up and looked at Cassie with a contempt she was sadly familiar with. It was like staring into the eyes of a younger Don. And, just like Don, he quickly smoothed a cool smile onto his face to conform with expected polite behavior.

Cassie looked him straight in the eye and returned the thin, insincere smile. "Hi, guys. Is there anything else you two need today? I don't want to chase you away, but we're doing inventory and we'll be shutting down the coffee machines."

The girl rushed to apologize. "I'm so sorry. We're ready to go." She glanced across the table, suddenly uncertain. "Aren't we, Tristan?"

He sat back lazily and shrugged before slowly standing. "I guess so. If we're gonna be thrown out." There was challenge in his eyes, and Cassie didn't blink.

"I'm not throwing you out, but we do need to shut down. We won't be able to serve you."

He jerked his head toward the girl and she leaped to her feet as if he'd tased her. He turned his back and tossed his words over his shoulder as he opened the door.

"Whatever. This place sucks anyway."

The girl hurried to follow, whispering a quick "I'm sorry" as she passed Cassie. They left, and Cassie stood by the door, filled with regret. That girl was in trouble, and Cassie hadn't done anything to help. She went outside to the sidewalk, but they were gone from sight. She'd missed her chance. She rejoined Nora and Cathy.

"Is there any kind of shelter for abused women around here?"

Cathy shook her head. "Not in Gallant Lake. But there's a place over in White Plains, probably half an hour or so away. Why?"

"I was just wondering. It's too bad there's not some-place closer." It would have been nice if she could have at least handed that poor girl a number to call for coun-seling. She'd have to check out the shelter and learn more about it. Maybe even volunteer. She didn't help that girl, but maybe she could help someone else.

Nora lifted the trash bag out of the bin behind the counter and Cassie reached for it. She needed the dis-traction.

"I'll take it out, Nora. You two get started counting cups and spoons and whatever else we have to count."

She was barely three steps out of the back door when she heard a frightened cry.

"No, Tris, stop! That hurts!"

The boy's voice was rough and angry. "It oughtta hurt, you stupid cow! I heard you apologize for me to that bitch in there. Don't you *ever* make apologies for me again, you got it?"

It was the kids from the coffee shop. He'd yanked the girl around the corner of the building and pushed her up against the empty bakery two doors down. Cassie dropped the trash bag and headed toward them. He con-tinued to berate the girl, and was raising his arm in the air when Cassie reached them.

He never saw her coming, and let out a yelp when she grabbed his wrist and twisted his arm behind his back before releasing him with a shove that sent him stumbling a few steps.

"What the hell are you doin', you crazy…"

Cassie nodded toward the girl, now wide-eyed and silent. "Go!"

Tristan avoided Cassie's grip, keeping his distance as he glared. "Shut up! Daynette, don't you listen to her!"

Daynette looked between Tristan and Cassie, crying and confused. Cassie kept her voice level.

"Daynette, this isn't the first time he's hurt you, is it? I saw the bruises on your wrist. Let me guess—he always says he'll never do it again, right? And then he does?" Cassie took a step toward her. "And then he makes it your fault, right? Blames *you* for making him mad?" She could see in the girl's eyes that her words were hitting home. "He's never going to change, Daynette. I've been where you are, and I can tell you he's never going to change. Get out while you can."

Tristan sneered. "And who's gonna stop me from chasing after her? *You?*"

Cassie ignored him. "Daynette, do you have someplace safe to go? Is home nearby?" The girl nodded. "Okay. Go there. Talk to someone about this. And stay away from this jerk."

The boy stepped forward. He was thin, but solid, and Cassie knew she'd have her work cut out for her if he got physical.

"Don't you leave, girl. Don't you walk away from me."

Daynette hesitated, then looked at Cassie, searching her eyes for the promise of something better. Cassie nodded toward the street.

"Go."

Tristan moved to grab Daynette when she ran off,

but Cassie elbowed him hard in the ribs. He grunted, then jumped away.

"Lady, you are batshit crazy!" He grabbed her arm, and Cassie could hear Nick's steady voice in her head. *Lower your center of balance. Don't try to outpower him, just go after the pain points.* She didn't try to pull away, surprising him by stepping into his grip, coming close enough to bring her heel down on the top of his arch. He cursed and let go of her arm. Adrenaline was pounding through her veins. She should walk away, but she wanted to push him onto his ass and kick the living daylights out of him right there in the parking lot. Before she could decide between the two options, she was shoved aside.

By *Nick*.

All Nick saw was red. He was driving back to the resort when he saw some punk kid drag a girl around the corner and into the lot behind Cassie's apartment. It took him a minute to turn around and swing back there to make sure the girl was okay. The last thing he expected was to see this guy grab *Cassie* and yank her around. Nick jumped out of the Jeep so fast he wasn't even sure if he'd put it in Park. Cass was fighting back—he saw her stomp on the guy's foot. The kid didn't have time to straighten before Nick grabbed the little piece of garbage and slammed him against the brick wall.

He looked like he was ready to soil his underwear when he got a look at Nick pulling back his fist. He started talking, and fast.

"No, man! You got it all wrong! My girl and I had a little fight, and this lady thought I was going to hurt Daynette, and I was explaining that I'd never do that! We're cool! Everything is cool, man, I swear!"

Cassie pushed past Nick, wagging her finger in the boy's face.

"Liar! You've been using that girl as a punching bag, and that's going to stop. You don't own that girl, and you don't put your hands on her again. Got it?"

"Cassie, damn it, get back! I got this."

"No, Nick, I *had* this before you got here. And why the hell *are* you here?"

The teen struggled, and Nick twisted his shirt up at his throat.

"I'm gonna let you go now, and you're gonna apologize to this lady and walk away. And whoever you were using as a punching bag? You stay the hell away from her. Got it?"

"Yeah, yeah, I got it. I'm sorry, lady." He took off like he was on fire.

Nick turned to Cassie, trying not to think about how many ways this scene could have gone wrong. "Are you okay? What the *hell* were you thinking, going after that guy?"

"Why do you keep insisting on being my knight in shining armor?"

"Most women *want* a knight in shining armor, don't they? Why are you mad at *me*?"

"Because I don't *need* your help, Nick! Wasn't that the whole point?"

"The whole point of *what*?" Nick raked his fingers through his hair.

"Of *us*!" Cassie gestured angrily between them. "I was your little pet project, right?"

"What the hell are you talking about?"

"Come on, Nick. You wanted to be a hero for teaching me a few self-defense moves, and you got a little fun between the sheets on the side. Big man, right?"

She stepped back and looked him up and down, hands on her hips, eyes flashing with emotion. "Well, I don't want to be your project anymore, Nick. I'm an independent woman and I can take care of myself!"

Nick's mouth fell open, but he couldn't form any words that he trusted. But Cassie didn't have that problem.

"I've already been with a man who controlled my every move. And *he* tried to tell me it was for my own good, too. But it *wasn't*. It was all for *him*. To make him feel like a big man. And you're doing the same thing. You've got some kind of hero complex..."

Anger rushed through his veins, white-hot. "I am *nothing* like your ex."

"You're *exactly* like him!" She threw her hands in the air. "You're trying to tell me what to do and how to think and where to be..."

"I would never hurt you!" His voice echoed off the brick wall. There was a time when shouting made Cassie flinch and stammer. That time was apparently long gone. Now she stepped right up to him, shaking her finger in *his* face this time.

"You hurt me *today*, by not trusting me!"

Guilt punched him hard in the gut, but he pushed it aside.

"I'm not Don. I'd never put a hand on you."

She blinked, lowering her hand slowly. Maybe she was finally hopping off the hissy-fit train. Her voice steadied, but there was still fury and hurt in every trembling word.

"Fine. You'd never hurt me physically. But the broken bones weren't the worst thing Don did to me, Nick. Stealing my self-worth, sucking away my confidence, changing who I was—*that's* the most serious damage he inflicted. And now you're doing the same thing."

"Cassie…"

She spun away, her shoulders so tight and straight he thought she'd snap. And he'd made her that upset. But how? By wanting to keep her safe? How could that be so wrong?

He scrubbed his hands down his face with a growl, staring at the ground. *Damn it.* She accused him of stealing her self-worth? He'd taught her how to defend herself and stand up for herself. Sucking away her confidence? She'd climbed a fucking mountain with him. Change who she was? He'd made her a better person…

His shoulders dropped. But was it his place to do that? She said he had a hero complex. Jada used to say the same thing. She'd died because of his hero complex. And look what he was doing to Cassie now. Christ, he was such a screwup. He looked up and found her staring at him. And he couldn't help defending himself, because…screwup.

"I thought I was helping. I thought that's what you wanted. I thought you…"

I thought you loved me.

But he couldn't say that out loud, not when she was staring at him with so much anger and hurt. This wasn't the time to tell her he was in love with her. He might be stupid, but he wasn't *that* stupid. He couldn't throw those words out there when there was a very good chance she'd stomp on them and fling them back in his face.

Cassie's arms wrapped tightly around her own body, as if holding herself together. He wanted to be the one to do that. He started to step forward, but she shook her head sharply, stopping him in his tracks.

"Don't. I can't..." She shook her head slowly. "I...I don't trust my feelings right now, Nick. Maybe I'm mixing you and Don up in my head. Maybe I'm lashing out at you because I never had the chance to lash out at him. Or the *courage* to lash out at him. Or maybe you deserve every bit of it because you built me into something you don't seem to like very much."

"That's bullshit, and you know it."

"Is it? You didn't want me to be a victim anymore because you don't like victims. But victims are the ones who need a hero's rescue. So if I'm not a victim anymore, you no longer have a role to play. I don't need you to save me, because you taught me how to save myself. You taught me that I don't need a hero. So where does that leave us?"

His mouth opened, but he had no idea what to say to her convoluted logic. If he *loved* her, it was his job to protect her, right? But then, why had he taught her how to protect herself? His brain was spinning faster than tires on ice, and his frustration boiled up again.

"You've got all the answers, Cassie. You've clearly psychoanalyzed me and come to your own rock-solid conclusion. So why don't *you* tell *me* where it leaves us?"

Her eyes hardened.

"So now the big, bad cop is refusing to take a stand. Who's the victim now?"

He bit back the angry words begging to be said. They'd reached the point in this argument where someone was going to have to walk away before they burned down any hope of repairing the damage already done. His jaw tightened. It galled him to be the one walking. It galled him to quit before a winner was declared. But he could see it in her eyes. She was drunk on her newfound ability to take a stand, and she wasn't going to back down.

He got it. For years, she hadn't landed even a glancing blow on her asshole of an ex. She was going to stand and fight now just to enjoy the adrenaline rush of getting her punches in. But it wasn't in his nature to be someone's punching bag.

They could finish this conversation when they were both more reasonable. He turned for the Jeep, his parting words spoken over his shoulder to the woman he loved.

"I think we're done here."

Chapter Seventeen

I think we're done...

Those words rolled around in Cassie's mind on an endless repeat cycle as she stared into her morning coffee.

We're done.

She hadn't slept at all, tossing and turning until the sheets were in a twisted heap. After Nick left, she'd sent a text to Cathy, saying she had a bad headache and begged off from the inventory. Then she'd quietly gone up to the apartment to assess what just happened.

Done.

She didn't know where all that rage had come from. One moment she'd been standing there, feeling like an Amazon warrior after setting Tristan back on his heels. And the next, it was as if Nick had snatched all of her power away. After teaching her those skills, he'd been furious when she'd used them. And something inside of her had just…snapped.

She brushed a fresh wash of tears from her cheeks. How many tears could a human body produce, anyway? She'd been crying all damn night.

All the hurt and rage of a decade had risen to the surface like lava in a volcano yesterday, and she'd unleashed it on Nick. It was frightening to be so completely out of control, with no ability to hold back words she wasn't even sure she believed. Wasn't sure if they should be aimed at Nick or at Don. Or perhaps even at herself.

The one person who could help her sort it all out, and the only person whose opinion mattered to her, had ended things yesterday. She sniffed back the tears threatening to drown her again.

I think we're done here.

Just like that, after she'd attacked him one too many times, he'd walked away.

We're done.

The man she was in love with, the man she *thought* loved her back, had declared them over. In a way, it may have been best that he'd left, as the argument had been racing toward a flameout. She'd kept throwing his words back at him over and over, until he finally said the one word she didn't have the strength to repeat.

Done.

Had Nick truly given her strength only to resent her for having it? That might not be fair. He came upon the situation with Tristan and Daynette without knowing what had happened. If the first thing he saw was Tristan's hand on Cassie's arm, it wasn't unreasonable for him to assume the worst. He wasn't wrong to want to protect her. But it *felt* wrong. It felt like he didn't want her to step up and be strong, even though that was all he'd been talking about since they met.

Her coffee had turned cold enough to make her grimace when she took a sip. A sad realization pressed down on her. Nick might never be able to see her as anything other than a victim. If she was going to start a new life as a new Cassie, she might have to do it somewhere other than Gallant Lake. Somewhere where no one knew her past. Where people would know only brave, strong Cassie. She glanced at her dusty go-bag by the door. She wouldn't be running away. She wouldn't be hiding. She'd be looking for a place to blossom and grow and be her best self. That would be a good thing. So why did the thought of leaving Gallant Lake, of leaving *Nick*, make her heart hurt?

Another one of those damned Sun Tzu quotes came to mind, and it stung.

Who wishes to fight must first count the cost...

Was losing Nick really a price she was willing to pay?

Her phone started vibrating across the stone counter, making her jump so high she almost fell off the kitchen stool. It wasn't Don, thank God. It was Blake Randall. She glanced at the clock and swore. She was late for work. She looked down at the sweats and cami she was still wearing. Whom was she kidding? She wasn't going to work today. She couldn't possibly face Nick in the office until she had some kind of control over her thoughts. Until she had some sort of plan. Or at least until she stopped crying.

Blake's call was on its third ring before she swiped to answer.

"Um..." She had to clear her throat and dislodge the tears. "Hi, Blake."

"Hi, Cass. Did you have a Friday off I'd forgotten about?"

"No. I should have called, sorry. I know I took time yesterday, but I need a personal day. Will that be a problem?"

"Of course not. Well, it's always a problem when I have to take care of my own damn self, but…" He paused, waiting for her to laugh at his little joke, but she didn't have it in her to even try. "Are you okay? Has something happened?"

"Yes. I mean… No, nothing's happened, and yes, I'm fine." She cursed the shaky breath she took and hoped he couldn't hear it. "I just…need a day."

"Just a wild guess—does this *need* have anything to do with the dark bags under Nick's eyes this morning and his general air of stay-away-or-I'll-stab-you?"

Cassie's chest tightened. Nick had been the one to end things, but at least he was paying a price for it right along with her. Was it wrong if that knowledge gave her a small dose of satisfaction?

"Cassie?"

"Oh…um… What?"

"Yeah, that's what I thought." Blake sounded resigned. "Is this going to be a problem?"

Does a broken heart qualify as a "problem"?

"At work? No, of course not. I just need a day, okay?"

"Don't be surprised if you have company shortly." Was Nick on his way over? Why? He'd said they were finished. She started to rise until Blake continued. "Amanda took one look at Nick this morning and managed to deduce everything in about five seconds. She scares the shit out of me when she does that, because she's never wrong. She called Nick a few choice names and flew out of here a few minutes ago. Odds are she's headed your way."

As if scripted, there was a sharp knock at the door.

She opened the door to find Amanda standing with hands on hips. She gave Cassie a quick once-over and stepped in for a sneak-attack hug. Cassie didn't bother pretending she didn't need it right now. She even returned it, and felt Amanda flinch in surprise. They stood in the doorway like that, and Cassie did her best to hold back the tears that threatened yet again. It was Amanda who stepped back first, wiping something from her face before meeting Cassie's gaze.

"How bad is it? Do I have to hire a hit man? Should I make Blake fire him? Banish him to Bali? Tell me and I'll make it happen."

Cassie couldn't stop the laugh that bubbled up. She'd never had a friend who had her back like this. It eased the pain, if only for a moment.

"Bodily harm won't be necessary." Although, to be honest, she had no idea how she'd be able to face Nick at work every day. "Let's face it, this was inevitable. I was never going to be able to trust Nick not to hurt me somehow, and he was never going to be able to see me as anyone other than a victim. It's better for both of us that it happened now instead of…" The words choked her into silence.

Instead of after I told him I loved him.

"That's a load of bull. You two are crazy for each other. And if it makes you feel any better, he looks even worse than you do, so there's no way he's thinking this is a good thing. Come on, pour me some coffee and tell me what happened."

Nick called and texted Cassie a dozen times with no response Friday. Ignoring him was childish, and it irritated him. Sure, the fight was bad, but pulling the silent treatment on him was ridiculous. He sent another text

near the end of the workday, basically saying exactly
that. Half an hour later, the boss's wife walked into his
office and made it clear that he'd be putting himself in
mortal danger—from *her*—if he bothered Cassie again
for at least the next twenty-four hours.

"I get that you already regret breaking up with her,"
Amanda said, "and you *should* regret it, but leave her
the hell alone for a few days. That kind of hurt doesn't
go away with an *I'm sorry*. And as far as I know, you
haven't bothered to actually say you were sorry yet."
Nick frowned, going over his texts and messages in
his mind. He'd apologized. Right? He must have apologized. Or had he just talked about how they "needed
to talk" before he started chastising her for not responding? Damn, he was really bad at this relationship business.

Blake appeared in the doorway, an amused smile on
his face as he slid his arms around his wife.

"Is there a problem here, honey?"

She twisted her neck to look up at him, then leaned
back into his embrace. Nick felt a pinch of pain in his
chest at the look of intimacy between them. It was the
same type of look he and Cassie had shared more than
once.

"Nothing serious, dear. Your idiot of a security chief
made an ass of himself and hurt the woman he loves,
but he's going to make it better. Right, Nick?"

...you already regret breaking up with her...

"Wait...did you say I *broke up* with her? We had a
fight, and it was ugly, but..." He tried to rewind their
argument. They both said hurtful things, sure, but not
that. "Did she tell you I broke up with her?"

It was the first look of hesitation he'd seen in Amanda's
blue-eyed glare since she'd spotted his unshaven, dishev-

eled appearance that morning, then looked to Cassie's empty desk and lit into him for obviously being the reason for her absence. She tipped her head to the side, her eyes narrowing again.

"Are you telling me you didn't tell her you two were 'done'—" she lifted her fingers into air quotes "—before you stormed off?"

"I..." Nick's mouth stayed open, but no more words came out. *Had* he said that? No. Well... Yes, he had. But...

"I didn't mean it that way." He knew that sounded bad, and Blake's sharp laugh confirmed it.

"Dude. You told the woman you love that you were done in the middle of a fight, but you 'didn't mean it'?" Now it was Blake's turn to do air quotes. "How does done not mean *done*? There aren't that many ways to interpret the word."

"I meant the *argument* was done. I was done *fighting*. I figured we needed to stop before it got worse, so I declared an end to it." He knew without hearing Amanda and Blake's sharp intake of breath that he sounded like a controlling asshole. Kinda like the guy Cassie had accused him of resembling last night. He scrubbed both hands down his face in aggravation. "Okay. Maybe I was wrong." Amanda's brow lifted sharply. "Okay, I *was* wrong. But damn it, how could she think I'd end us like that?"

Amanda started to answer, but Blake rested his hand on her shoulder.

"Let me field this one." He sat in one of the chairs in front of Nick's desk, pulling his wife onto his lap. He gestured for Nick to take the other chair. "You're in love with a woman that..."

"Okay, why do you two keep throwing the *L* word

around here like it's some foregone conclusion? I've never told you I'm in love with Cassie."

Amanda bristled, but Blake chuckled and held her tight.

"It's okay, babe. I was the same damned way. I refused to admit the truth about my feelings for you. I didn't ever *want* to be in love, so I clearly *couldn't* love you. Don't you remember?"

Her eyes softened and she patted his arm. "We both had a lot of denial going on back then."

Blake nodded. "And that's where Nick is right now. He doesn't *want* to need anyone, so he won't admit he needs that woman more than he needs air to breathe."

Nick straightened. "'He' is sitting right here."

"Yeah, you are. And she's sitting alone in an apartment in town. And you both feel like shit. I've been there, Nick." Blake glanced at his wife. "*We've* been there. You ask how Cassie could believe you'd end it, but the question is—why would she believe you *wouldn't*? Have you told her you love her?"

Nick didn't need to answer that. They all knew he hadn't.

"Okay. Have you thought about her past?"

"I'm the one who taught her self-defense, remember?"

"That's nice. But have you *really* thought about it? How deep it goes?" Blake sat back and sighed. "Look, I knew about Amanda's past, and her issues with trust, once we got involved. We'd talked about it, and everything was cool in my mind. What's done is done, right?" Nick saw the flash of pain that crossed Amanda's face, and Blake must have sensed it, because he pulled her close again. "Then Amanda thought I'd lied to her about something. I hadn't lied, despite all the evidence to the

contrary. I *told* her I didn't lie, but her past taught her
that men weren't to be trusted. I was so butt-hurt that she
wouldn't believe me that I got pissed off and left, basically proving she was right—men couldn't be trusted."
Blake shook his head, lost in the memory of what was
clearly a bad time for them.

Cassie had accused Nick of having a hero complex.
Of refusing to see her as anything but a victim to be
rescued. That he wanted to rescue her and simultaneously resented her need for rescue. How twisted up his
beliefs were with what happened to Jada. He glanced
at her photo on the bookshelf. If Jada were here right
now, she'd kick his ass six ways from Sunday for being
such a lunkhead.

He frowned. She'd kick his ass for a lot of reasons.
And at the top of the list would be the guilt he'd carried
around for two years. The way he'd avoided Shayla since
the funeral. The anger he'd been carrying toward Beth
Washington. The way he ran from LA, trying to flee
all those memories. The way he'd projected all of that
baggage onto Cassie, when she was already carrying a
full load. He stood, but Amanda jumped up before he
could bolt out the door.

"Give her some space, Nick. You're both exhausted
and hurting right now. Spend a little time thinking about
things, and give her time to do the same." She turned to
smile at Blake behind her. "Those days we spent apart
were brutal, but, looking back, I think we needed that
space to decide if we were both willing to change. Tomorrow you'll be thinking more clearly and can come
up with a way to win her back."

He looked at Blake. "Is that what you did? You won
her back?"

He was hoping for a few pointers, but Blake laughed.

"Nope. She beat me to it. Chased me down and basically dared me *not* to be in love with her." He shrugged. "It worked."

Everything in Nick was telling him to run to Cassie, but he resisted. He looked at Jada's photo again. He was no good to Cassie if he couldn't confront his own demons. He slapped Blake on the back and tapped Amanda under the chin with his finger.

"Thanks, you two. I'm still new in the corporate world, but I'm pretty sure this conversation is way above and beyond what's expected from an employer. I appreciate it."

Amanda smiled, but there was a steeliness in her eyes. "That's great. Just make sure you know what you want. And don't hurt her again, Nick. Or you'll be dealing with me."

Blake laughed again. "Okay, Rocky, let's go. Good luck, man."

Nick went home and sent one last text to Cassie.

I'm SORRY. We're NOT done. Let's talk when you're ready.

He was frustrated, but not all that surprised, when she ignored that text, just like she'd ignored the others. For all he knew, she'd turned her phone off after he'd kept hounding her earlier. Saturday passed without a word, but he didn't text her again, even though he checked his phone at least fifty times.

He poured a glass of whiskey and sat on the deck Saturday night, watching the sun setting over Gallant Lake. The ice cubes were almost melted before he finally picked up the phone and dialed. Shayla's voice was surprised and guarded.

"Hello? Nick?"

"Hi, Shayla." Silence stretched taut while he watched a blue heron walking on the lakeshore, pausing every other step to stare into the water, looking for dinner.

"It really is you. Is something wrong?" He pictured Shayla, her hair long and wild with curls, the way Jada liked it. Shayla was the light and energy to Jada's practical and, yes, controlling ways. Jada had been all business, the consummate professional police officer, while Shayla was the free-spirited dance teacher. They'd both had to compromise their ways to make the marriage work, and they'd done it without a second thought. At least it seemed that way.

"Hello? Look, Nick, if this is a drunk dial, I don't have time for it. I've got a recital tonight at the school..."

"I'm not drunk. I mean...I'm drinking, but it's my first one of the night. Do you have a few minutes?"

He heard her snort of laughter. "If you're gonna *speak*, I got an hour. If you're just crying into your whiskey, I ain't got the time or temperament for it, Nick. I haven't heard from you in more than a year..."

"I'm so sorry, Shayla."

There was a beat of silence. "Sorry for *what*?"

The heron was on the other side of the dock now, frozen on one leg, head tipped to the side as if he was waiting for Nick's answer, too.

"For every damn thing. But mostly for taking Jada from you."

There was a sharp intake of breath on the other end of the call, then he heard a rustle of fabric as if she was sitting down.

"Earl Washington took Jada away from me. From us. I told you at the funeral not to listen to those idiots at the department, didn't I? That you weren't to blame?"

"If I hadn't gone to that house..."

"If you hadn't gone there, Beth Washington and those kids would be dead. Is that why you haven't called before now? Is that why you left LA? Because you think you're responsible for me being a widow?" She paused. "I absolved you of that two years ago."

His short laugh had no humor in it. "It didn't take, Shayla."

"Clearly. Where are you?"

"I'm in the Catskills. I took a security job for a chain of resorts based here."

"Putting that master's degree to work, eh? And today, out of the blue, you sat down with a drink and decided to beg my forgiveness for Jada's death?"

"Pretty much, yeah."

"Why?"

Nick smiled. Shayla had picked up some of Jada's directness in their brief time together.

"Someone... Someone's been pushing me to face my past."

"In other words, you've met a woman who called you on your bullshit?"

The heron struck out, its head diving under the surface of the water, coming up with a wiggling minnow. Nick chuckled. "You sound just like Jada. Straight to the point."

"That's why you were so good together. You didn't take any shit from each other, and you almost knew what the other one was going to do before they did it. Jada said you two were like one person when you worked together."

Nick thought back to the years he and Jada worked together. Once they'd hashed out their initial power struggle, they really were like a well-oiled machine.

They broke up a sex-trafficking ring. They moved a drug gang out of a residential neighborhood so children could feel safe playing on the sidewalks. They solved dozens of murders. Probably hundreds of crimes. As weird as it might sound, they'd had a great time doing it. It just worked.

Until it didn't. Until he saw Jada falling from the blast of Earl's shotgun. Once Nick had everyone out of the house, he'd rushed back in to hold Jada in his arms. The sound of her rattling breaths drowned out the screams of the children and the wail of approaching sirens outside.

"Her last words were about you."

"I know, Nick. You told me. You came to me and repeated every word she said, just like she'd asked you to do." The tremor in her voice betrayed her tears. "Are you sure this isn't a drunk dial?"

He shook his head and took another swig of whiskey.

"You listen to me, Nick West. Jada's death is. Not. Your. Fault. She was a police officer following up on a domestic violence call. That's as unpredictable and dangerous as it gets. She knew that as well as you did. She used to tell me all the time that sometimes bad shit happens, and you can't always control it."

"She didn't have her vest on."

"That's not on you. She hated that vest. We used to argue about it all the time. Jada did whatever the hell Jada wanted, and she wasn't going to be bossed around by you or me or anyone else. The vest was her choice. And as high as the shot was, it may not have saved her anyway. Nick, you gotta let go of the guilt. It's too much to carry."

Cassie had told him basically the same thing. *Too much to carry.* Maybe he needed to start listening to

the women in his life. He heard a rustle on the phone…
Tissues? Shayla sniffled, then her voice steadied again.

"What if the situation was reversed?"

"What do you mean?"

"What if you were the one killed, and Jada survived?
Would you have wanted her to be burdened with guilt
over it? Would you want her quitting the force, running
away, torturing herself over some made-up idea of being
responsible for controlling your actions or the actions
of a madman with a gun?"

He didn't answer right away. He couldn't. It was too
much truth to take in. If Earl Washington had come
in the front door, behind Nick, it would have been *him*
shot in the back. And Jada would have been the one
watching in horror. He'd trade his life for hers in a
heartbeat, but that's not what happened. Earl came in
from the back of the house, behind Jada. And there
wasn't a damn thing Nick could do to roll back time
and change it.

"Nick? What would you want if it was reversed?"

He drained the whiskey, welcoming the sharp burn
of it sliding down his throat.

"I'd give anything for it to have been me who died
that night. I'd want Jada to be alive, you two to be together, having that baby you dreamed about. But no, I
wouldn't want her feeling responsible for me."

"Because…?"

"Because sometimes bad shit happens, and we can't
always control it."

Neither of them spoke for a moment, then Shayla
sighed.

"I've gotta go get the kids ready for this recital tonight. But Nick, you should know that I'm adopting a
little girl. It's what Jada and I always wanted. Tamra's

four years old, and I swear to God she's a reincarnation of Jada." Nick smiled at the thought. "She's all spit and fire and power, and she's gonna take over the world by the time she's ten if I'm not careful. I miss Jada every single damn day, but seeing love in this little girl's eyes keeps Jada with me in a *good* way. I honor her memory by loving someone the way she loved me. You should do the same. Maybe with this woman who's got the brains to tell you to straighten the hell up."

Chapter Eighteen

Cassie scrolled through Nick's messages for the who-knows-how-many-eth time. It was Sunday afternoon, and she hadn't heard from him since Friday night. His final message said they *weren't* done, but it sure felt that way from the silence. On Friday, silence was exactly what she'd wanted. He'd been driving her crazy with all the texts and messages. Just like he'd driven her crazy trying to run her life.

She stared out the window of the apartment—the *love shack*—as cars passed below on Main Street. She wasn't being fair. He said they'd talk when she was ready. He was giving her control. He wasn't intentionally trying to run her life. Or maybe he was. She dropped her head back against the overstuffed chair. The whole thing was such a confusing mess!

On one of their hikes a few weeks ago, Nick had pointed out a small whirlpool in a mountain stream.

A maple leaf was swirling around and around in the water, unable to break free. That's what she and Nick were like. Neither could break free from their individual whirlpools.

Whoa. That was deep.

She grinned to herself as she reached for her wineglass. Teatime had ended yesterday when she declared it sadly ineffective. Last night's bubble bath was equally unrewarding, since it only reminded her of Nick standing in a tub full of bubbles. Not productive at all.

Wine was doing a much better job of freeing her mind to drift, as well as dulling the pain when she bumped up against a painful memory. Every kiss. Every moment between the sheets. Against the wall. In the tub. On the sofa. In the Jeep. On the mountain. In the gym. She took a sip of wine. Okay, maybe a gulp of wine. It was more effective than tea, but not effective enough.

She was going to have to go to work tomorrow, and Nick would be there. Nick, who hadn't reached out since Friday. Amanda said he was a mess then. Was he still a mess? Awash in guilt and regret? Anger? Or was he tucking it all inside, as he so loved to do, ignoring the truth? Would he pretend everything was fine, the way they tried to do after their first kiss? Would he confront her and defend his controlling ways?

She frowned. Not fair again. And it had been especially not fair for her to compare him to Don. Those mysterious hang-up calls had put her on edge Friday. Then she saw Tristan and Daynette, and Cassie just flipped. And it felt *good*.

It felt good to help someone instead of being the victim. It felt good to see Tristan back down. Yes, he was just a kid, but she'd been drunk with power at that moment, and she wasn't seeing Tristan anymore. She'd been seeing Don. She'd been imagining making *him* back down. Making *him* stop hurting her. Following her. Stalking her. Frightening her. Having power over her.

And then Nick robbed her of all of that by swooping in to the rescue. And she was so damned angry that he took her power away. Except... He hadn't. Not really. Not on purpose. Don worked at making her powerless. Nick did the exact opposite. He wanted her to be strong. Did she really expect a man, especially an ex-cop, to *not* rush to help if he thought the woman he... Cassie closed her eyes. She was so sure he loved her. Just as sure as she knew she loved him. Of course he'd leaped to the rescue.

And what had she given him in return? All that rage that she'd been holding on to for Don. She'd just spewed it all at Nick. He hadn't deserved it. Yeah, he was over-protective. But he'd watched his best friend die in his arms. He'd convinced himself that Jada's death was his fault. It made sense that he'd react by wanting to protect the people he cared about from any chance of harm.

Cassie stared at her wineglass. Damn, this stuff was making her pretty smart today. Maybe after she had another she'd have the courage to call Nick and tell him to come over so they could work it out. Better tonight than tomorrow in the office, with Blake and Amanda watching them and playing matchmaker.

But that third glass of wine only made her sleepy. Or perhaps it was the fact that she'd hardly slept in two nights that made her fall asleep in the big chair. The apartment was dark when she heard her phone ringing on the counter. By the time she woke up and got to it, the ringing stopped. Her heart jumped. Was it Nick? She didn't recognize the number, but she knew the area code. Milwaukee. She ignored it and checked the time. Almost eleven.

She and Nick would have to figure things out tomorrow after all. It was too late and she was too tired to do it now. Her phone chirped with an incoming text. It was from the same mystery number that had just called. That was new—she hadn't received any texts since leaving Cleveland.

Cute little place you found there.

No. It couldn't be. A dagger of ice hit her heart.

She didn't touch the phone, willing it to stay silent on the counter. It chirped again.

Nice little waterfront tourist town.

Don couldn't have found her. Not now. The comments were vague, though. Maybe he was just fishing for information. She picked up the phone, hoping he was done. Several minutes passed before the final chirp.

Gallant Lake sure looks pretty in the moonlight.

Cassie dropped the phone onto the counter. Don was *here*. In Gallant Lake. He didn't mention her apartment, but if he was in town, it wouldn't take long for him to find her. She glanced at the go-bag by the door. She didn't want to run. But if she didn't, Don would ruin everything. Again. And he might hurt the people she cared about. Aunt Cathy. Nora. Amanda. Blake. A chill swept over her. Don would kill Nick. There wasn't a doubt in her mind of that. There was only one way to keep everyone safe. She grabbed a jacket, leaving her phone in the kitchen. If he was tracking her with it, she had to leave it behind. She'd buy a burner phone and call everyone tomorrow, once she was safe. Once *they* were safe.

She went to the door, picked up the duffel bag and flipped off the lights. It looked like she'd be making that fresh start in a new place after all. But this time she would go there unafraid of the shadows. She wasn't the same person anymore. She'd found her strength. She'd found her heart. She blinked back tears as she locked the door behind her. That heart wouldn't be coming with her, though. Because she'd given that heart away.

Nick knew walking into the office on Monday morning that the day would be tough. Cassie was probably still angry with him. After all, she'd never responded to his final text. Maybe he really *had* ended things, simply by being an idiot. He stood outside his car and gave himself a stern lecture.

He loved her, and he'd do whatever it took to make sure she understood that. He'd earn her love in return if it took him the rest of his days to do it. He'd make sure she knew how much he respected her. How strong he knew she was. How willing he was to let her stand on her own without him hovering around like a bodyguard. Although that last one would be tough. But he'd do it for Cassie. She said he'd taken her strength away, and he needed to give it back.

It wasn't until he started walking toward the resort that he noticed her car wasn't there. He stopped behind her parking spot and frowned. It hadn't occurred to him that she wouldn't show up. Blake would have let him know, wouldn't he? Nick checked the time. His sleepless night had him up and moving earlier than usual.

It was barely seven o'clock. She'd be here. And when she arrived, he was going to bring her into his office, close the door and kiss her senseless. Then they'd talk. It was going to be fine.

But three hours later, Cassie still hadn't arrived. Wasn't answering her phone. Wasn't answering *any-one* on her phone. Amanda and Blake were in his office, looking as worried as he was. Amanda called Nora, who said Cassie's car was gone. Blake didn't wait for Nick to ask.

"Go. I'll call Dan Adams and see if he's heard… anything."

He didn't want to think about what the deputy sheriff might have heard. Maybe there'd been an accident. Or maybe she'd had car trouble somewhere. Maybe she was at the auto shop out on the highway. Maybe she'd broken down on the way to work.

"Nick?" Blake was holding the phone, staring at him. He'd been frozen in place as his brain tried to solve the mystery of Cassie's disappearance. Nick gave Blake a quick nod and left.

Cathy and Nora were already in the apartment when he arrived. The police-detective part of his brain was annoyed that people were traipsing around, possibly destroying evidence of what happened. Where Cassie went. But then Nora motioned to the phone sitting on the kitchen island.

"We didn't touch anything, Nick. I knew you'd want to see everything the way we found it. She left her phone. And…she took her bag."

He spun to look by the door. Her go-bag was gone.

"That doesn't make sense." He refused to believe she'd go without a goodbye to anyone. To him. "That was her panic bag. Why would she take that instead of packing her stuff and talking to someone?"

Cathy folded her arms. "You *know* why."

Thinking she was referring to Friday's argument, he held his hands up in innocence. "It was just an argument. We'd have worked it out. She wouldn't have run away because of a fight."

Cathy's eyes narrowed. "I wasn't talking about any argument, but I'd definitely like to hear more about that. I was talking about that crazy ex-husband of hers."

"He's in Milwaukee," Nick said.

"Is he?" Cathy walked over to the phone.

"He's on probation. A restraining order…"

"And those always work, right?" She twirled the phone and slid it across to him. "Her pass code is 1111."

Nick grimaced. "Original."

"It's her birthday."

"It's four ones. Not a very secure passcode."

Nora threw her hands in the air. "Oh, my God. Stop debating cybersecurity and unlock the phone!"

It opened to Cassie's text screen. It was a number he didn't recognize, and the words chilled him to the marrow of his bones.

Gallant Lake looks nice in the moonlight.

Innocent words on their own, but on Cassie's phone, from a Milwaukee area code, they dripped with danger.

Don had found Cassie somehow. And he'd managed to convince her he was in Gallant Lake. And she *left*. Nick walked to the windows and looked down to the street. If someone *had* been out there watching, she would have been an obvious and vulnerable target fleeing in the middle of the night. Although she'd certainly give Don a better fight now than a few months ago.

But something didn't feel right. His instincts told him Don was still in Milwaukee. That the bastard was playing head games with Cassie for his own amusement. He could have an accomplice, of course, but that didn't feel right, either. Don was in it for the game. He wouldn't want someone else to have the fun. Abusive husbands didn't hire out their dirty work. Like Earl Washington, they wanted their victory all to themselves.

Cathy walked up beside him. "She said if she ever had to use the bag, she'd buy a throwaway phone the next day and call to let us know she was okay."

"She promised she wouldn't leave without me."

"I know, Nick, but we don't know what happened. All we can do now is wait."

He nodded mutely. Waiting wasn't his thing. But he had no idea where she'd go. Farther east? North to Canada? Catch a flight to the West Coast? None of that felt right. And she would have left in the middle of the night, so how far could she have gone? As a detective, he'd always trusted his gut. And his gut was telling him she wasn't far away. He turned and strode to the door.

"I'm going to drive around and see what I can find."

Cathy's hand rested over her heart. "What you can find? You think Don…?"

Nick shook his head, but it was Amanda who answered, walking through the door with her phone in her hand and looking ticked off.

"Don's not in New York," she said. "I just talked to the sheriff. He called and talked to Don's probation officer in Milwaukee. The probation officer went to Don's place with the police. He was at home. They found three burner phones he was making calls from. The idiot had them sitting right there next to his chair, along with a bottle of scotch. They're charging him with violating his probation, among other things."

"So Cassie's not in danger? Thank God." Cathy sat at the kitchen island. "Maybe my heart can start beating again."

Cassie might be safe from Don, but she didn't *know* that. She was on the run.

He headed for the door. "I've got to find her."

Amanda turned to walk with him. "I'll pick up Blake and we'll head west if you want to go east."

Nora walked over and gave Nick's hand a squeeze. "I have to get back down to the shop, but my husband, Asher, knows the area really well. I'll have him head north toward Hunter. We'll find her, Nick."

Nick hadn't prayed in a very long time, but he did his best to plead his case with whoever might be listening as he drove out of Gallant Lake. He was desperate for some clue of where she might be. He passed the mountain road that led to the walking trail up Gallant Mountain. It didn't make sense that she'd hike the mountain alone at night. But he couldn't ignore the nagging thought that he'd find her there. After driving less than a mile farther down the highway, he pulled a U-turn and headed up the winding road. He turned onto the rutted track that led to the base of the Kissing Rock trail.

His head told him her little car probably wouldn't have made it up here, but his heart told him he was getting closer to her. Sure enough, when he pulled into the clearing by the gate, her compact car was there, covered with mud. It was empty. He smiled and looked up the trail. She was on Gallant Mountain.

He took his phone out of his pocket as he grabbed his small pack from the back seat, texting Blake. No sense in everyone else searching. Even if he didn't have eyes on her yet, he knew Cassie was here.

Got her.

As he went through the gate, he thought of her going up the trail in the dark. It was a decent path, but steep, and through dense woods. She might be here, but was she okay? He'd just picked up his pace when Blake's response came.

I'll let the others know. Amanda says make sure you KEEP her this time.

Nick shook his head. He deserved whatever Amanda threw at him. And whatever Cassie threw at him once he found her. He'd been an idiot, and he'd almost lost her. But that would never happen again. He tapped a quick reply as he hurried up the trail.

Tell her to count on it.

Chapter Nineteen

Cassie had watched the sunrise from the top of the Kissing Rock. Actually, she watched the effects of the sunrise, since it came up behind her. It cast the shadow of Gallant Mountain on the lake and the smaller mountain on the opposite side, but that shadow receded slowly as the sun climbed higher. Pretty soon she'd be warmed by its light, and she wouldn't mind that one bit.

In her panic, she'd left everything in the car before climbing up here in the silver predawn light, including the go-bag with her jacket in it. It was amazing she'd made it here in one piece, but someone must have been watching over her as she did her best to remember the trail and not walk smack into a tree.

She stretched her legs in front of her. There was water and granola bars in the bag, too. The bag that was in her car. She really should have thought this through a little bit better. She didn't dare go back, in case Don somehow found the car. Highly improbable, but even if he *did*, he'd have no idea where she'd gone. Unlike Nick, Don *hated* the outdoors. She'd left the apartment in such a mad blur of panic after Don's texts. Then heartbreak took over as she drove out of Gallant Lake and away from Nick. She couldn't leave him. She couldn't bring herself to *go* to him, either. She'd said some awful things to him. His last text said they *weren't* done, but... What if they were?

Her flight out of town had been horrible. The road out of Gallant Lake led past the resort and the large estate called Halcyon, both on the lake. She'd slowed by the resort, filled with regret that she wasn't going to be able to say goodbye. At two in the morning, the lake had been black as ink beyond it. She didn't want to wake Blake and Amanda at that hour. What would she say?

Hello, I'm an idiot who chased off the only man I've ever loved and I don't know how to fix it. I thought I was tougher now, but I freaked out when my ex tried to scare me. So clearly I'm not tough. I'm just stupid and I don't know what to do... Help!

She could imagine the expression on their faces if she woke them up with that little pity party in the middle of the night. Amanda would do her best to make her feel better, but...no.

Cassie was so afraid Don would find her that she panicked every time she saw headlights. She'd finally turned off the main highway and started on the twisting mountain roads. It wasn't long before she was hopelessly lost, with no cell phone to call for help. By some miracle, she'd recognized the road Nick used to get to the Kissing Rock trail. She slowed until she found the opening in the trees to the dirt road leading up the mountain. Up to the place where she and Nick had kissed for the first time. Where they'd made love under the stars just last week. Where she'd felt like she was on top of the world. Invincible. If there was any place on this earth where she could figure out what to do next, this was it. And Don would never find her here.

The first hint that she wasn't alone made her pulse jump. She heard footsteps. Rustling branches. Was it Don? Maybe a hiker? A bear? She glanced up the rock wall behind her. She had no idea how to climb it, but if a bear strolled out of those trees, she might just give it a try. She scooted across the rock, wishing there was more cover, and knowing if she stood she'd be even more visible. She caught a glimpse of blue in the trees. Not a bear.

Nick stepped out from the shadows and stopped, looking straight at her as if he wasn't the least bit surprised to see her. She rolled her eyes at herself—duh, he'd seen her car, of course. But how had he known where to look? And what was that expression on his face? Anger? Relief?

"Do you mind having company up there?"

She shook her head, straightening against the cliff again. "Not if that company is you."

He climbed that little path up the side of the rock like it was nothing. He hesitated, then sat next to her, with his legs out in front of him like hers were. He looked out at the lake. Not at her. Her heart fluttered in her chest. They sat like that for several minutes before he spoke, his voice like honey and electricity in her veins.

"Don was never in Gallant Lake."

"I got texts. He knew where I was."

"I saw the texts. He knew about Gallant Lake, but he's not here."

She turned to him in surprise. "You opened my phone? How?"

"Seriously?" He gave her the first glimmer of a smile. "Your password is 1111. It wasn't that hard. He's not here, Cass. He's in Milwaukee. They arrested him there this morning and found the phones he's been using. You're safe."

She didn't answer. All that panic. For nothing. She was overwhelmed with exhaustion.

Nick nudged her shoulder with his. It was an innocent move, but the contact instantly had her nerves on end. His eyes met hers.

"That was pretty smart, hiding up here. But it doesn't surprise me. You're a pretty smart lady. You can take care of yourself." He grew more solemn. "You've always been able to take care of yourself, Cassie. You never needed me. Not now. Not before."

She let those words settle in. She hadn't realized how much she needed to hear them. She thought she could dismiss their argument and forgive everything. But forgiving wasn't the same as forgetting. It meant a lot to know he'd *heard* her on Friday.

"Thank you for saying that. I'm sorry about what I..."

He put his finger to her lips. "You were right. About everything. I mean, yeah, you twisted me up a little too closely with Don, but I get it." His words came out in a rush. "I was all tangled up with my guilt over Jada and the anger I hadn't dealt with... And then I fell in love with you and it scared the daylights out of me. The stronger my feelings got, the more I kept thinking that I couldn't lose someone *else* like that. I couldn't stand having you out of my sight, and I smothered you. I know that now. I see how it could make you think I was doing it for all the wrong reasons..."

Cassie moved his finger aside so she could speak.

"Say that again."

His brows rose.

"All of it?"

"The only part that matters." She needed to be sure she'd heard him right. He looked at the ground for a second, rewinding his rambling speech. Then his mouth curled into a smile, his eyes deepening to the color of hot, black coffee. He cupped her face with his hand and leaned in, repeating the words against her lips before he kissed her.

"I fell in love with you."

She sighed and let him kiss her. Let him pull her onto his lap and tip her back and kiss her until she was dizzy. When he lifted his head, she was clinging to his shoulders. Then she released her hold, fell back and grinned up at him as she stretched her arms out wide. It felt as if she was dangling over the edge of the mountain, with the lake glistening blue beyond them. Nick was bemused.

"Whatcha doin', slugger?"

"I'm letting you take care of me, Nick." She glanced up at him before gazing back out at the dizzying upside-down view. "I *am* able to take care of myself. And I *will* take care of myself. But it's okay to lean on the arms of the man I love and trust him to keep me safe."

Nick pulled her upright so fast she gasped, resting her hands on his arms.

"Say that again." His voice was thick with emotion. Their smiles mirrored each other.

"All of it?"

"Just the part that matters."

"I love you, Nick. And I trust you." He kissed her again, scattering her thoughts until all she felt were his lips and his hands sliding under her shirt and up her back.

"God, Cassie, I love you so much. Don't ever leave me again. You promised you wouldn't."

She pulled away, pinched with guilt at the pain she saw in his eyes.

"I'm so sorry. I didn't know where we stood after that horrid fight. I was afraid I'd blown everything. When I saw that kid grab his girlfriend and threaten to hit her I...kinda lost it. The mistake was that I lost it with *you*." She gave him a quick kiss. "I got a little carried away with my newfound independence and daring-do, and it went to my head. Then the text came through last night and..."

He placed his lips on her forehead and stayed there, as if reveling in the moment, before he answered.

"I went all caveman on you. I took your victory away. I get it. But from now on..."

She snuggled into his arms and finished the sentence. "From now on, you and I will talk things through and trust each other. I'll trust you to take care of me without making me feel helpless..."

"And I'll trust you to make the right decisions for yourself, even if they aren't the decisions *I'd* make." He kissed her. "I'll trust you to love me, even when I'm an overprotective husband."

"*Husband?* Did I miss a question somewhere?"

"The question won't come until there's a ring in my hand, but trust me, it's coming."

"O-kay. Then I'll trust you to love me, even when I'm a stubbornly independent wife."

"Sounds like we may be having a few...um...fun discussions down the road."

"Maybe. But as long as we remember the love-and-trust part, I think we'll be okay." She cupped his face with her hands. "You were wrong earlier, Nick. You said I didn't need you, but I do. I need you as much as I need the air I'm breathing. When those 'fun' discussions come up in the future, and I'm sure they will, we have to remember that need. That promise to love and trust."

He pulled her close. "We'll write it into our vows." He grinned. "I'm sorry, that sounded bossy, didn't it? I *suggest* we put it into our vows. Only if you agree, of course."

She chuckled against his chest. "I think that's a very good 'suggestion.' And now to a more important question…"

He looked down at her, one brow raised, waiting.

"Do you have food in that pack of yours? Because I am starving!"

Nick laughed and reached for the pack while cradling her in his other arm.

"You know I do. And water, too."

"I can always count on you, Nick."

With a quick twist, he laid her back on the rock and rested on top of her, his hand running down her side and around to her buttocks, pulling her up against him.

"Yeah, you can always count on me, babe. Don't ever forget that."

She knew what he was thinking, and frankly, she was thinking the same thing.

"What if someone hikes up to the Kissing Rock this morning?"

"On a Monday? Highly unlikely. I think we're safe." He kissed her. "Well, I don't know if *safe* is the right word. I never feel safe with you, because you make me crazy." He kissed her again. "I love you, Cassidy

Zetticci. And I'll never stop loving you. You still hungry?"

"Oh, I'm hungry, alright. Hungry for you. I love you, Nick West."

"Don't ever stop loving me, Cass. It'll break me."

"I couldn't stop loving you if I tried. Always."

He kissed her.

"And forever."

* * * * *

COMING SOON!

We really hope you enjoyed reading this book. If you're looking for more romance, be sure to head to the shops when new books are available on

Thursday 3rd October

To see which titles are coming soon, please visit

millsandboon.co.uk/nextmonth

MILLS & BOON

Coming next month

CINDERELLA'S PRINCE UNDER
THE MISTLETOE
Cara Colter

Imogen could tell Luca's experience with snowballs was limited. The ball was misshapen and did not look like it would survive a flight through the air.

"Yes, Your Highness," she said with pretended meekness, "please remember I'm injured." Then she swatted his snowball out of his hand. Before he could recover himself, ignoring the pain in her foot, she plowed through a drift of heavy, wet snow. She snatched up a handful of it, shaped a missile, turned back and let fly.

It hit him smack dab in the middle of his face.

She chortled with glee at his stunned expression. He reached up and brushed the snow away. But her laughter only lasted a moment. His scowl was ferocious. And he was coming after her!

She tried to run, but her foot hurt, and her legs were so much shorter than his in the deep snow. He caught her with incredible swiftness, spun her around into his chest.

"Oh, dear," she breathed.

"What would an ordinary guy do?" he growled.

Kiss me. She stared up at him. The tension hissed between them.

"Cat got your tongue?"

She stuck it out at him. "Apparently not." Then she wriggled free of his grasp, turned and ran again. And she suspected her heart beating so hard had very little to do with the exertion of running through the snow and what felt like it was a near miss of a kiss!

With the carefree hearts of children, the air was soon filled with flying snowballs — most of which missed their targets by wide margins – and their laughter. They played until they were both breathless. Imogen finally had to stop as her foot could not take another second of this. Though with her hands on knees, breathing heavily, she decided it was well worth a little pain.

He took advantage of her vulnerability, pelting her with snowballs, until she collapsed in the snow, laughing so hard her legs would not hold her anymore.

"I surrender," she gasped. "You win."

He collapsed in the snow beside her and a comfortable silence drifted over them as the huge snowflakes fluttered down and landed on their upturned faces.

Finally, he found his feet, and held out his hand to her.

"We're both wet, we better get at that snowman."

She took his hand. "Before the dreaded hypothermia sets in."

He tugged and she found her feet and stumbled into him. His hand went around her waist to steady her, and he pulled her closer. She could feel a lovely warmth radiating through the wetness of his jacket. She could feel the strong, sure beat of his heart. His scent filled her nostrils, as heady as the mountain sweet crispness of the air around them.

She looked up at him: the whisker-roughness of his chin and cheeks, the perfection of his features, the steadiness in the velvet-brown warmth of his eyes.

They were back at that question: what would an ordinary guy do?

But despite his clothing, he was not an ordinary guy. A prince! She was chasing through this mountain meadow with a prince.

Would kissing him enhance the sense of enchantment or destroy it

Continue reading
CINDERELLA'S PRINCE UNDER THE MISTLETOE
Cara Colter

Available next month
www.millsandboon.co.uk

LET'S TALK

Romance

For exclusive extracts, competitions
and special offers, find us online:

 facebook.com/millsandboon

 @MillsandBoon

 @MillsandBoonUK

Get in touch on 01413 063232

For all the latest titles coming soon, visit
millsandboon.co.uk/nextmonth

MILLS & BOON

HISTORICAL

Awaken the romance of the past

Escape with historical heroes from time gone by. Whether your passion is for wicked Regency Rakes, muscled Viking warriors or rugged Highlanders, indulge your fantasies and awaken the romance of the past.

MILLS & BOON

Desire

Indulge in secrets and scandal, intense drama and plenty of sizzling hot action with powerful and passionate heroes who have it all: wealth, status, good looks… everything but the right woman.

JOIN US ON SOCIAL MEDIA!

Stay up to date with our latest releases, author
news and gossip, special offers and discounts, and
all the behind-the-scenes action
from Mills & Boon...

 millsandboon

 millsandboonuk

 millsandboon

It might just be true love...